TALMAN PRIME

INTERSTELLAR FLEET

BOOK ONE

J.J. GREEN

READER GROUP

Sign up to my reader group for exclusive free books, discounts on new releases, review crew invitations and other interesting stuff:

https://jjgreenauthor.com/free-books/

I know well what I am fleeing from but not what I am in search of.

— Michel de Montaigne

One

As Setia Zees stepped into the lift to begin her journey to a new life on a new world, she nervously checked over her shoulder. People crowded behind her, waiting to travel up to the spaceport. Men and women, young and old, no faces looked familiar. It was a great relief.

She turned to face the closing doors, squeezing into the remaining space with her single suitcase, and took a final scan of the crowd. There seemed to be no sign of Arief. Now she was on the emigrants side of the admissions area he should not be able to follow. She was safe.

The doors closed, the elevator announced the destination, and the ascent began. Almost imperceptibly, it rose smoothly upward to the passenger processing section.

This elevator and its partner were the only ways to reach the section other than from the air. The extremely limited accessibility was designed to deter people from sneaking in illegally. A berth on any of the three colony ships finally ready to depart after decades of preparation was worth a fortune on the black market. Desperate and crafty would-be stowaways had been discovered within engine housing, supply containers, animal crates, and even furniture—someone had hollowed out a bed about to be flown up to a ship and hidden inside it. One particularly foolhardy individual had fashioned a makeshift spacesuit and tried to strap himself to a shuttle's hull, unsuccessfully. The image of the small figure plummeting to the ground had made all the news channels.

The elevator slowed to a stop and disgorged its passengers. Clutching her case, Setia was carried along in the flow. Only when the crush dissipated was she able to take in her surroundings. The long, wide concourse was enclosed above and to one side by a transparent shell and filled with hurrying travellers, the noise of their chatter and footsteps echoing.

She was not in any particular rush. She'd left plenty of time to make her appointment. But the general excitement coursed through her too. Everyone here was about to embark on a life-changing, historic voyage, a voyage from which there would be no return.

A man bumped into her. She moved out of the flow of traffic and walked to the outward-facing wall. The processing centre was a bubble protruding from the mountainside. Resting her hands on the rail, she took in the view of the valley, lush and green as it spread to a far horizon under a clear, sunny sky. Unless she changed her mind within the next hour or so, this would be her last sight of Earth.

She had no intention of turning aside from her path. She had to leave this world, and participating in humanity's first deep space colonisation expedition was her only means. Remaining on her home planet meant living a life she'd grown to hate yet couldn't otherwise abandon. It meant living a life that wasn't hers.

At the end of the concourse, double doors led to a small balcony where a few fellow travellers stood. Dragging her case, she went to join them. It would be a long time before she would breathe fresh air again.

A stiff, chilly breeze hit her as she walked out, taking her breath away. Here, the mountainside was visible. She hadn't realised she was so high up. Fine, powdery snow clung to the rocky slopes, and ice coated the handrail. She blinked as her eyes watered, squinting in the now-unfiltered brilliant sunshine.

"Mommy! Mommy! Look! There's another one."

The small child with her two parents was pointing at the sky. A shuttle was arriving. Setia had never seen one in real life. Slim-nosed and snub-winged, the giant, red Antarctic Project logo emblazoned on its tail, the silver craft slipped noiselessly through the atmosphere and disappeared over the shoulder of the mountain. The shuttles had been flying for weeks, ferrying passengers and cargo to the starships as they prepared for departure. In a couple of hours, she would be on one of them.

"We have to go now, honey," the child's father urged. "We mustn't miss our slot."

"But I want to see another plane!"

"We don't have time," said the mother.

When further cajoling didn't work, the parents picked up the little girl, now in full meltdown, kicking and screaming. The woman rolled her eyes at Setia. She smiled back indulgently, secretly hoping her cabin wouldn't be anywhere near the family. The parents carried the child out and Setia had the viewing area to herself.

She breathed deeply, savouring the clean, icy air. What would it be like living on a starship? She'd never been on one. Though she'd watched the vids she'd been sent after paying the final instalment of the fee, she found it hard to imagine the actuality. She guessed it was something like being on an aeroplane, only with more room to move around. Hopefully, a lot more room. She'd only been able to afford the smallest, lowest class of living accommodation, barely more than a bunk. She would be spending most of her days in communal areas.

At least there was no need to enter cryosleep anymore, not since the skein mappers had discovered—

"Setia. How nice to see you again."

She started and turned. "How did you...?" She hadn't heard the doors to the viewing area open. Neither had she heard any footsteps.

Arief smirked. "I am capable of many things. I'm surprised, after all these years, you aren't aware of that."

"I'm fully aware what you're capable of," she muttered. She'd almost forgotten how, when they'd first met, Arief had seemed to appear from nowhere. He *had* appeared from nowhere. She'd racked her brains afterwards, wondering if she'd been mistaken that the alley she'd run down to escape her intended murderer had really been a dead end. But she was sure she was right. Arief had stepped out of thin air, and now he'd done it again.

Scowling, she told him, "You want to persuade me to go back. Forget it. I've paid my passage with my own money that I earned through honest work, fair and square. I don't owe you anything."

"But Elek needs you." His tone was light and teasing. He wasn't even trying to pretend he meant what he said. "And, I might add, you signed a contract."

"Elek has a whole security team to protect him, fully trained by me. And I don't even remember signing a contract." Yet she didn't doubt that one existed—a contract signed in a moment of 'forgetfulness'. Such moments always occurred when she refused one of Arief's requests.

"Irrelevant. You need to come back with me, my dear. Forget all this nonsense. Your place is here, not on some godforsaken planet." Arief gazed out across the landscape, the wind lifting his silver-grey hair, his long, sharp nose turning pink. He'd spoken lightly, as if not fully convinced of his own words. He seemed to be looking at something in the middle distance, though she could see nothing.

She should leave. She should walk away, return to the warmth of the inner building and the safety of the crowd, but she couldn't. Her feet were fixed in concrete. *He'd* fixed them, somehow. "Let me go."

He faced her. "I have plans that remain unfulfilled. Plans for you and Elek. You must..." His head swivelled forward and his eyes lost their focus.

She tried to move. Yet though something was distracting him, his hold on her remained firm. Hopelessness invaded her heart. She'd thought she'd made it. After sneaking out this morning and travelling to the launch site, paying her fare with cash so it couldn't be traced, she'd felt confident that she'd successfully pulled the wool over Arief's eyes. How had he known she was here? Had he discovered she'd applied to the colonisation project months ago, and he'd known about her escape attempt all along? Had Elek spilled the beans? She'd thought he'd forgotten about her proposal to come with her.

"Let me go," she repeated in a whisper. With a great effort of will, she managed to wrench one foot off the floor.

Arief fixed her with a piercing stare. "Where do you think *you're* going? I haven't given permission for you to leave."

She gritted her teeth. "I'm going to my processing appointment, and then I'm getting on a shuttle that'll take me up to the—" She gasped.

He'd grabbed her wrist. A band of iron seemed to have fastened around it. The band was squeezing tighter, cutting off her circulation. She panted, responding to the pain and also the effort of trying to move away.

Why was he doing this? If he wanted to force her to obey he only had to confuse her with a brain fog, the same as he had so many times before.

Amusement flickered within the adamantine shell of his gaze. He was enjoying himself.

"Damn you, Arief! What did I ever do to you? Haven't you tortured me enough? Find someone else to mess with and leave me alone!"

"How ungrateful. If it wasn't for me you would be dead, a corpse rotting in the back alley of an insignificant city."

"I didn't ask you to save me or do whatever it was you did to give me my abilities, and I've paid you back with my service many times over. I'm not your slave. I deserve to live my own life."

"You deserve nothing." He leaned over her, his hold on her wrist increasing to agonising tightness.

He might have frozen her feet but he wasn't controlling the rest of her. With her free hand she slapped him. His head jerked to the side with the force of her blow—he *had* made her preternaturally strong, after all.

When he turned back fury had sparked in his features. "*Bitch*. You won't get away with that. If you refuse to come back with me, the least I can do is return you to the ground, the fast way." He yanked her wrist upward, lifting her from her feet until she dangled in his grasp. He was going to throw her off the balcony!

There was a flutter of wings and a bird landed on his shoulder. Bright-eyed and sharp-beaked, it was some kind of bird of prey, standing as tall as the top of Arief's head. Setia wasn't sure who was more shocked, her or him. He stared at the animal in disbelief. The bird must have flown across from the mountainside, but why it had landed on him and what it intended was unclear.

He released her wrist and she dropped to the floor. He tried to shoo the bird off, but it jabbed his hand with its beak.

She could move. Quickly, she took several steps back. Arief noticed but he was too busy dealing with the bird to do anything. It was lunging at his eyes, its talons digging deep into his shoulder. He batted it and ducked and swerved as he tried to avoid the pecks. "Oughh!"

She should take her chance to get away, but the spectacle of the strange bird had transfixed her. And what the hell was Arief looking at now? He was ignoring the bird. The invisible thing in the middle distance had claimed his attention again. The bird pecked his ear and he winced. His face twisted in exasperation. "Oh, all right!"

Arief became...*smudged.* His body began to dissolve. As Setia stared, he became indistinct, transforming into a black haze.

Its perch gone, the bird beat the air with its wings to fly away. But rather than returning to the mountain it headed toward the passenger area.

Setia could not take her eyes off Arief.

He was nothing more than a vaguely man-shaped blur, a dark cloud the wind was rapidly breaking into threads.

In another second he was gone.

After staring for a long moment at the empty space, Setia grabbed her suitcase and turned toward the exit. She didn't know what the hell had just happened, but she was going to get away while she could.

A young woman dressed in an AP crew uniform stood in the

doorway, the bird on her shoulder. But it was not attacking her. In fact, it seemed relaxed and comfortable.

The woman held her gaze. "Who was that guy? What did I just see?"

Setia shrugged. "Your guess is as good as mine." She didn't want to get into any conversations about Arief, and she didn't want to be associated with strange phenomena at the processing centre, not when she still had final checks to pass. "Aren't you worried about that bird?"

"Loki? He won't hurt me."

"He's yours?"

"He helps me out sometimes. That man seemed to be bothering you, so..."

"That was you? Thanks. He *was* bothering me, but he isn't anymore." She looked at the space where Arief had stood. She'd known he was capable of all kinds of things, but not transmogrifying into vapour. Who knew?

And why had he given up on trying to make her go back to her old life?

"Which ship are you on?" she asked the woman.

"The *Bres*. You?"

"The same. Thanks again for helping me. I have to go for my interview now."

The woman stepped aside and Setia edged past her. "Maybe I'll see you around."

But Loki's owner was already walking away.

Two

The ID checks were extensive. First, Setia had to submit blood and hair root samples, and her inner cheek was swabbed. They took her fingerprints and scanned her retinas. Even her breath signature had to be verified. These were all in addition to the background checks the assessors had undertaken in the hours before she arrived at the processing point. After all, it had been months since her application had been accepted. Who knew what crimes she might have been accused of, what loans she might have defaulted on, or what dependants might have come forward in the intervening time? The assessors certainly did not, and one thing was for sure: if there was the slightest suspicion she was not who she claimed to be or she had unfinished business on Earth, she would not be leaving the planet.

The medic nodded at a door. "Waiting room's at the end of the corridor."

"Is that it? When I pass I can go to the shuttle?"

"Huh? Didn't you read the information we sent you yesterday? Psych evaluation next, then your final interview."

"But I did a psych evaluation when I applied..."

The medic had buzzed the next applicant in and was looking

pointedly away from her. Taking the hint, she stepped towards the door he'd indicated.

"Your luggage, ma'am."

She collected the suitcase she'd forgotten. Another head check and another interview? She'd assumed that once her ID was confirmed that would be it—she would be on her way to her tiny cabin aboard the *Bres.* She'd been too excited and anxious yesterday to thoroughly read the passenger processing document. Surely everything would be okay. She had no psychological issues. What would the final interview be about? Was there still a possibility she might lose her berth? No doubt there was a clause somewhere in the fine print that would allow them to refuse passage in certain circumstances. The voyage would take months. They couldn't risk an unhinged, vengeful, or malicious passenger jeopardising it. But she was none of those.

Everything's gonna be okay.

The waiting room was nearly full. Only a couple of seats remained empty. A buzz of quiet conversation momentarily stilled as she entered, faces turned to her, and then the chatter resumed. Tension laced the subdued murmurs. One man's knee jigged. A woman drummed an interface with her fingertips.

Setia sat down between a petite, nervous-looking woman, who was holding hands with her partner, and a large, burly man with shoulder-length hair sitting in the corner. She pulled her suitcase in front of her as everyone else had done. They were allowed to bring only ten kilos of belongings for the shuttle flight, though additional baggage items could be shipped separately for a fee. She had shipped no additional items.

The man leant uncomfortably close, pressing his muscular shoulder into her arm. She understood why no one else had taken this seat. His rank body odour had wafted out at the slight movement.

"Runner or seeker?" As he spoke, he revealed yellow, plaque-encrusted teeth and enveloped her with halitosis.

Burnap's balls. The astronomical price of a ticket for a colony ship should have screened out people who couldn't get their act together sufficiently to keep themselves clean, but apparently not. His question implied he was mentally unwell too. An array of sympathetic and amused glances arrived from around the room.

Tilting her head away from him and shifting closer to her other neighbour, she replied, "What?"

"Are you running or seeking? It's a simple enough question." When she didn't answer immediately, he went on, waving a hand expansively, "Everyone in here, everyone on those ships, is leaving Earth for a reason. Some are running away from something. Escaping. Others are seeking something out. Seeking a dream, a wish, a hope. Which are you? Runner or seeker?"

"What I am is none of your business."

"Ha! It might be my business. We'll all be right in each other's business up there." His eyes turned upward.

Setia grabbed the handle of her suitcase and pushed it to the opposite side of the room, where there was another empty seat. The odorous man didn't seem to take offence. He ignored her once she was out of his immediate vicinity.

Gradually, people were called in for their evaluations and new people arrived to wait. Finally, it was her turn. She was led to an enclosed cubicle and sat down in front of an interface. There were two hundred questions to answer.

When was the last time you were angry? Why?

What do you think you will miss most about Earth? Give reasons.

It was tempting to write answers that sounded good. *I hardly ever get angry. Can't remember the last time. The only thing I'll miss about Earth is ice-cream.*

But the assessment software would be sophisticated, instantly detecting and flagging anything anomalous for the psychiatrists to take a closer look. And she wasn't a good liar. In fact, her frank honesty had landed her in trouble more than once. Had she been angry when Arief had tried to prevent her from leaving? Yes. She'd been scared and frustrated, but also angry. Sighing, she gave a short version of the story, leaving out the part about him dissolving into thin air.

An hour later she gave the instruction to submit, hoping she hadn't come across as a lunatic. When she stepped out of the cubicle, the assistant took her to another room. Three people sat behind a desk, two women and a man. A second, fairly elderly man sat in the corner behind a console.

"Setia Zees?" asked the woman in the centre of the three. Her salt-and-pepper hair was short and neatly styled. The man sitting next to her was about her age and wore a military uniform.

"Is there any doubt anymore?" Setia quipped.

This was met by a frosty stare. The younger of the two women covered a yawn with the back of her hand.

"Please take a seat," said the older woman. As Setia complied, she went on, "I am Kate Lineton, Chief Purser of the *Bres.*" She gestured left. "This is Lieutenant-Colonel Markham, and my other colleague is Wulandri, Colonisation Coordinator."

Setia's ears pricked up. The coordinator was from her part of the world, typically being known by a single name only. But though Wulandri had to have made the same connection, she didn't express any sense of solidarity. Mid-thirties and her black hair in a tight bun, she seemed tired and bored.

"Before we start," Setia said, "I want to ask, is there still a chance I won't make it onto the ship? I mean—"

Lineton snapped, "The Antarctic Project reserves the right to deny transportation to any person up to and including the day of depar—"

"All right, I get it," Setia grumbled.

"It's in the terms and conditions."

"Of course it is. What do you want to ask me?" If they were going to pull her off the list she wanted to get it over with. Maybe Arief wouldn't find out she was still on Earth, though she had a strong feeling he would.

"You have an interesting history, Ms Zees," Markham commented. "There aren't many people who can say they've worked closely with the great Elek. And you've been with him right from the start of his career, as I understand it."

She winced. She'd known this would come up. Yet she didn't have, and had never had a rational-sounding explanation for her involvement with the cult leader. For that's what Elek was, though he would never admit it. "I was asked about that in my first interview. You must have my response in your records. Do I have to go over it all again?"

"If you wouldn't mind." Lineton leaned back in her chair and rested her hands on her lap.

Markham fixed her with a piercing stare. Wulandri twiddled her thumbs.

Setia gritted her teeth and began her usual condensed and redacted version of her meeting with Arief, him introducing her to Elek as a new bodyguard, and Elek's slow but steady rise to national and then international fame via his in-person speeches and events. As always, she left out the most outlandish parts of the story, especially the unnatural strength, agility, and skills Arief had somehow imbued her with. The words to make that sound believable in any way did not exist.

When she finished her story Lineton had a follow-up question. "And what made you apply to be a colonist?"

Again, her answers had to be on file, but Setia chose not to point it out. The mood in the room seemed to have shifted. She had a feeling her place on the colony ship had become less secure over the course of her story. But perhaps she was being paranoid. It made sense that they would want to check her answers matched the ones she'd given earlier. If they deviated it might imply she was lying about something. Fortunately, she had memorised them.

"I've always been fascinated by the idea of living on another planet, ever since I was a child. I was so happy when I found out the Antarctic Project had been delayed and there might still be time for me to join it."

"You grew up in Spiral City?"

Setia jerked her head to face Wulandri. It was the first time she'd spoken, and Setia had almost forgotten she was here. "That's right. I was an orphan and far too poor then to even think about applying. Luckily for me, my circumstances changed."

Wulandri's lip lifted, betraying disgust. *That* was why she'd been ignoring her. She'd pegged her as low class and unworthy of attention.

"What attracts you to deep space colonisation?" Lineton asked.

"Several things. The challenge, discovering what it's like to live somewhere other than Earth, and...I have to confess...the honour and renown of being among the first humans to do it. I know I'll only be one of tens of thousands, but it'll be something to tell the grandkids, right? Assuming I find someone to settle down with." She smiled brightly.

Lineton nodded. "Perfect."

Setia's smile widened. She'd done it. Her next stop would be the shuttle to the *Bres.* She'd passed, and she was confident her psych assessment answers had been good too. They'd been similar to the first one she'd done, and she'd passed that so...

"Almost word for word what you said at your first interview," Lineton continued. "You have your generic, meaningless answers down pat."

Setia's smile faltered.

"I admire your determination, Ms Zees, but I'm afraid I have to inform you—"

"No!"

"Your application has been unsuccessful—"

"No! You have to let me on the ship. I've left my job, I've..."

"We will cancel any shipments you've ordered."

"You can't do this!"

"I'm very sorry."

Lineton didn't look remotely sorry. Markham was glaring at her. Wulandri was picking at her nails.

"I understand you must be disappointed," said Lineton, "but

I'm sure you know we can't take any risks. You haven't been forthright with us. This was your last opportunity to give your true reasons for wanting to join the project. The fact that you won't divulge them, despite being given several opportunities, is suspicious. Your real reasons may be innocuous or you may be a saboteur, a religious fanatic, or have some other nefarious motive. As I said, I'm sorry. Now, we have many more interviews to conduct today, so if you wouldn't mind...?"

"I *do* mind! I'm not leaving. I'll tell you why I'm here." But if she told them, would they believe her or would they think she was making it all up?

"It's too late," Markham barked. "If you won't leave I'll call security and have you thrown out."

"Please, give me a chance."

Wulandri said languidly, "Don't make things harder for everyone. It's over."

A soft cough sounded in the corner of the room. Setia had forgotten about the elderly man. He'd been silent throughout the interview. Lineton appeared to have forgotten about him too. Her eyebrows lifting in surprise, she turned to face him. "Is something the matter?"

"She stays."

"She..." Lineton checked her interface and then glanced at her fellow interviewers, who looked equally nonplussed. "Are you sure?"

He didn't answer, as if he should not have had to repeat himself. Setia's impression of the hierarchy in the officials present suddenly shifted. She'd thought Lineton was the one in charge, but it was this man.

Lineton's shoulders sagged. Markham's expression became inscrutable. Wulandri looked furious.

"Welcome to the Project, Ms Zees," the elderly gentleman said. "Step through that door and follow the signs to the shuttle departure point."

Setia got to her feet. "Thank you. Thank you so much." She walked across to him to shake his hand.

Appearing bemused, he took her offered hand.

"Can I ask who you are?"

"I'm Mapper Robins. Now hurry up and get aboard the shuttle. It leaves in five minutes."

Three

Setia had nabbed the final place. The people behind her in the queue would have to wait for the next shuttle flight, arriving in an hour. She could feel their jealous gazes on her back as she mounted the steps to the passenger door. As she stepped inside, she exhaled. Tingles ran through her. Over the last ten minutes she'd gone from a burgeoning hope she'd finally escaped Arief, to shock and despair, to overwhelming relief. She was on her way to the *Bres* at last. The future yawned wide, dark and mysterious.

"Baggage in the forward hold, ma'am," the attendant said.

A windowless tube confronted her, filled with people taking their seats in pairs across a central aisle. There were no overhead lockers. A place in front of the passenger section was assigned for luggage. The attendant helped her push her small suitcase into the only remaining space, and then she walked down the aisle, scanning for an empty seat. It would be aboard a vessel like this she would fly to a new planet roughly nine months from now. These people would be her fellow colonists. She'd been so focused on getting away from Earth she'd barely begun to think about what lay ahead.

Every seat seemed to be taken.

As she squeezed past someone taking off their coat, a shriek burst out. The couple with the small child were here, already sitting down.

The little girl was fighting her father, trying to get up. "I don't wanna go! I don't wanna go! I wanna go home. I wanna see Gramma!" The mother, who was sitting in front of her, leaned over the back of her seat, shushing her daughter.

From the expressions on surrounding faces, plenty of people were thinking the same as Setia: was the little terror going to scream the entire flight?

A sharp-faced young woman poked her head out from behind the child. Locking gazes with Setia, she beckoned and indicated an empty place next to the bulkhead. "I didn't want to sit against the wall," she explained. "Feels weird not being able to look out."

After some manoeuvring, Setia sat down. "Thanks. *Oh.*" Her safety harness had slid out and over her shoulders and waist automatically, closing in a comfortable fit with a soft snick.

"Cool, isn't it? I heard they're bringing them in on commercial aircraft. Of course," her neighbour added confidently, "the *Bres* and the rest of the fleet will have the latest of everything. Though it'll soon be out of date once we're a few weeks into the voyage."

Setia wasn't sure if the woman was referring to the effects of time dilation—that time would pass comparatively faster on Earth as the starships built up speed—or the general pace of technological innovation, which was so fast these days it was hard to keep track of. She didn't feel like talking, however, especially not over the noise the kid was making, so she just nodded.

The crew had sealed the passenger door. Everyone was seated. The aircraft gave a small jerk.

"Looks like we're on our way," Setia's companion announced.

The shuttle rolled forward and began to turn. It *did* feel weird not being able to look out. So the view she'd been enjoying when Arief arrived really had been her last sight of Earth forever. She would have liked to savour the experience, to commit the landscape to memory. If only Arief hadn't spoiled it.

"Uhhh..." Her seat companion pointed at her armrest.

An ear comm sat in a small depression. She popped it into her ear.

The pilot was in the middle of an announcement. "Our estimated flight time is seven hours thirty-five minutes, and that's a good estimate. We're expecting a little turbulence soon, but once we're out of the Earth's atmosphere it'll be plain sailing, so to speak." He paused, perhaps imagining a chuckle from his audience. "You may experience a very short period of weightlessness as the a-grav comes on line, and an adjustment in cabin pressure. Nothing that some determined swallowing won't sort out. If you have any concerns or issues, please speak to one of the cabin crew, who will be happy to assist you. Otherwise, sit back and enjoy the flight."

Setia relaxed and closed her eyes. Almost imperceptibly, the shuttle lifted into the air. Soothing music played from her ear comm. Shrieks and scuffles continued to emanate from the kid but she managed to screen the sounds out.

Memories flickered across her mind. She recalled hugging Elek goodbye. He hadn't known it would be for the last time. She hoped he would be okay. He should be, despite the growing rowdiness of his audiences. His security team had been the best she could find. An earlier memory arose, when she'd met him for the first time. Lanky and hairy, he'd reminded her of an orangutan. She lifted the corner of her lip. What had he made of her? Smaller than average, a simple local woman, he must have wondered what had got into Arief's head to prompt him to recommend her as a bodyguard.

She stepped back in time. She was running drugs for Pratam again, taking her life in her hands every day, though she hadn't known it. She been too young, too naive. Back then, the job had felt exciting, and it had been about the only way for someone with no education or connections to make a decent living. She'd felt no guilt about it, quick to dismiss the effects of Pratam's shit on addicts. If *she* hadn't been a go-between, someone else would, right? She shifted uncomfortably.

She was younger now. Dad was feeding her steamed rice from a banana leaf. He looked hungry, but he didn't take any for himself. Somehow, she'd sensed his hunger, yet it didn't stop her from opening her mouth for more. What had happened to her mother? She had no mental image of her at all. Then Dad was gone.

"I'm not doing it!"

Her eyes snapped open.

The annoying kid's father was on his feet. "Turn the shuttle around! I want to go back."

For a brief moment, Setia was utterly confused. It was as if the toddler and her dad had swapped places, the child's energy flowing into her parent.

"Sweetheart..." the man's wife gently remonstrated. "Sit down or—"

"*You're* the one who wanted to do this, not me. This is all *your* idea. Why should *I* have to go along with it, huh?"

"Sir!" exclaimed the flight attendant, running up the aisle. "I must ask you to take your seat immediately."

"Let me off the flight!" He clambered over his child. "I want to get off!"

"That isn't possible, sir."

His partner reached out and grabbed his arm. "Sit down, for god's sake!"

"Mommy!" The girl began to wail.

"Shut up!" her father screamed. "Shut up-shut up-shut up! You've been crying ever since we left home. I can't stand it!" He tried to snatch her out of her seat, but her safety harness held her in place. He fumbled with it—Setia couldn't see what he was doing exactly. There was a snick as the straps sprang apart, and he yanked the kid into the air.

"Put her down!" yelled the mother.

The father gave the child a shake. "Shut up!"

Setia unfastened her harness.

The mother leapt to her feet and tried to retrieve her daughter but he wouldn't let go. Mad rage filled his eyes. He started to shake his daughter harder.

Setia climbed over her neighbour, who was frozen in open-mouthed disbelief.

"Sir!" said the flight attendant, "I must insist..."

Setia didn't hear the rest. She was distracted by the approach of another figure. A man was racing from the front of the craft. That wasn't so surprising in itself. The crew member would clearly need assistance in restraining the hysterical passenger. What *was* surprising was what was happening to the man. A dull grey liquid was gliding over his shoulders and flooding down his arms. The metallic fluid surged around his chest and hips and spilled down his legs. As he lifted one foot, the substance ran beneath it. A liquid hood appeared on his head. A grey wave rushed over his cheeks and gushed down his neck. Within seconds, he was enveloped in a solid yet flexible protective suit, an eye slit the only opening.

The kid had become a red-faced wreck, her mouth wide open and screaming blue murder. Her head snapped backwards and forwards as her father shook her. The mother couldn't break her partner's hold. The armoured man slid to a halt at the scene, but the attendant was in his way.

"Sir! Sir! Please—"

Setia punched the father behind his ear.

Instantly, all tension left his body. As he collapsed, the mother grabbed her daughter from his opening hands. Setia took a step back. The guy was a lot bigger than her and she saw no reason to break his fall. The shuttle would have to make a return journey to drop this nutcase and his family off, inconveniencing her and everyone else. The father sprawled in the aisle, out cold.

A shocked silence reigned. Even the kid made barely a whimper as her mother hugged her close. When Setia's attention returned to the armoured man, his protective shield was flowing away, going back to wherever it had come from.

The attendant helped the mother and child back into their seats.

The formerly armoured man's gaze turned to Setia. "Nice punch. That wasn't by accident, right?" His dark brown hair was close cut and matched his keen eyes. He was military—shipboard military, assigned to the shuttle in case of exactly the kind of passenger breakdown they'd just witnessed.

She shrugged a non-committal answer. After nearly losing her berth, the last thing she'd wanted to do was attract attention, but she'd felt sorry for the kid.

Her seat companion stood to allow her to edge past and return to her place. As the soldier stooped to grab the unconscious man under his armpits, he caught her eye again. "Fancy joining the ship's guard?"

She gave her head a little shake and looked away.

"If you change your mind, talk to Lieutenant-Colonel Markham. Military personnel get special perks."

"I'll think about it." She hoped her reply would make him leave her alone.

"I apologise for the recent disturbance."

The disembodied pilot's voice sounded in her ear, making her jump She'd forgotten about the comm. She reached up to remove it.

"We will be returning to our departure point, and once—"

Placing the comm in the armrest depression, she leaned back.

"Wow, that was something," said her neighbour. "The psych evaluations weren't as good as I thought."

"Guess not," Setia murmured.

Four

Displayed on the seatback screen in front of Setia was a metallic disc, its edge thickened. The *Bres*'s hull was drab —no need for polish where metal wouldn't rust and there was no one to impress—though the Antarctic Project logo stood out clearly.

The colony ship had once been a gigantic corkscrew, she'd heard, wrapped around a central propulsion system. The turning of the screw would have mimicked Earth-like gravity, essential for the health of the colonists on the long voyage. Revelations resulting from the Britannic Alliance's encounter with extraterrestrial life forms on a foray into deep space had changed all that. Now, with the invention of a-grav, there was no need for the ship to spin. The time it would take to reach the first colony planet had been drastically shortened too, from years to months, meaning no cryosleep chambers.

The re-built *Bres* resembled a doughnut without a hole. It was impossible to guess her size but it had to be vast. Twenty thousand colonists would inhabit this vessel alone. The smaller, more distant, shapes of her identical sister ships, the *Balor* and *Banba*, hung in the void like ancient coins resting on glitter-speckled black velvet.

"You're awake?" Setia's neighbour remarked. "I don't know how you could sleep at a time like this."

Setia gave her a tight-lipped smile as she inserted her ear comm.

The image of the *Bres* disappeared from the screen, replaced by a red *AP*. They'd arrived. She pretended to focus intensely on the pilot's spiel while the shuttle docked. Breathless, excited chatter rose around her, bursting in a crescendo when the announcement arrived to unfasten safety harnesses and prepare to disembark. Applause erupted. Setia's companion joined in enthusiastically. They rose to join the queue to leave the ship, taking their comms with them as instructed by the pilot. The devices would be theirs for the duration of the voyage.

Taking her suitcase from the storage area, Setia felt as though she was dreaming. The babbling of her fellow passengers sounded muted and distant, their forms hazy and indistinct. Mechanically, she approached the exit, nearly last in line.

"Amazing, isn't it?" asked her seat companion.

"Yeah."

"What section are you in?"

"D."

"Cool. Me too. What number?"

"I don't know. I'll have to check." Setia knew full well her cabin was in D12.

"Maybe we'll be neighbours aboard the *Bres* as well. I'm in D12. It would be a cool coincidence if your cabin's there too, right?"

"Right."

The line shuffled forward. As Setia stepped through the passenger door, the chill air of the shuttle bay hit her, laced with an odd scent. A mild perfume to mask other odours generated aboard starships perhaps? Food smells, the sweat of twenty-thousand bodies and who knew what else would be hard to filter out entirely.

Three more docking spaces stood empty in the vast bay, awaiting returning shuttles. The footsteps of the disembarking passengers echoed tinnily from the steel walls, ceiling, and floor.

"I hope the rest of the ship is prettier!" her seat neighbour remarked.

Setia hurried down the steps, itching to put distance between herself and the sharp-faced woman. She didn't have anything against her per se. She just needed to be alone.

Half an hour later she got her wish. The induction to living on the ship had only taken fifteen minutes, just information on where to eat, how to get around, and what communal facilities were available to all passengers—some were only available to higher classes. Then they were free to go. She managed to lose her would-be friend on the way to Section D12. In the labyrinthine network of passages, she located cabin 42 and pressed her thumb against the panel. The door slid back, and she stepped inside.

A single bunk occupied half the space. Above it hung an interface. Another screen sat at an angle on the desk. Opposite the desk and accompanying chair was a set of drawers. There was more storage space under the bed, and a long shelf hung over it. A second door led to a tiny cubicle containing a shower, washbasin, toilet, and small cupboard.

Her living quarters for the next nine months occupied roughly eight square meters, and they had cost her every penny she'd had, all she'd saved during her lucrative career as the great Elek's primary security agent. But, of course, the fee didn't only cover her passage. It was a ticket to the future of humanity, and, for her, the only escape possible.

She pushed her suitcase under the bunk and lay down, putting her hands behind her head.

Nine months in this cubby hole?

Considering the alternative, she could do it.

Talman Prime slowly rotated in the centre of the auditorium. It was not a holo of the actual planet, naturally, but an approximation of its appearance derived from data sent back by probes.

"Though our new home is somewhat larger than Earth it has less overall mass," Wulandri explained, standing at a podium in the first ring of seats, "which means the gravity is slightly lower. Point eight-three-five of Earth's gravity, to be precise."

"Will we be able to fly?" a high-pitched voice called out.

Even at some distance from her countrywoman, Setia could see irritation flit over Wulandri's features.

"Over the course of our voyage the gravity aboard ship will be gradually reduced, so that by the time we arrive you'll be accustomed to it and shouldn't notice any difference. I would like to draw your attention to the largest land mass. Most research has been focused on this area as the site best suited to colonisation. As a young planet, Talman Prime is more volcanically active than Earth, but all the fault lines appear to run beneath the oceans. The main land mass seems stable. We will attempt the first settlement inland, far from potential tsunamis, yet near liquid water. Average temperatures in this area range between..."

Setia began to lose interest. There would be plenty of time to learn about Talman Prime before they arrived, and new data was being transmitted back from probes all the time. What Wulandri was telling them was probably already out of date. Mildly regretting her decision to come to the information talk, her gaze roved the audience. Perhaps more important to the success of the project wasn't conditions on the planet, but her fellow colonists.

A familiar face leapt out, eliciting surprise and disgust. The cleanliness-challenged man from the waiting room was here. How come? Surely he should have failed the psych check. He appeared to be ignoring Wulandri too. He had an interface open and he was tapping it.

She spotted someone else she recognised. Seated opposite the speaker in the lowest tier was Mapper Robins. His legs crossed and one foot jigging, he focused on the spinning globe, his expression thoughtful.

"Found you!" The woman from the shuttle sat down. "I've been looking everywhere for you. Did you find your cabin okay?"

"Uh huh."

"What section number?"

Setia inwardly cringed, but lying was pointless. "D12."

"Snap! I knew it. I knew you would be in the same section as me."

"It's fine. A place to sleep." She waited for the inevitable question about her cabin number, anticipating that Burnap was playing a joke on her and that the woman would be living at 43.

But instead she said, "You know, I don't think we ever got around to swapping names. I'm Miriam. Miriam Belby."

"Setia Zees."

"Pleased to make your acquaintance, Setia," Miriam said in a singsong tone. "It's good to have friends when you have a big trip to take. Helps to pass the time. Maybe we can have dinner together. I can't wait to try the food."

"I'm not hungr—"

"Oh, cool, look!" Miriam was peering down at someone in the audience. "Mapper Robins is here."

"You know him?"

"You don't?"

"I'd never heard of him, and I would remember a name like that."

"A name like what? Robins isn't unusual."

"No, Mapper. Who would think it was a good idea to call their kid Mapper?"

"That isn't his name, silly. It's his title. He's a skein mapper. We have a few aboard the ship, but he's the most famous."

"*Ohhh.*"

Skein mappers were part of the new order. They traced the connections between people, links on a hitherto unknown plane of existence. Other than that, she didn't know very much about what they did.

As if sensing someone was talking about him, Robins turned and his head lifted to survey the audience. He saw her and their gazes locked. For a split second Setia was deeply and keenly scrutinised. Then his attention moved on.

"Hm, he certainly seems interested in you," Miriam remarked.

When the talk was over, Setia made her excuses to her new friend about dinner, though she wasn't sufficiently quick-witted to think up a reason to avoid meeting for breakfast. Feeling a little churlish—there was nothing intrinsically off-putting about Miriam, it was only that she would inevitably ask about Setia's past, and she didn't want to talk about it—she set off to find an alternative place to get a snack before retiring for the 'quiet shift'. There would be no more night-time for the next three-quarters of a year.

The arterial routes linking the sections accommodated the electric buggies used for travelling long distances as well as pedestrians. Setia walked at the edge of the route. Somehow, she'd managed to pick a path that went against the general flow of traffic. She dodged people walking in pairs and groups, parents holding hands with their children, couples with their arms wrapped around each other.

Most of the colonists seemed to have come with companions. Singletons like her and Miriam were relatively rare. Perhaps she shouldn't be so standoffish.

A shout rang out.

There was a disturbance down the passageway. Ripples ran out from it, waves of irritation, annoyance and disquiet. The roar of rowdy young men hit. The crowd parted and she saw them: four men carrying a fifth on their shoulders, weaving unsteadily. They staggered sideways and nearly dropped their burden. Giggling loudly at his complaints, they hoisted him higher. The near-accident wasn't because they were struggling to carry him. All the men were burly. But the four bearers appeared as drunk as their load, possibly drunker. The man suspended between them was calling out directions with some accuracy even though his head hung upside down.

"Hostiles at two o'clock," he stated, referring to a stationary cluster of flamboyantly dressed women, staring disapprovingly. "Take evasive action."

Setia rolled her eyes and pressed her back to the wall to give them room to pass.

As the leaders of the group drew level with her the carried man blurted, “Whoa, hold it. Abort mission. I said, abort mission.”

His buddies were slow to respond.

“Put me down, guys.”

He landed with a thunk.

“I said put me down, not drop me,” he complained, rising haphazardly to his feet while his friends doubled over with laughter, clutching their guts.

Now he was upright, she recognized him. He was flushed and sweaty and his minimal hair was somehow messy. He was also out of uniform. But she was sure it was the soldier from the shuttle.

He put his hands on his hips, rocking slightly. “It’s One Punch Girl!”

She cocked an eyebrow. “Girl? I’m thirty-two.”

The other men had begun to wander away.

“Hey, guys, it’s One Punch Girl. The woman I was telling you about, remember? Screaming kid. Crazy dad. Pow!” He mimed a punch. “Crash!” He pretended to fall down. “Guys! Guys, come and meet her. We need to persuade her to enlist.”

His plea drew no response from his companions, who were now several metres away. Two were lifting a third between them, his arms around their necks, their forearms under his thighs.

The soldier from the shuttle pointed at her, thumb extended, and clicked his tongue. “Catch you later.” He ran off to join his friends.

It was going to be a long voyage.

Five

"So you see, colonising Talman Prime is going to mean most of us becoming accustomed to an agrarian lifestyle. For all their merits, neither the *Bres, Balor* nor *Banba* is a manufacturing plant. Sure, they're carrying spare parts for the machinery we're bringing along, but those items are in finite supply, and once they're used up, we're on our own. There won't be any sending to Earth for replacements. The distances are simply too great."

"But it's only nine months away!" a voice in the audience objected.

Their lecturer, a broad-chested man in his fifties who had introduced himself as Papa Paulus, shook his large head. "Nine months by one of our magnificent ships. You must know the plan is for all of them to venture onwards to other potential colony planets once Talman Prime is established." He grinned good-naturedly, exposing a fine set of white teeth. "They aren't delivery services!"

The audience had mostly been in the palm of his hand since he'd started speaking, and they chuckled, all except the portly man who had made the objection. He frowned and folded his arms over his chest.

"We're used to living in a highly developed, technological society," Papa Paulus went on. "Supply chains for all our resources are well-established—the minerals mostly from offplanet these days. Do any of you know the materials required to make an interface?" He surveyed the blank faces. Setia didn't have a clue either. "Or a printer? How about this table?" He tapped the surface of the one he'd propped himself on. "Or those benches where you sit?" After pausing a beat, he explained, "All the resources used to make everyday objects and devices have been mined and processed, or perhaps grown, or perhaps retrieved from an ancient landfill. Though we've managed to automate many of the production systems, they don't happen by magic, and hundreds of thousands of people are still involved in providing the luxurious lifestyles we had on Earth."

"Luxurious!" the portly man spluttered. "I scrimped and saved for this opportunity right from when I was a kid. I deprived myself of everything except bare essentials all my days, and now you're telling me I have to be a farmer!"

Setia gritted her teeth. What exactly had he expected he would be doing on humanity's first colony planet? Bathing in asses' milk while being fed grapes by naked women? She looked with sympathy at Papa Paulus. How would he handle the dissatisfied customer?

"The anticipated lifestyles of project participants were laid out clearly in the information packets," he replied gently. "We will be creating a new society from scratch without the backup of a huge population or well-established, wide-reaching infrastructures. Naturally, things will be tough sometimes. We will have to get used to roughing it and doing without. But think of the benefits—a pristine environment, living organisms completely new to science, the chance to build a new civilisation in the wilderness. Imagine, on the first night after we set foot on Talman Prime, you will see new constellations in the night sky. Surely, any sacrifice is worth those rewards?"

The objector didn't appear convinced, though Paulus's words had inspired some looks of awe in the rest of the 'students'.

"Right from its inception," said Papa Paulus, "the goal of the Antarctic Project was to establish autonomous, self-sustaining colonies on extraterrestrial planets. Talman Prime won't be an offshoot of Earth society, a lonely outpost like we have on Mars and Ganymede, it will be its own entity, entirely self-contained, with its own history, customs and—who knows?—maybe eventually its own culture."

A hand rose. "Will we be expected to breed with the aliens?"

Paulus blinked. His expression tightened as if he was struggling to keep a straight face. A titter ran through the audience.

"Even if that were possible, I can say with some confidence that we're unlikely to encounter intelligent life. All the probe data indicates only very small animal organisms, no bigger than rats, inhabit Talman Prime, and nothing highly evolved. Certainly nothing you could..." He gave a small cough followed by a forced smile. "Moving on. Today, we're going to look at... Yes?"

Another hand had risen. A woman's haughty voice asked, "You said at the beginning that *most* of us will be involved in agriculture. What are the other jobs, and how do I apply?"

"There are no other jobs as such. Some members of the ship's personnel are already involved in other aspects of the project—coordination, scientific research, supply management, human resource management, construction, and so on. Some are teachers, like me. These positions are already filled. There is no application process."

"Hmpf!"

Another dissatisfied customer.

"All of this should have been very clear to you months ago," Paulus said in an even tone.

In truth, Setia hadn't studied the details very well either, but her sympathies were with the teacher and not his class. What had they imagined their lives would be like on the new planet? Their expectations seemed wildly unrealistic. On the other hand, most of them had to be from extremely privileged backgrounds. Despite her humble beginnings, she'd been wealthy herself, but she'd only just been able to afford her passage. The costs of financing the project had been astronomical, and they had been reflected in the fees.

Had anyone else in this room ever done manual labour? Did they know one end of a spade from the other? Papa Paulus had his work cut out.

"Let's start with the basics," he said, and then gave the command to open a holo. A field of wheat filled the front of the room. Brilliant lights shone down on the golden stalks. "On Earth, most farming now takes place underground, leaving the surface to reassume a wild state. On Talman Prime, things will be different. We will be reliant on good weather, the same as the farmers of old, and we must tend to our crops, weeding them and treating any infestations."

"Ugh, bugs?!" someone said. "I can't do that. I have a phobia."

"There are many tasks involved in farming. If insects aren't your thing, there's plenty else to do. I'm sure you'll be able to find something you like. The first years will be a settling-in period. It will take some time to establish what crops grow well in the new soil and climate. We may discover some indigenous edible plant species we can exploit."

"I'm not eating foreign muck," said a disgruntled voice.

Papa Paulus took a deep breath and then slowly exhaled. "All these challenges can be overcome with time, patience and perseverance. After all, our ancestors managed it, and they didn't have a fraction of our knowledge. We might not have access to support from Earth, but we have something almost as useful." He tapped his head. "Scientific understanding going back generations. Some of the best scientists in their respective fields are coming along on our voyage. With people like that and the combined efforts of you good folk, we can't go wrong."

Someone muttered, only just audibly, "I can't believe I paid good money to grub around in the dirt."

Someone else said, "This isn't at all how I imagined it would be."

How *had* they imagined it would be? Setia sighed. Papa Paulus had revealed an awful truth. These bankers, heads of multi-national companies, business moguls, media giants, and heirs of fortunes would have to actually work to put food on their tables. They must have read the project literature but not cottoned on that it applied to them—that, for once in their lives, someone else wasn't going to do all the unpleasant stuff.

The portly man shot to his feet. "I demand to speak to the captain!"

"Yes," said the haughty woman who had asked about jobs, also jumping up, "me too! This is outrageous. I've been misled. We've *all* been misled, and something must be done about it. Why can't robots grow the food? I want to enjoy my time on Talman Prime, not spend it dirty and smelly, covered in sweat, and not knowing where my next meal is coming from."

Paulus lifted his hands. "Please, sit down, and we can talk about this. No doubt, eventually we will achieve a similar standard of living as on Earth, with similar leisure time, but in the beginning—"

"Look," drawled a new voice, "you seem like a nice guy and all, but you don't understand where we're coming from. We're all very important people. We aren't *labourers*. You seem to want us to pick up all these new skills but I'm too old for all that. This old dog ain't learning any new tricks. All I want is somewhere to retire. A place in the sun to live out the rest of my days in peace and quiet. Not...I don't know...picking cherries and milking goats. Heck, no one would want to rely on *me* in order to eat."

Papa Paulus appeared to be at a loss for words. Then he said, "If everyone would sit down, I'd be happy to discuss your expectations."

"Screw that!" exclaimed the portly man. "Who cares what you say? You're just a teacher."

The audience was fragmenting, talking among themselves and turning away from Paulus. The haughty woman icily asked the other people in her row to move out of her way as she edged by. The portly man was also leaving. The class began to descend into chaos.

Setia decided to leave too. She felt sorry for Paulus but she couldn't help him. He'd been given an impossible task, to turn humanity's soft-handed elites into productive human beings. Silently wishing him luck, she slid out of the room.

There would be plenty more classes to prepare them for their new lives before they reached their destination. She'd thought of something else to do. Ever since Mapper Robins had saved her from being culled from the ship's manifest, her curiosity about why he'd done it had grown. There was only one way to find out the reason she'd been spared, and that was to ask him.

Six

Robins's door slid open, revealing a scene that, though it only lasted the briefest of moments, remained vivid in Setia's mind for months to come.

The lights were off and the interior was dark, but for a single source of illumination: a web of fluorescent green threads, filling the room from side to side and floor to ceiling. Bright blobs of green glowed where the threads crossed, some larger and brighter than others. The threads differed in thickness too. Some were gossamer-thin, others strong, broad bands.

Robins sat facing the web, leaning back in his seat, feet up on his desk, regarding the display with half closed eyes. The glow lit up his face at an angle, causing crazy shadows to run up and over it. Even at the distance from the door to the reclined man, Setia caught a glimpse of a tiny, shining web, impossibly fine and intricate, reflected under his eyelids..

The scene vanished.

The lights had come on. The web was gone.

Robins took his feet down from his desk and sat up. "Setia! I was wondering when I would see you. Come in, come in."

He'd recognised her straight away, even though he must have met thousands of passengers.

"Am I disturbing you?" she asked. "I could come b—"

"Absolutely not. Take a seat."

Devoid of the display, his office was mostly empty and seemed too big for its purpose.

Cautiously, she sat down. "That thing I just saw. Was it...?"

"A skein? Yes. Sometimes it helps to get a visual of an issue, you know?"

"Was I...? I mean, was *I* on it? Were you looking at something to do with me?"

He chuckled. "Totally unrelated."

"Right. I've heard about skeins but I don't really know anything about them or how they work. I'm grateful you helped me out in my interview—very grateful—but I don't know why. That's why I'm here. I want to find out. I don't understand exactly what you do or what your role is on the *Bres.*"

"Tell me what you know and I'll fill in the rest, though only to a point."

"As I understand it, skeins are the underlying connectedness between all things. They allow..." the words felt clumsy in her mouth "... I mean, they show how things can affect other things that appear independent from each other."

He nodded.

"And people are connected too, and events, and... That's about it. I must seem pretty ignorant. I've been busy these last few years. I haven't had time to keep up with the new developments."

His eyebrows lifted. "You've been busy indeed."

"So you know all about what's been going on with me?" she asked, her gut tightening, the vision of the web flashing into her mind's eye. Did he know about Arief and the struggle at the passenger processing centre? "I don't get it. How is that even possible?"

"You aren't as anonymous as you might think. Even if I weren't a mapper, I could easily find out all about you with a standard search, the same search that was undertaken when you applied to join the Project."

"Yeah, of course." She relaxed somewhat. "But you know more, right?"

He gave a non-committal shrug. "All matter and energy is connected. That's the principle. My job is to see how they're connected and to guess—and I stress *guess*—why. The connectedness isn't random, we don't think, and as time moves forwards, events seem to tend towards certain ends. My role aboard this ship is to map the skein of the Project, the people in it, the relations between them, how they develop, and what might be the repercussions of decisions taken and events that occur."

"You can predict the future?"

"Everyone can predict the future. I have a better chance than most of getting it right."

"Did you know I was coming here today? And if you did, why weren't you ready for me?"

He guffawed, his head tilted backwards. He wiped an eye. "I like you, Setia Zees."

"Seriously, I want to know why you spoke up when I was about to be kicked off the Project."

"I'm afraid I cannot tell you, except to state the obvious—that you are significant. I forecast deleterious results if your presence were removed from the skein."

"When you say you can't tell me, do you mean you don't know or you aren't allowed to tell me?"

"Neither. I cannot reveal the nature of your significance without potentially impacting later events, possibly in a negative way. Also, I can't tell you because I don't know your future for sure, and it wouldn't be fair to mislead you."

She paused to digest this information, and Robins watched her gravely. The potentialities of what he did were vast. A storm of implications rained down. "Can you... Do you know when someone is going to die?"

Silence was his answer.

"Have you...? I'm sorry, but I have to ask this... Do you know...?"

"Predicting my own death would be rather morbid, don't you

think?" His gaze had turned steely.

She swallowed. She'd been rude, and her cultural hangover of always respecting her elders loomed large.

Burnap's balls. What had she been thinking to ask him such a question?

His revelation that she was significant to the outcome of the Antarctic Project had unsettled her, even though she'd kind of guessed that must be the case. Otherwise why had Robins saved her from being thrown out with the rubbish?

He reached out across the desk and laid his bony hand on hers, all stoniness gone from his expression. "I understand your curiosity about your place in the skein. It's natural, and I feel bad for disappointing you. Let me show you something that may make your visit worthwhile." He rose to his feet. "Come with me."

He led her out of his office and along the passageway, right to the end. They turned the corner and halted between two doors facing each other at a dead end. If they'd been in D12, the left-hand door would have been her cabin.

He lifted a hand to the security panel, but before touching it he said, "You may have been told it's impossible to see outside the ship. That isn't exactly true."

"You mean it's a lie."

His features turned thoughtful. "Strictly speaking."

He placed a hand on the panel, and the opening door revealed the tiny space Setia had been expecting. In place of her bunk was a narrow bench. The room was otherwise empty, except for another security panel on the far wall.

"It's hard to get your bearings on so large a ship," Robins said. "This room abuts the hull, believe it or not."

"And that panel opens a window?"

"A small one." Sitting down, he beckoned her and gestured that she should join him on the bench. "If I were to open the panel, what do you expect we might see?"

"Space, of course. Stars."

He gave her a look.

"Or maybe not. Is that why they tell everyone we can't see outside?"

"The psychiatrists already have their work cut out. Why up the ante?"

His comment reminded her of Papa Paulus and the lecture about farming. "Do the higher-ups realise that most of the colonists are completely unsuited to, to...colonising?"

He sighed. "Ua Talman was a great man, but he was also an out-and-out capitalist. People were just cogs in a machine to him, to be slotted in, taken out, and moved around however was best to make the machine work and provide the biggest output—in other words, profit. The criteria for selecting participants—namely, that their wealth was equally as important as their health—is one of the project's greatest flaws, and something I must take steps to counteract. Yet perhaps it was unavoidable. Without the financial input of Earth's richest citizens, deep space colonisation probably couldn't happen." Smiling wryly, he added, "My colleagues back home are seeing the widening effects of removing so much of the upper echelons of Earth society all at once."

So the organisers already knew about the problem. Concluding there wasn't anything *she* could do about it, Setia said, "You were going to show me what's outside the ship?"

"I think you will find it less alarming than most, and definitely interesting."

They sat on the bench and he placed his palm against the panel. The covering of the portal slid away.

The *Bres*'s hull had to be metres thick, yet somehow the engineers had created a visual illusion in the panel. The view was similar to looking out an aeroplane window.

Horizontal streaks of light crossed the scene, and the space between them was not black but deep red. There was no appearance of motion. The streaks were immobile and the red a consistent, unchanging colour.

Setia stared.

"If you were to don an EVA suit and step outside," said Robins, "that's what you would see. It's a passage through a vein of less, uh, temporally-resistant material than ordinary space. The discovery was made not long before our departure, and modifications were made to the ships at the last minute to enable them to travel along it. This new route should reduce our journey time considerably."

"We'll arrive in less than nine months?"

"We will 'arrive' when the captain judges the colonists to be ready for the trials lying ahead."

"That could be a lot longer than nine months. Are we already there?"

"Not quite."

Her gaze was riveted to the view until at last she said, "Could you close that thing?"

Robins's estimation that she was stronger-minded than the average colonist was misplaced. The sight was deeply disturbing. As the cover slid shut, she rested a hand on a wall and closed her eyes. Why had the mapper allowed her the special privilege, revealing the truth about the length of the journey? She opened one eye and regarded him. Was he manipulating her?

His expression was mild. "I hope you don't mind me mentioning it, but I believe you haven't made many friends yet?"

She straightened up, about to reply, *Actually, I do mind* when he continued, "If you're ever feeling lonely, I would suggest re-acquainting yourself with Carys Ellis. You might find you have some things in common."

"I don't know anyone called Carys Ellis."

He frowned. "You've already met."

"I'm pretty sure we haven't."

"She runs the aviary? Deck Eight."

"I haven't been to... Ohhh. Does she carry a bird around on her shoulder, like a pirate?"

"I've never seen her in person, but—"

"She's connected to me in some way. I get it. I thought you weren't supposed to influence future events?"

"Sometimes it doesn't hurt to give them a little shove."

Seven

Setia was floating in the ocean, suspended in warm water, sunlight hot on her face. The waves gently lifted and lowered her. Underwater bubbles vibrated in her ears. Her lips held a salty tang. She wasn't sure why she was here, but the sensation was pleasant and relaxing. She eased into it, letting her mind drift along with the current. She could almost fall asleep.

Something slid beneath her.

A long, smooth-skinned animal brushed its body against her back, dragging its form against her skin. It was cold and sinewy and its muscles undulated as it moved.

In her panic, she rolled onto her front and her head dipped beneath the water. She reared up, gasping and choking, flailing wildly, batting the surface as if that might somehow help her stay afloat.

Where was the creature?

Where had it gone?

Was it going to attack?

There was nothing but empty ocean all around.

How had she got so far from the shore?

What was she even *doing* here?

A head broke free from the waves, thin and snake-like. The

vertical slits of its eyes focused directly on her. The jaw dropped open, revealing rows of jagged teeth.

Setia turned to swim, though she knew it was hopeless. A sea animal like that would catch her in a second. She pushed a hand into the water, but the liquid had turned viscous. It clung to her like glue.

"Bleep, bleep, bleep," the creature said.

She turned back, treading water, forcing her legs through thick fluid.

"Bleep, bleep, bleep."

The mouth hadn't moved. The noise had come from the throat somehow, like an intercom or speaker. The creature seemed frozen in position. The sky was darkening. The ocean began to solidify.

She could not move at all.

"Bleep, bleep, bleep."

As she woke, she groggily realised the sound was an alarm. She had learned about the different kinds during her induction to living aboard the ship. There were different sounds for the various potential emergencies: depressurisation, fire, attack...

Rubbing her eyes, she sat up. Her cabin light had already turned on automatically. It dimmed and brightened, dimmed and brightened, matching the rhythm of the bleeps.

Which alarm was this?

"This is your captain speaking. I regret to inform you we have recently discovered there is a stowaway aboard. For your safety, you are required to return to your living quarters immediately. If you are already in your cabin you must remain there. I repeat, all passengers are confined to their cabins until further notice. If anyone unauthorised attempts to enter your living space, please report it. Thank you for your cooperation."

For your safety Setia mentally scoffed. Though she guessed it was possible the stowaway might be dangerous, they were locking down the ship in order to find the man or woman more easily. That was clear. Everyone with a ticket had a place to sleep. A stowaway did not, but while passengers were out and about he or she could get away with slumbering in various places without attracting attention.

Anyone would assume it was just someone having a nap. With the public areas empty, it would be hard to find a place to hide.

She lay down again and settled in for a wait. She wasn't sleepy anymore, not after that horrible nightmare, so she pulled down the overhead interface to watch a vid.

The drama became a blur of meaningless images and voices, however, as her mind drifted back to the current crisis. What would they do with the stowaway? The ship could hardly turn around. There was probably a brig somewhere, a place to put passengers or crew who had committed a crime. But after they arrived at Talman Prime, what then?

Would the first building constructed on the new planet be a prison?

What a statement about human nature that would be.

Her stomach rumbled and she placed a hand on it, regretting her decision to skip dinner. None of the options had looked enticing. As a passenger of the lowest class, she could only eat at the free diners, which offered a basic range of dishes. All were filling and nutritious, but they were not imaginative. She missed her country's cuisine already. Her palate had become more refined during her years working as Elek's head of security, too. Further lowering of her expectations would be required in the years to come, no doubt, while the colony established itself.

She re-started the vid and tried to concentrate. The story was a wild one. A group of runaways had a brilliant business idea and they were trying to make a success of it, but international conglomerates stood in their way, trying to force them to sell their secret and also resorting to nefarious means to defeat the ambitious youngsters.

Setia rolled her eyes. All the street rats *she'd* ever known, herself included, generally survived through drugs, prostitution or a combination of both. The vid drama was a fantasy.

She sighed and checked the time. A couple of hours had passed since the captain's announcement. How much longer would it take them to locate the stowaway?

Turning off the drama and the light, she tried to go back to sleep.

After a while, she managed to achieve a light doze despite the complaining of her stomach. But then a new noise disturbed her. A voice. She blinked wearily. It wasn't another captain's announcement. The sound was coming from outside her cabin, and there wasn't one voice, but two.

One was whiny, the other stern and kind of odd. She forced herself fully awake and listened. The reason the stern voice sounded strange was because it was being broadcast, not spoken.

The whiny voice became louder and more insistent. "Do you have any idea how much I paid to be on this ship?!"

"Sir," said the stern voice, "if you don't return to your cabin immediately, I will be forced to—"

"If you lay a finger on me, I'll report you. What's your name, soldier?"

"This is your final warning, sir."

"DO YOU KNOW WHO I AM?"

There was the sound of a scuffle.

Unable to resist a peek at the disturbance, Setia padded to the door, still in her pyjamas.

Two figures wrestled in the passageway. She recognised one of her neighbours, a young guy, hefty and sleek like a slug. As soon as he'd found out what cabin she was in, he'd looked down his nose at her and walked the other way whenever he saw her around the ship. She wasn't cut up about it.

The other figure was in an armoured suit like the guard on the shuttle. He twisted slug-guy's arm behind his back and forced it up. Her neighbour shrieked.

"Don't hurt me!" he sobbed. "I'll go quietly. Let me go! This is all a big misunderstanding."

The soldier didn't release his hold as he pushed the man towards his cabin.

But then he halted. The helmeted head swivelled to face Setia. The dark eye slit seemed to pierce her. "Return to your cabin, ma'am."

She took a step back and her door closed.

It had been hours since the alert about the stowaway, and there hadn't been any further announcements. Setia was annoyed. She expected an update at least, and she was getting seriously hungry. Surely they wouldn't let passengers starve in the cabins for however long it took them to find their uninvited guest?

And if *she* was annoyed, she couldn't imagine how the more self-important passengers were feeling. The captain would be inundated with complaints once the crisis was over.

Her tiny cabin was no place to spend long periods of time. It was little bigger than a prison cell, and that was certainly how it was starting to feel. Should she comm someone to see if she could find out what was going on?

Who could she comm?

She didn't really know many people, except to nod at and smile at in passing.

She was almost tempted to comm Miriam Belby.

Almost.

In fact, thinking about it, she was surprised Miriam hadn't contacted her.

What about Mapper Robins? He'd seemed friendly.

She smirked, wondering how the stowaway fitted into Robins's skeins. How come he hadn't known all about him or her?

Her door chime sounded and she started. A visitor? But no one was allowed out.

"Meal ration, ma'am," the door speaker announced. "If you wouldn't mind opening up?"

"About time," she muttered, getting to her feet. She hoped it was something nice. Maybe the captain would have ordered a tasty dish to help take the edge off the passengers' irritation.

A soldier stood at the entrance, suited up. He turned to take a box from a trolley, but then swung back to look at her. His helmet melted away from his face, beginning at the eye slit and then disappearing down to his neck. It was the guard from the shuttle, the one who had been drunk with his buddies.

"Hey," he said, "it's One—"

"Don't call me that." She held out a hand. "Can I have my meal?"

"Sure, sure." He picked up a box but didn't give it to her. "I'm glad to see you again. I want to apologise for my behaviour."

"I'm not interested in your apology. I'd like my food, please."

"Of course. I was disciplined, you know. We all were."

"I'm not surprised." Her hand fell to her side. Now it came down to it, she was reluctant to end the encounter. "I suppose high spirits at the start of a long voyage are only to be expected."

"Yeah, we were only letting our hair down. My CO didn't see it that way, unfortunately. Okay, I'd better deliver the rest of these rations." He gave her the box.

"Do you know how much longer it's going to take to locate the stowaway?"

"We're sweeping the ship, but she's a big girl. It shouldn't be too long now, though. Enjoy your—"

"Do you know anything about this person? How did they know he or she was aboard?"

He shrugged. "It's a he, but they don't tell us much more than they tell the passengers. The rumour is Mapper Robins alerted the captain that an anomaly had appeared in the skein."

"It had appeared? Wouldn't he have noticed it from the beginning?"

Another shrug. "Like I said, I don't know much more than you."

"Hmm. Thanks for the food. I won't keep you any longer."

The soldier's helmet returned, flowing over his head and face like an incoming tide. She was tempted to ask him about it, but perhaps that was a conversation for another time.

"Don't open your door to anyone else," he said as he walked away, pushing his cart. "Especially not a tall, skinny, middle-aged dude with a pointy nose. He's probably not dangerous, but you never know."

Setia caught her door before it closed. "What did you say? Something about the stowaway?"

"Tall dude. Pointy nose."

"You know what he looks like?"

"Oh yeah, he's been caught on camera. That's how we know he's definitely not supposed to be here. No one matching him on the manifest. Look after yourself, One Punch Girl."

Setia narrowed her eyes as the soldier disappeared around a corner.

Could it be...?

It couldn't.

Yet she had a vision of a man dissolving into a cloud, melting into vapour, and being blown away on the breeze.

If Arief could do that, it wasn't beyond the realms of possibility that he might also have defeated all the defences against stowaways. Maybe he'd even arrived from space.

She ate her food, wolfing down the box's contents without really noticing what they were.

When she'd finished she got dressed, put on her shoes, and slipped out.

Eight

Deserted, the *Bres* was like a different ship. The passageways seemed wider, the social areas looked more spacious, brighter and cleaner—the microscopic sanitation bots must have caught up on their work while the humans were absent—and everywhere was much, much quieter. Setia's footsteps faintly echoed as she walked the tiled corridors.

Underlying the enveloping hush was an almost-indiscernible hum. Was she hearing the engines for the first time? Did they make a noise? She had no idea what type of mechanism drove the ship through space or, rather, not space, but the strange void Mapper Robins had revealed. Perhaps it was only the whine of the environmental control units.

Now she'd taken the decision to find Arief herself, the enormity of the task was only just beginning to hit. How could she hope to locate him in the vast vessel? The entire ship's military had failed so far.

Why was she even looking? When she'd realised the stowaway was probably Arief, she'd assumed he must be here for her. But if he was, he would have come to her cabin. He'd known she was at the passenger processing centre. He seemed to know exactly where she was at any time. Yet he hadn't approached her, so she was not the reason for his presence. There was no need for her to go out and meet him.

But he had to be here for her. What other reason could he have? If he'd wanted to be a colonist he could have done it in the usual way and bought a ticket, the same as everyone else. Maybe he was teasing her. He'd always been mischievous, deriving malicious pleasure from others' confusion and anxiety. In which case, she was playing right into his hands.

She had the feeling she was being watched. Halting, she looked behind her. The empty passageway curved out of sight, white-tiled floor gleaming, walls and ceiling a calming pale green, blemish-free.

She should return to her cabin. What would she even do if she found Arief? She couldn't fight him. He was more powerful than her. She couldn't force him to leave. He would do what he'd always done—exactly as he pleased. She could report his position to the captain, she supposed, but then what? How would he confine someone to the brig when they were able to dissolve into cloud?

She walked on. Her search was pointless, but, somehow, she felt responsible for Arief's presence. He was her problem, though she didn't know how to fix it.

A second passageway crossed hers, and she was debating which way to turn when noise emanated from the right. Many boots pounding on tile resounded, drawing quickly closer. She shrank backwards, but there was nowhere to hide. No doorways opened nearby. The best she could do was to retreat beyond a curve, out of sight of the junction.

The boots grew loud and she tensed, waiting to be discovered. But the guards didn't appear. They hadn't turned into her passageway. She leaned cautiously out and caught a glimpse of the armoured rear of a soldier before he vanished. While she waited for them to move away, a realisation struck and she craned her neck to look into the corners of the ceiling.

No cameras were visible but they had to be here, too small to be seen but keeping watch on the passengers. The ship's officers had to know she was out of her cabin, and soldiers had passed within a few metres of her. Why were they allowing her to wander about when a potentially dangerous stowaway was on the loose?

A chill hit. The atmosphere had grown damp and misty. Cool breezes wafted across her skin. She touched her cheek. It was cold and wet. The air current seemed to be coming from behind her.

There was a vent close to the deck, about the size of a personal interface. Grey, hazy vapour was pouring from it.

She backed up until she hit the wall. Palms pressed against it, she waited, regretting her decision to leave her cabin. As she'd feared, the vapour began to coalesce, becoming vaguely man-like. The nebulous, translucent mass solidified further. Its edges tightened, the shape became opaque, colours burst from the grey, until seconds later, Arief stood in front of her, smirking mockingly. "I knew you wouldn't be able to resist when I called."

"You didn't call me," Setia retorted. "I just guessed you had to be the creep they were talking about. Get off this ship. I know you can. That's how you got here, right? Melting away to nothing and floating around wherever you want. How do you do that? What *are* you? No. Forget I asked. Just leave. Whatever you've come to tell me I don't want to hear it. Get out!"

Arief took a step closer. Setia pressed her back into the wall. The passageway to each side was empty. Where were the soldiers when you needed them?

Arief said quietly, "You don't get to boss me around, little Setia. Don't try, or it will make me angry. I wanted to enjoy more time aboard this ship of fools, but the authorities seem determined to deprive me of my fun, so I might as well do what I came here to do. I want to make a proposal. Listen while I explain. We do not have much time."

She looked up into his eyes. As always, his stare held her in place. She didn't want to hear his proposal but she had no choice.

"It must be blindingly obvious to you by now that I am not human. My species is older than yours, aeons older, and we call several planets our home, though in fact we can live wherever and however we please. I want to take you back with me, Setia, to a place where you can live forever in peace. And when I say forever I mean it. I can extend your lifespan as long as you have the will to live. You may have anything you want—luxuries, foods, experiences you may only have dreamed of. You will not be lonely. I can create any companion you desire. In your terms, it would be like heaven. You could avoid the necessity to slave and toil and suffer all the trials involved in settling a new world and live for eternity. What do you say?"

"I'd say there's a catch you aren't telling me about. You're forgetting how well I know you. The answer's no. I'd be crazy to accept your proposal. Now leave." She willed herself to move away but her feet were rooted to the deck.

"If I'm leaving," Arief hissed, leaning in, "then you're coming with me." He grabbed her shoulder. His fingertips dug into her flesh like pincers.

"Smart answer, Setia," said a new voice.

Mapper Robins appeared from around the curve in the corridor. He drew to a halt and fixed Arief with a hard stare. "Let go of her."

"Or you'll...?" Arief retorted derisively.

His fingers dug deeper and Setia winced.

"You have no right to be here," said Robins. "None of your species has. That was the agreement."

"That was the agreement about Earth. As you may have noticed, we are not on Earth."

Agreement? What were they talking about? She had no idea, though she was deeply relieved Robins had arrived. She had a suspicion Arief would have been able to take her, regardless of her wishes, across the void to the fake 'heaven' he'd proposed. He might still do it, but at least Robins was trying to help.

The mapper moved closer. "That was the agreement about humanity." He placed a hand on Arief's arm. "Release her."

"And if I do not?!" Dark rage suffused Arief's face.

"Then my brother leaves your world, and so does Arthur."

Another new voice.

Setia swung her head around.

It was the woman with the bird. What had Robins said her name was? Carys...something.

"What would your friends have to say about that?" Her falcon companion sat on her shoulder, its bright, intelligent gaze focused on the alien.

"Good point," said Robins. "Thank you." He returned his attention to Arief. "What *would* they say?"

He didn't reply, but his hold on Setia didn't loosen.

"You have no place here," Robins announced. "Depart this ship, leave us to continue our voyage in peace, and cease your interference in our affairs. We have fulfilled our side of the contract. Your species must fulfil yours."

"Wrong!" Arief barked. "We do not *have* to do anything. But I *choose* to abide—for now."

His fingers opened. Setia gasped and sagged against the wall, lifting a hand to her painful shoulder. Dark bruises had to be forming where his fingertips had bit.

Arief was melting, dissolving once more. He ballooned into a dark grey mass of particles, and then swept into the vent as if sucked by a vacuum, until there was nothing but empty space where he'd stood.

"Has he really gone?" asked Carys.

Robins replied, "There's no way of telling for sure, but I don't think he will be back for a while." He noticed Setia where she slumped against the wall. "My dear, I'm so sorry. Let's get you to a sick bay."

"I'm okay, just a bit sore."

"We had to allow you to make yourself bait, I'm afraid, to draw him out. Otherwise he might have lurked inside the environmental control system forever. I didn't want to put you in danger, but you were already in a perilous position. He might have taken you at any time. The agreement seems to be holding him in check, however, for now anyway. He seemed to need your acquiescence before he took you away."

"Could he do that?" asked Setia, continuing to rub her shoulder. "Across space and without a ship, I mean?"

"He must be able to, or else why would he suggest it? Though we aren't exactly sure what they can and can't do."

"What's the agreement you were talking about?"

"It was recently forged between humans and Arief's species, but it would take a long time to explain. Perhaps Carys could..."

Except for Setia and Robins, the passageway was empty.

Carys had gone.

Nine

Setia found Carys Ellis topping up a bird feeder in the aviary. The young woman stood next to the wide dish atop a pole, scraping chopped fruit from a plate. Her avian companion was absent. Trees surrounded the feeder, reaching up to the brilliant lights in the ceiling, and parrots and cockatoos were already swooping down to eat. Carys took a step backward and watched them for a few moments before leaving.

Setia hesitated to follow. Twice, they'd both been involved in an altercation with Arief. Twice, Carys had slipped away, as if to avoid her. Was it personal, or was the *Bres*'s bird expert only shy and reclusive?

It had taken several days of puzzlement coupled with the tedium of shipboard life to prompt Setia to seek Carys out, and now she was here, indecision re-surfaced. Rather than follow the enigmatic woman, she set off in another direction.

It was her first visit to the aviary. One of the areas reserved for higher passenger classes, it had been out of bounds, but Mapper Robins had 'tweaked' her permissions. He was keen on the two of them becoming friends, though he continued to refuse to explain why. But she wasn't about to turn down a free upgrade.

A flock of small birds burst from bushes and soared upwards, twittering and squabbling. On a nearby branch, love-birds rubbed beaks. Hidden pigeons or doves cooed incessantly, and from somewhere more distant came the caws of crows. The environmental control units kept the atmosphere a tad warmer and moister than the rest of the ship, and the greenery was thriving. The place brought back memories of home, and Setia resolved to return here often, regardless of the standoffishness of Carys Ellis.

She turned a corner and instantly recoiled. What might once have been a chicken dangled by its feet from a rope. Crows attacked the corpse, ripping off shreds of flesh and fighting with each other, clinging precariously and batting their wings.

A couple approached from the opposite direction.

"Gross!" exclaimed the man, and they turned back.

Setia also reversed direction—and came face to face with Carys.

The birdwoman, as Setia had come to think of her, had her hands on her hips. She waggled a finger. "I know why you're here. Robins sent you, right? Look, I can't stop you from coming here as often as you want, but I'm telling you now, we're not friends."

"Hey, I—"

"And I'll tell you something else, if your weird former boss turns up again, I'm not helping you with him. I'm done with all that shit."

"Okaaay..."

"So we're clear, right? I'm not going to be your bestie on the ship or after we reach Talman Prime, and I'm certainly not going to be your saviour if—"

"I don't need saving, thanks," Setia snapped, finally overcoming her surprise at the unexpected tirade.

"Huh, it didn't look like it. You had both situations *totally* under control."

When Setia didn't answer, for in truth she *had* no answer, Carys continued, "Sorry, I didn't mean that the way it came out. What I meant to say is, your business isn't my business. I came on this voyage to get away from all that, and I can't help you with your problems anymore. So it's best if we stay out of each other's way. That's all I'm saying."

Get away from all what? Setia wanted to ask. This woman seemed to have a better understanding of 'her business' than she did. But she was damned if she was going to spend another second with Carys Ellis, who seemed to hate her for no reason. "Staying out of each other's way sounds great to me. Don't worry, you won't see me again."

She about-faced and marched towards the exit. It was a shame to leave the place. She liked it here, birds fighting over carcasses aside. But she very obviously wasn't welcome. The next time Mapper Robins mentioned that she should become better acquainted with Ellis, she would tell him where to shove his suggestion.

As she stepped into the passageway, a comm arrived.

"Setia," Robins said.

Just the man she wanted to talk to. She took a breath, preparing to chew him out.

"Go to the shuttle bay immediately. I will meet—"

"The shuttle bay? Why?"

"Please keep your voice down. We don't want the other passengers knowing about this. I'll see you there." He cut the comm.

She halted, trying to figure out what was going on. Passersby walked around her. Why the shuttle bay? She comm'd Robins back but he didn't answer. It felt as though he'd given her an order, but she'd paid her fare. She was a passenger, not an employee. What gave him the right to tell her what to do? Reluctant to obey, yet curious to find out what was happening, she slowly continued.

Carys Ellis overtook her. Predictably, the woman didn't offer a word of acknowledgement. Setia was certainly not going to say hello. Carys proceeded purposefully, arms swinging, ponytail bobbing. There was a flutter of wings, and the falcon landed on her shoulder. Setia followed the pair through several junctions until it became apparent they were travelling in the same direction.

Awkward.

At the bay, the four slim tubular craft that had ferried the *Bres*'s passengers from Earth sat in their spots, but there was a fifth vessel Setia hadn't seen before. A squat, six-legged spacecraft comprised of connected spheres, it looked tougher and more utilitarian than the other shuttles. A jack-of-all-trades ship. It reminded her of a giant bug.

Robins stood next to it along with a group of men and women in fatigues. Setia was a few steps behind Carys when they arrived. Robins rubbed his hands. "Glad to see you two are getting to know each other better."

Carys looked over her shoulder and frowned.

Setia gave her a little wave. "We're getting along like a house on fire. What's this about?"

"A short trip. A speculative expedition, so to speak. Providing you're interested, that is. I mean you, Setia."

"*I* don't get a choice, I suppose?" Carys asked bitterly.

"As a member of the ship's personnel..." Robins shrugged in apology.

"A trip where?" asked Setia.

"Why, to—"

"To the planet surface, of course," Carys interjected. "Are we already in orbit?"

"We will be dropping into normal space imminently. Your journey time will be approximately six hours. What do you say, Setia?"

Carys caressed the bird on her shoulder and whispered in its ear. It took flight and fluttered out of the bay.

"I-I don't know," Setia replied. "You said it's a speculative expedition. I don't get what you want me to do. I thought we already knew a lot about the planet from the probes. What would I do down there? I'm not a scientist or an engineer." She hadn't even been to school, though that was something she never told anyone.

"You're right, we do know a lot, but nothing beats being there in person. Scientists and engineers will be coming with you. They're on their way right now. Your inclusion in the mission is speculative. You won't have any duties to perform as such. Just take a look around.

You'll be one of the first human beings to ever set foot on an exoplanet."

"It's a great honour," Carys said in a sour tone. "Why would you say no? Apart from the risk of dying, that is."

She was trying to put her off.

Setia said, "Sure, I'll do it. Why not?"

Ten

If there was a change in the *Bres*'s motion as she dropped from deep red twilight into ordinary space, Setia didn't feel it. All she knew was the shuttle pilot had announced they were about to depart and everyone must take their seats. The colony ship must have arrived at Talman Prime.

There had been no general announcement.

No burst of fanfare to celebrate the end of the voyage.

No flurry of preparations to begin the colonisation.

The passengers were being lied to, and Setia wasn't sure how she felt about it. It was clear they were nowhere near ready to begin their challenge, if they would ever be. On the other hand, if they found out about the subterfuge, she feared the reactions of a bunch of people who were used to being in charge.

The final arrivals were moving through the shuttle cabin, slotting into vacant places. The military contingent was already seated, so the newcomers had to be scientists and engineers. A tall, skinny, shaggy-haired man appeared—the hygienically challenged guy. He had to be some kind of expert, and that was why they'd let him on the ship.

He moved behind her and sat down.

Lieutenant-Colonel Markham appeared and stood at the front

of the cabin. He cleared his throat, and the shuffling and murmuring died down. "Ladies and gentlemen, I apologise for the short notice regarding this mission. I'm sure you understand we must keep things under wraps as far as possible, and I appreciate your discretion. To those who are not under any obligation to be here, let me extend my thanks. My men and women have been briefed, but I'd like to say a few words to the civilians before you set out."

He nodded at two flight assistants, whose arms were filled with small, plain bundles. In response to his gesture they began to distribute them to the non-military personnel.

Markham continued, "You're about to receive an EVA suit. As you know, Talman Prime's atmosphere is expected to be safe to breathe, but until on-site tests are conducted we don't want to take any chances. Your suit will supply you with a couple of hours of air as well as protect you from falls and other accidents."

A hand rose from among the seats, grasping one of the bundles. "Are these like the new military armour?"

"Similar. Your suit attaches to your body via shoulder straps, whereas military suits are contained within the uniform and activated by voice command. To activate yours, you must press a button on one of the straps." He lifted a palm to his audience. "Please, wait until you're about to disembark before putting on your suit. The material is smart, but it requires some room to work. You must lift your feet to allow it to flow under them and complete the seal. You will see a heads-up display with a range of information, including how much available air you have left. Ensure you return to the shuttle at least fifteen minutes before you're due to run out. In case of an emergency, there's additional air in the containers you're taking with you."

Setia's bundle arrived in her lap. She inspected it curiously.

"It conforms to the size and shape of the wearer," said a voice.

She turned her head and got an unpleasant whiff. Halitosis Man was leaning over her seat back.

"One size fits all," he continued to explain.

"Uh, thanks." She faced forward in the hope of putting a quick end to the encounter.

But he wasn't deterred. "Made up your mind yet?"

"About what?" she replied irritably.

"About what the heck you're doing here."

Before Setia could tell him to buzz off, Markham said loudly, "I repeat, civilian personnel must not exit the shuttle until the perimeter fence is constructed and electrified. Most of you have clear objectives for your time on the surface. The few who are along for the ride, just make sure you don't get in the way. That's it. Good luck, everyone. I'm jealous as all hell that I'm not going with you, but maybe next time."

He raised a hand in a gesture of farewell and left. The pilot reminded the passengers to strap in, which made Setia's unwelcome conversation partner sit down.

As the shuttle flew to Talman Prime, the annoying question from Halitosis Man turned into an earworm, digging a hole in her brain.

What am *I doing here*?

Not on the colonisation project. It had been her only escape from Arief, though *that* hadn't turned out too well. But why was she on this mission? She had no burning desire to be one of the first arrivals. She couldn't care less about her name going down in history. Neither was she a sensation seeker. Let the adrenaline junkies and the military take the risks. Though she was somewhat curious about what was down there, she was content to take a look after the place had been assessed and safety measures taken.

She'd had the proposition sprung on her so quickly, she hadn't had time to think. Mapper Robins had obviously asked her for a reason, but he hadn't explained it. And then Carys Ellis had goaded her...

Burnap's balls.

She was here because Robins wanted it and because Carys Ellis didn't. Her decision wasn't anything to do with what *she* wanted. It was like the last decade of her life, playing out all over again. But this time it wasn't Arief controlling her. Two new puppet masters had arrived, though only one was deliberately pulling the strings. The other didn't want anything to do with her, and that pissed her off.

She folded her arms tightly over her chest. If she could have ordered the pilot to turn around and take her back to the ship, she would have. But there was no going back. She would just have to grit her teeth and get through it.

The view beyond the shuttle exit was a vertical, steel grey, fast-flowing blanket of water.

It was raining on Talman Prime. If you could call it rain. Watching the downpour, Setia mused that the colonists might need to think up another name, something better suited to describe the perpendicular river that was precipitation on the exoplanet.

Was it wise to step out of cover? Maybe it would be a better idea to wait until the 'shower' was over. But most of the soldiers had already disembarked and the scientists were following. Even reluctant Carys Ellis had left the craft.

Setia hesitated, almost last in line.

"Better press the button," a voice warned from behind.

Oh, man.

The Odour Monster was like a little devil sitting on her shoulder. He literally hung around like a bad smell.

She thumbed the button on her shoulder strap and a chill spread out from her back, flowing along her arms and legs, surging over her chest and up her neck. She recalled Markham's advice and lifted each of her feet in turn. The silver material encased her shoes and left no mark at the joins. The substance melted together and became whole. As it enveloped her head, a spasm of claustrophobia hit. With a sudden sensation that she was suffocating, she tried to tear the covering from her mouth and nose, but her fingers only met a smooth, unyielding surface.

How was she supposed to *de*activate the suit? No one had explained.

The HUD flashed to life. Figures and words floated on the edge of her peripheral vision. As she looked at them in turn, they grew brighter and more distinct. The data she understood included the external temperature, air remaining—currently one hour fifty-nine minutes—a distance measurement to 'home', which she guessed was the shuttle as it read zero, a list of gases and percentages that had to be the planet's atmosphere, and stated under Comm was Incoming, General, One-to-One, and External. 'Incoming' was brighter than the rest, though she couldn't hear anything. She was unsure how to operate the comm until she saw another sign that read Deactivate Suit and, in brackets underneath it, Focus 2 Seconds. So to return the EVA suit to its pack she had to stare at Deactivate for that length of time. A similar rule had to apply for the comm, along with a voice command, perhaps, if you wanted to speak to someone one-to-one.

What if you were unconscious? How would you remove the suit? There had to be an outer control.

Someone poked her shoulder.

She knew who it was and didn't turn around. Empty space was all that remained between her and the exterior. The rain had not abated one iota while she'd waited in line.

She stepped out.

The deluge hammered on the top of her helmet and her shoulders, the sheer weight of water pushing her feet into the muddy ground. The thrum of the pelting raindrops penetrated her suit. She could barely see a thing. Blurred shapes moved around her, close by and in the distance. The people nearby were the experts carrying out their experiments, taking readings and samples. The figures farther away were probably soldiers at the fence. There were also large, solid cubes. Storage containers. She looked beyond the fence, barely making out a grey-brown landscape.

She tilted her head back. Water instantly obscured the view through her eye slit. Returning her attention to ground level, she squinted, trying to focus on the far distance, trying to see something —*anything*—other than rocks and mud.

But there was nothing.

Talman Prime.

What a shithole.

"Please move to the fence. All passengers move directly to the fence. Preparing to depart."

She recognised the pilot's voice but she was confused. Where was the shuttle going? No one had mentioned a second trip. He couldn't be going back to the *Bres*, and if someone had decided to try a different spot—somewhere dry and preferably sunny—shouldn't everyone re-board?

Two people were climbing the steps.

She walked towards them, reluctant to abandon her only means of returning to safety, but a hand grabbed her arm.

"Gotta get over to the fence, Ms…" a pause "…Zees."

Another familiar voice. It was the soldier who insisted on calling her One Punch Girl. She hadn't known he was here too. "What's going on?"

"Shuttle's gotta make another stop. Quake scientists need to install their seismometers. It'll be back soon. No need to worry. This way, ma'am."

"Thanks, but I know how to find the fence."

He released her arm and she stomped away. From behind came the faint noise of the shuttle engine permeating the endless drumming of the rain. Black, horizontal fence lines became more distinct. As she reached the boundary she turned. The shuttle was lifting off the ground. Its six landing pads retracted into their slots, and then it disappeared into the haze.

They were alone, for the time being. Alone on the surface of this strange, alien planet.

There had been no celebration of their arrival other than some light clapping in the cabin when they'd touched down. No bottles of champagne had been popped. No speeches had been made. No partying had occurred.

It was Deep-Space Colonisation Lite.

The real celebrations would begin when the once-rich and mighty arrived. There would be a big show then. Then, and not before. Setia peered through the electrified wires and the corner of her lip lifted as she imagined the colonists' reactions when they set eyes on their new home.

The ground began to shake.

Eleven

Earthquakes hadn't been unusual in Spiral City. While the rest of the expedition members ran about—running *where* Setia didn't know, as no one could get outside the fence—grabbed each other in hugs and gesticulated wildly, she only moved away from the fence, parted her feet for balance and waited for the tremor to pass. She wasn't sure why everyone was over-reacting. They'd been told that Talman Prime was a young planet and many areas remained volcanically active. The vibrations were probably only the margins of a ripple spreading out from a far-distant epicentre.

To be fair, this tremor's a strong one, Setia mused, the reverberations running up her legs. The origin point might not be far away. Maybe the scientists' estimation of the safe zones was wrong. Up until now, they'd only had probe data to go on. Still, unless a fissure opened up there was little danger. The greatest threat from an earthquake wasn't the quake itself but falling buildings, and the only construction here was the fence. Luckily, no one was stupid enough to stay close to it.

The vibrations were fading. People began to stop running and relax. Their hands fell to their sides and they stood around uncertainly. The downpour was easing too. The thrumming on Setia's helmet, which hadn't let up all through the excitement, was growing quieter and, for the first time, she had a clear view of the landing site and the landscape beyond it.

They were standing on a plateau, the surrounding land sloping downward to lowlands dotted with lakes. So this was to be the site of the first human settlement? She could see the reasoning. The ground was flat and firm, and the rainwater was quickly draining away along rivulets and streams, heading for the lakes. They could farm crops and graze animals in the fields, and perhaps generate electricity from water moving down the levels.

She blinked. What she'd thought was odd-coloured soil on the lower ground was actually shrubs and weeds. They were all shades of purple. The vegetation of Talman Prime was *purple*. No one had mentioned that in the information sessions. She lifted her gaze to a far-off mountain range, which she'd thought looked purple due to the distance, but maybe the slopes were cloaked by plants.

Turning on the spot, she tried to find the sun, but all she could see was a patch of bright cloud high in the sky. It had to be roughly midday, yet the new world seemed so dark. Perhaps it was only due to the still-falling rain.

Within the fence, the scientists had returned to their experiments and readings. Soldiers stood guard, facing outward, rifles at the ready. Some scanned the skies. Their efforts seemed overkill. Nothing moved above or on the ground. Apart from the vegetation, Talman Prime appeared to be lifeless.

She crossed to the other side of the site for a different view. The landscape was similar, a bit more rocky. She imagined the first little town, but all she could conjure up was a damp, depressing place, the streets and prefab buildings huddled under a grey sky, the settlers' days spent in tedious toil. *Her* days spent in tedious toil, with only disappointed, disillusioned, disgruntled fellow colonists for company.

Her previous life suddenly didn't seem so bad.

She gave her head a little shake.

What am I thinking? Even *this* was better than living under Arief's control and doing a job she hated.

Sighing, she wondered how long she would have to wait before returning to the *Bres*. With nothing to do and very little to see, the trip seemed a waste of time. She had no idea what Robins was on, thinking her presence would be useful.

Her gaze lit upon a purple shoot poking up through a crack in a slab of stone. She squatted down to take a closer look at the alien plant. But what caught her attention wasn't the plant but a long indentation running next to it. The groove seemed too regular to be natural. She ran a gloved fingertip along it, wondering what had caused it. The line extended across the rock and—she peered closer—onto the next rock. She moved sideways on her haunches to see how far it went.

It disappeared into loose pebbles and shards. She pushed them aside. There it was. The line continued on, dead straight and at the same depth of half a centimetre. Odd. It didn't seem natural. How had it been made? Nothing lived here except species just beginning their evolutionary journey.

She rose to her feet. There had to be geologist among all these scientists, but how to tell who was who among the silver-suited figures? Should she try a general comm?

But what if she was wrong? She didn't want to look stupid among all these highly educated folk.

She checked the line again, following it in the opposite direction. There was another line branching off from it, and another!

She took a step backwards, almost colliding with the electrified fence. The more she looked, the more lines she saw, dipping in and out of patches of mud and scree. Most of them were not straight. They curved, spreading wider and wider across the site, glistening on the wet ground.

Tilting her head and squinting, she began to see a pattern, or rather, not a pattern, but—

The ground began to shake again.

Another tremor so soon?

She braced herself, hands on hips. People didn't seem so panicked this time, though really a bit of fear was warranted. Two tremors close together signalled something more serious than a little shake.

The vibrations intensified, and Setia struggled to remain upright. She sank down onto her bum and wrapped her arms around her knees as the ground moved violently. A deep, resonant rumbling filled her ears. The last time she'd experienced a quake like this she'd been a kid. Many buildings in her home town had crumbled, killing or trapping hundreds of people. The ground had been lifted and moved, roads torn apart and bridges destroyed.

If the site was too disturbed the shuttle might not be able to land.

Crack!

A fissure was opening.

Her jaw dropped. The surface was pulling apart along a jagged line. Stones slid and bounced into the widening gap. Boulders lifted and tumbled onto their sides. Mud undulated like a wave. The ground was rising, pushing her over. On the far side of the site, the electric fence toppled, posts ejected from the ground or snapped at their bases.

She scooted away from the hole, hoping the crack wouldn't extend farther.

How much longer was the quake going to last?

It was insane. If this was what a 'safe zone' was like, there was no way Talman Prime was fit for human colonisation. They would have to give up and fly onward to another of the identified potential worlds.

She inhaled sharply.

A soldier had fallen—fallen into another crack. The new fissure had opened suddenly, right beneath the man's feet. It might not extend far below ground level, but if it jerked closed… She swallowed. The result didn't bear thinking about. She leapt up and ran over on wobbling legs. Staring down, she gaped and her eyes grew round. The fissure was deep, so deep she couldn't see the bottom. It disappeared into darkness.

The soldier was clinging to the edge by one hand, swinging the other up, trying and failing to grab the disintegrating soil. His legs scrabbled feebly on cascading stones.

He was losing his hold. She stepped closer and reached down, trying to avoid tumbling into the fissure herself.

The rock he was holding onto one-handed split under his fingers.

He fell.

She slapped her hand against his forearm and her fingers closed around it, digging in. She feared he would slip from her grasp, but the gloves of the EVA suit seemed specially textured for a good grip. On her knees, pressing her other hand into the unstable soil for purchase, she hauled the man upwards. She leaned back, gasping, and then dug in her heels to slide away from the hole, dragging his upper half out. He managed to climb out by himself and crawled forwards until his feet were clear of the crack. Then he dropped onto his stomach.

Setia lay on her back, catching her breath, hardly daring to move.

The vibrations were easing once more.

"Holy shit! Thanks. That was close."

She guessed she was hearing the man she'd saved. Her stomach sank as she recognised his voice. In the heat of the moment she hadn't even thought she might already know him. Everyone looked the same in EVA suits. "No problem."

"Seriously," the soldier continued, "if it wasn't for you I could be dead."

"Don't worry about it."

He turned onto his side. "What I can't figure out is, how the hell did you *do* that? I must be twice as heavy as you."

The ground was still. The quake seemed to be over. Setia sat up. Devastation surrounded them. The place was wrecked, as if a giant cultivator had gone through it, upending rocks, churning mud. Two large fissures had opened and the site was now uneven. One entire side of it had lifted. Would the shuttle even be able to land?

"Please remain calm," said a different voice. "Needless to say, the mission is cancelled. When our transportation returns, we will be evacuating immediately. Pack up whatever you can of your equipment but stay away from holes and large rocks, which may be unstable."

While the colonists slowly moved, gathering up their items and stowing them in containers, Setia stayed where she was.

The soldier got to his feet and held out a hand. After a moment's hesitation she grasped it and he pulled her up. Slapping her back, he commented, "You might not be the friendliest girl I ever met, but I'm sure glad you're here."

Twelve

Setia burst into Robins's office. The old man, who was crouching over an interface, looked up, eyebrows lifting in surprise. She was reminded of her joke—how come he hadn't known she was coming? Pushing aside the thought, she was about to speak when he beat her to it.

"Setia, I'm glad you weren't hurt in the earthquake. But if you've come here to complain about my invitation to participate in the mission, I can only say—"

"I saw something. I think I know why I had to go there. I saw something on the ground and I think it's significant."

He leaned back in his seat and folded his hands on his lap. "What kind of something? I would have thought there were many strange things to see on an exoplanet."

"Then you'd guess wrong." She pulled out a seat and sat down opposite him, leaning her elbows on his desk. "Talman Prime is about the most boring, depressing place I've ever been. The only strange thing about it is the vegetation. It's coloured like the vomit of a dog with a nasty disease. You know, there's going to be hell to pay when our privileged passengers get down there and see the place they've paid a fortune to live in. But that's beside the point. I think I'm beginning to understand why I'm significant in your skein. I saw something, and I don't think anyone else did. Everyone else was too busy, either keeping guard or doing experiments. I'm not sure what I saw, but it has to be important."

"All right. Describe this thing."

She opened her mouth to speak, but he held up a finger. "Wait a moment." He gave the voice command to set his interface to record.

"It was a pattern," she said. "It took up most of the site, and it was faint, just lines on the surface. In some places it was covered by patches of mud or loose rocks, but if you followed the angle from where a line disappeared, it always reappeared in the right place. I swear it wasn't natural. Something or someone carved it."

"A regular pattern?"

"Not exactly, or at least, I don't think so. It looked symbolic, but naturalistic."

"Symbolic *and* naturalistic?"

"It's hard to explain. I was still trying to figure it out when the second tremor struck."

"So you only caught a glimpse of this thing?" His tone held a note of scepticism.

"More than a glimpse. I saw enough of it to realise what I was looking at wasn't natural cracks in the rock."

"Could you draw it?"

The desk top interface in front of her lit up and a slot slid open, containing a stylus.

"Uhh..." She'd never drawn anything in her life. "I'll try." The stylus felt weird in her fingers. She pressed the tip against the screen and scraped a line.

"You don't have to press so hard," Robins said gently.

Easing the pressure, she tried again. But what she produced looked very little like what she'd seen. "This is wrong. How do I erase it?"

"Never mind. I just remembered your EVA suit camera will have recorded everything you saw. We can check the vid."

We? Who else would be verifying her story?

One time, when she'd been running drugs in Spiral City, she'd been picked up by the police and interrogated. It had been horrible. The authorities rarely stuck to the rules once you were behind closed doors. They hadn't gone anywhere near as hard on her as they could have, according to what she'd heard, and, luckily, she'd already handed off the last of her delivery minutes before she'd been arrested. They had no evidence. When it became clear they weren't going to get an easy confession they'd released her. Nevertheless, the experience had left a deep impression, and it was one she didn't want to repeat.

She got up. "Okay, you do that."

"You're leaving? Is something wrong?"

"Everything's good. Like you said, you have my suit's vid. You don't need me."

Robins's brow lowered. "I feel I have offended you in some way."

"I'm not offended. The vid can tell you all you need to know." She was halfway to the door.

"For what it's worth," said Robins, "I believe your presence on Talman Prime was significant for another reason."

She halted and turned to face him.

"You saved a young soldier's life."

"Oh, that."

"Preventing a death in any circumstances has wide repercussions, wider than—if I may say so—a perceived pattern on rock. And I can see from the skein that your thread and the man's have been somewhat entangled recently."

"Entangled? Is that what you call it? He keeps turning up in my life, like that smelly guy. I don't see how they can be important. They certainly aren't important to me."

"Smelly guy?"

"Burnap's balls, you have to know him. Furry teeth, bad breath, armpits like last year's dirty laundry, the works. He must be one of you guys or else he would never have got on the ship."

Robins chuckled. "You mean Dr Jacobs."

"He's a *doctor*?"

"Head of the psychiatric team. I believe his personal hygiene habits—or lack of—are a ploy."

"A ploy to make people avoid him and ease his workload?"

"To unsettle his patients. If something is distracting them, they're less likely to put up defences. I believe he thinks he can get to the heart of their difficulties faster."

Setia was speechless for several seconds before saying, "Anyway, that soldier—"

"Corporal Sheldrake."

"Him and Jacobs, I hope our paths have crossed for the last time. I hope your skein's wrong."

"It's neither right nor wrong. It simply is."

She left.

Screw Robins and his stupid skein.

Marching along the passageway, she debated where to go. The trip had been exhausting. She should go back to her cabin and try to get some sleep. But her berth had come to feel cramped and dismal, like a coffin. On Earth, where she'd had a lot more money than most, she'd grown used to expansive apartments and luxury hotel suites. On the *Bres*, she was back to the tiny living space of her childhood, and it wasn't great.

I was trying to be helpful.

She'd gone on the mission, and she'd reported back with what she'd thought might be useful information, only to be disbelieved.

If that was Robins's attitude, if whatever she told him had to be 'verified' by nameless others, she wouldn't bother. She would keep her head down and just get on with the colonisation. The next time he invited her to participate in something dangerous, her answer would be no.

She needed food. Something to eat and the presence of other people would help to reset her mood.

"Hey, watch out!"

A figure had appeared from nowhere right in front of her. They collided.

"Ever thought of looking where you're going?" Carys Ellis snapped. "You should try it some time."

"You walked right into me!" Setia protested, though, in truth, she wasn't sure who was at fault. But it felt good to take her frustration out on someone.

"Yeah, right," Carys muttered, moving away.

"Whoa, wait a minute." Setia grabbed her arm.

"Get off me!" She tore her arm from Setia's grip. "What the hell's wrong with you?"

"What's that on your shoulder?"

Carys was wearing her fleet uniform. Up until now, Setia hadn't paid much attention to the crew's clothes. She vaguely knew that each section wore a different badge, and that the badges had three sides or parts, representing the three ships: the *Bres*, the *Balor*, and the *Banba*. The Engineering Section badge was the only one she remembered, after seeing it in a documentary. It was the Penrose Tribar, a weird triangle that could only exist as a drawing, not as a solid object.

Carys's badge displayed three rabbits chasing each other in a circle, their ears pointing to the centre. Like the Penrose Tribar, it was another illusion. Each rabbit appeared to have two ears, but there were only three ears in total.

"The hares?" Carys asked, touching the badge.

"Hairs?" It took Setia a moment to realise her mistake. "I thought they were rabbits."

"Right." Carys narrowed her eyes. "Well, it's been fun chatting."

"Hold on a minute." She grasped Carys's arm again.

When Carys glared at her hand, she let go. "Sorry. And I'm sorry I bumped into you just now. But I'm interested in the symbol on your badge. Do you know what it means?"

"It's supposed to represent a few things. Why do you want to know?"

"I think I..." She hesitated. After Robins's response, she was reluctant to talk about her experience to anyone else.

"You think you...?"

She exhaled, puffing air between loose lips. “It doesn’t matter.”

“In that case, let’s not waste each other’s time, huh?”

Setia watched Carys’s retreating figure, unable to shake the impression that the image of the three hares running had been the pattern she’d seen inscribed on the surface of Talman Prime.

Thirteen

It wasn't until she began piling her plate at the buffet counter that Setia realised she was ravenous. She scooped up spiced rice, curry, fried seaweed, dumplings and steamed slices of lotus root. The fare at the free-to-all cafeteria was especially good today. Perhaps the purser, Lineton, was easing up on rationing. After all, the *Bres* had arrived at her destination months earlier than anticipated. Or perhaps it was an attempt to boost morale. Grumbles and complaints from the passengers had been on the increase. Maybe the reality of what colony life would really be like had begun to hit.

The place was busy, and it took her a minute to find an empty seat. It wasn't until she was sitting down she realised Miriam Belby sat opposite. She greeted her awkwardly.

"Setia, great to see you. I was wondering where you'd got to. Never seem to see you around, which is funny, considering we're practically neighbours."

"Oh, you know." She shrugged. "I'm not big on socialising. How have you been?" She mixed some curry with rice and forked it into her mouth. It wouldn't hurt to let Miriam chatter on while she ate. The woman was harmless.

"Pretty good. Well, no, that isn't true. I'm bored. Can you

believe it? There are so many things to do, so much entertainment to keep us occupied, but all I can think about is Arrival. I thought this voyage would be like a cruise, and, to be fair, it is in a lot of ways, but on a cruise you stop off at different destinations. The *Bres* only has one destination, and it's all I can think about. Nothing else interests me, not the sim suites, vids, exercise classes, bars, live shows, games, lessons on building the colony…" She rolled her eyes. "If I have to listen to Papa Paulus explain how to grow yet another crop, I might scream." She chuckled. "Not really. But you know what I mean."

Setia had managed to eat more food during this monologue, and her hunger pangs were easing. "I suppose so. What do you think living on Talman Prime will be like?"

"Hmm…" Miriam knitted her fingers and rested her chin on her knuckles while her gaze roved upward speculatively. "My family has a beach house on a tropical island. We would always spend at least a month there every year. It was so cool, lazing on the beach, drinking cocktails and eating fresh seafood. I think the life on the new planet's going to be something like that."

Setia almost sprayed her mouth contents over her companion. She hastily swallowed and said, "What gives you that impression?"

Miriam had been to at least one information session about Prime. Setia knew it because she'd been there with her. There had definitely been no mention of tropical beaches or cocktails. "It seems to me we can expect a harsh environment."

"That's what they *say* but it can't really be like that. Otherwise how could they justify charging us so much money? I understand we'll have to do a little work at first, until things get established. Not everything can be automated, and humans will be needed for some tasks. But it's obvious they're trying to lower our expectations so when we arrive we get a nice surprise. Under-promise and over-deliver. It's a marketing tactic, and a good one. My family is in business. I know all the tricks."

"Right." Setia stabbed a dumpling and transferred it to her mouth before chewing stoically.

"Don't worry. Colony life is going to be cool."

A cafeteria bot had toddled over to their table. It must have spotted Miriam's empty plate. One of its arms snaked out and grabbed the plate in its pincers. When it had gone, Miriam checked to her left and right and leaned forward before whispering something, but the hubbub and clink and clatter of cutlery drowned her out.

"What?"

She repeated louder in a conspiratorial tone, "Have you heard the rumour?"

"Uhh, I doubt it."

Miriam leaned so close her upper half was almost lying across the table. "Some people are saying we've already arrived, way ahead of time, due to new tech, or space pathways, or something."

Her fork poised halfway to her mouth, Setia stared at her. "*Some people*? Do you know who?"

"Does it matter?" asked Miriam, straightening up. "Do you think it could be true?"

Continuing to eat, Setia weighed her words carefully. "If we've arrived, why wouldn't they tell us?"

"I'm not sure. They could be getting things ready. You know, surveying the sites, building houses and roads, shops, offices and hospitals, that kind of thing."

"Don't you...don't you think we would have noticed the people doing all that work aren't here anymore?"

"Not necessarily."

Setia had a vision of a world where only the rich truly existed, where builders, shop assistants, admin staff, medical professionals, all the people who did the actual work, were non-player characters. Burnap knew how Miriam saw sanitation operatives. Probably not at all.

"There are twenty thousand of us. If a hundred or so have left the ship, who's going to notice?"

"A hundred or so? Is that how many you think it would take to..." She could hear her tone rising. She shut down her ire.

Miriam couldn't help it. She wasn't to be blamed for how she'd grown up.

But it didn't matter anyway. Miriam hadn't noticed her reaction. "Or it could be they want us to complete our training before we go planetside."

Finally, she was starting to make sense.

"The lecturers like Papa Paulus will be under contract," she continued. "They have to deliver all their classes or they won't get paid."

Setia threw down her fork and folded her arms over her chest.

"Is something wrong?"

"Get paid? You understand there won't be any currency, right? Everyone will be living on rations for years until the colony is established. What are the lecturers going to do with their wages? They would have to go back to Earth to spend them."

"I, er... I didn't think of that." A flush spread up Miriam's neck and over her face.

"It's okay. Don't worry about it." Setia resumed her meal.

"Maybe they will go back to Earth."

Tired of the conversation, Setia didn't reply, keeping her head bent over her plate. She would be finished soon, and then she could get away.

"I mean, if we *have* arrived, if the time it takes to travel the galaxy has shrunk *that* much, then it wouldn't be a big deal for one of the ships to make the return journey."

"That's not going to happen. The Fleet was built for colonisation. The ships aren't ferries. Like it or not, we'll be staying on Talman Prime. The only way off the planet will be to wrangle passage on the onward journey."

"Like it or not? What do you mean?" When Setia didn't answer, she continued, "You don't seem to think my idea of colony life is realistic."

Setia's gaze flicked up.

"I'm not stupid," Miriam went on. "I can tell you think I'm an idiot. I can feel your contempt radiating out at me right now."

"That's not..." Setia sighed. "You're right. I *don't* think your expectations are realistic." *I know they aren't.* "But you're not alone, not by a long stretch. Hardly anyone seems to understand what they've got themselves into. Sorry if my attitude comes across as contempt. If it helps, I don't have a lot of respect for myself either."

A bot was trying to leave the cafeteria, its pincers full of dirty plates and cutlery to be taken to the washer. But a burly guy with a bushy beard stood in front of it. Whenever the bot tried to go around him, he stepped into its path. The bot's simple algorithm caused it to speed up to outpace the moving obstacle, and the game was attracting attention. Each time the man managed to manoeuvre into the bot's intended path, a cheer went up. He was clearly enjoying himself as he defeated the machine.

Setia rolled her eyes. Teasing bots was something most kids grew out of by the time they reached adolescence. This man still had some growing up to do, and his audience had to be very bored of life aboard ship to find him entertaining.

"It's okay," said Miriam resignedly. "I'm used to it. My parents never liked me much. That's why I'm here. There wasn't anything for me back on Earth."

Their gazes met, and Setia gave her a small smile. "Everyone on this ship has a story, right?"

"Uh huh. You never told me yours."

She wasn't going to get into the Arief affair. She didn't want to sound crazy. "It isn't interesting."

Miriam waited in expectant silence. It felt wrong not to offer something to reciprocate her opening up. Setia leaned forward and beckoned the woman closer. Background noise from the commotion in the corner of the cafeteria would prevent eavesdroppers from overhearing them.

"You know that rumour you were talking about?"

Miriam nodded, eyes widening.

The bot made a dash for it and almost made it around the man, but he was a sore loser. He kicked its little flexible legs sideways and the machine hit the deck with a thunk. Plates and cutlery burst from its grasp and scattered everywhere. Howls of laughter erupted from the diners.

The bot clambered upright and stooped to begin to gather the dropped items. Leftover food smeared the floor and spilled drinks had made puddles. Grinning, the man walked to the bot's rear and kicked, punting the machine onto its front.

Cheers and clapping echoed around the room.

With an air of stoical patience, the bot drew its legs in and pushed itself upwards once more. This time, it didn't even have a chance to grab a single plate before the man kicked it again.

"*Stars,*" Setia murmured. "What an idiot."

"What were you going to tell me?" asked Miriam.

Setia got up and walked over to the man, reaching him as he was aiming yet another kick at the machine. She stepped between them and faced him. "Cut it out. Sit down and eat your dinner, or leave if you've finished. You're making a mess."

Behind her, the bot finally made it to its feet and its pincers snaked out to pick up the plates.

"Who the fuck are you?" The man thrust his face into hers. Alcohol wafted from his breath.

"Just sit down and stop making a fool of yourself."

"Oh, yeah?" He tilted his head and pulled an ugly face, but then his features relaxed. He waved a dismissive hand. "Whatever."

As Setia turned away, he swiped a leg against her calves. She landed on her backside, the jolt jarring her spine.

Leaping up, she drew back a fist and punched the man's jaw. At the last split-second she managed to soften her blow a smidgen. Nevertheless, his head snapped backward and he stumbled, clutching his face and looking shocked.

After regaining his balance he flew at her with a roar.

She ducked down, preparing an upper cut to deck this idiot loser once and for all, but a hand fastened around her biceps and a forearm moved across her chest, dragging her away. She went limp and allowed it to happen. It was a stupid, pointless fight. Other diners had grabbed the man and were holding him off while he struggled and fought.

Guards ran in—where had they been five minutes ago? She was handcuffed. "I didn't do anything. He assaulted me!"

One of them replied, "We'll let the captain decide that, ma'am."

"Setia!" Miriam called out as she was being led away. "What were you going to tell me?"

"Never mind."

Fourteen

If anyone could be said to have the weight of the world on her shoulders, it was the captain of the *Bres*. Or rather, if not the weight of the world, the weight of a gigantic, state-of-the-art colony ship and 20,000 passengers.

The woman's desktop—an expanse of polished wood—reflected her tired features. Great bags drooped under her grey-blue eyes and deep lines ran from the corners of her mouth to her jawline. Her hair was frizzy, a white halo around her aged face. A burn scar, pink and shiny, marked her right cheek.

Captain Bujold's seen some shit.

The captain didn't need to look so ancient. Cosmetic surgeons performed wonders these days, turning worn-out old hens into spring chickens. And though Mapper Robins could have easily chosen to look younger too, his appearance was sprightly and vital. Bujold looked like life had done a number on her, yet she hadn't corrected her looks. Maybe she just didn't care about her appearance, or maybe, as with Dr Jacobs and his off-putting poor personal hygiene, she had an ulterior motive.

Was that why the captain hadn't said a word for five minutes, ever since the guard had brought Setia into her office? She'd only lifted a finger, signalling a request to wait, and then gazed into the middle distance while listening to a comm. Was she trying to make a point about her time being much more valuable than an unruly passenger's? She didn't look angry. In another situation and different clothes, and minus the scar, she might have been someone's grandma not wanting to miss the final climax of an audio show.

Setia turned her attention to the wall screen, which was scrolling through a sequence of images. Lonely landscapes lit by low sunlight —moorlands, mountaintops, polar wastes—flashed up, hung around for a few seconds, and vanished, replaced by the next picture. Every so often a military starship put in an appearance. One of the ships was an earlier iteration of the *Bres* from the time when she'd been a giant spiral. Images of people were rare in the sequence and only one was familiar: Lorcan Ua Talman, founder of the colonisation project. How strange that, after dedicating most of his life to his dream, he'd changed his mind and decided to spend the remainder of his days on Earth.

Captain Bujold relaxed in her chair and folded her hands on her lap, resting a steady, calm gaze on Setia. A muscle under her left eye twitched repetitively, like the beat of a drum.

Instantly unnerved, Setia stared back.

"Ms Zees," Bujold said mildly, "I don't think I should need to point out to you or any other passenger on this ship that your recent behaviour is unacceptable." *Twitch, twitch, twitch.* "One of the paramount requirements for living on a starship is the absolute avoidance of conflict, especially physical conflict. Were the *Bres* a domestic aircraft or shuttlecraft, I would have diverted her to the nearest airport and had you and your brawling partner removed." *Twitch, twitch, twitch.* "The safety of the passengers is my prime responsibility, and I will not tolerate any threats to it."

Setia had been almost mesmerised by the tic coupled with the captain's soft, world-weary tone, and had barely registered what she was saying. There was an absence of true conviction in Bujold's words, as if she was repeating a speech she had given many times.

"Be sure," the captain continued, "that if you don't manage to keep your emotions under control and become involved in a similar incident, I will be forced to confine you to the brig."

She was silent. Setia's attention switched from the captain's malfunctioning muscle to her eyes.

"That is all. A guard will escort you to your cabin. If you take my advice, you will remain there and sleep away your—"

Setia lifted her cuffed wrists.

Bujold blinked uncertainly.

"Take them off," Setia explained.

"When you're in your cabin, the guard will—"

"Now. You must have the device to do it."

The captain's twitch sped up and her lips thinned. She said quietly, "If you think you're in any position to order me around, you're sadly mistaken."

"Remove my handcuffs, or I'll tell every single person on this ship that we've already arrived at Talman Prime."

Bujold's mouth opened and closed. Then she said, "You'll find it very hard to speak to anyone while incarcerated."

"How long will you keep me locked up? It was only a small fight that I didn't even start. *He* hit *me*, not the other way around. And, believe me, I can speak to a *lot* of people while being dragged to the brig."

Indecision seemed to war in Bujold's features. Then she puffed a sigh and pulled a slim rod from a drawer. She inserted the wand into a hole in the cuffs and they sprang apart. "You know I could have you sedated so you wouldn't be able to speak to anyone until you were locked in a cell? None of the guards would be interested in your ranting."

"I guessed you could, but I was betting on you not being a fool. No one could get to your position by being unreasonable or dumb."

Bujold snorted. "You'd be surprised. But you're right, I'm not stupid or unreasonable. However, what I said earlier stands. I will not allow fights on this ship, regardless of the circumstances. So if you think you can convince me that what happened in the cafeteria wasn't your fault..."

"I wasn't the one being a prick."

"I've seen the security recording. There was absolutely no reason for you to confront that man. You could have ignored him, reported his actions, or done any number of things other than challenging him. I'm familiar with your background, Ms Zees. Given your wealth of experience, I'm surprised you thought what you were doing could turn out well for anyone concerned."

Setia, who had been about to snap back a retort, was silent.

"As this is your first offence, I'm prepared to let it go with only a verbal reprimand. Cause me more headaches and you will find my response very different. Is that clear?"

"You know this colonisation is going to be a disaster, right?"

Bujold shifted uncomfortably. "You aren't here to give me your opinion about our mission."

"Well, you're going to get it anyway. And it isn't an opinion, it's a fact-based prediction and better than anything Robins could come up with. You said you know my background? I bet you don't know half of it. But in my time as Elek's security person I encountered the worst of the worst. I'm not talking about the crowds at his shows. I'm talking about the entitled, rich dickheads who thought they could buy his attention or his friendship, hoping some of his shine would rub off on them. I know those people. They're lazy, arrogant, and egotistical. Not all of them. A few were okay. Usually the ones who'd worked hard for every cred they had. But most of them were useless. Absolute liabilities in any situation. And what did I find when I boarded the *Bres*? A whole ship full of them."

"Oh, please." Bujold waved dismissively. "You're exaggerating."

"How much time do you actually spend with the passengers? This is the first I've seen of you."

"I have many demands on my time. Getting to know everyone on the manifest is very far down my list of tasks."

"Maybe you should give it a higher priority, though there's no point now. What's done is done. But if you think your colonists are going to get their hands dirty and work up a sweat building houses and tilling fields, think again, because that isn't going to happen. As soon as they realise what they've got themselves into, they'll be furious. It's going to be mayhem down there. Chaos."

"The plan to create the colony was very clearly outlined in the—"

"You don't get it. I bet half of them haven't read the information. The other half think it doesn't apply to them. Haven't you received feedback from the lecturers and trainers? What's Wulandri told you?" The Colonisation Coordinator must have surely informed Bujold about the passengers' attitudes and mistaken beliefs.

The captain pursed her lips. "I have heard one or two disquieting reports, I admit. But that's only to be expected. I have no doubt there will be challenges ahead for all of us. Yet I have every confidence that, with time, everyone will adjust to the new way of living and the colony will succeed."

Setia shook her head. There was no point in giving a view of the future to someone who refused to open their eyes. Besides, arguing with someone of Bujold's age made her uneasy. She should have more faith in someone who had lived so long and done so much. "Whatever you say, Captain. Am I free to go now?"

"You may leave, but I ask that you avoid speaking to Mr Kaminski, who is waiting outside. And if you see him around the ship, please avoid him."

"Don't worry. I don't want anything to do with the moron." Setia got to her feet, but then a sudden idea occurred. She dropped back into her seat and leaned across Bujold's shiny desk. "Assuming the Prime colony does start to establish itself, the *Bres* and the other ships are going to continue their voyages, aren't they?"

"That is the plan. We will part company with the *Balor* and *Banba* and travel to a new destination."

"Which is?" Setia asked hopefully.

Bujold's eyelids lowered. "Confidential." *Twitch, twitch, twitch.*

"What if... what if I wanted to stay on the ship and come with you? What would I have to do?"

"Your ticket bought you passage to Talman Prime and Talman Prime only."

"You mean some people have tickets to other places?"

"I fail to see why I should discuss the ship's business with you. That is all. Enjoy the rest of your evening, Ms Zees, and, please, try to stay out of trouble."

Setia slowly stood up. Should she tell her about the running hares motif? There didn't seem to be any point. The captain wasn't receptive to her ideas, and the glimpse of the pattern had been fleeting. Maybe she'd imagined it. The badge on Carys Ellis's uniform might have only added weight to the illusion. "If the situation changes... I mean, if there's a chance I could miss the colonisation and stay on the *Bres*, would you let me know?"

"Goodnight, Ms Zees."

Fifteen

S*etia, please come to my office at 14.00.*

She read the message from Robins twice before deleting it. Why did the mapper want to see her? Why hadn't he put the reason in his note? He was being deliberately enigmatic. He must know that if he told her why he wanted to talk to her, she wouldn't come.

Which meant she should ignore his summons. He probably intended to persuade her to go on another risky mission to the surface. If that was the case, he needn't have bothered with his subterfuge. It didn't matter what he said. Whatever arguments he made, her answer would still be no.

It wasn't only because the last time she'd gone to Talman Prime she could have died. It also wasn't due to the fact that the colony planet was the most bleak, boring place she'd ever been. It was mostly because Robins had ignored her report of the thing she thought she'd seen. His scepticism still stung. Even if he was convinced she was talking nonsense, he could have listened. He could have at least pretended to pay attention. She'd been trying to help. He could have appreciated it.

More than a week had passed since she'd told him about the running hares. He'd had plenty of time to look at the recording from her EVA suit, but he must have found nothing. That wasn't what this meeting was about or he would have mentioned it.

This was about something else.

She wouldn't go.

At 13.55 she found herself outside Robins's office. No doubt he already knew she was here, either from his door camera or—the corner of her lips lifted in a wry smile—from his skein.

There was still time to turn around and walk away. He couldn't force her to see him. But the same indecision and curiosity that had been plaguing her all day remained. Like a fly fatally attracted to the tantalising interior of a carnivorous plant, she was finding Robins's request for a meeting impossible to resist.

She lifted a hand to press the chime, but running footsteps distracted her.

A soldier was pounding down the passageway.

Burnap's balls.

Robins had told her the man's name. What was it? Shell-something. Shelley? No, Sheldrake. That was it. He was a corporal, and their paths had crossed far too many times for her liking.

Corporal Sheldrake drew to a halt and looked her up and down, frowning. "It's you again."

"I was thinking the same."

He faced the door, hands folded behind his back, before side-eyeing her and shuffling a little away. "Did you let him know you're here?"

"I was just about to. Ugh, I don't believe it." She'd just spotted another arrival.

Carys Ellis was approaching. Their gazes met simultaneously. Carys grimaced. In silence, she completed her journey. She hadn't brought the bird.

Sheldrake asked, "You're here to see Mapper Robins too?"

Carys leaned her back against the opposite wall. "Uh huh."

"Do either of you know what this is about?" Setia asked. If she didn't like the answer she could leave now and avoid an awkward refusal.

The corporal replied, "I'm guessing it's a top-secret mission. I was told not to mention it to anyone."

Carys shrugged.

"Top secret mission?" Setia lifted a finger to the chime button again, hesitated, and then pressed it.

"Come in, come in." Robins sat at his desk, waving them over.

Four chairs had been set out. One was already filled. The woman had her back to them, but a sense of familiarity hit Setia. She knew this person.

The woman looked over her shoulder.

"Miriam?! What are you doing here?"

Miriam Belby grinned excitedly. "No idea. Mr Robins hasn't explained anything yet. He said he was waiting for the other attendees. I didn't expect one of them to be you. This is so cool."

Carys stomped to the seat at the far end of the line and parked herself in it, folding her arms over her chest.

"Permission to sit, sir?" Sheldrake asked.

"I'm not your CO, Corporal. You don't have to ask my permission. For the purposes of this meeting, please act as a civilian."

"Understood, sir." He sat down but remained bolt upright, his spine rigid and his knees bent at perfect right angles.

Setia sat next to Miriam in the only vacant chair. Miriam flashed her a brilliant smile.

"Thank you all for coming," Robins said. "For two of you, your attendance wasn't compulsory, but I had a good feeling you would turn up anyway." He winked. "As you know, I've been mapping the course of the colonisation project and, according to the skein, you four are closely involved."

"Miriam as well?" Setia asked, hearing too late the puzzlement and disbelief in her tone.

"Why wouldn't I be involved in something to do with you?" asked Miriam.

"Oh, no reason, it's just..." Setia grappled for an answer.

"We sat together on the shuttle from Earth," Miriam went on. "We're practically neighbours. We have lots in common."

"We have?"

Miriam's eyes widened in surprise. "We haven't?"

Carys snapped, "Robins, could you get to the point? I have an aviary to run."

"Of course." He cleared his throat. "Setia, Carys and Sebastian, you already know that we've arrived at Talman Prime."

"We have?!" exclaimed Miriam. "I knew it! Wait." She faced Setia. "Why didn't you tell me?"

Robins explained, "She wasn't at liberty to divulge the information."

"She could have given me a hint."

"Not even a hint."

Miriam didn't appear mollified.

"Anyway," said Robins, "now you know. I can also tell you that there's been an expedition to the surface for the scientists to conduct on-the-ground observations. Though the expedition was somewhat marred by an adverse event—"

"Adverse event?" Carys scoffed. "We could have died."

"Sacrifices in the line of duty are to be expected," said Sheldrake.

Miriam asked Setia, "Did you go on the expedition too?"

"I'm pleased to report," Robins continued, "that the results from the scientists' sampling and tests are in, and there's nothing to indicate the colonisation can't go ahead."

"Hallelujah," said Carys sarcastically. "It's nothing to do with the fact that the project has cost quadrillions of creds, right? Or that the passengers will sue the Antarctic Project into bankruptcy if we don't make the attempt."

Setia said, "They're going to sue if we *do* make the attempt."

Robins cleared his throat. "As we speak, preparations have begun to construct the first settlement."

"I hope they picked a different place from the one we went to," said Carys.

"It's in a place far from the site of the initial investigation."

"See?" Miriam challenged Setia. "They *have* begun to build a settlement secretly, and no one's noticed those people are missing."

"At the moment," said Robins, "only some surveyors, civil engineers and a handful of scientists are on the surface, along with a platoon of soldiers. It's very early days yet. The colonisation proper isn't expected to begin for several months. In the meantime..." He rubbed his hands.

Here it comes.

"...I have a proposal. As I said earlier, your threads in the skein are closely interlinked. The confluence intrigues me, and I would like to explore it further. I would like to propose another expedition to the surface, but involving you four only. You would be given all the equipment and supplies necessary for a month's stay, and your tasks would be minor—only to explore and report what you find. Reconnaissance, if you will."

"Why?" Carys asked. "What's the point of sending us? If our supposed destinies are entwined, won't they play out naturally? Why should we go down to Prime? If you want us to spend time together we could do that on the ship. I mean, personally I would rather choose my own friends, but if you want us to get to know each other it's going to be a helluva lot safer doing it here than down there."

"The skein maps the colonisation," Robins replied, "not life aboard the *Bres.* You all remaining on the ship would be useless for my purposes."

"I don't get it," said Setia. "Isn't what you're proposing interfering with the operation of the skein? Didn't you tell me you can't do that?"

"I understand your confusion. Let me explain. Everything we do 'interferes' with the skein. Each action we take and everything that happens alters it. The quake that occurred during the first mission sent out ripples that vastly affected it, though only for a short time. Lately, it has settled back to something similar to its former state."

"Couldn't you tell the quake would happen?" It was such a

major and dangerous event, Setia couldn't imagine how he couldn't see its approach.

"I saw a disturbance, yes, but no threads ended there. As it turned out, no lives were lost. It's impossible for me to tell what a disturbance might be. It might have been a good thing—a major, beneficial discovery, for instance."

She slumped in her seat. Robins's skein mapping seemed a waste of time.

"Though generally I try to avoid interfering," he went on, "as I don't know for sure what effects might occur, when I see a strong indication of a positive outcome I sometimes try to enhance it. Though, I confess, skein-mapping is a very young science. I am probably the most skilled reader and adjuster of my profession but even I still have much to learn."

Miriam asked, "So you see a positive outcome if the four of us go on this expedition? None of our 'threads'..." she wiggled her fingers "...get cut off?"

"That's right."

"Then I'm in. Let's do it, guys."

"Tell them the rest," Carys said darkly. "Tell them the truth."

"What truth?" Setia turned to Robins. "What does she mean?"

"I believe Carys is referring to the point I made earlier. Every action affects the skein. The fact that your lives don't currently appear to be in danger doesn't mean that your safety is guaranteed. There's a small possibility that by sending you to the surface I alter the course of the future."

"You mean it doesn't matter what the skein says right now, we could die anyway?"

"The future is not fixed. It is constantly in flux. There are no certainties."

Miriam said, "Well, any one of us could drop dead of a heart attack right now."

"Not me," Sheldrake retorted. "I'm in prime physical health."

"Even you," Miriam replied. "I say we do it. It'll be fun."

"Fun?" Carys snorted with scornful laughter.

Setia was inclined to agree. Miriam hadn't been to Talman Prime.

"I accept the mission, sir," Sheldrake announced.

"You don't have a choice," said Carys, "and neither do I."

All attention turned to Setia. For some reason she couldn't fathom, she said, "All right. Count me in."

Sixteen

"You have EVA suit packs," Robins said, "though you don't actually need them. All the tests indicate Prime's atmosphere is fully breathable and contains nothing toxic to human health."

"Nothing *identifiably* toxic," Carys interjected. "They can't test for things they don't know exist."

"We've also had people on the surface breathing the air for days with no ill-effects."

"Yet."

Robins shot Carys a look that indicated she was wearing the patience of a patient man very thin.

They were back in the shuttle bay, waiting for their equipment to be stowed. Setia eyed the boxes, backpacks and packages with interest. She'd never been camping. She'd gone from the streets to sharing a room in a drug den with other runners, to living in a series of luxury hotels while Elek worked his circuit of speaking engagements. Camping was something that families and couples did. Normal people with ordinary lives.

"Will we be armed, sir?" Sheldrake asked.

"Sidearms have been included in your baggage, purely as a precaution. As you know, none of the probe data implies predatory or even large life forms on the planet, and on-the-ground observations back this up. You also have a portable electric fence to protect your campsite, but it's extremely unlikely you will need to defend yourselves. Perhaps you can run through some basic weapons training with the others once you land, Corporal."

"It'll be a pleasure, sir."

Setia said, "I don't need any training."

"Where exactly are we going?" Miriam asked. "Is it near a beach?"

"That would be a little too risky," Robins replied. "Talman Prime is more tectonically active than Earth. There's a small but real danger of an undersea tremor."

"Well, if it's underwater, why would that affect us?"

"Earthquakes make waves," Carys said. "Big waves. Big, land-swamping waves that will wash you and your deckchair away." She waved her arms dramatically. The bird on her shoulder dug in its talons to hold on.

"Are you bringing your pet?" asked Setia.

"He isn't a pet, and, yes, Loki's coming too. That's non-negotiable." She'd addressed the latter remark to Robins, as if they'd had a discussion about it. "He's imprinted on me and he's still young. I can't leave him alone for more than a day, definitely not for however long this ridiculous mission will take."

"You will be in constant comm contact with the primary site," Robins said, smiling before adding, "I would say 24/7, but Prime's day length is 20 hours 15 minutes, and no one has decided how long a week will be."

"Twenty hours?" Miriam shook her head. "That's going to take some getting used to."

"It's just one of many adjustments colonists will have to make. The scientists predict everyone will adapt over time. Circadian rhythms are strongly governed by light/dark cycles, and, naturally, there is day and night on Prime."

Setia recalled the dim light that passed for 'day' on the planet.

"Where are you sending us, and what's the weather like down there? If it's another monsoon, I might change my mind."

"The shuttle will set you down at the main site, where, I've heard, the weather is currently clement. Where you go from there is up to you. My advice is to travel wherever your natural impulses take you. Think of it as an adventure. You will be the first explorers of Talman Prime."

"I can't wait," said Sheldrake.

"Wouldn't it be better to send scientists on this expedition?" Carys asked. "Or a military unit? Or, you know, someone who knows what they're doing?"

Robins replied, "You are all extremely capable, in your own way, including you."

Huh? Setia furrowed her brow. Arief had forced certain abilities on her, and Sheldrake was trained, but Miriam didn't seem familiar with anything except sipping cocktails. Not unless you counted her thorough knowledge of marketing and sales, which, for the life of her, Setia couldn't imagine might be useful in a survival situation. And what did Birdwoman have to offer?

Loki's head swivelled and fixed her with his piercing gaze.

Okay, she mentally conceded in response to the bird's stare, *Carys did help me with Arief. But that was because she had you. Are* you *going to save us if a volcano opens up under our feet*?

As if reading her mind, Robins said, "The new area for settlement is fifty kilometres from the nearest coastline in one of the most seismologically stable areas of the main landmass."

"Isn't that what you said last time?" Setia asked.

"We've been able to take many more readings since then. Even so, what happened on the first mission was anomalous. A freak event."

Miriam asked, "What happened on the first mission?"

"You don't want to know," Setia replied.

The settlement site was little more than scattered tents and poles stuck in the ground. Lots and lots of poles. Caterpillar-wheeled robots crawled the place, some of them dragging trailers. It wasn't as rocky here as the location of the first mission to the surface. The soil, where it peeked from between tussocks of low, spiky plants, was moist and black. Beyond the flat plain the ground rose to rolling hills on one side and fell to a distant river on the other. Grey clouds blanketed the sky. Setia studied them darkly.

A red-cheeked, bearded, burly man approached while they were hauling their equipment from the shuttle's hold. "Our intrepid explorers!" Grasping each of their hands in turn, he shook firmly.

Setia's knuckles were briefly ground together before he mercifully released his grip.

"Feel free to hang around for a few days before you set off. Acclimatise yourselves and whatnot." Perhaps in response to their bemused expressions he added, "I'm Ahmad, site manager. Make yourselves at home. Though it's not much of a home just yet. Would you like a hand setting up your tent?"

Tent? Setia scanned the baggage. "We only have one tent?"

Robins hadn't said anything about the sleeping arrangements and she hadn't thought to ask. There would be no escape from her companions.

"It doesn't make a lot of sense for each of us to have our own tent," said Sheldrake. "Unnecessary weight. Don't worry. I'll carry it. Wouldn't expect anyone else on the team to..." He faltered. "I mean..."

Setia wasn't sure what was bothering him. "If you're volunteering, that's fine. Don't let me stand in your way."

Carys told Ahmad, "We should make a start today. We'll set up our tent at our first camp. The sooner we get this over with the better."

Loki had already flown away and was presumably doing his own exploring, though where he might set down Setia didn't know. No trees marked the landscape.

"Why are the plants that horrible colour?" asked Miriam, her lip curling as her gaze wandered the view.

"I heard it's something to do with wavelengths in the daylight," Ahmad replied. "You would have to ask one of the botanists if you really want to know. I'll let you guys sort yourselves out. If you need anything, I'll be in my office." He indicated a marquee-style construction in the centre of the site. "I'd appreciate if you would give me a heads up before you set out."

"I'm going to double-check the supplies," Sheldrake declared. "It won't hurt to be prepared."

"You do that," said Setia. "I'm going to take a look around."

She'd walked for half a minute before she noticed she wasn't alone.

"We shouldn't split up," Miriam explained apologetically from two steps behind. "This is a new place for all of us. Who knows what might happen?"

Setia surveyed the empty plain. "I doubt there's anything dangerous out there. The surveying team has been here for days, and the area would have been scanned thoroughly before they arrived."

"Still..." Miriam giggled nervously "...like the army guy said, it doesn't hurt to be prepared."

"If you're worried that something might attack, you should stay at the shuttle with the others." *Or maybe you shouldn't have come along in the first place.*

"Somehow, I feel safer around you."

Setia heaved a sigh and continued walking. She was heading for the hills to get a better view of their surroundings. She was also—though she hardly admitted it to herself—on the lookout for more strange symbols embedded in the landscape. In this soft dirt it seemed unlikely she would see anything, but she couldn't shake the deep-down feeling she hadn't been mistaken. A second sighting would confirm she *had* seen something the first time around.

Apparently emboldened by Setia's silence, Miriam caught up to her and marched by her side.

"What do you think of Talman Prime so far?" Setia asked.

"It's...it's different from how I imagined it."

"No beaches or cocktails?"

"No beaches or cocktails," Miriam echoed weakly. "And it's so dark and humid and quiet."

"And purple."

"Yeah. Purple."

Seventeen

Sheldrake had comm'd, telling them everything was ready and it was time to set out. Setia tightened the straps on her backpack. The pack didn't feel heavy at all, but she hadn't expected it to. Whatever Arief had done to her meant that few things were heavy to her anymore, yet she didn't like to advertise the fact. She couldn't explain it better than anyone else, and she already felt like a freak without the stares and questions that would result from revealing her unnatural strength.

"Oughhh!" Miriam exclaimed, knees bending as she shouldered her load. She straightened up before adding, "I hope we aren't going far today."

Sheldrake said, "I can re-distribute our equipment and supplies if you want. I divided everything up according to my estimate of your body weights. I might have miscalculated how much you can comfortably carry."

"You estimated our body weights?" Carys scoffed. "Weird, but you do you." Her bird had returned and perched next to her ear, grooming her hair with his beak.

Setia tried but failed to stifle a snort of laughter. The irony of the woman calling someone else weird was impossible to ignore.

Carys glowered. "Did I say something funny?"

"Not at all. Miriam, do you want me to take some of your stuff?"

"I'll be all right, I think. I just need to get used to it."

"If you change your mind, let me know."

In the distance, the shuttle was taking off. It lifted from the ground, retracted its legs, and zoomed forward and up, quickly vanishing into the cloud cover. Ahmad had returned to his business. The rest of the scientists, engineers, workers, and military stationed at the site went about their tasks, ignoring the explorers.

"That's it," said Sheldrake, his gaze returning from the spot where the shuttle had disappeared. "Let's make a start. We should try to cover at least ten klicks before sunset."

"Why?" Carys asked. "This isn't supposed to be an endurance trek."

"Because..." the cogs of the corporal's mind seemed to whirr "... we need to explore as much new ground as possible. There might be important discoveries to make. Things no one knows about yet. Useful information that will help with the colonisation."

"I'm not sure I *want* to discover things no one knows about." said Carys. "I'd be happy staying right here. In fact, if it weren't for the fact that Robins will find out and get me into trouble, I would."

Setia muttered, "No need to remind us. Everyone knows you didn't want to come. You've made that clear."

Carys was about to fire something back when Sheldrake interrupted. "Which way are we heading? River or hills?"

Miriam replied, "We have to follow the river, right? Otherwise, what do we do for water?"

"Water's no problem," said Sheldrake. "We have condensers. They'll draw all the water we'll need for drinking and washing from the air, especially in this humidity. It has to be near ninety percent."

"Don't worry," Setia said, scanning the skies. "I bet we'll soon have more water than we want."

"All the more reason to begin walking immediately," Sheldrake urged. "River or hills? I say hills. We can see pretty far down that river and there's nothing of interest in sight."

"River," said Carys. "The land's flat. It'll be easier going."

"On the other hand," Miriam said nervously, "if there are dangerous predators we don't know about, they could be aquatic and that's why no one's noticed them yet. Maybe we should stay away from water."

Carys rolled her eyes. "Maybe you should make up your mind."

"Hills it is," Sheldrake announced. "Let's go, people."

He marched resolutely in the direction of the high ground. Miriam followed and, after a moment's hesitation, so did Setia. When she looked back a few minutes later, Carys was trudging in their wake.

It was around midday, but the sun was only a patch of lighter grey among the clouds. The air was heavy with moisture. Dew-speckled alien vegetation snagged at Setia's boots as she waded through it, quickly wetting them. There also seemed to be some kind of exudation from the leaves as trails of pink slime appeared along with the water.

The going wasn't easy without a trail, and the land soon began to climb. Sheldrake appeared intent on leading them up the highest hill. He didn't explain his purpose. It would have made more sense to travel along the lower slopes, especially as it was their first long walk after months of living on a starship. Miriam's puffs of exertion were already loud. Setia looked over her shoulder again. The settlement had receded, Carys had dropped behind and her bird had flown away.

"Sheldrake!" Setia called out.

Without pausing, he replied, "Yeah?"

"Where are you taking us?"

He pointed up the slope. "View from high ground."

"We'll be able to see all around," panted Miriam. "Great idea."

Setia said, "But we already have..." She didn't bother completing her sentence. They had a detailed map of the surrounding area derived from satellite and ship's scan data, and if they managed to reach the edge of the scanned territory they could download more information from the *Bres.* But she guessed it wouldn't hurt to set eyes on the wider landscape.

She still wasn't sure what she was doing here. Perhaps it was only that life aboard ship was boring, especially with her poor person's limited access to activities coupled with—she was forced to admit—her general reclusiveness. Perhaps this activity was only a diversion. And maybe she was mildly curious about Robins's observation that somehow her life was tied up with her companions'. But she didn't have a lot of faith in the mapper's profession. His predictions were so vague any event could be attributed to them.

Miriam was flagging, dropping back. Setia waited for her to catch up, and then thrust an arm under her elbow to support her. Miriam smiled her thanks, too out of breath to speak. They were less than halfway to the summit.

"Ellis!" Sheldrake yelled.

Setia, whose gaze had turned to her feet to avoid tripping on thick plant stems, looked up. The corporal had halted and was glaring downward. Carys had dropped even farther behind.

"Keep up!" Sheldrake added.

"Let's have a rest," said Setia. "Don't forget we aren't as in shape as you."

His expression softened. "Makes sense. Five-minute halt. While we wait for Ellis."

"Ten minutes. To give her time to catch her breath."

He didn't answer, only softly tutted and shook his head. They watched Carys toil upward, a dark look on her face.

"Where's Loki?" Miriam asked.

Carys only shrugged. When she reached them, her chest was heaving. She slipped her shoulders out from under her backpack's straps and let it fall to the ground. Then she rested, hands on hips. "Whose stupid idea was this again? Oh yeah, Robins. Remind me to ask Loki to pay him a visit when we get back."

"It isn't too bad," Miriam said. "We're some of the first humans to set foot on—"

"An exoplanet. Whoop-de-doo. Anyway, Prime isn't the first extra-Solar world humans have been to. An expedition set out to another planet a while ago. It just didn't make the news."

"Huh?!" Miriam exclaimed. "It didn't make the news? But that's the story of the century. Of the millennium. I don't believe you. You're making it up, teasing us because you're grumpy about being here."

"You think I care if you believe me? It's true whether you believe me or not. The voyage wasn't reported in the media. It was hushed up."

What a strange assertion. Setia didn't know what to make of it, or the fact that Carys was telling them this now. She certainly was 'grumpy', as Miriam put it, but there seemed more to it than that.

"Even if it is true," said Miriam, "why would *you* know about it? You're only a worker. You didn't pay for your passage, so you can't be rich or important. How would you know secret information?"

"I just do."

"If that intel is classified," said Sheldrake, "you're landing yourself in a world of trouble by revealing it, so I'm gonna pretend I didn't hear you. And my advice to everyone else is to do the same. Halt's over. No more stopping until we reach the top." He strode away, marching forcefully through the clinging vegetation. Pink slime coated his boots and his trousers to his knees, as if he'd been wading through a field of marshmallows.

Setia chuckled.

"Laughing again?" Carys asked. "I'd love to know what you always find so funny."

"No reason. It's just my sunny temperament."

Miriam set off and Setia did the same, leaving Carys to bring up the rear once more.

Almost immediately, Miriam gave a small shriek and fell onto her backside. "Ow! Oooh…" She edged backward.

Setia bent down. "Did you slip? I'll help you up."

"It moved!" Miriam was staring at something.

When Setia looked closer all she could see was a hole in the black soil. "Was it an animal?" She hadn't spotted any creatures yet, only plants. Prime was only supposed to host simple life forms, low on the evolutionary scale. "Or an insect?"

"No," Miriam said, "it was a—there it is!"

A yellow tendril had crept from the hole and was waving cautiously, as if probing the air for danger.

Thump, thump, thump. Sheldrake arrived. "What's the hold-up? On your feet, soldier." Reaching down, he grasped Miriam's upper arm.

"Let go of her," Setia snapped. "None of us are your soldiers, so you can cut that shit out right now. She saw something, and you just scared it back into its hole. Don't move or you'll scare it again."

"She's right," said Miriam. "I did see something. Oh, look, there it is."

The probing tentacle had reappeared. Another joined it, and soon an array of slim, yellow fingers were poking from the hole. Finally a stem that joined them emerged. When it was fully extended from its hole, the organism was about thirty centimetres tall. It gently swayed, though there was no breeze.

"Huh, never seen anything like that on land." Carys was crouching beside them. Unlike Sheldrake, she'd managed to avoid scaring the creature.

"You've seen it somewhere else?" Miriam whispered. "On Earth?"

"Only in vids. It looks like a hydra. In water, those arms would catch food that happened to float past. I'm not sure what it could catch here. Maybe flying insects? If you look in the centre of the arms you can see its mouth."

It was the first time Setia had heard Carys speak minus her usual bad attitude. Her bird was back and her expression was full of interest.

Miriam asked, "Is it a plant or an animal? And is it safe?"

"I don't see how it could hurt us," said Carys. "It's too small, for one thing. I suppose it might be venomous so we should probably keep away from it. I know it doesn't look much like it, but it's an animal."

"Cool! We've seen the first animal on Prime."

Carys straightened up. "The xenozoologists will have catalogued plenty already. Don't get too excited."

Miriam's face fell. "Yeah, they must have."

Sheldrake had an interface out and was taking photographs. "I'll send these up to the ship, then we move out. We need to complete our recon and decide our route for today."

"Yes, sir!" Setia replied.

Sheldrake didn't seem to notice her tone. He gave a stern nod and turned to continue his climb.

At the summit of the hill a purple sea spread out, undulating into the distance on three sides and descending to the river. The beginnings of the settlement looked at odds with the rest of the place, like a pimple on otherwise flawless skin. They decided to head for what could best be described as a forest, though really it was only an area of the landscape where plants grew much taller than the others. They would be walking west, toward the lowering, hidden sun.

After a short rest and a drink of water, the corporal led them on a fast hike for an hour. Gradually, Miriam began to struggle to keep up and Carys lagged farther and farther behind, until Sheldrake was forced to slow to a medium pace.

After another hour, Miriam seemed to be on her last legs, though she was bravely trying to struggle on. Carys, on the other hand, was behaving very differently. She'd passed Setia and Miriam and walked level with Sheldrake, though a couple of metres distant. Anger appeared to be lending her energy.

"We need to stop," Setia said.

"Another halt?" Sheldrake asked irritably.

"No, a stop. We should set up camp here." The ground was fairly level and the vegetation was low, soft and springy.

"But we're nowhere near the forest," Sheldrake protested.

"It was you who decided we had to reach it before sunset, and it's a completely random target. The reason we're here is to spend time together, according to Robins. We don't have to explore all of Prime."

Sheldrake looked about to argue, but Miriam said quietly, "I *am* quite tired. I wouldn't mind stopping if everyone agrees."

"Well...okay. You all sit down while I set up the perimeter wire and tent."

Carys barked, "Some of us do know how to set up a tent, you know."

Setia was happy to let the corporal and whiny Birdbitch do all the work. She kept quiet and gave Miriam some water and snacks while the other two prepared the campsite.

The sun was dipping below a nearby ridge, casting them into shadow. The air began to chill and grow even more humid. Leaving Miriam to eat and rest, Setia wandered around while Sheldrake was hammering stakes into the ground and Carys spread out the tent.

They'd spotted more of the tentacle animals on their journey. They'd even seen one snatch a flying creature from the air and force it, wriggling and struggling, into its mouth. She wondered if there were any here too. She saw a few, withdrawing into holes as she approached.

Then she saw something new. A white, bulbous form protruded from the ground, stark against the generally purple background. The organism was round and smooth and sat about five centimetres high. As soon as she'd seen one she quickly saw others. On Earth, she might have said they were mushrooms except they had no gills or stems.

A *snap* sounded, quickly followed by the rush of fast-moving fabric.

"Tent's up," Carys announced before immediately crawling inside.

"Awesome," said Miriam and went over to join her.

That night, after they'd eaten their self-warming dinners and taken part in the awkward conversations of people who didn't know each other very well, they climbed into their sleeping bags for an early night.

Miriam was the first to fall asleep, her gentle snoring filling the silence not long after her head hit her inflated pillow. Sheldrake was next, his deep breathing indicating he was accustomed to noisy bunkmates. Carys didn't sleep for a long time, and Setia was tempted to indulge in a hushed conversation. But the woman's prickliness and clear personal dislike put her off. Eventually, soft, rhythmic exhalations signalled that Carys had fallen into slumber too.

Setia lay awake, staring into the darkness.

What are you doing here?

She'd escaped Arief, apparently. No sign had been seen of him since their confrontation on the *Bres*.

Now what?

Was this to be her life? Would the remainder of her existence be spent on Prime? Bujold hadn't been open to the idea of allowing her to take part in the onward journey, yet the prospect of remaining on this dark, dull world wasn't inviting.

The heaviness of approaching unconsciousness began to steal over her mind. Her eyes drooped closed. As she slipped into sleep she thought she heard whispering, but perhaps it was only Loki grooming his feathers or the beginning of a dream.

Eighteen

The first thing Setia heard in the morning was the sound of someone opening the tent. She peered over the top of her sleeping bag. It was Carys. With the tent flap open, she held her gloved fist up to Loki on his perch, and he hopped onto it. Then she carried him outside. A quick beat of his wings and he was gone. Carys collapsed the perch and thrust the slim pole into her backpack before also stepping through the opening.

Setia turned onto her back and stretched. Sheldrake and Miriam remained asleep. Dull Prime sunlight was shining in. What time was it? If a day was twenty hours and fifteen minutes long, did that mean they would wake up later and later, until finally they would be waking up when the sun was setting? She blinked. It was too early for musings of an arithmetical nature.

She sat up, pulled on her jacket and put on her boots, and then went out. Carys was nowhere to be seen. Setia deactivated the fence, opened a section to step through it, then reactivated it.

They'd camped in a hollow among the hills. Slopes rose all around, blocking a wider view. With surprise, Setia noted the sky was clear. It was the first time she'd actually seen the sky of this new world. A rosy hue suffused it, deeper in one section where the sun had to be rising beyond the hills. The purple vegetation drooped under the weight of moisture, jewel-like drops speckling every leaf.

She decided to climb a hill to loosen up and get a better view of their surroundings.

As she was scaling the lower slopes, however, Carys called, "Setia!"

Setia paused. For Carys to willingly address her was surprising enough, but there had also been an urgent tone in her voice. "What?"

In answer, Carys beckoned.

Bemused, Setia descended the short distance to the bottom of the hill, sliding somewhat on the wet plants.

"I'm glad someone else is awake," Carys said breathlessly when she reached her. "I wasn't sure whether to wake anyone else. I suppose there isn't anything we can do about it now."

"Do about what?"

"This way." She led Setia in the direction of the fence.

Sheldrake had constructed the circle several metres from the tent, driving two-metre poles into the ground at intervals, and strung wires thirty centimetres apart. The whole thing was electrified by the power pack.

Carys said, "I probably should have told someone before I left. But I was amazed and I wanted to try to follow their trail, maybe catch sight of them."

"What are you talking about?"

"Look!" She pointed at the ground. The vegetation at the rear of the tent, beyond the wires, had been trampled flat. Stems had been broken in half and bruised foliage oozed pink, milky sap. Something —or things—had stood here during the night. "I didn't hear anything. Did you?"

"No, I didn't hear..." Setia frowned, recalling the whispering.

"As soon as I spotted the damage, I set off to try to find out what had done it. Reckless, I suppose, but I wasn't thinking straight. The trail quickly peters out, though. I carried on in the same direction but I couldn't see anything. So I thought I would head back and tell you guys. What do you think?"

Setia had never heard Carys utter so many words all at once. She seemed to have forgotten her animosity in her excitement.

"What do *you* think it could have been?" Setia asked, squatting down to take a closer look at the damaged plants. The trail she and the others had created yesterday hadn't been so devastating. Whatever had trodden on this vegetation must have been large and heavy, or it had stood here a long while and moved about.

"I can't even imagine. Something at least as big as us. Maybe more than one of them."

"Do you think they were trying to get through the fence?"

"I suppose so? I don't know. I can't see any marks on the wires, but anything that touched them would have been instantly shocked. All I can say is, I'm bloody glad we have this fence. I thought Sheldrake was being annoying yesterday, playing soldiers. Thank the stars he put it up."

Setia rose to her feet. "You and Miriam need to do some target practice."

After a quick comm ruled out the unlikely possibility that people from the settlement site had paid an overnight visit, there was no other conclusion to draw—an unknown creature or creatures had arrived at the campsite and dawdled at the boundary while the travellers slept.

Setia handed a breakfast ration to Miriam, who nervously ripped the seal, activating the heating function. Picking out a cheese omelette for herself, Setia joined the others on the ground sheet Sheldrake had put down. As soon as he'd been shown the evidence of unknown visitors, he'd ordered everyone inside the fence.

"I don't understand," said Miriam. "There aren't any big animals on Prime. Wulandri stated that clearly at one of the information sessions. She was certain."

Setia snorted derisively. "I'm not sure Wulandri's even been here yet. I wouldn't take a whole lot of notice of what she says. She's going from what the scientists tell her, and they got most of their 'facts' from probe data. They might have quite a few surprises in store as they investigate the planet."

"Do you think those things are dangerous?"

"Impossible to know," said Sheldrake, "but we're not taking any chances."

"So we're going to head back to the settlement?" Miriam asked hopefully.

"Uhh, that's not what I meant."

"Thinking about it," said Carys, "we don't have any reason to be scared. To be predators the creatures would need something to eat, but we haven't seen any herbivores or anything like that around. The only prey animals are insects, in which case we don't have anything to be worried about."

Sheldrake nodded. "Exactly. Today we complete the trek to the forest, and maybe go further."

Setia wasn't confident about Carys's conclusion. She wanted to say, *No herbivores around that we've seen.* After all, they hadn't caught sight of their surprise visitor(s) yesterday either. But she didn't want to worry Miriam, and neither did she want to return to the fledgling settlement or the ship. For the first time since boarding the *Bres,* she felt energised.

She squeezed the remainder of her omelette into her mouth and ate it before saying, "Carys and Miriam, I'll give you some weapons training while Sheldrake packs up the camp."

Carys was scanning the skies.

"Are you looking for Loki?" Miriam asked.

"He should be back by now. He'll be hungry."

"I'm sure he'll show up soon," said Setia. "If you've finished eating, get your firearms and join me."

She took them through the basics, mainly gun safety and aiming at near and far targets. It would have been good to give them practice at shooting moving targets but that wasn't an option. The pulse rounds exploded the target plants into clouds of steam, though rarely set them on fire, and any flames that did appear quickly died down. The place was too wet to sustain prolonged burning. Miriam proved a better shot than Carys. Though Miriam's temperament was more timid, a gun in her hands improved her confidence tremendously, whereas Carys seemed to find it hard to concentrate, and she reacted with irritation to advice and suggestions.

When Sheldrake's huffs of impatience as he stood waiting with their full backpacks were too hard to ignore, she brought an end to the session.

Loki still hadn't returned and Carys was visibly anxious.

"Maybe we should wait here for the bird," Miriam suggested.

"It won't make any difference," Carys said. "He'll find me wherever I am."

"So he isn't lost?"

"No way." Her brow wrinkled, she peered into the heavens.

The sky had remained clear so far, but a band of dark cloud was moving in from the west. Already, tendrils of rain trailed from it.

"Can he fly in wet weather?" Setia asked.

"He will if he needs to, but..." Carys's frown deepened.

"I know where he is," Sheldrake announced. "He's in the forest. Where else could be? He's perching in a tree. Waterproofs on, everyone, before that hits." He jerked his chin at the distant clouds. "Then we head out."

As they marched, Setia's thoughts returned to their overnight visitors. Clearly, the animals had to be nocturnal, but that didn't explain why none of the probes or the ship's scanners had picked them up. Animals would give out heat and the equipment was sensitive to infrared. Perhaps the species was extremely rare and it was pure chance individuals hadn't been noticed. Sheldrake had sent extensive recordings of the trampled ground to Ahmad at the settlement and to the *Bres*. Maybe they would hear back today about the scientists' conclusions.

When the rain arrived it hit suddenly. One minute the sky was empty, the next near-darkness fell as the cloud quickly closed in. Visibility shrank to a few metres and the distant forest was lost behind a grey shroud.

"Talman Prime," Setia said. "Gotta love it."

"Where's my cocktail?" asked Miriam.

Before the rainstorm arrived they'd been descending the last of the hills and about to enter the flat land leading to the forest. Setia soon wished they were still walking on an incline. On the lower ground the soil was boggy and the rain wasn't making the situation any better. Through the sound of falling water came the repetitive *squelch*, *slurp* of their boots sinking into mud and then wrenching free. If there was a dry path through this quagmire, Sheldrake wasn't finding it.

"Not far now!" the corporal called out.

As the heaviest person carrying the heaviest pack he was sinking deepest into the mud. Sometimes, his legs disappeared almost to the knees. Setia had a vision of him vanishing entirely.

"Should we turn back?" Miriam asked, raising her voice to be heard over the constant pitter-patter. "Try going around?"

Sheldrake replied, "Just a little further."

Setia's head was down to keep the falling water away from her face, meaning the only person she could see was the corporal, who trudged in front. Other than him, her vision was mainly filled with bog plants. A faint smell wafted up at each step she took. It reminded her of playing in the warm water from outflow pipes on the beach bordering her home town. It was not a good smell, and she wondered what had possessed her, as a child, to play there.

She looked back. Carys had fallen way behind again. Letting Miriam go past, she waited for Birdwoman. Her head was down and she shuffled along, not making any effort to keep up. She seemed to be in a world of her own.

Setia stared. There was something behind Carys. A grey shape, the same hue as the rain but denser and more solid, appeared to loom only steps beyond her companion.

"Carys!"

Setia blinked and focused, but the figure was hard to make out. It was humanoid in shape but she couldn't see a face or clothing. It was a homogeneous blob without definition.

"Carys!" she repeated. "Hurry up!" She didn't want to alarm the younger woman, especially as she wasn't sure if the thing was real or just a trick of the light.

Carys's head lifted and Setia caught a glimpse of a scowl before it sank again. Carys's pace didn't increase.

Setia swung around and ran—if you could call it running in that bog—to Sheldrake.

"I don't want to sound crazy, but could you take a look at Carys?"

"Huh? If she's slacking again—"

"That isn't what I mean. Please, take a look behind her."

Reluctance in his features, the corporal halted. He turned, frowned, and then his mouth dropped open.

"Holy shit!"

He tore open his jacket and thrust a hand inside, pulling out his gun.

"Get down!" he yelled at Carys, aiming at the grey figure.

Miriam froze. Carys looked up, confused.

"I said, get down!"

"But we don't know..." Setia hesitated. Did the figure pose a danger? It was impossible to tell, but she understood Sheldrake's reaction. An eerie dread had crawled over her. The *otherness* of the alien sparked a visceral fear.

Following the direction of Sheldrake and Setia's stare, Carys turned. She didn't seem to see anything. Perhaps she was too close to her pursuer. Maybe distance was needed to be able to make it out. She faced them again. "What the hell are you doing?!"

Setia sucked in air sharply. There were more of them. It was so hard to see them in the blinding downpour, but seven or eight of the grey phantoms hovered only metres behind the first. Their forms were so vague, she wasn't sure if they'd been there all along.

She grabbed Sheldrake and pointed.

At the same time, the figures moved closer, apparently floating along without the use of legs.

Miriam screamed.

Carys's head snapped back to her rear, and she finally seemed to see the threat. She stumbled forward.

Sheldrake fired. The pulses hit but passed right through the first grey thing. It and the others sped up their pace. Sheldrake fired again but the rounds had no effect. It was like he was trying to kill the rain. "Run!" he yelled. "Everyone, head for the forest!"

A mad scramble followed. Battling through the clinging mud, they ran. Sometimes, someone would trip and fall into the mire, and their companions would stop to help them up. Setia threw regular fearful glances over her shoulder, but in the deluge, rain streaming into her eyes, she was never sure of what she could see.

Something like a tree appeared out of the mist, branches reaching up, torrents of water streaming down its trunk. There was another. And another. The trees grew closer, and their canopy closed overhead, screening out the rain.

Miriam dropped to her knees. Then she tumbled onto her side and gasped, "I can't do it. I can't go any farther."

Setia looked back again.

The trunks of the forest trees crowded closely, and there was no sign of the grey ghosts.

NINETEEN

"If I tell you to get down, you get down!" Sheldrake yelled.

Like Miriam, Carys had also collapsed. On her knees on the forest floor, drawing in great gulps of air, she was unable to answer.

Sheldrake leaned over her, hands on hips, face puce with exertion and fury. "You could have been ki—"

"Cut it out," Setia snapped. "Now's not the time." She was still scanning the trees for signs of pursuit. It had only been due to the thick rain they'd been able to see the figures. Here, beneath the canopy where the rain fell less heavily, they should be easier to distinguish. Yet, thinking back, the creatures had seemed to be *made* of rain. Could they even exist except in a downpour?

"And...the next time..." Carys gasped "...you point...a gun at me..."

"I said cut it out!"

Under the trees—if they could be called that—the low light had dimmed further. As well as the rain clouds, the sun was struggling to penetrate the canopy of drooping leaves. They hung swollen, lumpy and disconsolate, like the fingers of an empty glove, endlessly dripping. They were not marked by veins or serrations like tree leaves on Earth, and the striated tree trunks stuck up from bare soil, not leaf mould, as if the leaves never fell. The ground was dryish, certainly drier than the bog. Deep channels cut through it, ferrying the water away.

"I'll give Robins a SITREP," Sheldrake announced. "Zees, keep watch." He turned on his heel and stomped away from Carys, broadcasting his disgust with every step. Mud had made it all the way up his body and splashed his face, which was etched with fatigue. He unsnapped the waist belt of his pack and, with a grimace, slid his shoulders out from under the straps.

"Are we going back to the *Bres* now?" Miriam asked, sitting up and also taking off her backpack.

"I'm not sure how that's going to happen," Setia replied. "The shuttle can't land among all these trees or, I'm guessing, on marshy land. It's too heavy. It'll sink right in."

"You mean we'd have to trek all the way back to the hills? What if those grey things attack us again?"

"I don't think the shuttle could land there either. It needs reasonably level ground."

Dismay filled Miriam's face.

While Sheldrake murmured at his interface Carys also took off her pack. She sat on it, resting her elbows on her knees and her chin on one hand. Miriam gazed intently at the surrounding trees.

"If you two can keep a lookout," Setia said, "I'll set up the tent. We can shelter from the rain and take off our waterproofs." Like everyone else, she was caked in mud.

Deep in a whispered conversation, Sheldrake didn't object when she retrieved the tent from his pack. She was in the middle of spreading it out when he said, "Robins wants to talk to you." Without waiting for her answer, he thrust his interface into her hands and took over the erection of the tent.

The mapper's mild expression as he gazed at her from the screen was a welcome calming influence in all the turmoil. "Setia, Corporal Sheldrake has delivered a rather alarming report. I would like to hear your perspective, if you don't mind."

"On what? Strange nocturnal creatures hanging around outside our tent or being chased by rain monsters?"

"I have plenty of information about your overnight visitors. I was alluding to the 'rain monsters' as you put it. Could you tell me exactly what happened, as you remember it?"

Setia related the sequence of events, from spotting the figure behind Carys to halting in the forest when the others couldn't run any farther.

"I see. How would you evaluate the threat these aliens posed?"

"What do you mean?"

"I mean… Where are you? Is our conversation private?"

The tent was up and Miriam and Carys were inside. Sheldrake sat at the entrance, a grim, mud-caked sentinel.

"I'm just going a little farther into the forest," she told him.

He nodded. "Stay in sight."

She returned a short way along the route they'd travelled. "No one can overhear us now."

"I'm trying to decide whether to order your group's return. Do you believe you are in serious danger? To be frank, the corporal believes there is a high level of threat yet he's keen for your expedition to continue. That seems paradoxical. Risking your lives is unacceptable. I was hoping you could provide another viewpoint to help me make my decision."

"I've already told you what happened. I don't know what else you want me to say. How can I assess the threat when there are so many unknowns? This is new territory for all of us." His question was unfair. If she told him it was safe to continue and then someone died, how would she live with herself?

"As Elek's Head of Security you must have faced many challenging situations with a range of unpredictable variables. I'm calling on your experience and expertise. I think I understand your reluctance to answer. To be clear, whatever happens I will take full responsibility."

"That's easy to say. Not sure it'll change how I feel if someone gets killed."

"Nevertheless..."

She sighed. "Looking back, there weren't any obvious signs we were in real danger. Whatever visited us at the tent had to be quite big but the fence deterred it, and those things in the rain..." she frowned "...all they did was come closer. If they'd reached any of us, I'm not sure what harm they could have done. They seemed to be made of water, so maybe they could have drowned us, I suppose?"

"Made of water," Robins echoed. "Remarkable. What a shame none of you was recording during the incident."

"We were kind of preoccupied with slowly running away."

"Slowly?"

"Have you ever tried running through a bog?"

"So the beings could have caught you at any time, but they didn't."

"Once we took off no one was checking what they were doing. It was only when Miriam and Carys couldn't run any farther that we stopped and looked back."

"Can I ask, if the creatures weren't particularly threatening, why you ran at all?"

"Honestly, it's hard to say. I suppose we were spooked. Those things are creepy as hell."

The mapper's expression turned thoughtful and he didn't speak for several moments. "If all of you are in agreement, I would suggest that you continue on your expedition. It must be a unanimous decision, however. Otherwise, you have my permission to return to the settlement and await transfer back to the ship."

"Carys will never agree to stay. She's been bitching about everything ever since we landed. And Miriam's had a wakeup call about what Prime is really like. If there's a chance she can return to the comfort of her cabin on the *Bres*, she'll jump at it."

"I thought that might be the case, with Carys anyhow."

"What's her problem? If the chip on her shoulder was any heavier she'd be walking lopsided. And you told me to be her friend, but she hates me. A leper would get a better reception."

"Carys Ellis had rather a difficult childhood."

"She's not the only one. Some of us don't take it out on everyone else."

"It's more than that. It wouldn't be fair for me to explain. It's up to her whether she tells you more about her history, but it may be that she bears some animosity due to what you represent. It isn't personal."

"It *feels* personal."

"I'm sure she will come around with time. Deep down, she is kind and self-sacrificing to a fault."

"Well, she'll be the reason you'll be seeing us again in a day or two. There's no way she'll spend a second longer on this planet than she has to. Sheldrake's going to be so pissed. He's in his element."

"Corporal Sheldrake will do what he's told. If he argues, tell him it's an order."

"Got it. Hey, you never told me if you saw anything in my cam recording from the first trip."

"Ah, no, we did not, and the ship's computer couldn't come up with a pattern. Which isn't to say I don't believe you thought you saw something."

"But you think I was imagining it."

"I didn't say that. What I can say is, your recent experiences demonstrate there's more to Talman Prime than meets the eye, and I'm glad I played a wild card with your expedition."

Back at the tent, Carys and Miriam had taken off their waterproofs and cleaned up, and Sheldrake had constructed the electrified fence. He held out his hand to take back the interface, looking annoyed when he saw the screen was blank. "What did Robins say? We continue the mission, right?"

"I have to talk to Carys and Miriam. Why don't you get changed?"

"What's there to talk about?"

Setia glared at him.

"All right. Keep a lookout for hostiles, okay?"

"Just leave us alone for a minute."

After he'd disappeared into the tent, she said to her remaining companions quietly, "Mapper Robins has said we only have to carry on if we all agree. He'll call off the expedition if that's what any one of us wants, regardless of the others' wishes. I think our military friend is going to put up a fuss, so we have to present a united front."

"A fuss about what?" Carys asked.

"About returning to the ship, of course."

"What if no one wants to?"

"Wh...?" Setia frowned. "You haven't stopped complaining since we landed. In fact, the complaining started before we even took off. Now you're saying you don't want to go back?"

"I'm not leaving without Loki."

For a brief moment, Setia had imagined their prickly companion might have begun to feel a smidgen of comradeship. But no. Yet her objection made perfect sense. Setia had forgotten about the bird. "What about you, Miriam? If you've had enough of Prime now's your chance to get off it. Until you have to be an official colonist, anyway."

"Even if you all go back," Carys interjected, "I'm staying."

"You've made that clear. Miriam?"

"I...er..." She looked between Setia and Carys. "I'll do whatever everyone else wants."

"Not upset about no beaches or cocktails?"

"Beaches and cocktails are overrated. I admit that this place is about as far from what I expected as you can get, but it's fun hanging out with you guys."

Setia blinked. "You're having fun?"

"Well..." Miriam shrugged and smiled weakly.

What to do? Sheldrake's vote was a no-brainer. "So it's down to me?"

Rain phantoms and overnight creepers versus a cramped living space and a limited range of boring activities. Now she thought about it, the choice was easy to make.

Twenty

Sheldrake was rummaging in his pack. "I'll break out the heater. You all need to get warm. We'll eat and rest a while."

The rain hadn't let up, but they were inside and wearing dry clothing. A steady *drip-drip-drip* tapped the tent roof.

They clustered around the cylindrical heating device, which gave out an even warmth as well as a subdued yellow glow. The light was comforting, as was the intent, no doubt. Yet a morose mood overhung the group, despite the implicit decision to continue their expedition. No one seemed to have anything to say.

Except Miriam. "I'm sure Loki will turn up soon."

Carys's shoulders drooped. Then she moved to the open tent flap and sat down cross-legged, her back to the group, looking out into the gloomy forest.

Sheldrake broke out the rations and they ate in silence.

Drip, drip, drip.

"We need to figure out tomorrow's route," Sheldrake said.

"Not right now," said Setia. "We have the afternoon and all evening."

"You're forgetting that days are shorter here."

"I'm not forgetting anything." She was conscious of Carys's focus on the outdoors, which hadn't changed while she'd been eating. Chatting about what they would do next seemed to imply the bird wouldn't be coming back, and they would be moving on without him.

"If we have a concrete plan," Sheldrake persisted, "based on the map—"

"Can't you give it a rest, even for a minute?"

The corporal snatched the empty food packet from her hands and bundled it up with his own and Miriam's. Wordlessly, Carys tossed hers out through the flap. The packets would dissolve in the environment within a few days. Nevertheless, Sheldrake dipped out to retrieve it and add it to the others in the rubbish bag. Carys ignored him.

"Now we're warm and fed," said Miriam, "how about we go and look for Carys's bird?"

"That's a great idea," Setia said. In some ways it was a terrible idea. Their chances of finding Loki among the sodden trees were slim. Carys had told them if he could return to her he would, so he wasn't nearby. It also meant putting on their waterproofs and venturing out into the chilly downpour. The only upside was that their efforts might make Carys feel better, for a short while anyway.

Sheldrake's expression said it was a waste of time. "We should split into pairs to maximise the search area. Miriam, you're with me."

Hours later, Setia returned with Carys empty-handed to the tent, chilled and hungry once more. They'd explored a large area to the west of the campsite while Sheldrake and Miriam covered the east. Night had fallen and they'd been forced to don night vision goggles to make their way in the darkness. The wooded area spread for many square kilometres, and in all their searching they hadn't spotted any animal life at all, let alone Loki.

The place reminded Setia of a painting she'd seen when, to escape the summer heat, she'd snuck into a museum. The picture had represented a dream world, the artist's imagining of the place lost souls lingered after death, trapped between life and their final destination, wherever that might be. Rank upon rank of thin, straight, black trunks rose to branches that overhung the ground, as if ready to grasp anyone who wandered beneath them.

The oppressive silence emanating from the painting had been replaced by the unending patter of raindrops here, but the effect was the same. Pressure of ceaseless noise closed in. The forest seemed to say, *Go home. You aren't welcome.*

It was no surprise they hadn't found Loki. If the bird had any sense it would have flown back to the settlement, where humankind had begun to shape the unforgiving landscape.

Sheldrake and Miriam were already back and changing out of their waterproofs. There was no need to state the failure of each pair's mission. They had been in comm contact throughout the afternoon. The heater was re-started, and for the second time the group gathered around its soothing glow.

"We can work out tomorrow's route after dinner," said Sheldrake in the tone of someone making a concession.

"Or in the morning," said Setia. "We aren't on a schedule."

A muscle in the corporal's jaw twitched. "Time to eat. Then I suggest we get an early night, ready for an early start. I've turned on the fence so nothing should bother us."

"Would those rain things be able to pass through it?" Miriam asked. "They aren't solid from what I could tell."

"Good point," said Sheldrake. "We should keep watch. I'll go first. Then Setia, Miriam, and Carys. If anyone sees anything out of the ordinary, wake the rest of us immediately. We can't take any chances."

"Out of the ordinary?" Setia scoffed. "This whole place is out of the ordinary. Burnap's balls!"

"What did you say?"

Sheldrake's face held such a strange mixture of annoyance and puzzlement, Setia couldn't help giggling, and Miriam began to laugh too. Even Carys managed half a smile.

The corporal spluttered, "Whose...?"

Setia gave a great guffaw and doubled over, wiping her eyes.

After gazing at his amused companions for several moments, Sheldrake's lips twitched and then he chuckled. "I guess that's a saying where you're from."

"Something like that," Setia squeezed out. She managed to get herself under control. "Let's eat."

"And after we eat," said Miriam, straightening up, "I have a little treat to share." She reached inside her jacket and pulled a tall, slim, plastic bottle from an inner pocket.

"What's that?" asked Sheldrake.

"Tequila."

A glow suffused Setia that hadn't come from the heater. The tequila had been very drinkable when mixed with crystals of lemon flavouring they had to break the monotony of drinking water. In fact, she mused, she may have had more than her fair share of Miriam's 'cocktail'. There was no making up for it. The bottle now lay empty on the groundsheet, drained of every drop.

Carys sat cross-legged, resting an elbow on a knee and her chin on her palm, staring into the heater's warm yellow light. Miriam had retreated to her sleeping bag and gently snored. For all her talk of living the high life, when it came to drinking she seemed something of a lightweight. Sheldrake was mainly unaffected, though he'd mellowed somewhat. He hadn't chided anyone or insisted on discussing plans for a while.

The rain had finally stopped. Gentle rustles came from outside—the noise of the breeze stirring the strange vegetation of the forest. The electric fence was up, and if curious alien creatures had gathered outside it they made no discernible sound. The tent flap was closed, sealed against the night.

Setia was lying on her side. "Carys."

"Yeah?"

"You told us we weren't the first humans to land on an exoplanet."

"We aren't."

"All right. But how do you know?"

Sheldrake broke in, "If that information's classified..."

"What?" Setia asked, a little slurred. "What if it is?"

"Aww, never mind."

Carys heaved a heavy sigh and her gaze drifted from the heater to meet Setia's eyes. Her face reflected the golden rays. "That's a long story, and you might be better off not hearing it."

"So it *is* classified information," said Sheldrake.

"I didn't mean you, general," said Carys. "I meant her."

Setia sat up. "Me? What's it got to do with me? I don't know anything about people going to another planet."

"I know you don't, but you're connected to all of the sick, sorry mess. The mess I was trying to escape by joining the Fleet. Only I can't. It's followed me around all my life. Wherever I go, there I am. Trapped by stuff beyond my control."

"So *that's* why you hate me—because I'm part of what you're trying to escape?"

"I don't hate you. I hate what you represent. It isn't personal."

Setia was getting tired of being told that, but she bit her tongue. She'd begun to get an inkling of what this was all about. "Is Arief tied up with this?" Carys had been present both times he'd attacked, and there was definitely something otherworldly about him and his abilities, including what he'd done to her.

"Who's Arief?" Sheldrake asked.

"The stowaway. I knew him in my old life."

"You did?"

"Ugh..." Carys shook her head. "If I'd known what he was that day at the passenger processing section, I might not have intervened. The last thing I wanted was to get mixed up with all the bullshit again."

"I'm glad you did," said Setia. "If you hadn't I wouldn't be here. They would have been scraping me off the side of the mountain."

"I don't think he would have actually killed you."

"He tried to kill her?" Sheldrake blurted. "Who is this guy?"

"I think he was only trying to frighten you," Carys continued. "He wouldn't have destroyed his prize piece so easily."

"I was his prize piece?" asked Setia. "What does that even mean?"

"Yeah," said Sheldrake.

"I mean..." Carys paused, her eyes downcast "...it's hard to know where to begin. And, like I said, I'm not sure I should tell you. They say ignorance is bliss."

Setia said, "Now you have to tell me."

Twenty-One

Carys began her story in the dark times of the Crusader Wars. Setia remembered them well, though the cult hadn't made it as far as her country. Yet she was older than Carys. She recalled the emergence of Dwyr Orr and her fanatical following, the spread of the Earth Awareness Crusade across Europe, the fall of Old France, and the invasion of the Britannic Isles.

"I'm from West BI, you see," said Carys.

Sheldrake commented, "The last country the assholes conquered."

"No, Orr moved into the Caribbean after that, with Lorcan Ua Talman's help. She had Jamaica entirely under her control until the Alliance managed to get her out."

"Talman?!" the corporal exclaimed. "The owner of the Antarctic Project? No way."

"His involvement wasn't widely known at the time, and it's been hushed up since, for obvious reasons. He did the right thing in the end and switched sides to the Alliance."

Setia said, "You seem to know a lot about it, but you must have only been a kid."

"I learned about it all afterwards when I got back from Australia."

"You got back from…" Setia was getting confused. The conversation had jetted all over the globe within about a minute.

"Holy shit!" Sheldrake's eyes widened. "You were one of the Displaced Children."

It took Setia a moment to recall the reference. When understanding hit, she said, "I'm so sorry. That must have been terrible."

Carys shrugged. "It was a long time ago."

She had been wrenched from her home country—her parents either dead or imprisoned—and taken to a secret encampment in Australia, where she'd lived while the war raged. The Crusaders had indoctrinated the children into their cult, giving them new names and forcing them to accept new beliefs and a new worldview. The kids were starved, beaten, and made to work in harsh conditions, growing crops and tending to animals in secret, deep within the vast Australian bush. Many hadn't survived.

Setia's heart was wrung with pity. When Robins had told her Carys's childhood had been tough, he hadn't been exaggerating. But what was the connection between Carys's background and her assertion that humans had already visited another exoplanet? Setia hesitated to ask her to clarify. It felt unfair to probe someone who had been through so much.

"Nasty business," said Sheldrake, "but what's that got to do with the intel you claim to know?"

"Don't hassle her," Setia admonished. "Carys, you don't have to go on if you don't want to."

"I might as well get it off my chest, and you deserve an explanation for why I've been such a bitch."

"I wouldn't put it like that."

"I would. When I got back to West BI I discovered I was an orphan. Luckily, a kind woman, whose children had also been displaced, took me in and made me part of her family. She was great, really great. She'd been involved in the war too, and she'd helped to find the encampment in the Outback where her kids and I were being held."

Carys reached out to the empty tequila bottle and idly spun it.

"It was through her I learned what had been happening behind the scenes. What it was all about. The Crusader War and the secret weapon the Alliance used to defeat them. I know you'll find this hard to believe, but aliens were behind it all. They arrived on Earth thousands of years ago, and they've been messing with human affairs for their own amusement ever since."

Thinking of Arief, Setia didn't find it hard to believe, but Sheldrake gave a dismissive *pfft*.

"They were responsible," Carys went on, "in part at least, for the formation of the Earth Awareness Crusade. They love to stir up conflict and strife, setting country against country, inciting wars. To them, it's fun."

Setia gave a gasp. "That's why Arief helped Elek!"

Carys nodded. "You're getting it now. Elek wasn't the first person the aliens made famous and powerful. They pick people to play as pieces in their game. Elek must have been one. You were another, right?"

Setia was silent. Carys's words were throwing a whole new light on what had happened to her.

"The thing is, I thought the bad part of my life was all over. I'd lost my parents, but at least I'd escaped from the Crusaders. The Alliance had won the war. We had peace at last and the world was a better place." Carys swallowed. "I had a home, a family, a job I loved. Everything was just about perfect. Then it all came crashing down. I can't tell you the whole story. It's too long, and it isn't mine to tell. But the Alliance decided to confront the interfering alien species on their home turf. They wanted to get them to leave us alone, to stop brewing conflict in human society. My adoptive mam, brother and sister left to travel to the aliens' planet, along with a guy Mam knew. A Royal Marine."

"You couldn't go with them?" asked Sheldrake.

"I was invited, but I didn't want to. I had enough of that shit to last me a lifetime."

"So that's the other exoplanet you were talking about," said the corporal. “Still, you don’t know if they made it. We might have reached Prime before them.”

“They made it. Robins told me. They were on their way back when the Fleet left Earth.”

“You didn’t want to wait for your adoptive family to return?” Setia asked softly.

“For how long? With the effects of time dilation, I would have waited years. I’d waited years after they left before I could apply for a job on the *Bres*.” She heaved another sigh. “It’s hard to explain, mostly because I don’t understand it properly myself. But, for one thing, how would I ever be a part of that family again? They’re related by blood. I’m just some stray they picked up along the way. And they’d gone through something huge together, something life-changing, and I wasn’t a part of it and never would be. I would always be an outsider looking in, seeing their special bond. They were good people. They would have tried to include me. And I know it will upset them to discover I’ve left, but it’s easier this way.”

Setia wasn’t sure it was easier. But she hadn’t lived Carys’s life. Who was she to say what was right or wrong for her?

“And I just couldn’t stand to be a part of all that alien bullshit again. They would be full of stories when they got back, stories I wouldn’t want to hear. My parents were murdered by Crusaders and my life was torn apart. My adoptive mam’s kids were young when we were living at the camp, too young to really understand what was going on. The youngest one doesn’t even seem to remember. I was older than both of them. I saw things, heard things…” She wiped her eyes. “I’m sorry. It brings it all back.”

“It’s okay.”

“Sounds like PTSD,” Sheldrake announced. “You know you can get treatment for that?”

“Oh, shut up,” Setia snapped.

Carys said, “Setia, when I saw what that…thing…did at the passenger processing centre, I realised what it was, and that I’d somehow become mixed up with the exact same shit I was trying to escape. Robins tells me I am. He says that's what the skein indicates. I don't get a choice. Doesn't mean I have to like it, though."

"So Arief is one of *those* aliens?" She knew he was an extra-terrestrial being. He'd revealed that much already. But it was hard to grasp that he and Elek were tied up with something so ancient and perverse in Earth's history, or that it somehow all connected with this young woman sitting in front of her.

"I know he is. Robins said so."

"And I'm one of the pieces in the game he's playing?"

"If he came all the way out to the *Bres* to find you, I think you have to be. You're important to him. But Robins told me the aliens had agreed to stop interfering with humans, and your friend was breaking that agreement. Maybe you won't hear from him again."

You have no right to be here, Robins had said. *None of your species has. That was the agreement.*

Arief had replied, *That was the agreement about Earth. As you may have noticed, we are not on Earth.*

"I certainly hope I never see Arief again," Setia said. "I never liked him, even when I thought he was human. Thanks for explaining. Things are clearer now. I can see now why you didn't want anything to do with me."

"The tall dude was an alien?" Sheldrake asked. "Whatever happened to him? All I heard was they'd caught the stowaway."

Carys replied, "I think he went back wherever he came from."

"But how?"

"Who knows?"

Sheldrake's brow wrinkled. "I'm not sure you should be discussing this information. Neither of you should talk about it in front of Miriam when she wakes up."

Setia and Carys shared a look.

"Don't worry," Setia said. "Everything we've discussed is on a need-to-know basis only."

Sheldrake nodded sagely. "Copy that."

Carys asked, "Do you think there's another bottle of tequila in Miriam's jacket?"

Twenty-Two

It was impossible to tell whether the overnight visitors at the previous camp had returned for another look. The soil on the forest floor was bare and rain had fallen in the early morning. Any tracks would have been washed away, as their own had been.

Pausing as she helped to pack up the camp, Setia gazed into the heavens. The sky was a clear, pale rosy pink through the lattice of canopy. It wasn't the hue of sunrise. The sky seemed to stay that colour all day, judging by the glimpses she'd caught through the ubiquitous clouds.

"Looks like we've escaped the rain for a while," Miriam said cheerfully.

"But for how long? I'd heard of water planets but I didn't think Talman Prime was one."

"It isn't that bad."

"Isn't it?"

"My, someone woke up grumpy this morning."

Setia frowned. She *did* have a little bit of a headache that *might* have something to do with drinking possibly more than her fair share of the tequila. But she didn't think it was affecting her opinion of Prime's predominating climate, which was based on solid experience. "Tell me something, Miriam."

"What?"

"How do you manage to stay relentlessly upbeat? I mean, you had the highest expectations of this planet. You should be the most disappointed of all of us. You also seem...if it's okay to be frank... pretty timid. Yet when you had your chance to go back to the ship you didn't take it and, despite everything threatening us, you're stubbornly optimistic. Why is that?"

"I don't know. I've always been like this, as far back as I can remember. I suppose you could call it my special power."

Carys was also scanning the treetops, but she wasn't assessing the weather. There was still no sign of Loki.

Setia doubted they would see the bird again.

"Oh seven hundred," Sheldrake announced. "Time to move out."

The plan was to explore deeper into the forest. The dense vegetation had yielded the least scan data, for obvious reasons, so there was greater potential for discoveries. The only places the scientists knew less about were deep rivers, lakes, seas and oceans. The forest held another attraction—it would provide cover when rain inevitably began to fall. According to the forecast, precipitation wouldn't be heavy but it made sense to avoid it. The rain phantoms of yesterday's downpour also hovered at the back of Setia's mind, and she didn't think she was alone.

Sheldrake took the lead again, though this time there was no need. His bulk wasn't required to force through vegetation today. He only had to navigate a path through the trees and labyrinthine water channels.

The easier going meant everyone could travel faster. Setia's headache faded, the daylight increased, and she began to feel better about Prime. She was growing used to the weird trees and odd light. Maybe the strange rain figures they thought they'd seen had only been an optical illusion.

Sheldrake slowed down as he neared a channel crossing their path. It was too wide to simply step over, and it stretched into the distance on each side. If they didn't want to climb one of the trees with branches extending over it, they would either have to go a long way around or take a leap. Sheldrake barely broke his pace. He jumped across the barrier, saying over his shoulder, "We can do twenty klicks today, easy."

Carys halted at the edge. "You can if you like. We aren't trying to break any records." She took off her backpack and threw it to the other side before also leaping across.

"The more territory we cover," the corporal reasoned, "the more we'll learn about the planet. We might uncover vital intel."

Setia asked, "Can you *have* intelligence about a natural environment?" She bounded over the channel easily. "Don't you mean information?"

"When you're doing recon," Sheldrake replied, "everything counts. You never leave anything out. Never know when something might be important. Everyone has their recorders turned on, right?"

Miriam was hesitating, looking uncertainly at the water that ran between her and the others, cloudy with dark sediment.

"Throw your pack over," Carys suggested.

Miriam unsnapped the waist belt and slowly slipped her arms from the straps.

"If you have any tequila left," quipped Carys, "throw that first."

Smiling, Miriam hefted her backpack into the air and tossed it toward the farther bank. It didn't quite make it, hitting the side and sliding into the stream.

"Whoa!" Setia snagged one of the straps and hauled the pack out. Water ran from it, creating a puddle.

Miriam was clutching her face in both hands, her mouth a silent O.

"Don't worry," said Setia. "It'll dry out fast, but be careful when you jump. I don't want to have to drag you out too."

"Hold on." Sheldrake strode to a nearby 'tree'. Like all the rest, its branches drooped forlornly and divided into turgid fingers. He grasped one the thickness of his arm and jerked it downward, clearly intending to break it off. But the branch bent like a child's balloon figure, folding neatly where it joined the trunk. "Huh," he mused.

"Feels weird. Rubbery." He tried again, twisting and tugging the branch this time. Tension lines formed on its skin but it didn't break. Grunting with effort, he gave the branch another vigorous twist.

Pop!

The branch had parted company from the tree. Water spurted from the wound. The gush hit Sheldrake in the face. Stilled by surprise, he just took it, the branch hanging limply from his hands.

Carys gave a great whoop of laughter, fell to her knees and folded in half, shoulders shaking. Setia had clamped a hand over her mouth and her eyes filled with tears as she tried to not laugh.

"Please," Carys gasped. "I think I'm gonna wet myself."

The corporal stepped out from the path of the flow, which remained as steady as a fountain.

His efforts to help Miriam had proven useless. Without internal water pressure the branch had lost all rigidity. It was little more than a long, soggy rag. Meanwhile, the water continued to spurt from the tree, which slowly sagged.

"Oh dear," Miriam said sadly.

"Dry yourself, soldier," Setia told Sheldrake. "I'll handle this." She took off her backpack, put it down, and then jumped back over the channel to join Miriam. "Get on my back."

"Huh? No! You can't possibly get across carrying me too."

"I can. I'm stronger than I look. Trust me."

"No way. I'm sorry, I know you're trying to help but..."

"What happened to Ms Optimistic? I promise you, I can do it."

Sheldrake had taken off his jacket and unfastened his shirt. "She probably can."

Miriam shook her head. "It's okay. I think I can make it on my—"

Setia picked her up in both arms like she was cradling a baby.

"Wait! Don't...Ough!" Tossed over the stream, Miriam landed on the farther side.

As the morning wore on a light drizzle started up, but the rain didn't get any heavier. It only coated everything in a thin layer of wetness. Miriam's attitude to Setia had changed. Where she'd once been friendly and talkative, she was now reserved and quiet around her. She'd tried switching her attention to Carys, but Carys's earlier mirth had quickly dissipated and she'd returned to her usual morose state. No doubt she was worried about her bird. Sheldrake wasn't interested in idle chatter while on a mission, so Miriam was forced to remain mostly silent like everyone else.

Sheldrake treated Setia the same and, after initial surprise, Carys had taken Setia's feat in her stride too. Only Miriam had been truly shocked. It was to be expected. Setia didn't want to offer a long explanation. Perhaps she would only ask Miriam to not mention anything to anyone else when they got back to the ship.

So things continued for another few hours until Sheldrake announced a halt. "Thirty minutes to eat and rest, then back on your feet. Let's see how far—"

"I swear," Carys snapped, "if you don't drop the military bullshit, I'm gonna punch you in the face."

The corporal began to splutter a retort, but Carys spoke over him. "Even better, I'll ask Setia to do it, and she'll knock your bloody head off."

Sheldrake's mouth snapped shut. Then he muttered sullenly, "Thirty minutes."

He pulled out a ground sheet for them to sit on. There was nothing else. No rocks, no tree stumps. Setia wondered what happened to the trees when they died. Without water to keep them plump did they shrivel away to nothing?

Each traveller took something to eat from their packs. She selected beef noodles and pulled the seal. They'd walked deep into the forest. The trees grew so thickly their branches crowded together, cutting out most of the sky. They'd left behind the water channels a while ago.

All through their trek no one had spotted a living thing other than the trees. No insects, none of the weird moving plants with tentacles, nor any of the white, bulbous, fungus-like things she'd seen at the first camp. Perhaps it was sometimes like this on young planets—a single species predominating in a landscape. It certainly didn't make for an interesting excursion.

Setia's lunch packet was warm. She opened it and tipped it up, slurping some of the contents into her mouth. Sheldrake was busy on his interface, keen to get his report in. He bent intently over it, staring at the screen, swiping it and murmuring to himself, growing agitated.

Miriam had noticed his odd behaviour too. "Is something wrong, Corporal?"

He ignored her. Suddenly, he looked up. "This is broken. Ellis, can I borrow yours?"

"I'm eating. Can't you wait five minutes?"

In answer, he got up and strode to Carys's pack.

"Hey," she half-heartedly protested as he dug inside it. Retrieving the device, he put it in front of her face to open it. She poked her tongue out at the screen.

Sheldrake carried the interface to his former position and sat down. Crouched over the new interface, he worked with impatience, swiping and prodding it. "This can't be right."

"What?" Carys asked.

"This one isn't working either."

"They can't both be broken."

"You try, then." He reached out to give her the interface.

With irritation, she put down her lunch and took it. "What were you trying to do?"

"First, I tried to comm the *Bres.* When I couldn't get a connection, I tried the settlement. No dice. So I looked up our position, wondering if topography might be affecting the signal. Only I couldn't even bring up the map. There's nothing."

Twenty-Three

Miriam put down the tiny screwdriver and brushed the hair out of her eyes before lifting the back off the interface and staring at the interior.

"Never would have pegged you as a tech whizz, Belby," Sheldrake remarked. He sat close beside her, elbows resting on his lifted knees.

"Maybe that's because I'm not a tech whizz."

"I don't see anyone else carrying a tool kit around with them. Zees? Ellis?"

Setia and Carys shook their heads.

"Point taken," said Miriam. "I *do* know a little about computing. It isn't something I like to advertise. You suddenly find you're tech support for everyone and his third cousin."

"See anything?" asked Carys.

Miriam peered closer. "Can someone get me a light? It's so dark under these trees."

The shorter Prime days meant the light was beginning to fail. They could have managed another couple of hours of walking before it became dark, but there was no point in continuing when they didn't know where they were or where they were going.

Sheldrake searched in his pack and pulled out one of the small tent lights. Crouching over the opened interface, he shone it into the workings.

Heavy foreboding had settled in Setia's stomach. She watched Miriam inspecting the interface with scepticism. The chances of even one of them breaking were low. The *Bres* and the other Fleet ships were carrying state-of-the-art tech, the very latest and best quality money could buy, not ancient knock-offs purchased at a street stall in Spiral City.

The chances of *two* of them going wrong at the same time?

Infinitesimally small. So small as to be virtually impossible.

Something else was happening.

Everyone was thinking the same thing, no doubt. Only no one wanted to say it. Setia was also confident that the trackers they wore around their necks weren't working either.

"Hmm..." Miriam murmured, "I can't see any broken or loose connections but I might not anyway, and some of the functions are quantum. Let me check a few things." She looked through her little kit.

Carys got to her feet. "I'm going to look for Loki."

"Don't wander off," said Sheldrake. "It's easy to get lost in this type of terrain, and without a working interface we won't be able to locate you."

Setia offered to go with her. Carys didn't answer, but neither did she object.

As soon as they were out of hearing of the others, Setia said, "We're screwed."

"That's what I was thinking. Do you know the way back to the settlement?"

"Not a clue, and we haven't left a trail to follow. The damned near-constant rainfall washes everything away."

They continued in silence until Carys said, "I wish I knew what happened to Loki. If this is going to be it, I'd like to see him again."

"It's a long way from being *it*. We have food and camping equipment. We even have a power pack. And we have an endless supply of water. We could last weeks. We might find our way back. I bet the boy ranger has survival skills coming out the wazoo."

"If survival was our only problem you might be right."

"You mean the interfaces?"

"You know that's what I mean. It's no coincidence they both failed at the same time."

Silence fell between them once more.

The trees were clustered only a few meters apart. When Setia looked back the way they'd come Miriam and Sheldrake were already out of sight. She took out a knife and scored a shallow cut in a tree trunk. Water dribbled from the wound.

"What are you doing?" asked Carys.

"Something we should have done ever since we set foot in this place."

A short distance on, she made another cut.

The branches above intertwined, bare and lumpy, with no sign of a bird sitting among them or any other creatures.

"What do you think happened to Loki?" asked Setia. "You seemed so sure he would come back."

"I was. I can't explain it. He thinks I'm his mother, and it goes against all his instincts to not return to me. Even if we didn't have that bond he knows I'm an easy source of food. He can't hunt properly yet. I was teaching him, but—"

"Watch out!" Setia put out a hand to hold Carys back.

She had been walking a little ahead of Carys, and her foot had just sunk to the ankle in mud. She pulled at it but the mud clung like glue. With some effort she finally dragged herself free, the ground giving her up reluctantly like a child holding onto a favourite toy.

The ground in front of them had appeared to be the same as the rest, but now she looked more closely she saw it gleamed wetter than its surroundings. The patch stretched to the nearest trees.

"I wonder how deep it is," Carys mused.

"I don't know and I don't want to find out. Let's go back."

When they returned to Sheldrake and Miriam the two interfaces lay on the ground, whole once more. Judging from the looks on their faces, Miriam's efforts had been unsuccessful.

"No luck?" Setia asked.

Miriam shook her head. "What happened to your foot?"

The remnants of Setia's accident coated her boot and the hem of her trouser leg. "Uh, yeah. We need to be careful. There are places around here where the mud is really deep, and they're hard to see."

"Copy that," said Sheldrake. "I'll set up the tent and we can settle in for the wait."

"The wait for what?" Setia asked.

"Rescue, of course. We've lost comm contact and we don't know the way back. So we sit tight and wait. Standard procedure in non-combat scenarios."

"What makes you think they'll find us?"

He reached inside his shirt and pulled out his tracker. "Forgot about these, huh? Ahmad is expecting us back in four days, five at the latest, as pre-arranged. As soon as we don't show, they'll start looking. Our heat signatures will show up like a beacon in this terrain, especially with no other large life forms around. Drones will pick us up easy. We shouldn't have to wait too long. Just to be on the safe side, we'll halve our food intake. That way, we'll have enough supplies to last us a week. Plenty of time for a team to reach us."

"Hold on," said Setia. "Back up. What makes you think the trackers are working?"

"What makes *you* think they're not?"

"Because whatever killed the interfaces probably killed the trackers too. Right, Miriam?"

"Hmm... If something like an electro-magnetic pulse had taken them out, I might agree. But if that was the case they would be dead. They aren't. They just can't connect to anything."

"So neither can the trackers."

"I don't see why not. Though I don't have anything to test them with, unfortunately."

Setia's gaze travelled from Miriam to Sheldrake. "Don't tell me you think it's coincidental that both the interfaces lost comm."

"It has to be a coincidence," said Miriam. "What other explanation is there?"

"What explanation is there? Are you forgetting the trampled vegetation outside our campsite? The things in the rain? We're on an alien planet. We have no idea what's here."

When Sheldrake and Miriam's expressions remained blank, she went on, "Something has obviously done something to cut us off from the rest of the colonists. If I was planning on attacking someone, the first thing I'd do is remove their ability to call for help. Whatever the aliens did to the interfaces, they must have done the same thing to the trackers. We should get out of here as fast as we can."

Sheldrake smirked. "You're sounding a little paranoid, Zees. We've had an equipment failure, that's all. No need to blame it on bogeymen."

"I'm not blaming it on bogeymen. We're on a freaking exoplanet." Setia swung to Carys. "You agree with me, don't you? There's no way those interfaces simultaneously broke."

"Wait," Miriam interrupted before Carys could speak. "There *is* a simple explanation. The interfaces could be from the same manufacturing batch. If they were faulty, they could have failed within a similar time period. We walked for a few hours before Sheldrake tried to make a report. We don't know they lost their ability to connect at exactly the same time."

"It was near enough the same time. And, besides, they would have been tested at least twice. Once before they left the factory and then when they were brought onto the ship. They didn't break, they—"

"Then it could be an environmental factor," Miriam interrupted. "We could be in a blackspot, or something in the atmosphere might have—"

"There are no blackspots. The planet's ringed by satellites already. And you're seriously suggesting that something in the air corroded *just* the comms and nothing else?"

"We're forgetting another possibility," said Carys. "What if the interfaces are working fine, but there's nothing out there for them to connect to? What if the satellites and everything else was destroyed and we're the only ones left?"

Even Setia was struck dumb by this notion.

After a moment's pause, Sheldrake said, "Man, you're full of great ideas. You know that?"

Setia said evenly, "Putting aside the prospect that we've lost comm because everyone else has been killed, we need to decide what to do. I don't agree that we should sit here like wannabe victims. We need to try to make our way back. If we can just make it out of this forest we'll stand a better chance of defending ourselves. We might even be able to contact the settlement or ship again."

"Until we have a clear indication of hostiles," said Sheldrake, "we follow procedure and stay put."

"You don't get to decide what we do all by yourself," Setia snapped. "I'm not putting my life in danger because you're too dumb to see what's right in front of your face."

"It's my duty to protect you—"

"I don't need protecting, thanks very much."

Speaking between clenched teeth, the corporal repeated, "It's my duty to protect you and I'm going to do that whether you like it or not. You're staying here."

"You think you can stop me from leaving? Try it." She got to her feet.

Sheldrake reached inside his jacket.

"No guns!" Miriam shrieked. "Please don't draw on her."

The corporal bristled, but his hand remained inside his jacket.

"Sit down," urged Miriam. "We can talk this out."

"There's no time," said Setia. "Whatever took out our comm could be on its way right now. Or surrounding the place, cutting off our escape. If you all stay here, you're fools." She walked several paces before turning back. "Carys, are you coming with me?"

Carys bit her lip. "We only have one tent. I think the big guy's gonna fight us for it. And if we leave this place, are we any better off? If something does attack we can defend ourselves easier here. We can set up the fence, take turns keeping watch... I agree that something's definitely off. But there's strength in numbers."

"Carys is right," said Miriam. "And Sheldrake's right when he says someone will come and find us soon."

"I don't want to leave," said Carys, "and I don't think you should either, Setia."

The light drizzle was turning to heavy rain. Drops of water hit Setia's nose and eyelashes. The already dim light was darkening. She faced the forest. Unknown assailants could already be out there somewhere, waiting among the trees. Even if they weren't, as Carys had pointed out, she had no tent. She turned to her companions, crouched on the ground sheet, watching her.

With a sigh, she stomped back to the group.

Twenty-Four

Sheldrake took first watch. Setia was supposed to be next, catching a couple of hours of sleep before taking over. She lay in her sleeping bag, hands behind her head, focused on the soldier's back as he sat at the open tent flap, gazing into the night. Carys and Miriam had quickly dropped off, but slumber would not come to her.

The small matter of the fact that she expected an attack at any minute was bothersome, as well as the knowledge that if she did fall asleep she would have to wake soon. Though she possessed many abilities and skills in the field of security, she was not military trained. Soldiers probably all became accustomed to sleeping at a moment's notice, snatching rest while it was available.

She sat up. Sheldrake glanced over his shoulder and then returned his attention to the outdoors. After pulling on her jacket, she padded to his side and sat down. "Seen anything?"

He whispered, "What are you doing? It's more than an hour before your watch."

"Can't sleep. I'll finish yours."

"Catch some shuteye while you can. If you're right about the comms—"

"I know I'm right."

"All the more reason to sleep while you can."

"We should all be awake and watching."

"We can't do that indefinitely. And we've had no other sign of enemies, not in the last day or so anyway. But if there are hostiles in the area we're gonna need everyone at one hundred percent."

"I can't magic myself to sleep."

Their conversation had been undertaken in a hushed tone. Setia checked Miriam and Carys. They didn't seem to have been disturbed. Beyond the tent only the immediate area was visible, the wet ground lit by a single, small tent light. Cloud blocked the starlight and Prime had no moons. Sheldrake was wearing night vision goggles.

"I mean it," she went on. "I'll finish your watch. Have you seen anything odd?"

"Negative."

She stuck a hand out of the tent. To her surprise, it came back dry.

"The rain stopped a little while ago," said Sheldrake.

"Now that *is* odd." It looked like the corporal wasn't going to leave his watch. "Do you want a drink?"

"Okay. Just some water."

"It's a shame we drank all the tequila."

"We should have rationed it."

Setia got Sheldrake a drink, glad that they were getting on better. She didn't dislike the corporal, only found him somewhat annoying and narrow-minded. But his heart was in the right place. She gave him his water and sat down.

"Zees, can I ask you a question?"

"Can I stop you?"

"That stuff Ellis was saying about aliens on Earth and the stowaway, the tall guy, being one of them. And you're involved in it all. Is she right?"

"Her story explains a few things that have happened to me, Arief included. He could do some shit no human could ever do. Him being an extraterrestrial would make a lot of sense."

"Do you think that guy has something to do with what happened to our comms?"

She blinked. "It never occurred to me, but you could be right. He might be able to do something like that."

What was it Arief had said to Robins? That the 'agreement' his species had made with humans only applied on Earth. Was Arief stalking them, playing games with them? It would be just his style. Carys had said his kind loved to toy with human emotions.

"If it is him," she continued, "I don't know what we can do about it. He seems able to turn himself into different forms—gaseous forms. He could be here right now, listening to us. Laughing at us."

Sheldrake put down his water and drew his firearm, resting the gun in his lap.

"I honestly don't think that'll stop him."

"Only one way to find out."

But talking about Arief hadn't prompted him to appear.

Silence and darkness yawned wide.

After a while Sheldrake said, "Can I ask you another question?"

"Might as well get it all out."

"How come you're so freaking strong? I couldn't believe it when you hauled me out of that fissure."

"So that's what changed your attitude to me?"

"I found out there's a lot more to One Punch Girl than I thought."

She lightly punched him.

"Hey, watch out. I need that arm."

Taking a breath, she considered what to say. She'd never told anyone about what had happened all those years ago in a back alley in Spiral City. Who would have believed her?

She exhaled. "I used to run drugs. Before you judge me, I was just a kid and I didn't know what I was doing, okay? It was the only way I could survive. One day, I got on the wrong side of my boss. What happened wasn't my fault but that didn't matter. Maybe he wanted to make an example of me to the other runners. He sent someone out to kill me. That would have been it, except Arief turned up and saved me. Only, he didn't exactly save me. He did something to me, gave me the strength and ability to fight back and save myself." A lot more had happened afterwards, but that story was too long to tell. "I've been the same ever since."

"He *gave* you strength? How?"

"He put his hand on me and something flowed into me."

"Right."

"You asked. I answered. There's nothing I can say to convince you, and I don't really care to anyway."

"I guess it makes as much sense as someone your size being able to toss someone over a stream, or pull a hundred and eighty-pound beefcake out of a hole."

Setia snorted with laughter, then quickly checked she hadn't woken up Carys or Miriam. They continued to sleep soundly.

"Tossing a woman over a stream isn't *that* funny," Sheldrake remarked.

"What about you?" Setia asked. "I don't know anything about you, apart from your beefcake status I mean."

"What else is there to know?"

"Where you're from, what got you into the military, what made you join the Fleet. The usual stuff."

"I only have the usual answers. Nothing interesting about me. Certainly not anything about strange guys injecting me with special powers."

His words rang hollow but Setia didn't push, though she was slightly annoyed that after she'd given him her big reveal he wouldn't reciprocate. Yet she also didn't feel entitled to know his background. Maybe it was too painful to tell.

"Holy shit!" Sheldrake leapt to his feet and pointed his gun into the dark. "Halt! Who goes there? Don't come another step closer or I'll shoot."

Setia found herself standing too. She squinted into the night, peering in the direction Sheldrake was aiming.

"What's happening?" Miriam asked sleepily.

"Be quiet," Setia hissed. "There's someone out there."

She saw something. Darker than the surrounding darkness, a large shape stood a few metres away. She was reminded of the rain monsters. It was indistinct, seeming to merge with its surroundings.

"Whoa," said a deep, male voice. "Take it easy, soldier."

The voice was familiar but she couldn't place it.

"Zees, turn on the main light," Sheldrake commanded.

As she did so, he tore off his night goggles and tossed them. With his other hand he maintained his aim on the newcomer.

It was Ahmad, the site manager at the settlement.

"Phew!" Miriam exclaimed, making Setia jump. She'd walked to her side, barefoot and therefore soundlessly. "You gave us a fright."

Sheldrake was returning his gun to its holster. "Man, you need to be more careful. Announce your presence. Don't sneak up on folk. I could've shot you."

"My apologies."

Carys had arrived at the tent entrance too. "What are you doing here? How did you find us?"

"It was our trackers, right?" Miriam asked. She turned accusingly to Setia. "I told you they were still working."

"That's right," said Ahmad. "When I couldn't reach you I thought something might have happened. Thought I would check up on you. Make sure you were all okay."

"We're fine," Miriam said. "We just happened to lose comm on both our interfaces at the same time."

He grimaced. "Bad luck."

"You're telling me. I had a helluva time convincing the others it was just a coincidence. Come inside before it starts raining again."

Miriam stepped back to allow Ahmad to enter the tent. As Setia also moved out of the way, Carys caught her gaze with a troubled look. She was worried too. Was Carys thinking the same as her?

How had Ahmad reached them so quickly when they were days from the settlement?

Why had he come alone?

And how had he managed to walk right through an electric fence?

Twenty-Five

Ahmad's rounded stomach protruded from his open jacket and hung over his trouser belt as he sat down. He scratched his beard and took off his hat, placing it on the ground sheet. "You guys had us worried for a while there. How have you been doing? Seen anything interesting?"

"You mean apart from the mysterious rain aliens?" asked Miriam.

"Yeah, uh, apart from them. Crazy, right?"

"Has anything like that appeared at the settlement?"

"Absolutely not. Or, at least, no one's reported anything. We have a lot of people on site, and it's rained a lot. I suppose it's possible someone noticed something but didn't quite believe it and decided not to mention it."

"We struggled to make them out at first," said Miriam. "In fact, thinking about it, I'm not sure there was anything there. It could have been a trick of the light. Can I get you something to eat or drink? You must be exhausted."

"No, nothing. I'm fine." Ahmad looked from face to face. "But how are you guys? Holding up okay?"

"Sure," Sheldrake replied, tension in his tone. "Why wouldn't we be?"

Ahmad raised both hands. "Just asking."

While this short conversation had been going on, Setia had slipped away to her pack and, her back facing the rest, taken out her gun and slipped it into a pocket. Her hand on the grip and her finger on the trigger, she said, "Can *I* ask *you* something? How did you arrive so fast? Our comm hasn't been out long enough for you to notice then travel all the way here."

He chuckled, and his belly jiggled. "Now I have an explanation for a couple of suspicious faces. We have buggies for travelling overland. I left mine at the edge of the forest and hiked in."

"We have buggies?" Miriam exclaimed. "You mean I've been lugging my pack for miles for no reason? How come we weren't assigned a buggy?"

"You'll have to ask Robins that, but they're in short supply. We've only brought two down from the ship so far. As site manager I get to say who uses them."

Setia frowned. "A buggy would have sunk in that swamp we walked through to reach the forest."

"That's why I went around it."

"And you went around the hills too?"

"Man, I thought I was doing you guys a favour coming out here to check on you. I didn't expect an interrogation. The buggies can manage quite an incline, but I did have to take a less direct route than you."

"And you didn't bring any supplies Where's your stuff?"

"Of course I did. They're—"

"In the buggy," Setia finished for him. "Naturally. Can you explain how you managed to get through our fence?"

"Setia!" Miriam admonished. "Ahmad was trying to help us. Why are you treating him like a criminal?"

"It's a fair question," said Carys. "I'd like to know the answer too."

Ahmad nodded. "I can see how it looks. You're right to be wary." He reached into his jacket.

"What are you doing?!" Setia exclaimed, pulling out her gun. "Keep your hands where I can see them."

"Stars!" Miriam leaped up and backed away. "What's wrong with you?"

"No one move," Sheldrake ordered. "Setia, put down your weapon."

"The fuck I will."

Ahmad said, "This situation is getting entirely out of hand. Carys, please come over here."

"Uh, no?" The characteristic way Carys curled her lip at the suggestion almost made Setia smile. The woman's disdain for nearly everyone and everything was beginning to grow on her.

"I want you to take something from my jacket," said Ahmad. "It will explain my apparently magical ability to defeat electrified fences."

Carys looked doubtful.

"I'll do it," Miriam volunteered.

"No." Setia's grip on her gun tightened. She didn't like the idea of anyone approaching Ahmad, especially not naive, trusting Miriam. If anyone was going to be used as cover it shouldn't be her. "Sheldrake can do it."

"Good call." The corporal rose to his feet. His considerable height dwarfed the older, chubbier man sitting on the ground.

"It's in the right hand, inner pocket," said Ahmad, craning his neck.

Sheldrake approached him, squatted down and fished inside the jacket. Setia watched Ahmad closely, especially his expression. If someone was about to do something violent their faces often changed a split second beforehand. But Ahmad's features remained neutral.

"Is this it?" asked Sheldrake, drawing out a small, slim black object half as wide as his palm.

"It's a remote," Ahmad explained. "We have the same set up for nocturnal defence as you guys, only on a larger scale. It's a pain in the ass to walk over to the control centre to switch it on and off, so I had one of the electrical engineers rig up remote access for me." He fixed his gaze on Setia. "Does that answer your question?"

"So you're saying you saw the fence, turned it off, climbed through it and walked over to our tent? Why not just call out to one of us?"

"I didn't climb through the fence." He patted his belly. "Not sure I would have managed that and held onto my dignity. I pulled up a stake at the join and walked through the gap. I didn't call out because I wasn't sure what I might find. Until I saw you were all okay, I didn't know what might have happened."

"That makes sense," said Sheldrake. "If something had attacked us it could still have been in the vicinity. It might have attacked you as well."

"The possibility did cross my mind."

"Setia," said Miriam, "he's explained himself perfectly. Would you please put your gun away now?"

Unease continued to darken Setia's mind, but she couldn't come up with another objection to Ahmad's sudden appearance. She slowly returned her weapon to her pocket, keeping it within her grasp.

The tension inside the tent lowered a notch.

"Did you replace the fence stake?" Sheldrake asked.

"Yup, and I turned the power back on. You don't have to worry about any more surprise visitors tonight."

"In that case," Miriam said brightly, "how about we have a little snack and then go to sleep? I don't know about everyone else, but all this excitement has worn me out. Do you have working comm, Ahmad?"

"I do indeed. I have my own and a spare interface you're welcome to take with you."

"Cool. And now we know that if we lose contact again, someone will come and find us. We can continue our expedition."

Miriam's proposal met with general agreement. Food was brought out and eaten. At the same time, they talked with the newcomer about what they'd seen and done since leaving the settlement. Setia wasn't sure what Sheldrake had already reported back, but Ahmad seemed interested in everything they had to say. She didn't speak much, unable to overcome the disquiet that niggled in her guts. Carys was reserved too, but that was her normal behaviour. Setia couldn't tell if she'd believed Ahmad's story or if she also continued to harbour doubts.

Finally, in the early hours of the morning, it was agreed that it was time to turn in. There was no talk of setting a watch. Setia climbed into her sleeping bag and the others did the same. Ahmad made do with his jacket and spare clothing from their packs. He'd announced that he would return to the settlement in the morning.

As soon as her companions began to fall asleep, new questions for Ahmad popped into Setia's mind.

Why had the site manager himself come out to check on them? Why not send someone less important?

Was there no message from Robins about losing comm contact? Didn't Ahmad need to reassure the mapper immediately that everyone was okay?

How had he managed to navigate the trees in a buggy?

Her memory of the local map was hazy, but she was fairly confident they were kilometres from the forest's edge. His lone effort to find them in unexplored territory, not knowing why they weren't replying to comms, seemed reckless.

Nothing added up.

She shifted position until she had a good view of the man, or as good a view as she could get in the half light from the single, dimmed lamp. He was a bulky shadow in the darkness. Her hand hadn't strayed far from her gun since the earlier confrontation, and she maintained a loose grip on it. She was determined to remain awake all night, watching and waiting, though for what she didn't know.

Time passed. It felt like hours. The others snored, shifted position, and muttered to themselves in their dreams. Ahmad didn't move and Setia only did slightly to ease pressure on her joints. Despite her intentions, sleep began to creep up on her, forcing her eyelids to close. Her mind began to wander paths inhabited by strange images: a cauldron overflowing with glittering liquid, a woman's face, grimacing, one of the hares from Carys's uniform insignia, tumbling head over heels into a hole.

Her eyes snapped open.

Ahmad had moved.

The mounded form had altered shape. An arm emerged. He was slowly pushing away the clothes covering him. He drew out his legs and gradually sat up.

She held her breath, watching. There was no sign of the approach of dawn, but it was possible he only wanted something to eat or drink. If that were so it would quickly be obvious from what he did.

He turned onto his hands and knees and began to crawl away from his spot.

He didn't head for the supplies.

She observed him another few seconds to be sure she was right.

He continued to crawl towards the exit.

As he reached it and unfastened the opening, she scooted out of her sleeping bag, raced the short distance to him and launched herself at him. As she landed on his back he collapsed, arms and legs sprawling.

"Where are you going, huh?" she demanded, one knee on his spine.

Ahmad heaved upwards, throwing her off and turning over. She jumped on him again, shoving his shoulders to the ground.

They struggled. Ahmad didn't say a word. He only glared at her, his mouth twisting. The commotion woke the others.

"Setia!" called Miriam. "What are you doing?"

Ahmad writhed and fought but she managed to stay on top of him. Fury sparked in his eyes. He lifted his head close to hers. Their gazes were clamped.

His face changed.

His features melted and transformed. Suddenly, it was Sheldrake looking up at her, ferocious. She gasped but her hold didn't lessen. At the same rapid pace, Sheldrake became Carys, venom lacing her expression. Then Carys was gone and Miriam's visage flitted in.

Then Ahmad's face became her own.

She was staring at herself. Her *angry* self. Her livid, raging, violent self.

Her arms grew weak.

Ahmad's face returned and he threw her off.

Numbly, she landed on her backside and sat helpless, her mouth agape, as the man tore open the tent flap and ran out into the night.

Twenty-Six

"It wasn't Ahmad!" Setia protested. "How many times do I have to tell you?"

Her three companions regarded her doubtfully. Talman Prime's questionable dawn was breaking, the weak sunlight filtering through the trees, lighting up the open tent flap with an ethereal glow.

At least, that was how it looked to Setia. A sense of unreality had settled on her. She was still recovering from the shock of seeing their strange visitor's face transform into her own. Its metamorphosis into the others had unnerved her enough. Seeing herself but not herself—another Setia, full of deep loathing and hatred of a kind she didn't think she'd ever felt—had shocked her to her core.

After Not-Ahmad had run out all she'd been able to do was to stare into the darkness impotently, utterly dumbfounded.

"But it was," Miriam said gently. "I'm sure you believe what you're saying, but we've been over this. We all *saw* Ahmad. We talked to him, ate with him. He was the same man we met at the settlement when we landed. This story you've told us... You have to admit, it doesn't make a lot of sense."

"All right. I know how it sounds." Setia put her head in her hands. Then she thought of a point that might convince them. "If it was Ahmad, why did he run off? He said he was here to help us. Why go away, leaving us without any comm?"

"If I was to hazard a guess," Miriam replied, "I'd say maybe because you attacked him? If someone jumped on me in the middle of the night, I wouldn't stick around either. You'd already pulled a gun on him. The poor man was probably in fear for his life."

"I didn't..." Setia swallowed and started again. "Okay, I did jump on him. He was trying to sneak off and I wanted to stop him."

"How do you know he was trying to sneak off? Maybe he only wanted to answer a call of nature. Not everyone can wait until morning."

"It's a fair point," said Sheldrake. "If he was going out to take a leak and you pinned him down, he might have been freaked and cleared out. Now he knows the situation with us he can send other personnel in to help. But they'll be warned one of us has a screw loose."

"I don't have a screw loose!" Setia swivelled to face Carys. "*You've* seen this before, right? What Ahmad did is like something Arief could do."

"Not exactly," said Carys. "Your alien friend could dissolve into a gas. I never saw his face change. Not that I don't believe you," she added hastily, "but you have to admit it was dark, and in the position you were in, you would have been blocking the light. Plus you had just woken up. You could have been in a dream state and imagined it all. Like Miriam said, if someone attacked me for no reason, especially someone who was freakishly strong for their size, I'd be spooked. I'd get out, fast. Who wouldn't?"

Setia's jaw tightened. "I didn't imagine it." She considered putting the questions to them she'd thought about last night, such as why the site manager himself had come to find them and not someone less important, but she dismissed the idea. These three weren't going to accept the truth without concrete evidence. She had to concede that, in their position, she would be dubious too. "I know," she said, standing, "let's see what that thing did after it left. It should be light enough now to get a good look at the ground."

Miriam heaved a sigh. "If it'll make you happy..."

They exited the tent.

Predictably, a fine rain was falling. The forest floor was spongy and slippery. The tracks they'd made yesterday were already losing definition, their footprints melting into the mud. It wasn't possible to tell what belonged to the creature that called itself Ahmad and what were their own.

Setia cursed. There was no doubt in her mind they were all in danger. Whatever had visited them last night, its intentions hadn't been good. It had been checking them out, assessing their weaknesses. Perhaps its species was trying to figure out the best way of destroying the human invaders.

Perhaps they would start with the four vulnerable humans, far from help.

"Nothing to see here," said Sheldrake. "We could check the fence stakes."

"Yes!" Setia exclaimed. "It said it had deactivated the fence and pulled out one of the stakes. Did you get a close look at the remote?"

He shook his head. "I gave it back as soon as he explained what it was. It did look like a remote, but I guess it could have been anything."

Heartened that the corporal was finally taking her seriously, she went with him to the section of encircling fence where it joined. The join was complete and the fence was live. They squatted down.

The soil was smooth and unmarked.

She asked, "Does that look like someone's pulled out a stake twice?"

Sheldrake peered at the wet ground but didn't answer.

"Would someone leaving in a hurry have time to turn off the power," she persisted, "pull out a stake, replace it and reactivate the fence?"

Straightening up, Sheldrake put his hands on his hips and surveyed the surrounding vegetation. "The guy looked exactly like Ahmad," he murmured.

"I thought so too. But he wasn't. He was something else."

"But what?" Sheldrake focused on her with a questioning gaze. "What was he?"

"Something that could transform into Ahmad and sound like him. But he didn't talk much about the settlement, remember? We discussed what we'd been doing. He hardly mentioned what's been happening at the settlement at all."

"It'd be good if we could comm them. Find out what's been happening there. Speak to the real Ahmad."

"I doubt they could tell us anything."

Carys and Miriam joined them.

"Find anything?" Carys asked.

"Nothing," Setia replied. "There's no trace of that thing leaving. Whatever it is, it passed right through an electrified fence. The story it made up about a remote was bullshit."

Miriam said, "Maybe the rain washed away—"

"There's nothing here!" Setia interrupted. "We need to break camp and try to make it back to the settlement. It's not safe."

"I'm not sure what's going on," said Sheldrake, "but I'm with you."

Finally!

"Pack up, everyone," he went on. "Moving out in five."

She gritted her teeth. The corporal's penchant for ordering them around hadn't wavered, but at least he was finally seeing sense.

Miriam stomped to the tent, muttering to herself.

It took a little longer than five minutes to pack up, but they were ready to depart in record time. Even Miriam seemed to feel that something wasn't right.

"We had the sun behind us yesterday morning," Sheldrake announced.

"How could you tell?" Setia asked, squinting at the dull sky through the overhanging, lumpy foliage.

Ignoring her, he continued, "So we head toward it. We'll keep heading east until midday, then reassess. If anyone spots something that seems familiar, speak up. It'll be good to know we're going in the right direction."

He strode off without another word.

"You were right," said Carys as the women followed him.

"I know I was right," Setia replied.

"Not about Ahmad—though I'm not saying you're wrong about him. I meant what you said about the boy ranger having survival skills coming out the wazoo."

Miriam giggled. "What's a wazoo?"

At first, Setia was tense with anxiety as they marched through the forest, attempting to retrace their steps. The thing pretending to be Ahmad appeared to lurk in every shadow. Every tree trunk seemed on the verge of mutating into him. She even cast nervous glances upwards, expecting him to drop from a branch.

But Ahmad was conspicuous by his absence.

Then the gruelling nature of their journey took her attention, and worry was replaced by misery and fatigue. Her tiredness wasn't physical, it was mental. She wore her mind out with endless speculation about their mysterious visitor and their loss of comm. Sheldrake stopped and checked the interfaces every half hour, without success.

Conversation among the companions ceased as they hiked quickly and relentlessly eastward, stepping around trees, leaping streams, Sheldrake supposedly leading them in a consistent direction. Nothing Setia saw sparked recognition. The forest was utterly monotonous. She hoped the corporal knew what he was doing.

Inevitably, Miriam was the first to flag. She had quickly dropped to last in line and as time passed the distance between her and the others increased. Setia took her pack and carried it for her. Even lightened of her burden, Miriam couldn't keep up and stumbled several times. Setia had to repeatedly tell Sheldrake to wait.

When midday arrived and they stopped for a rest, Miriam was pale and sagging with exhaustion. Setia was torn. It was clear that the woman couldn't go much farther. The pace they were setting was simply too much. On the other hand, it was vital that they return to the settlement as soon as possible, assuming they could find it.

As they were eating lunch Miriam said, "You know, I'm happy to stay here while you all go on ahead."

Silent surprise passed through her companions.

"That's a negative," said Sheldrake. "We stick together."

"But I'm slowing you down, and I can't go any faster."

"You'll feel better when you've had something to eat."

"No, I won't. I'm not as strong or fit as the rest of you. There's no denying it. I can wait here."

"That's not happening," said Setia.

"No way," Carys concurred.

"I'll be fine until someone can come out and rescue me." Miriam's shoulders slumped. "I don't think I can go on."

A pause.

No one could deny she was slowing them down or that the problem would only worsen.

Carys said, "I'll wait with you."

"What? No." Setia shook her head. "We're not leaving *two* of you behind. If we have to go slower, so be it."

Sheldrake said, "It would suck to split up the team, but it's vital that we report back to base as soon as possible. What we've learned could affect the entire colonisation. Maybe it isn't such a bad idea for Miriam and Carys to stay here. We could set up a camp, ditch everything except what's absolutely essential, Setia and me fast-trek all the way back. If we don't stop for sleep we might make it in twenty-four hours. There might be search parties out already. I've missed two scheduled check-ins."

"I'm *not* leaving anyone behind," Setia reiterated.

"Then you stay," Carys said.

"What?"

"You stay here with Miriam. The boy range... Sheldrake and I can go back to the settlement and send help. It makes sense. You're better equipped than me at tackling any new Ahmads who appear, and if I leave most of my gear here, I can do the fast trek."

Miriam heaved a sigh. "I feel terrible. Please, everyone, just go. I'll be fine. It's what I want."

"What happened to Ms Optimistic?" Setia touched her arm. "Actually, I don't mind spending another night or two in this forest. Whatever that thing that looked like Ahmad was, it didn't hurt us. We won't come to any harm." She wasn't convinced by her own words, yet she also didn't want to abandon Miriam.

"That *thing* knew at least one of us was armed," Carys said. "Maybe it didn't want to risk anything."

"Then it still knows we're armed," Setia countered.

Miriam clearly harboured doubts too, but she didn't object to the proposal.

"It's settled." Sheldrake slipped off his pack and began to take things out. "Carys, only bring what you absolutely need. The lighter we travel, the faster we'll get where we're going."

Did he know where he was going?

Setia didn't even know where they were right now.

Twenty-Seven

A pile of belongings sat in the middle of the tent, a physical reminder of Sheldrake and Carys. Setia could see her team mates in her mind's eye, striding through the darkness on their forced march back to the birthplace of a new human civilisation. Had they even left the forest yet? It would be a gruelling journey.

Naturally, rain had begun to fall. The corporal and the bird-woman would be contending with the downpour as well as the lack of light. And if they were out in the open there was the risk of the rain figures reappearing. Only they would be invisible in the dark. There was also the risk of the thing masquerading as Ahmad approaching. Maybe he would bring buddies.

Setia shivered and faced outward, peering through night vision goggles. Nothing moved within or beyond the electrified fence. She turned to check on Miriam, lying curled on her side in her sleeping bag.

Was she asleep?

It wasn't possible to hear her breathing over the noise of the rain. She hadn't spoken much since the others had left. Guilt was racking her, no doubt. Setia had tried to make her feel better, telling her the person who brought the tequila deserved a rest and making other jokes, but nothing she said had any effect.

She regarded the rain, wondering how she would ever get used to it. Perhaps it wasn't a year-round phenomenon. It had rained a lot in Spiral City, but not all the time. The relentless thrumming was mesmeric. A yawn forced its way up her throat and she lifted the back of her hand to her mouth, blinking her gritty eyes.

She hadn't slept at all last night, and she didn't intend to sleep tonight either. Their situation simply wasn't safe. If they were attacked Miriam couldn't defend herself.

But staying awake was hard, despite the danger. Setia blinked again and forced herself to focus. The monotony of the surroundings didn't help. Endless trunks of the strange trees rose from the ground within and outside the electric fence, fading into distance and shadows. The fence itself was faintly glowing, horizontal lines crossing her vision.

What had Sheldrake seen when Ahmad had arrived? The corporal hadn't said, and she hadn't thought to ask him. She stretched her back and arms and yawned for a second time. Maybe eating or drinking something would help.

As she reached for her pack, a small noise seemed to break the ceaseless patter of raindrops. Something between a click and a creak.

She froze and slowly turned her head. The scene through her goggles didn't seem any different. There were the trees, the fence, and the grey shroud of falling water.

No.

Something *was* different.

The outline of a tree standing within the fence had altered. It was fatter now. Wider.

It was growing wider still.

She picked up her gun. "Miriam! Miriam, wake up."

There was a rustle of fabric.

"What's wrong?" Miriam asked groggily. She gasped. "Can you see something? What is it?"

Setia's attention was riveted to the tree trunk. She'd been somewhat mistaken. It wasn't growing wider. It was opening, splitting down the middle like an overripe melon. Something was climbing out.

"Get your gun and come over here."

"What is it, Setia?" Miriam's voice was so quiet it was barely audible.

"Get over here!" A ripping sound came from behind. She spun around. A knife blade was running down the tent wall.

Miriam gawked at the blade.

"Get your gun out!" Setia yelled. "Shoot at it!" She swung about —just in time to see a large, dark figure running at her. The thing had emerged from the tree. She fired as it reached her. The pulse hit it right in the middle. It groaned and tumbled forwards, smacking into her, knocking her down, landing on top of her.

"Miriam!"

She caught a glimpse of something looming over her companion, stooping to grab her, and Miriam's horrified features. Her hands were raised but she was still, petrified.

Setia forced off the thing lying on her squirming and groaning. She could hear more of them.

Where was her gun?

The impact of the thing hitting her had knocked it from her grasp. She slapped around desperately but her hands hit only ground. Something brushed her arm. She threw a punch. Kicked. Flailed.

Somehow, she was on her feet. Miriam was being carried off through the gaping hole in the tent. Setia flew at her captor, but before she moved two steps hands fastened around her waist. She was lifted up. A face appeared. She slammed her fist into it. Another face. She jabbed the eyes.

Suddenly, she was free. Her knees struck a hard surface.

Miriam was gone.

Fingers dug into Setia's back. She wrenched herself around.

She was up.

She was off.

The fence zoomed closer.

A dark shape moved to her left. Another approached from the right.

She ran at the closest one, thrust her shoulder into it, raised it up and hurled it.

The figure landed on the fence, forcing the wires down, bending the poles. It jerked and the wire sparked.

Setia's boot hit its middle. Thrusting downwards, she leapt over the fence and landed running.

Dodging tree trunks, she sped away.

Rain soaked her hair and streamed down her face. Her feet slithered and slipped on the sodden ground.

She cast a look backwards.

Figures moved between the trees, pursuing her.

She ran on.

A torrent of streaming water crossed her path. She soared over it but landed badly. As her foot hit the ground it slid from under her and she landed heavily on her front.

On the far bank, the figures halted.

What were they?

They were humanoid but swathed, their faces hidden.

The mud was like oil as she attempted to climb to her feet, fighting for traction. Finally, she was up and gone, racing away.

Her hunters could not cross the stream. They would have to go around. Would they be able to track her through the forest. Not by her trail, surely. Not with the rain washing away her footprints. But perhaps they could trace her scent. Who knew what they might be able to do?

Miriam!

Setia's heart heaved. She'd been charged with protecting the woman and she'd failed. What would happen to her friend?

The rainy night pressed in. She had no idea where she was going, and all she had with her were the clothes on her back. No shelter, no supplies. She didn't even have her gun. She pulled up her hood. Water had already invaded at her neck. The dampness penetrated.

Though she wasn't cold yet, she soon would be. She would have to stop running eventually and she would cool down.

She would have to find a way out of the woods and all the way back to the settlement, alone. She didn't stand a chance against those things that had taken Miriam. She didn't even know where to find them.

Poor Miriam.

Setia could not imagine facing Sheldrake or Carys if she ever managed to get back.

She slowed her pace to a jog. There was no point in running when she had no idea where she was going. She could end up racing right into the arms of her enemies.

Damn these endless trees.

Damn Talman Prime.

Hate for the planet rose up in her. Of all the places she could have gone to escape Arief, why did it have to be here?

But there had been no other place to go, no way to get away from him without leaving Earth, and that hadn't been entirely successful. He'd managed to find her even aboard the *Bres.*

One thing did seem clear: the things that had Miriam were not anything to do with him. If he'd been one of them he would have declared his presence. He would not have been able to resist. He would have—

Her foot sank deep into the mud. Before she could stop herself she brought her other foot down. A heartbeat later she was up to her thighs and still sinking. Helplessly, she reached up to save herself, but there was nothing to grab. Her hands swiped empty air and she slipped in up to her hips.

She was submerged up to her chest and still she sank.

The mud was up to her armpits.

She twisted and kicked. The mud oozed into her clothes, slimy and clammy. It rose over her shoulders.

"No..." she breathed.

"Help!"

All around was darkness. The trees watched dispassionately.

Her chin hit grimy wetness. She tilted her head back, drowning her hood in mud.

Her arms were going under, legs stilled by the weight of the bog.

"Help," she gasped.

Outside noises turned muffled and grotesque as her ears slipped beneath the surface.

Just before her head sank under, she took a breath and closed her eyes.

She was in a world of dirt and water. Fighting terror, with a supreme effort, she thrust a hand upward. It broke into air, into life. But there was nothing to grab.

She tried to swim, but her arms and legs could not make passage through the clinging mud.

There was no way out.

Seconds passed. Minutes.

Her ribs bucked as her lungs screamed for air.

A vision appeared before her eyes: her body, still and lifeless, entombed in the bog, lost and forgotten.

She couldn't help it.

Her mouth opened. She took a breath.

Twenty-Eight

She was shaking with cold.

Where am I?

Why am I still alive?

Feebly, she moved an arm. The mud was gone.

But she couldn't open her eyes. Air entered her lungs and she expelled it raggedly, something blocking its flow. She touched her face. Dried mud caked it. Breaking off flakes, she cleared her nose and mouth first, then picked off the clay covering her eyelids.

A blurred view appeared.

She was in a small room. The walls, floor and ceiling a dull earthen colour. Aside from her and a single light, it was entirely empty and there were no windows.

Where was the door?

She moved, and her joints complained. She was stiff, frozen, cramped.

There was the door. It was closed and there was no handle, only a square window with bars.

This wasn't any old room, it was a prison cell.

Fighting aching muscles, she straightened up. She'd been slumped against a corner.

Someone pulled me out of the mud and put me in this cell. I was put here.

Where was here?

There were sounds, but they were so distant they were hard to identify—people moving and talking, maybe.

Her clothes were solid boards of dry mud. Every movement she made, they shed particles. Her hair was thick with the horrible stuff. It coated every centimetre of exposed skin. She reeked of it.

She bent her arms and legs, though her teeth chattered with cold. Bracing herself with one hand on the wall, she slowly rose to her feet. Rigid creases in her clothes dug into her. She hobbled to the door and peered through the window. A corridor of the same beaten earth as her cell stretched to the left and right, interspersed with more cell doors.

"Hello!" She rested her chin on the bottom of the window and stuck her face through the bars. "Hello! Is there anyone there? Miriam? Are you here too? It's Setia."

There was a shout. A deep male voice had replied in a language she didn't understand.

She jerked her head away from the bars.

Burnap's balls.

Where she'd grown up it wasn't unusual for people to speak two or three languages as well as English, but they only spoke them in their local areas, in their villages or within their families, not when talking with strangers.

If it hadn't been for the events of the last few days, she might have guessed that she'd heard someone from one of the other ships. Colonists from the *Balor* and *Banba* were settling other parts of Talman Prime. Some might have ended up in the forest somehow, but why would they respond in their mother tongue? Besides, the Fleet would not have constructed a prison on Prime and had no reason for putting her in one.

Hurrying footsteps echoed down the corridor, and a torrent of figures burst from one end. Setia backed up to the wall opposite the door, alarmed at the flurry her shouting had provoked. A key rattled in the lock and the door flew open. People crowded in, facing her, staring.

They were swathed in similar garments to the attackers she'd fled at the campsite: dull-coloured trousers and leggings, knee-high boots, baggy tops and long outer garments with hoods. But the hoods were down and, for the first time, she could see their faces.

Sallow-skinned, brown-haired and dark-eyed—their eyes turned up at the outer corners—they looked oddly similar to each other. Even their body frames looked alike. Their hips and shoulders were narrow, their hands and wrists slim. Though they were undoubtedly human-*like*, there was something different about them. Something wrong.

They seemed as interested in her as she was in them, their gazes inspecting every inch of her as if she were a zoo animal.

How must she look, encased in a pie crust made of dirt? And she was freezing. She hugged herself. "Where's Miriam?" she murmured. "What did you do with my friend?" Then, hopelessly, "Let me go."

Another set of footsteps approached, a single set, heavy and measured.

The people drew away to let the newcomer in.

Ahmad.

Or, rather, Not-Ahmad.

"Who are you?" she demanded. "*What* are you?"

He chivvied the gawpers out of the door, complaining at them in a foreign language. However, he didn't make all of them leave. He touched a female's shoulder and she stayed.

He closed the door and faced Setia. "What's your name?"

"Let me out of here! And I'll take my friend with me, thanks. The one you kidnapped from our tent."

"Things will be easier if you tell me your name. I can find out anyway. I can force your companion to tell me if you won't. I know she's called Miriam. You must be Carys Ellis or Setia Zees. Which is it?"

She grimaced. Where had he got their names from? Not from

Miriam. She must have told him her own name, but not Setia's. Did he know from Ahmad?

She didn't want him to hurt Miriam. "I'm Setia," she replied sullenly.

He said something to the female. Setia heard her name repeated within the babble. The woman nodded understanding and gave her a long look before departing.

Setia had not been able to read her expression. She asked not-Ahmad, "So one of you pulled me out of the mud pit?"

"You were lucky we were trying to find you, or you might have been the first of your kind to die on this world."

"*My* kind? You aren't human? What do you call yourselves? What's *your* name?"

He didn't answer, only regarded her impassively.

"What did you do with the real Ahmad? What's happened to Miriam? Where are they?!"

When he continued to remain silent, she took a small comfort in his comment. If she could have been the first human to die on Prime, it meant Ahmad and Miriam were alive. Also, he'd thought she might be Carys, so Carys and Sheldrake hadn't been captured. They might make it to the settlement. Though what would any rescuers find at the campsite? A slit tent and scattered belongings. With the constant rain wiping away all traces of a trail, they would never find her or Miriam.

Someone spoke outside the door and Not-Ahmad opened it. The female had returned, bearing a bowl of water and some cloths.

Setia said, "It's gonna take more than that."

Twenty-Nine

Over the next couple of days she returned to a semblance of cleanliness. The female assigned to her even contrived to wash her hair, bringing several bowls of water to the cell. The clothes she gave her to wear were similar to her captors'. The baggy, black pants and loose shirt and jacket were made from slightly rough, unevenly woven fabric. It seemed natural in origin, not synthetic, but it wasn't cotton or wool and it didn't have the lustre of silk. She was allowed socks but not shoes. Her hiking boots probably remained in the mud pit.

Her body temperature had returned to normal when, after helping her to wash off the worst of the mud, the woman had brought her hot soup to drink. The main ingredient had seemed to be some sort of fish or shellfish. Setia hadn't registered more before consuming it, a sudden ravenous hunger seizing her as soon as she set eyes on it.

More meals arrived: meat, vegetables, starchy foods. She didn't recognise any of them, neither by appearance nor taste but she ate it all. A hunger strike was the last of her strategies for gaining her freedom. She was thankful she *could* eat, that her body didn't reject the foodstuffs of Prime.

Her attendant had also brought her bedding, consisting of a thin mattress, a single pillow and a blanket. It wasn't much, but at least she didn't have to sleep on the floor. On the other hand, she seemed to be in for a long stay.

Her basic needs met, her greatest challenge was boredom. She had absolutely nothing to do during the hours she spent alone. She would stand at the cell window, watching and listening, hoping to learn something useful. But nothing happened. The other cells seemed unoccupied. She called for Miriam and Ahmad. No one answered.

The female tending to her needs was her only company and source of interest. The woman didn't—presumably couldn't—answer any questions. Sometimes, she would issue instructions, but in her own language. Setia had to guess what she meant.

On the third day, the woman arrived with a bowl of stew on a tray. A guard unlocked the cell door and let her in before locking it again. She squatted down and attempted to give Setia the tray. "Eat."

Setia stared. "What did you say?"

The woman thrust the tray into her hands. "Eat."

She sat opposite Setia on the floor of the cell and watched her.

This behaviour wasn't unusual. The attendant would often spend a couple of hours in the cell. At first, Setia had spoken to her, demanding answers, complaining, and insulting the woman and her race. When it had become clear she couldn't understand what Setia said, she gave up. But she'd pondered over everything. How come Not-Ahmad could speak English but no one else of his kind could? He couldn't possibly have learned the language from the real Ahmad. There hadn't been sufficient time. Unless Not-Ahmad had been the person they'd seen at the settlement?

None of it made any sense.

"You can speak my language now?" she asked.

"Eat your food."

"*Eat your food*? That's pretty good, considering how long you've been listening to me." She put down the tray. "What else can you say?"

The woman picked the tray up and placed it in her lap. "You must eat."

Setia held her gaze. Her eyes were not an unusual colour, only a shade or two lighter than Setia's own. Their shape—the way they turned up at the outer corners in a style some women on Earth recreated with make-up—was more unusual, but not something Setia had never seen. There was nothing intrinsically non-human about the eyes, yet looking into them was unnerving.

She put the tray down again. "I don't want to eat right this minute. If we can communicate, I'd rather learn something about you. What's your name? How come you can speak my language?"

The woman blinked. "You..." she paused as if searching for the next word "...you do not...you must not ask questions."

"Oh really? I don't see how you're going to stop me. Whether you answer or not..."

They stared at each other.

"What's your name?" Setia repeated.

If she could build a rapport with this woman, it might help in her effort to escape. At the very least, she might have an ally if her captors decided she was no longer of any use to them.

She reached out to touch the woman's arm. "Why are you keeping me here? If you don't want humans on your planet, allow me to return to my ship. I'll pass on your message."

The woman's gaze had moved to Setia's hand. A shudder passed through her. Revulsion? Fear? She grasped Setia's wrist and lifted her hand off. Rising to her feet, she said, "Eat. I will return soon."

If building bridges wasn't going to work...

Setia also stood, picking up the tray of food. She hurled it into the wall. The bowl shattered. Stew spattered the surface. Tray, fragments of bowl, and spoon clattered to the floor.

The attendant stiffened in shock, her mouth gaping. Setia seized her and spun her around, fastening her hands around the woman's throat.

"Call for your buddies," she hissed in her ear. "Tell them that if they don't release me I'll kill you."

She forced her to the door and pushed her face into the bars. "Tell them!"

Booted feet were already approaching, their footfalls echoing along the corridor.

It was an act of desperation, but what else could she do? The longer she lay rotting in a cell, the longer her enemies had to capture more colonists, the more time the hostile aliens had to create a plan of attack. If their motives weren't malicious, why had they taken her and Miriam prisoner, and presumably Ahmad too?

She squeezed her attendant's neck, taking care not to squeeze so tightly she passed out, yet hard enough to render her incapable of fighting back. Like most of her kind, she was slightly built and easy to overpower.

The woman kicked backwards into Setia's shins, but she grimaced and held on. The woman twisted and squirmed. Setia squeezed a little tighter.

Four men arrived. Among them was Not-Ahmad.

"Good to see you," said Setia. "I won't need a translator. Open this door and let me out. She comes with me."

"Or?" asked Not-Ahmad.

"Isn't it obvious?"

The woman's sallow skin was turning purple. Setia was forced to ease the pressure and allow her to breathe just a little. Carrying an unconscious hostage would complicate things.

"You would kill her?"

"I could, and that's all you need to worry about."

His sombre expression darkened. He said something to one of the men, who stepped forward with a key. As he unlocked the door, Setia stepped backwards, dragging her hostage with her.

"Back off," she commanded. "All of you. That way." She jerked her chin at the left hand side of the corridor. Which way was the exit? She had no idea. But a fifty-fifty chance was better than rotting in captivity.

Not-Ahmad stood at the front of the knot of men, crowded into the narrow space. Setia held her semi-conscious captive in front as she stepped from the cell and walked backwards down the corridor. The woman had stopped fighting. She appeared to still be conscious but she'd gone limp, making Setia's escape effort harder. The lack of muscle tension had turned her into an unwieldy sack of potatoes.

Setia struggled on, not taking her eyes off Not-Ahmad and his fellow jailers.

She made it as far as the corner before something struck her hard on the back of her head.

Well, it was worth a try, she ruminated before passing out.

She came to lying on her side in her cell. The remains of her stew clung to the wall, drops spread out from the central explosion. The bowl shards were scattered on the floor, the tray lay upside-down, the spoon had somehow ended up right in the corner.

She sat up, wincing as pain radiated across her skull.

Outside, all was silent.

How long had she been out? Probably only a few minutes. In that time, Not-Ahmad, his cronies and her female attendant had left.

Would someone else be assigned?

She gingerly touched the back of her head, her fingertips registering a lump. Not knowing what else to do, she got to her feet and crossed again to the barred window. The corridor stretched from side to side, empty.

Should she shout her protests again? Call for Miriam or Ahmad? There didn't seem much point. They were clearly being held somewhere beyond earshot. She slumped, resting her chin on the sill, and pondered her next move. But try as she might, she couldn't come up with anything. She was entirely under these strange aliens' control and out of options.

Footsteps approached.

She straightened up and listened. The sound was coming from the left and appeared to be heading her way. Was Not-Ahmad returning? Or perhaps she was being taken somewhere else. Or maybe he'd decided she wasn't worth having around anymore.

Her gut twisted but something kept her at the window, peering out.

It was Not-Ahmad, marching at the front of a group of three. A female walked behind him, followed by one of the guards.

The woman wasn't wearing the aliens' usual attire.

She was wearing…

Setia's eyes widened. The woman was wearing her clothes. They'd been cleaned of all mud and looked good as new, right down to her hiking boots.

A greater surprise awaited. Setia lifted her gaze to the alien's face.

Holy shit!

She found herself looking into her own eyes.

Eyes, nose, mouth, hair…everything was the same.

She was looking at herself.

Setia fell back from the window and stared as the group passed by.

Thirty

How could I have been so stupid?

Setia lay on her side on her mattress, cradling her head with one hand to protect the lump on her skull.

Of course that woman was in here with me in order to 'copy' me, or whatever it is those aliens do. I knew Ahmad had been copied. I'd seen Not-Ahmad's face change as I tried to stop him leaving the tent. Why else would just one person help me get clean and bring me my food? She even learned how to speak English.

Burnap's balls, Setia. You're a moron.

On the other hand, what else could she have done? It wasn't like she was in a position to dictate who came into her cell.

Yet she shouldn't have been so surprised to see Not-Setia walk past. Had the little display been a big *Screw you*? She saw no reason they should have chosen to use that corridor. The place seemed almost deserted. Her cell wasn't en route to anywhere.

She got to her feet and crossed to the door.

Pressing her face to the bars, she confirmed her suspicion. Blank walls confronted her.

"Miriam! Are you there?"

Silence.

"Ahmad! Ahmad!"

Not a sound.

"Where are you guys?"

She gripped the bars. "Let me out! Let me out of here! Why are you keeping me here? What are you doing? Let me out!" She hammered the door with her fists. Then she kicked it. "Ow! Shit."

Pain had shot up from her toes. She slumped to the floor and rested her forehead on the door, her shoulders heaving.

Time passed. She didn't know how long. She remained in the same position, going over the events of her life. Her father dying, near-starvation on the streets of Spiral City, running drugs, Arief, Elek, the *Bres*... None of it seemed to be her choice. Every decision had been forced on her. Even Mapper Robins and his damned skein indicated she had zero free will. She'd thought she'd chosen to go on the expedition, but she'd been wrong. It was all pre-determined.

With only the artificial light shining from the ceiling, which never went out, she had no way of marking the hours. She no longer knew if it was day or night or how long she slept. All she knew was that sometimes she would feel hungry and more often than not food would arrive soon after.

She was hungry now, but no food had come. Would any ever come now that Not-Ahmad had what he wanted? She wasn't of any use anymore. Would they leave her to die?

The metal door was cold against her forehead. The chill penetrated, giving her a headache to match the ache at the back of her head.

Sighing, she sat up. Moping wasn't going to help her predicament. Easing her cramped muscles, she got to her feet and looked out into the corridor once more.

"Hello? Is there anyone there? Can anyone hear me? I'm hungry. Could someone bring me something to eat?" The word *please* rose to her lips but she swallowed it back down. She would not beg. Her begging days were over, even if it meant *all* her days were over.

She slumped on the floor and leaned her back on the door.

What had happened to Miriam? She kind of missed her sharp little face, her naivety, her open-heartedness.

Had Carys and Sheldrake made it back? Had Carys's bird found her? Probably not. That bird was long gone. Setia closed her eyes and recalled Carys Ellis in her workplace, scraping pieces of fruit from a plate onto a feeding tray.

Footsteps.

Someone was coming!

She leapt up. The window bars were solid against her face as she yearned to catch sight of the new arrival. As two guards rounded the corner, her heart sank. Neither appeared to be bringing any food. Yet their hands were not empty.

They were at the cell door. She took a step back. As soon as they were through one grabbed her, yanking her wrists behind her back. The other thrust a bag over her head. She was forced forward, a firm hand on each arm.

"Where am I going? Where are you taking me?"

No reply came.

She tried to keep track of the turns she made and the number of paces she took and steps she climbed up and down, thinking the information might come in handy, but she soon lost track. At one point, someone put shoes on her. Then she sat in an automated vehicle, but she couldn't have guessed what type. It seemed that a long time passed. All the while, her guards didn't say a word.

Perhaps three or four hours after being taken from her cell, the bag was removed from her head. She winced and blinked as bright lights hurt her eyes. Her wrists remained fastened.

She was in a large, white, windowless room—some kind of laboratory, judging by the equipment on the benches. Her guards loomed to each side of her, and in front stood an elderly man. He had the same tilted eyes as the other natives of Prime, but his hair was white and flowed below his shoulders. A web of fine lines marked his features. As with all the people of this planet, she found it hard to read his expression.

"I've been told you're called Setia."

"You speak my language?"

"I want to be very clear with you about your position here. You will not be returning to your people. You will live out the rest of your days with us. Perhaps when we have repelled the invaders and there is no risk from subversion, you may be allowed your freedom. Your behaviour will decide that. Until then, you will remain in confinement and you will give us all the information we need. If you refuse to help us, you will be executed. Do you understand?"

She opened her mouth, but she had no reply.

"You see, if you don't help us, we have no reason to keep you alive. In fact, it would be safer to kill you now. But the chances of you escaping and managing to contact your ship are vanishingly small. So we will take that small risk for the benefit of the useful intelligence you can supply."

She had no intention of helping the aliens, but to tell them so would result in a quick death. "I want to live. If I have to answer your questions, I'll do it."

"A good choice, quickly made. I see you are a pragmatic person. You will be treated decently providing you don't renege on our agreement. Be assured, if you do, we won't be slow in exacting your punishment." The old man spoke to the guards, then he said, "Tomorrow, we will begin our work."

The guards took her out of the laboratory to one of several plain doors with symbols above them, presumably numbers. She waited while they unlocked it. It wasn't until she was about to step inside that they removed her wrist bindings.

She'd been expecting another cell, but the new place was more like a modest, twin-bedded hotel room. One bed looked as though it had been slept in.

The door closed and was locked. She went to the window and opened the curtains. Beyond lay a dreary Prime landscape. Hills stretched to the horizon under a dull sky. Her room appeared to be four or five floors up, and the window was solid.

It was raining.

She turned away and was wondering if someone would bring her some food soon when the bathroom door opened.

"Setia!" Miriam flew to her and grabbed her into a hug. "Harold said you might come, but he didn't tell me you were coming today."

"You're okay?" Setia gently extricated herself from Miriam's grasp. "Did they hurt you?"

"No... Only a little bit, when they took me from the tent. I thought I would never see you again, never see anyone. Then Harold told me they found you and you might come here too. I'm so glad you did. I would have been lonely without you."

Setia was happy to see Miriam, yet she couldn't help feeling disappointed and annoyed. "You told them my name?"

Miriam hung her head. "I didn't see what harm it could do. Should I have kept it a secret?"

"I suppose it doesn't really matter, but... What else have you told them?"

Her companion's features twisted. She looked pleadingly into Setia's eyes. "We have to tell them what we know or they'll kill us. What choice do we have?"

Setia forbore answering, not knowing if the room was bugged. Besides, a disquieting realisation had hit. She studied Miriam closely. Nothing she could see indicated this wasn't the person she'd met on the shuttle to the *Bres*, the person she'd tried to avoid until fate—or rather Robins— thrust them together. But Not-Ahmad had looked convincing too.

"Is this bed mine?" Setia indicated the undisturbed one.

"If you want." Miriam sat on hers.

"Still no cocktails, huh?" Setia quipped.

Miriam chuckled. "Talman Prime definitely isn't living up to my expectations."

"What was the drink you smuggled on the expedition? I forgot."

"Tequila, of course. How could you forget a thing like that?"

"Yeah, that's right. Tequila."

The answer was correct, but Setia couldn't quieten the little voice asking her if this really was Miriam.

Thirty-One

"What I don't understand is," said Setia, "how our probes and scanners haven't spotted that Prime is inhabited with intelligent life. I mean, we're in a multi-storey building. It isn't exactly easy to miss."

The question had been growing in her mind all night. While Miriam slept peacefully in the adjacent bed Setia had found slumber hard to come by, despite her improved circumstances. Now it was morning, Prime's baleful sunlight was shining through the window and Miriam was awake, she'd taken the first opportunity to voice her puzzlement.

"Ha, that's simple," Miriam replied, hands behind her head as it rested on her pillow. "Have you taken a proper look outside?"

Setia climbed from her bed and peered once again at the landscape. "Oh look," she remarked. "It's raining."

A grey curtain was turning the view semi-opaque, yet it was exactly as she remembered from yesterday. High hills rose and fell all the way to the horizon, the weird purple vegetation sprouting from the slopes. "What do you mean? It's the same old—"

"Look closer." Miriam got up and joined her at the window, putting her head close to Setia's. She pointed. "See that hollow there?" Moving her digit, she added, "And there?"

Following the direction of Miriam's finger, Setia only saw patches of shadow, where daylight hadn't penetrated beneath overhanging foliage. "Umm, darker bits?"

Wordlessly, Miriam pressed a finger under Setia's chin, tilting her head up. Leaves edged the top of her view. Vegetation overhung their window.

Setia's jaw dropped. "Those are...?"

Miriam nodded.

"This is...?"

"We're inside a hill, and all those hills are inhabited."

"Burnap's balls."

Miriam returned to her bed and sat down. "It took me a day or two to figure it out, but it's obvious when you think about it. If you lived on Prime, would *you* live on the surface? Wouldn't it make more sense to live mostly under cover, out of the rain?"

"It would certainly be a helluva lot drier." Setia also sat down. "And if there are frequent tremors, living inside the landscape *might* be safer. It's flexible. No walls of heavy concrete to collapse on your head. But where do they grow their food? Where do they keep their livestock?"

Miriam shrugged. "I haven't figured out the whole answer, but the Primians' living habits must be the reason the probes didn't pick up evidence of intelligent life. We were looking for buildings, roads and so on. We were looking for evidence of how *we* would live, entirely blind to ways others live."

"What did you call them?"

"What? The people? Primians. Better than Talman Primians, right? I don't know what they call themselves."

"But what are they? They aren't human." Setia still wasn't sure that Miriam wasn't a Primian herself, but it didn't matter. If her companion was one of them she might say something enlightening.

"I've tried probing Harold." Miriam sighed.

She'd mentioned that name before.

In response to Setia's questioning look, she added, "He's an old guy, some kind of scientist who's been interrogating me. He doesn't give much away. He's all questions, no answers."

"What have you told him?"

Another shrug. "Pretty much whatever he asked me."

"Miriam!"

"What? What was I supposed to do?"

"Refuse, or lie, or *something*. Whose side are you on?"

"Mine. I'm on my side. I don't want to die. I joined the Fleet because I wanted to get away from my family and Earth. My life had no meaning there. I wanted a different way of living, to do something really significant. I'm not ready to give up that dream."

"And you think betraying your fellow human beings is the best way to go about it?"

"Is it really betrayal, though?" Miriam's expression turned pensive. "The Primians would find out most everything about us by themselves eventually. I'm not able to tell them anything important. I don't know any information about our military or defences. Nothing like that."

"I wouldn't be so sure. You don't know what they can find out by themselves, or what might be important if they plan to attack our settlements. But that's all beside the point. Don't you feel any loyalty to our people, the other colonists? If we were at war you would be a collaborator. Hell, maybe we're already at war."

Once more, doubt niggled at Setia. Was this really Miriam confessing she'd spilled the beans to the enemy? Or was it a Primian who looked like her spinning a tale in order to convince the captive to give up intelligence?

"Maybe this is how we avoid a war," said Could-be Miriam.

"Avoid a war? How do you figure that?"

"If we don't withhold information, if we tell them everything, all about who we are, where we're from, what we intend to do, the Primians will see we aren't so different from them. They won't want to fight us. Honestly, Setia, from what I've seen, their population isn't huge. There must be plenty of space on this planet for humans to settle, especially if we stay on the surface and leave everything underground to them. And I don't think their tech is as good as ours. We could help them develop. It could be a great partnership."

Setia burst into laughter.

"I don't see what's so funny," Miriam commented with uncharacteristic heat.

"You think this 'great partnership' is going to begin with you telling the Primians everything they want to know about us? I've never heard anything so dumb. Partnerships only exist between equals, with each side having power in the relationship. We know next to nothing about the locals here but, thanks to you, they know nearly everything about us. We're already at a huge disadvantage. If —more likely *when*—they attack a settlement, it'll be a bloodbath. How are you going to live with yourself? You'll certainly have done something *really significant*."

Just looking at Miriam made Setia so disgusted she wanted to vomit. She returned to the window. Now that she knew the Primians' set-up, she could see the openings in the hillsides that were actually windows. The hills and the ground between them had to be riddled with tunnels.

And, of course, so was the forest. When she and Miriam had been attacked, she'd seen a tree trunk splitting open and a figure emerging. The tree had been within the electric fence. The forest trees grew too thickly to avoid it. Their attackers must have travelled underground to reach them, and Not-Ahmad had done the same at their first encounter with the aliens. That was how he'd circumvented the fence. His story about turning it off with a remote had been bullshit, that much was already clear. But now his method of entry was explained.

Yet he'd known about fences and how they worked, and he'd made up a credible explanation on the fly. He'd also managed to convince most of the others that he was the real deal, not slipping up when it came to common knowledge about the colonisation. Could Not-Ahmad have learned all those details from the original? Had Ahmad been another Miriam, spewing intel to the enemy?

"Setia..."

"Don't talk to me."

"I understand why you're angry, but if you think things through—"

"I said..." Setia rounded on her. "Look, I don't know if you really are Miriam, or if you're an alien, but it doesn't matter. Either way, I'm not speaking to you anymore. I don't associate with traitors."

Miriam paled and her mouth dropped open. "Is that how you really see me?"

Setia faced the window again.

"I'm not a traitor! I'm just trying to do what's best for everyone."

A pause.

"Huh! You think you're better than me, don't you? You think that when you have to talk to Harold you're going to be so much braver and refuse to tell him anything. When you have to choose between death and revealing information, are you going to be so high and mighty then? Are you going to die to keep your integrity? When Harold asks you a question, what are you going to answer, Setia? What?"

THIRTY-TWO

The fact that Harold's laboratory was windowless made more sense now. It had to be deeper within the hill than the room Setia shared with Miriam. She watched the older man adjusting apparatus on a laboratory bench. The two guards who had brought her here waited each side of the door. They wore full body armour made of a thick material something like leather, and they carried sheathed knives as well as pistols in holsters strapped to belts. Their helmets were of the same black material as their armour, coming down low on their foreheads and covering their cheeks and most of their necks.

Defeating both of them would be tricky, and even if she managed it, where would she go? She didn't know how to get out of this place and had no idea where on Prime she was or how to get back to the settlement.

One of the guards met her gaze, steeliness in his look. She returned her attention to Harold.

"There's no need to be concerned," he commented, glancing over his shoulder. "This is nothing to do with you. Just a small experiment I'm conducting."

Setia lifted her eyebrows. She hadn't imagined that he might be planning to experiment on *her*. Was that a possibility? She still hadn't come up with an answer to Miriam's question. What would she say when Harold asked her about the colonisation? Her former friend had already paved the path for a full explanation. Anything she said that deviated from the truth could result in her execution. After all, Harold had Miriam, who had decided to be an absolute open book. He didn't need her, and each human they held presented a risk. Even following Miriam's lead might not save her. She might only stay alive if she offered something Miriam could not.

Harold approached, holding a small device. He flipped a switch and placed the device on a table.

"In case I forget anything," he explained, sitting opposite her. "We will begin with the basics to affirm what I've been told. If I find your answers satisfactory, we will move on to more complex subjects. Providing all goes smoothly you can expect to be here two to three hours. Subsequent interviews may last longer. I intend to eventually extract every iota of useful information you may have to offer. There will come a time when your knowledge is no longer important, after your species has left our planet. At that point, as I hinted before, you may be rewarded with your freedom. Needless to say, your compliance is key to your continued survival and eventual release from captivity. Do you understand?"

She chewed the inside of her cheek, her mind racing. "I understand."

What else was there to say?

"Excellent. Let us proceed."

He asked her about the Fleet, the ships, the number of passengers and crew, the steps of the intended colonisation. He asked her about the disciplines of the crew members, focusing predictably on the military contingent. He asked her about Earth, its population and levels of development, and plans for space exploration.

She answered honestly, loathing herself for every word that left her mouth. All she could do to mitigate her betrayal was to limit the range of her answers, only giving exactly the information implied by the question and absolutely nothing more. Harold didn't seem to know much about space travel and he knew next to nothing about humans and Earth apart from what Miriam had told him. Consequently, there were gaping holes in his understanding Setia didn't fill, and she would insist to Miriam that *she* didn't fill either. He appeared to be entirely ignorant of skeins and skein mapping. She didn't enlighten him.

After a couple of gruelling hours, he leaned back in his seat and nodded. "You've done well. I expected you to be more defiant than your companion, but you're wiser than your earlier behaviour indicated." He paused, lifting a finger to his lips. "I have another question for you..."

She gave an inward sigh. Concentrating on revealing only what she absolutely had to was exhausting.

"...What was your rationale for your escape attempt? You seem to be of at least average intelligence."

Thanks.

"You must have known you had no chance of success. Escape was impossible in the circumstances, yet you tried. Why?"

"I-I'm not sure I understand why you're asking. Isn't it obvious?"

"Clearly not."

"I could have been killed or tortured." *Or ended up in a situation like this.* "I didn't know what was going to happen to me. I had to try to regain my freedom. I had to take back control, even for a short time, even though—I suppose you're right—even though I knew it was pointless."

"Hmm. I think I understand."

Whatever it was he took from her statements, he didn't tell her. Why *had* she tried to escape? She wasn't sure she knew. The way he put it, it seemed stupid, but it had made sense to her at the time.

"Thank you for your cooperation so far," Harold said. "I would rather not order your execution if I can avoid it."

You and me both.

"Is that it?" she asked. "Have we finished?" She wanted to get back to Miriam and warn her about not revealing anything outside the scope of Harold's questions.

"Not quite. You have not mentioned anything about your superiors' plans regarding us, no doubt deliberately. I accept that this subject is sensitive, but it's also essential information. I insist that you tell me everything."

"My superiors' plans regarding *you*? They don't know you exist."

If Sheldrake and Carys had made it back this might not have been strictly true, but Harold seemed entirely ignorant on the subject. Miriam couldn't have told him more.

He frowned. "That is what your companion said. I warn you, my earlier threat stands. If you refuse to divulge the information we need, you will not live much longer."

"Look, Harold—that's what you want us to call you, right?—I'm not lying and neither was Miriam. We had no idea an intelligent species inhabited this planet. We sent probes but all they showed was wilderness. No buildings, no signs of agriculture. We really didn't have a clue about you guys living here. If we had, we probably would have picked a different planet."

"You're lying."

"Burnap's balls! Why would I lie, knowing you could kill me? I've been honest with you so far, haven't I? Why would I lie now?"

"Because information about your proposed eradication of us is vital to your plan's success. You've fed me unimportant tidbits in order to ensure your survival until you can be rescued. But you must hold back the most important details or the attack will fail and you will remain captive."

Setia opened her mouth to respond, but closed it again. He was making a lot of sense. "I don't know how to prove it to you that there is no eradication plan. Believe me, I don't want to die. I would answer you truthfully if I could. It's wild to me that you exist. You look so like us but we can't be the same. I don't understand how two species who are so alike evolved on planets many light years apart. Maybe if I was a scientist I could explain it, but I can't."

Blood suffused Harold's features. "I'm disappointed."

Setia stiffened. *More like angry.* What would he do? She couldn't tell him what she didn't know. There was a remote possibility that the Fleet was aware of Prime's intelligent inhabitants, but she doubted it. If it did know, she wasn't privy to that information. "I'm sorry, but—"

He rose to his feet. "The interview is over. I will see you again tomorrow morning. You and your companion have until then to reconsider your attitude. What you've told me so far may be accurate but that's irrelevant. The requirement to save your lives is that you must tell me everything I want to know, and you have failed."

He motioned the guards to take her away.

Thirty-Three

Miriam's face fell when Setia conveyed the news upon her return to their room. Despite her resolution to freeze Miriam out, she'd felt compelled to let her know her hours were numbered.

"But you answered his questions, didn't you?" Miriam asked. "I mean, apart from the last ones."

Setia was drawn once more to the dismal view from the window. Purple hills rolled into the distance under a glowering sky. "Of course I did. I didn't have any choice. Not after you paved the way to a full and complete disclosure."

"I don't understand."

"We can't tell him what we don't know."

"But..."

Setia turned to glare at her room mate. "They aren't playing a game. There are no rules. They can do what they like. And they will." She cast a glance around the room. "Unless we can think of a way out."

Miriam drew up her knees and wrapped her arms around them. Rocking back and forth, she murmured, "I don't want to die. I *really* don't want to die." To Setia, she said, "I thought if we cooperated everything would be okay."

"I don't know why you would think that. There's no telling what these people might do. They aren't our friends. Heck, they aren't even human."

"That's right," Miriam replied thoughtfully. "They look human, but..."

"They definitely aren't." Setia dropped onto her bed. If Harold followed through with his threat, it was likely neither she nor Miriam would see tomorrow night. There didn't seem much point in staying angry with her companion. "Humans can't turn themselves into doppelgängers, for one thing. And they can't pick up new languages by ear within a few days. It's odd that they think we know about them. Harold seemed to think we were on Prime in order to annihilate all his people. I'm only a lowly colonist. I don't know any of the project organisers—except Robins, I suppose—but I would swear no one was aware that Prime was inhabited by an intelligent species."

"But how can we convince Harold? I told him the same as you. He obviously didn't believe me either."

Setia got to her feet and returned to the window, a solid pane. She ran her fingertips around the edges, but it was firmly attached to the frame. Resting her forehead on the surface, she peered downwards. The drop was pretty steep but it was uneven and vegetation clung to it. If they could get out, they might be able to clamber down.

Then what?

She didn't know, but whatever happened was a better alternative than certain death. Picking up a chair, she tested its weight. The piece of furniture was light, but with sufficient force it might break the pane. Failing that, there were always the beds.

"What are you thinking?" Miriam asked.

"Never mind." The room could be bugged. There might even be cameras. She put down the chair.

The door opened. Two guards had arrived, one bearing food. His partner barked an order. Miriam seemed to understand. She got to her feet and took the tray.

Over the course of the afternoon, Setia thoroughly examined

their room, heedless of people potentially watching. It was natural that she and Miriam would want to escape. What else could their captors expect after Harold's threat? Yet she found no possible exit other than breaking a window. She'd contemplated attempting to overpower the guards, but even if she succeeded the outcome was likely to be the same as it had been at the prison. She and Miriam wouldn't get far inside the hill. If they made it out into the open, however, there was a small possibility they might get away.

She decided not to tell Miriam of her plan. She might be overheard and, regardless of listening devices, Miriam might not *be* Miriam. Even if she was, she was a blabbermouth. It wouldn't have been a shock if the woman demanded to be taken to Harold to confess all.

Prime's shorter rotation had screwed up Setia's sleeping pattern. What passed for the planet's sun had long set, the usual blanket of starless, impenetrable night had fallen, but she wasn't even drowsy. Which was just as well, considering.

Miriam was awake too. She hadn't spoken, but neither had her signature quiet snore begun.

Setia climbed out of bed.

"Can't sleep, huh?" Miriam asked.

Ignoring her, Setia felt for her jacket and shoes and put them on before picking up a chair.

"What are you doing?!"

She smashed the chair into the window glass.

To no effect.

Mustering all her considerable strength, she tried again, with the same result.

"Setia, someone will hear you! They'll punish us."

"They'll punish us *worse* than executing us tomorrow?" She tossed the chair into a corner, and then ripped the bedding and mattress from her bed.

"You're going to...?" Miriam's sheets rustled. She was moving.

"Don't you dare try to stop me."

"Not in my wildest dreams. I'm getting away from the window."

Setia hurled the bed frame at the window. A hollow thunk resounded. The frame bounced back, and its edge caught her on the temple before it clattered to the floor. She staggered backward and blood trickled into her eye. Her calves hit Miriam's bed and she tumbled onto it, encountering something soft and squishy.

"Ow!" Miriam moved out from under her.

Setia pressed the heel of her hand to her cut, trying to stem the flow of blood.

"I thought the glass might be unbreakable," Miriam commented.

"I should have too, I suppose," Setia muttered.

"Probably. Are you all right?"

"All things considered...? No." She added, "The bed hit me."

"Oh dear. Are you bleeding?"

"Quite a lot. Head wounds are bad for it."

"Show me where. Maybe I can help."

Miriam's questing hands touched Setia in the darkness. She guided them to her forehead and winced as her companion's fingers made contact.

"That feels nasty. Let me find something."

After some searching, Miriam used a thin hand towel from the bathroom to staunch the blood, tying it around her head. No one came in response to all the noise. It looked like they were on their own until morning.

In the lightless bathroom, Setia washed off the dried blood. Together, the two women put her bed back together by touch. She lay down, her head throbbing. After a while, Miriam began to snore. Setia marvelled at the woman's composure in the face of impending death.

Thirty-Four

By some miracle, Setia had fallen asleep. Harsh words in a foreign language woke her and she blinked in bright sunlight. *Sunlight*? The rays were warm on her skin, shining in through the window. She moved and grimaced as a wave of pain stabbed her head.

Two figures loomed over her—Primian guards in their black armour.

"What did you say?" she asked. "You brought breakfast? How nice. Thanks."

One reached down and yanked her upright by her elbow. He jabbed a finger at her shoes.

"Oh, I don't have to be executed barefoot? I'm honoured."

Miriam was already on her way out, flanked by two more guards.

"Are you going to pay Harold a visit?" Setia asked.

One of her guards cuffed her. Setia stifled a cry as he hit her wound. He jabbed again at her shoes. Setia eased one shoe on slowly, figuring out her best course of action. There wasn't any point in allowing herself to be taken to Harold. She had no answers to his most important questions, which meant he would carry out his threat. It was likely she'd seen Miriam for the last time.

The only—reckless, stupid, hopeless—course of action that

made any sense was to try to get away from these goons and escape this rabbit warren. Better to attempt to take back some semblance of control than go passively to her fate. If she didn't make it she might still get lucky and be killed quick and clean.

A guard barked something and kicked her leg. She picked up the other shoe.

Damn Arief.

Damn him for driving me to this godforsaken planet.

She put on the other shoe.

Walking between the guards, she exited the room. Miriam was already out of sight somewhere ahead. After a couple of turns, Setia realised they weren't going to Harold's laboratory.

During her recent long hours of wakefulness she'd contemplated feeding him a story. If she made up lies about the Fleet's intentions to eradicate the Primians, it would buy her time. She might make up a better escape plan than 'disable the guards and make a run for it'. Or another opportunity might have appeared. Or Harold might have changed his mind about killing her.

But they weren't going to his laboratory. Had he predicted she wasn't going to fold? Was she being taken directly to a place of execution where she would be given one last chance? Would she even be given one last chance?

Harold seemed hasty, but, she reminded herself, he wasn't human. She couldn't hold him to her own species' standards. The Primians were aliens. She had no idea what they might do.

Oh well, looks like it's 'disable the guards and make a run for it'.

She side-stepped, turned and kicked, sweeping the left-hand guard's legs from under him, causing him to fall flat on his face. Ducking the other as he made a grab for her, she snatched the downed guard's gun. It was surprisingly heavy. Hands fastened on her arms. She drove an elbow backward, but this only elicited a grunt as it impacted leather armour. She was dragged backwards. Meanwhile, the guard on the floor was getting up.

She thrust both feet down and pistoned her head into the chin of the guy behind. His cheek protectors dug into her skull, but the blow had the desired effect. She was suddenly free. Sweeping around, she aimed at the men in turn. Blood dribbled from the lips of the one she'd hit on the chin as he glared at her, hunched over.

She switched her aim to the other guy who crouched, halfway to standing, and the first one snatched his weapon from its holster.

She fired.

An explosion roared and her gun kicked back so hard she nearly dropped it.

External sound was replaced by a high-pitched whistle.

What just happened?

The man she'd fired at was down and writhing, a red pool spreading from his shoulder.

The other—

Something heavy and hard barrelled into her, flinging her onto her back. A hand tugged at her gun. In an effort to hold onto it, she accidentally pressed the trigger again. A second shot rang out, the bang piercing the whistling sound in her ears.

A fist slammed into her jaw, whipping her head around. Sparks flickered in her vision and darkness encroached. Again, the guard tried to wrest the gun from her grasp. She held onto it with a death grip—perhaps it would be a death grip.

The suffocating weight of a large man's body pressed down. Keeping hold of the gun, she got both hands under his chest and heaved. Then she brought up a knee and used that too. She threw him off and he thumped into the wall. The small distance allowed her to aim at him again.

The short struggle had left both panting.

His gaze slid to the gun.

She jerked it threateningly. "Move, and I'll shoot you like I did your buddy." Her voice sounded muffled and distant. The whistling was beginning to fade.

Keeping her gaze fixed on the unhurt guard, she clambered to her feet.

He watched her all the while.

She had to run. The noise of weapon fire would bring the entire hill's inhabitants here within seconds. But the moment she turned her back on this guy...

"Sorry."

She shot him in the thigh.

Then she was gone.

Another corridor crossed hers. Which way? Left or right? How to get out of this place?

Left. It was vaguely in the direction the window in her room had faced.

She needed an exit to the outdoors. Did one even exist? Or were the only ways into and out of this hill subterranean?

A right turn. No options here.

An open doorway and steps leading downward. But she didn't want to go down. She wanted to go *out.*

A sound was breaking through the whistle—running footsteps echoed from somewhere behind.

She took the stairs, which spiralled downward. She cursed. This had to be one of the main routes to a tunnel.

Someone was coming up.

She halted and turned. The footsteps behind her were louder.

Turning again, she flew down the steps, throwing aside a shocked Primian woman in her path. More footsteps, running up.

She was trapped.

Pressing her back to the wall, she waited, unsure whether to point the gun up the stairs or down. Figures appeared but ducked out of sight. Beyond her view, the two groups had halted.

"Setia Zees!"

She held her breath.

"Setia Zees, put down your weapon."

The voice was male.

Not-Ahmad.

"What's the point?" she shouted back. "You're going to kill me. I might as well take out as many of you as I can."

"No one wants to kill you."

"Well, you would say that, wouldn't you?"

"You were being brought to see me, not taken to your execution."

"I've already seen you, thanks. More of you than I wanted."

"You'd rather die than see me again?"

"That isn't what I said."

"Put down your gun. You don't stand a chance and, believe it or not, I don't want you to die."

"I *don't* believe it."

Not-Ahmad's voice had come from above. If any guards were to approach it would be from there.

She pointed the gun up the stairs. "I can't give you the information you want. It doesn't exist. So I'm useless to you and a liability. You've no reason to keep me alive."

"You've thought this through, I see," said Not-Ahmad. "But you're missing some vital information. Please disarm yourself. You've already wounded two of my men. Though I'd prefer it if you were to remain alive, I'm not prepared to take unnecessary risks. I will count to ten. If your weapon isn't clearly visible on a step, my men will shoot to kill. One... Two..."

She clasped the gun tight to her chest.

How was she to know he wasn't lying, just trying to make sure she was defenceless?

"Three... Four..."

It would be satisfying to see some of them go down before the end.

"Five... Six..."

And she would hate it if the final thing to pass through her mind was the realisation she'd passively allowed herself to be killed.

"Seven... Eight..."

On the other hand, death was death, no matter how you looked at it.

"Nine..."

And the chance of life was always preferable, no matter how slim.

"T—"

"I'm putting my gun down!"

Thirty-Five

Not-Ahmad was seated behind a long table when she saw him again. The guards had grabbed her, secured her wrists behind her back, and taken her away without the opportunity to put a face to the disembodied voice that had persuaded her to give herself up.

Two more Primians sat to his left and two to his right, making five in total. Harold was one of them. Like her interrogator, the other three were also unchanged into human form. Why hadn't Not-Ahmad reverted to his Primian appearance? Did it take a long time? Or maybe he was now stuck as Not-Ahmad forever. That would mean a Not-Setia would be permanently running around the place.

She shivered. Then a symbol high on the wall behind the seated figures caught her attention and her jaw dropped.

Not-Ahmad rested his elbows on the table and knitted his fingers. "I'm glad you made the right decision, Setia."

Dragging her gaze from the symbol, she looked him in the eyes. "I still don't know if I did."

"Perhaps I can convince you? It will help with our further discussions." He gestured towards a woman hovering in a doorway.

She exited and then quickly returned with Miriam.

"Setia! I'm so glad you're okay." Miriam ran up to her and hugged her tightly.

Setia awkwardly patted her back, reserving judgement on whether this actually was Miriam.

Then someone else entered and Setia's reservations leapt higher. She pushed Miriam away.

After a gasp, the woman asked, "What's wrong? What's the matter?"

"Who are you? Who's *that*?!"

A second Miriam had halted at the door, her hands behind her back.

Hugging Miriam swivelled to follow Setia's gaze and gave a second gasp. She returned her attention to Setia. "I'm the real one. *I'm* the real Miriam. Your friend!"

"Sorry, but as you can see..."

Not-Ahmad nodded at the Miriam by the door, and she left. "I understand this is confusing for you, but there's something urgent to discuss before we go into explanations." He reached down and picked up a box, which he placed on the table. "I would like your help with this creature. Please step forward and take a look at it."

"What? Why?" Setia was hesitant to do anything this man asked. She was reminded of a nightmare she'd had on the *Bres*, when a sea creature had beeped the ship's alarm at her. The excess of Miriams was making everything seem surreal. "How the hell can we help you with one of your animals? We aren't vets! We aren't even from your goddamned planet."

While she'd been spluttering her disbelief, Miriam had walked up to the table and was peering into the box. She gave a soft *Oh*! and turned to Setia. "It's Carys's bird."

"Loki?! So *that's* what happened to him."

She arrived at the table to see a sorry sight. The poor animal looked on its last legs. He hunched in the corner of the box, feathers dull and eyes half shut. Pity gripped her heart. "You bastards! You caught him and now you've nearly killed him. If you really want to help him, why don't you let him go?"

"We've tried," Not-Ahmad replied. "It won't leave the box."

Miriam suggested timidly, "Maybe it's too weak."

"Too weak *now*," corrected Setia. She glared at Not-Ahmad. "What have you been feeding him? Have you given him water?" She rolled her eyes. "What am I talking about? Of course he's had plenty of water, living here. What about food?"

"That's the problem," said Not-Ahmad. "It won't eat anything we give it. We've offered everything we could think of. Seeds, shoots, fungi, seaweed..." He shrugged.

"Seaweed? Why on Earth... Why on Prime would a carnivore eat seaweed? What about meat? Have you given him any meat?"

"Meat!" Not-Ahmad exclaimed. "It eats meat?"

"That's *all* he eats. Look at his beak, his talons. Burnap's balls! You couldn't figure out he's a predator? Get him some meat before he starves to death."

"Thank you." Not-Ahmad closed the lid of the box and handed it to an assistant, murmuring something.

"Little pieces," said Setia, holding up fingers to demonstrate the size. "Small enough for him to eat." The additional information shouldn't have been necessary but these people were clearly idiots. As the box was taken away she added, "That bird had better damned well live. He belongs to someone who'll rip out your guts if she finds out you killed him."

"The animal's natural food seems obvious now you've told us," said Not-Ahmad, "but you should understand that very few species consume other animals here. Most life forms are plants, deriving their energy from the sun."

"Now *that* I find hard to believe."

The woman sitting next to Not-Ahmad whispered in his ear.

He added, to Setia, "Or, as my colleague reminds me, decaying matter. Please, sit."

While they'd been discussing Loki, two chairs had been brought over.

Miriam sat down and, annoyed and worried, Setia also slumped into hers.

Not-Ahmad explained, "I've brought you here in order for us both to come to a better understanding."

"Uh huh." She folded her arms over her chest. She didn't look at Miriam. For all she knew, there could be two fake Miriams, or even more. The hill could be full of them.

"Setia, the person you saw a moment ago stayed with you last night in your room," Not-Ahmad said. "She has attested to the fact that you appear to be telling the truth when you say your species has no knowledge of us."

"Right."

"And so we will not carry out the threat of execution—for now."

"That's great!" exclaimed Miriam. "I was wondering why we'd been separated."

Setia self-consciously touched the bandage around her head that the Primian had applied. "You expect me to just believe all this shit?"

Not-Ahmad's expression darkened. "It isn't important to us whether you believe it. But I had expected you would be relieved you won't die today."

"How can I be relieved? How do I know what you're saying is true?" She jabbed a finger at him. "You look like a guy I met at our settlement site a week ago, but you're not." She jerked a thumb at Miriam. "She looks like someone I sat next to on the shuttle leaving Earth, but I've no idea who she really is."

"Setia!" Miriam exclaimed. "I thought I was more to you than just someone you met on a shuttle."

Setia continued to Not-Ahmad, "All of you are so close to human that if I passed you in the street I wouldn't look twice, but somehow you're here, light years from Earth. How's that possible?"

He gave her an inscrutable look.

"And another thing," she went on. "If you wanted to hear what I said in private, why didn't you bug my room? Why create a whole new Miriam just to spy on me?"

Leaning back in his chair, Not-Ahmad replied, "I'm not clear on what you mean by 'bug'. It's another word for insect, isn't it?"

"Why not go and ask the real Ahmad?" Setia snapped. "Where is he? Is he dead?"

"Your species isn't able to copy as we do. It makes sense that you don't understand the limitations, and that it was so easy to trick you at our first meeting."

"No, we can't *copy.* You didn't answer my question about Ahmad."

"He's alive."

"Is he okay? Is he here too?"

"Your friend isn't the subject of our discussion. As to how it happens that our species are so alike..." He turned to the people seated to his left and right and began to converse with them in their own language.

A timid hand touched Setia's arm. "I'm really me," said Miriam, "though I don't know how to prove it."

"Even if you really are you," Setia hissed back, "you're still the Miriam who spilled her guts to the enemy the first chance she got, right?"

The hand left her arm.

The discussion among the Primians was over.

Not-Ahmad said, "You asked how it's possible that two species who are so alike could have evolved on different worlds. We have wondered exactly the same thing, ever since you arrived on our planet. I would like to show you something that might explain it. Perhaps humans have something similar in their records or cultural history."

"I doubt it," Setia retorted. "I can't think of anything that would explain your existence. We have many cultures and societies, going back millennia. The only one I know in any detail is my own. I'm sure there's nothing there about intelligent aliens. But..." she narrowed her eyes at the symbol on the wall behind the Primians "... is what you want to show me something to do with that?"

Not-Ahmad looked over his shoulder. "I don't think so. Why?"

On a round plaque, high above the seated Primians, three hares connected by three ears ran in a circle.

Thirty-Six

Not-Ahmad led Setia and Miriam out of the chamber and down a spiral staircase. He took the lead and guards followed, but Setia and Miriam could walk freely, unbound.

"Who were those people you were sitting with?" Setia asked. "Who's Harold? Your chief interrogator?"

Not-Ahmad lifted an eyebrow as he glanced over his shoulder. "The man you call Harold is an Investigator, the head of the department in this district. The other people are council members."

"What does Harold investigate? Crimes?"

"Crimes? No, he's a scientist. I'm not sure what he's currently working on, but he put himself forward as the best person in the local area to question you and learn more about your species."

"How come he can speak our language, but he hasn't transformed to look human?" From what Setia had seen the Primians' metamorphosis included language skills as well as a physical transformation, but Harold confounded the pattern.

"He didn't wish to look like you. He has no reason to. But communicating with you is important, for now. He had to compensate for your disability."

"Disability?!"

"You're unable to take on another's likeness or language. That's a serious defect."

Setia was silent.

Not-Ahmad halted, resting a hand on the smooth wall. He held her gaze another moment before he went on, "It isn't necessary for us to change our bodies in order to speak to you."

"Can you choose to change only your appearance and not speak the language?" What else they transform into? Animals, presumably. Rocks?

Not-Ahmad didn't answer. He continued down the stairs until he reached a landing, where he pulled open a door. Opposite stood a familiar sight.

"You have lifts?"

The three sets of double steel doors wouldn't have looked out of place in any office building or hotel lobby on Earth. Setia was reminded of the very beginning of her long journey to this strange place, when she had stepped into the lift that would take her to the *Bres*'s passenger processing centre, mistakenly relieved that she'd escaped Arief.

Throwing her a frown, Not-Ahmad replied, "We must descend to the lowest levels of this section, and then descend farther. The place I want to show you is one of only a handful of similar sites on our planet, discovered in recent times. It's perhaps not a coincidence that our major population centres developed above them. Scientists like Harold haven't reached a consensus about that, but personally I think there's something in the speculation."

They stepped into a lift and descended several floors, the strange Primian numbers displayed above the closed doors. The parallels with human societies grew stronger the longer Setia spent with the aliens. They were so like and yet unlike humans.

At the lowest level, they entered an area of rough-hewn stone. The floor was finished but the walls had only been cut from the original rock.

"This excavation took place fourteen years ago," Not-Ahmad explained. "Archaeologists are still working on it. They uncovered a new section last year and that's what I want to show you. It's some distance from here."

A young Primian woman awaited them. Her gaze fixed on the human, she and Not-Ahmad had a short conversation, then she led them into the excavation. Beyond the entrance the tunnel walls were smooth and the floor sloped sharply downward. In some places there were stairs and handrails.

"It seems warmer here than up top," Miriam commented.

"Our planet is generally warmer below the surface," Not-Ahmad replied. "We create much of our energy by heating water below ground. The rest comes from fast-flowing rivers, ocean currents, and waterfalls."

"Figures," Setia muttered.

Though his reply appeared innocuous, its openness worried her. Knowledge of Primian energy sources could be useful to invaders in the event of a military conflict. Not-Ahmad didn't seem to think she or Miriam would ever be returning to their friends.

"This place is a labyrinth," Miriam remarked. "It would be so easy to get lost."

It was true. Many side tunnels snaked out from their route as they'd been walking along. Setia had become disoriented. "Are you going to tell us where you're taking us?"

"I told you already. An archaeological excavation. Perhaps an explanation. But you must interpret what you see yourself. I shouldn't influence you. But if I'm correct, it may be that there's a way your species will agree to leave my planet, and there will be no need for bloodshed."

"I hope you are correct," Miriam said brightly. "Right, Setia?"

She ignored her. "No matter what you've found," she said to Not-Ahmad, "I seriously doubt our people will halt the colonisation. They've come a long way at great effort and expense. They won't leave easily, even when they discover the planet is inhabited by an intelligent species."

She spoke heavily, her words tolling in her ears like a death knell. Humanity's history of colonisation was bloody and brutal. Her own country had been aggressively invaded more than once in its long history, and in recent times Crusaders had followed the same pattern. Humans had learned little from their past, and though a new age appeared to be dawning, the tendency to violence was a basic human instinct. Plus, the rich, spoiled colonisers were unlikely to give up their dream without a fight.

And while the wars were fought, she and Miriam would be trapped here, on the wrong side.

"Whether easily or not," said Not-Ahmad, "your people will leave."

The archaeologist had led them to a tunnel that descended vertically. A steel ladder was mounted into the wall. The scientist went first, followed by Miriam, then Setia, then the guards. At the bottom, more tunnels spread out at a variety of angles. They walked upward, stooping as the roof closed in.

"Believe it or not," said Not-Ahmad, "we're fairly near the surface. It's believed that at one time there was an external entrance to the caves I'm about to show you. It must have closed over, or at least it's never been found."

The archaeologist spoke to him and indicated a tunnel to the left.

"You've got to be kidding," said Setia.

The opening was at waist height and less than half a metre at its widest. They would be forced to wriggle on their bellies.

"It's very short," Not-Ahmad replied. "You'll be through it very quickly. This is the end of our journey."

The archaeologist climbed into the hole and disappeared. Not-Ahmad beckoned his captives.

"You first, Setia," said Miriam nervously.

Rolling her eyes, she followed the scientist. She was forced to shuffle forward on her elbows and knees. Soon, she heard Miriam puffing behind her.

The cavern at the other end was five or six metres wide and lit by standing lamps, their light reflecting from the walls.

The walls.

At first, the markings had appeared to be discolouration of the rocks, but soon Setia began to see patterns and forms. Pictures. Wherever she looked, all around and above, were pictures. All surfaces except the floor were covered in paintings in dun, natural colours like ochre and tan—animals, people, hands, primitive weapons and tools. Her mouth hung open. She'd heard of cave paintings but she'd never seen any in real life. She hadn't known they were so spectacular. A tingle ran down her spine. Ancient people must have created the artworks by torchlight.

Not ancient people.

Primians.

"How...?" She turned a circle, taking in the sight.

Not-Ahmad and the guards had arrived.

"How what?" Not-Ahmad asked. "These paintings are very old. They were made by our ancestors using pigments derived from plants and rocks."

"I know. We have similar paintings on Earth."

"You have? I thought that might be the case."

Setia shook her head. "This doesn't make any sense. We only invented interstellar space travel a few decades ago. I know our species are alike, but these paintings make us seem so similar it's as if humans came here somehow long ago. But that isn't possible."

"We aren't so alike," said Not-Ahmad. "Humans cannot copy as we do. That's a big difference."

"It is." She heaved a sigh. "I can't explain it. I'm not a scientist. I can't help you."

"This isn't all I have to show you. Look at this." Not-Ahmad stepped to a section of the wall, picking up one of the standing lamps on the way. "Tell me what you see." He held up the light, bringing the painted images into sharp relief. "We've established that these paintings are the oldest in this cave, and the oldest yet discovered on our planet."

Frowning as she scanned the faint markings, she began to piece together scenes. Everyone present crowded behind her. At the top of the wall was a depiction of people fighting. Arrows and spears flew through the air. Fighters hacked at each other with axes. Several figures lay prone, some headless, some with amputated limbs. One group definitely seemed to be the losing side.

Below the top picture was another scene. A third group of people had appeared, taller stick figures than the rest. They were herding the defeated into a house. Some had raised hands against the victors, who were turning to flee the scene of battle.

Setia crouched to peer at the next scene. The losers were exiting the house. Their attackers were gone and so were their saviours. The third group must have chased the aggressors away.

The final scene was at the bottom of the wall. Setia knelt down for a closer look. The picture mimicked others in the cave. People stood in water, spears in their hands, hunting water creatures presumably.

She straightened up.

"What do you make of it?" Not-Ahmad asked.

"Two sides were fighting, then some other people turn up, saved the losing side and kept them safe. When their enemy had gone, they came out of hiding and carried on living the same as normal."

He nodded. "That's one interpretation, but what do you think this is?" He pointed to the house.

She shrugged. "It's a..." She wrinkled her brow. She was no expert, but she didn't think people at that stage of development could build. "A house?"

"Is it?"

She squinted at the image. The thing was roughly oblong, it had walls, a curved roof and a couple of windows. What else could it be?

Then she noticed that the people near it stood on a lower level while the house itself appeared to hang in mid-air. "*Ohhhh.* Burnap's balls."

The archaeologist jabbered something at Not-Ahmad, her hand on her ear. News seemed to have arrived from the surface. She shot Setia a dark look.

Not-Ahmad's lips drew to a thin line. "It's begun. This has been a waste of time. You lied! You will be returned for further interrogation."

"Huh? What's begun?"

"One of our cities has been attacked. You did know about us. You've known our planet is inhabited all along, and now you've begun your extermination plan. I was a fool to believe you. You and your companion—" He swung around, his gaze sweeping the cave. "Where is she?" he demanded, glaring at Setia. "Where has she gone?"

While everyone had been focused on the cave paintings, Miriam had snuck out.

Thirty-Seven

"Where is she?!" Not-Ahmad grabbed Setia's shoulders and shook her, eyes blazing. "You two planned this, didn't you! As soon as you had the chance, one of you was to sneak away and learn all our secrets."

"Don't be stupid. How the hell were we supposed to know you would bring us down here? And what goddamned secrets could there be in these caves?"

With a grunt of frustration, Not-Ahmad thrust her away from him so hard she stumbled and fell. A guard was already on his way out of the chamber. Not-Ahmad barked at the others, causing them to hastily follow. He snapped another order. A single guard strode to Setia's side, grabbed her arm and hauled her to her feet.

Not-Ahmad and the archaeologist were deep in conversation.

Her guard's grip was so tight it cut off her blood flow. Her limb began to turn numb. She flexed her biceps to counter the effect. The guard's gaze turned to her questioningly.

She watched Not-Ahmad and the archaeologist, but there was nothing to be learned from their discussion in the foreign language.

Why had Miriam left? For someone so timid, her behaviour was odd. What did she hope to achieve? She wouldn't survive down here very long without food or water. Without food, at least. On Talman Prime, there was always water.

No doubt she would be found soon enough... or would she? The cave system was extensive. If Miriam had left as soon as their guards' attention was on the paintings rather than her, she had several minutes' start.

The conversation between the archaeologist and Not-Ahmad grew louder, and the woman gesticulated fiercely, jabbing a finger at Setia. Not-Ahmad's gaze flicked toward her. He spoke gruffly to her guard, who drew his weapon and poked her in the ribs.

It looked like they were leaving. With the guards' companions occupied in the search for Miriam, he was taking no chances of her getting away too. Now events had turned, she was in no doubt that if she made a move to escape she would be shot and killed.

All the way up from the cave system, her guard's attention hadn't wavered for an instant. He took her to a familiar room. Not-Ahmad was carrying out his intention immediately. She was to be interrogated again by Harold.

The older Primian moved from his experiment and sat opposite her, his hands knitted on his lap. Before saying anything, he regarded her steadily for several moments from under hooded eyelids. Setia's mind flashed back to Mapper Robins in his darkened office, a brilliant skein hanging in mid-air like a gigantic, intricate cobweb, and the miniature reflection in his eyes.

Robins and Harold might have much to say to each other if they were not different species separated by a gulf of conflicting desires.

Harold said, "Things have moved on quickly since we spoke."

Setia didn't know how to reply to this. She remained silent.

"It seems everything you told us was a lie."

What to say? The situation seemed hopeless. Sheldrake and Carys must have made it back to the settlement. The Primians' existence had been discovered, and the Fleet's military perceived them as a threat. She didn't condone the attack. As far as she knew, though the Primians had taken some hostages, they hadn't actually killed anyone yet. Launching an assault on a Primian city was an overreaction.

On the other hand, she was human. The Primians were the enemy. It would be wrong to give them more information. If she told Harold she'd been truthful before about the Fleet, the number of colonists, what Earth was like, and all the other myriad details she'd divulged, that might help the Primian cause.

She was in an impossible position.

"Are you going to confirm or deny the facts you revealed at our last interview?"

"Where's Ahmad?"

Harold took a moment to understand her. "He is safe."

"Send us back. Our military is attacking because they think you killed us. If you return us safe and sound, they'll call it off."

Harold softly clicked his tongue. "They don't think we killed you. That isn't the reason for the strike against our city."

"Why? They must think..." She recalled the Not-Setia walking past her cell. There was also a Not-Miriam. Perhaps there was a second Not-Ahmad walking around the new settlement right this minute. If the Primians had replaced all the humans they'd taken captive, and the replacements were doing a good job of slotting into their new roles, no one might have realised that she, Miriam and Ahmad were even missing.

Yet surely Sheldrake and Carys must have told them about Not-Ahmad's visit to their tent that night in the forest. Maybe no one had believed them, or they hadn't made it back as she'd thought. Maybe the Primians had been discovered some other way, perhaps by other colonists from one of the *Bres*'s sister ships. There were two more colonisation sites and Not-Ahmad hadn't specified where the attack was taking place.

"Besides," said Harold, "we can't send you back, not all of you. Where is your companion? What is she planning to do?"

Setia remained tight-lipped.

"It doesn't matter. She will be found, and if she is not and doesn't give herself up she will die a painful death. There's nothing in those caves to sustain her and every exit is secured."

"Let me help look for her. I'll be honest, I don't know why she slipped away. I'm worried about her."

"Out of the question. There will be no more excursions, no more opportunities for escape. From now on when you aren't here with me you will be confined to your room."

"So you aren't going to execute me if I don't tell you what you want to know? Things have changed, right?"

A flush permeated Harold's features and he clenched his jaw. It was his turn to dodge a question, but his reaction told her she was right. They probably intended to keep her, Ahmad and Miriam—if they found her—as hostages, bargaining pieces in the conflict.

He replied, "There are some things worse than death."

She flinched and her attention moved to Harold's 'experiments'.

"As you will find out if you refuse to help us defeat your people," he continued. "Think on it." He motioned to the guard. "When you return, I expect a full disclosure of the plans to take over our planet."

"Wait," she blurted as the guard marched over. "If you tell me more about what I saw in the cave I might be able to help you."

He held up a hand, signalling to the guard, who halted. "What difference could that possibly make?"

"Our species go back a long way, it seems. Am I right? Is that what Not-Ahmad thinks?"

"Not...? Oh, I see."

"That's what the cave painting shows, if I interpreted it correctly."

Harold dismissed the guard with a flick of his fingers and settled back into his seat. "Tell me what you think you saw."

She swallowed. "I think... I think you evolved on Earth too, but we were about to wipe you out." Though all her education had come from her own efforts over the years, even she knew there had once been a few kinds of intelligent ape-like species who walked upright, used tools, had culture and so on. Humans were the only ones who had survived to the present day, probably due to killing off their competitors. "Only aliens arrived and saved you. They took you into their spaceships and brought you to Prime a very long time ago. So long ago no one remembers, but the cave painting tells the tale."

A pause. "Go on."

"That's it. That's all I've got."

Or maybe not quite. In her mind's eye, three hares sharing three ears ran in a circle.

"Your interpretation is similar to Not-Ahmad's, as you call him. And a significant number of us agree with him, me included. We didn't understand fully what must have happened until you came here in your ships. Came here to finish off the work you started."

"No, no! That isn't true. I keep telling you, we had no idea Prime was inhabited. We didn't know you existed. We aren't here to commit genocide. We only wanted to settle here."

"Why? Is your world no longer habitable?"

"No, it is." If anything, conditions on Earth were the best they'd ever been. "We did it out of a spirit of adventure. The colonists want to explore new places, live somewhere different."

Harold frowned.

"Don't you have people like that? People who want to push boundaries and set off into the unknown?" Yet... that hadn't been *her* reason for leaving Earth, and she wasn't sure it was the majority feeling among the Fleet's civilians. It was more like they were so wealthy nothing excited their interest anymore. An interstellar voyage and a new world were just novelties to relieve their general boredom.

Harold seemed confused. Maybe the urge to discover new places didn't exist among Primians. She was confused too, and worried—worried about Miriam. Guilt over the woman's disappearance nagged at her. She'd been very cold toward her, and though it was justified, Miriam was sensitive. Their falling out could have been at least part of her motivation for slipping away.

"What you're saying makes no sense," said Harold, "which means it isn't true." He beckoned the guard again. "I want you to consider your way forward. If you refuse to tell me what I want to know, I will be forced to use other methods to extract the information."

Thirty-Eight

Twilight was falling along with a gentle, misty rain. Setia rested her forehead on the windowpane, staring out into the darkening landscape. The shadows on the opposite hills betrayed no sign of lights within the dwellings. There had to be some property of the 'glass' that kept light in while allowing people to look out. The Primians' technology was an odd mixture. They had comm, even deep within caves, yet they didn't seem to have invented bugging tech. Maybe they'd had no need of it.

They also had weapons, but they fired projectiles rather than pulses. Generating electricity wasn't a problem—Prime had plentiful resources for it—yet they hadn't made the leap to use the power offensively. They had lifts and presumably travelled underground through tunnels, yet they hadn't invented aircraft.

She narrowed her eyes at the rain. Maybe it wasn't so surprising they hadn't mastered flight. Hardly anything seemed to fly on this planet. And without aircraft, they wouldn't have been able to take the next step: space flight.

What did Primians make of stars? Did they know they were suns like their own, many of them orbited by planets? The arrival of the Fleet must have been a huge surprise. Then aliens very similar to themselves had descended to their planet. Intelligent minds like Not-

Ahmad and Harold's had drawn the credible conclusion that Primians were under threat. She couldn't blame them for their line of thinking. Humans on Earth probably would have reacted the same, assuming the worst about the new arrivals. The cave painting had only added weight to their guesswork.

What was the story behind the attack on a Primian city? There had to be more to it than an unprovoked assault but, naturally, Not-Ahmad and his buddies only saw their side of things.

What was happening on the *Bres* and her sister ships? The Fleet captains knew now that Prime was inhabited by an intelligent species. Surely there had to be more to their understanding. Someone as experienced as Bujold wouldn't order a military strike without a good reason.

Setia closed her eyes tightly. She couldn't tell Harold what he wanted to know. The situation had turned and made her look like a liar. Now he wouldn't believe anything that came out of her mouth. What tortures did he have in store? What a shame that, when Arief had imbued her with strength and fighting abilities, he hadn't also made her impervious to pain.

Alongside her fear of what lay ahead was the heavy foreboding that Prime was on the verge of war. How much death and destruction would take place? Humans had technological superiority, but Primians had far greater numbers and would be fighting on their home turf. The underground had to be riddled with their tunnels. Guerilla warfare could go on forever, fulfilling the prophecy Not-Ahmad had interpreted from the cave painting, that humans killed Primians and they'd arrived to finish the job they'd started.

A vibration ran through the floor, snapping her eyes open. Another tremor. Even here in a presumably stable area, tectonic activity plagued the place. She held onto the window sill. There was nothing in the room to fall on her. The vibrations built. The earthquake was a strong one—and she was glad. She looked over her shoulder. Would the tremor break the door from its surroundings, or maybe it would take out the power supply and deactivate the lock? But, no, the latter was unlikely. Unless the Primians were very dumb, a power cut should make the door remain shut, not open it.

The vibrations faded. Less than a minute after it started, the quake was over and she remained trapped. A sinking feeling in her gut, she returned her attention to the exterior. Dusk now hung over the hills. The rain had stopped and stars shone from between the threads of dissipating clouds. The tremor didn't seem to have affected anything but it was hard to tell. Shadows cloaked most of the ground in the dim light.

There was movement.

Something was moving in the darkness.

Some *things*.

Her breath seized in her throat.

What was she seeing?

Her mind flew back to the rain creatures, hulking, menacing beings made from moisture.

But it could not be them. There was no rain.

Pressing her nose against the window, she squinted at the indistinct forms. They were smaller than the rain creatures, though they were humanoid. Perhaps they were only Primians, outside for some unknown reason. They must go out sometimes. She recalled the trampled vegetation outside the electric fence after the group's first night's camp. That had to have been Primians investigating the newcomers.

Briefly, the head of one mysterious approacher rose into a bright patch of starlight, and she exhaled with recognition. She'd seen a helmet, the helmet of one of the armoured EVA suits the Fleet's military wore. She would have recognised that black eye-slit anywhere. Then it was gone.

Fleet soldiers were nearing the hill. Did they know it was inhabited? Were they reconnoitring the area, preparing for an attack? Or were they on their way to some other place? Was Corporal Sheldrake among them?

There was no way the Primians were not aware of the enemy

soldiers. After the assault on their city they would be on high alert. The troops were about to come under fire.

"Hey!" She hammered on the window. "Hey! Watch out! Get back! Fall back!" Her fists dully thumped the pane. There was no reaction from the soldiers. They couldn't hear her. "Retreat!" she exclaimed hopelessly, her hands falling to her sides.

But maybe it wasn't a bad thing that her warning had fallen on deaf ears. Maybe the military was here to rescue her and Miriam. Maybe they knew, somehow, about the captives inside the hill. It seemed unlikely but she was willing to hold onto the hope, knowing the alternative that lay in wait.

Clouds moved in, cutting out the starlight. Now, all was black, impenetrable night.

A scrabbling sound distracted her. It was coming from the door. Had a guard arrived to take her back to Harold? Was she being moved to another place as a precaution against the oncoming attack? The noise seemed to take too long for the simple opening of the lock.

She moved to the door and held an ear against it, trying to figure out what was going on.

The faint scratching sounds continued.

What could it be?

She had a vision of Primian mice, gnawing at the—

The door opened, banging into the side of her head.

"Ow! What the...? Miriam?!" She uttered the last word as a hiss, managing to moderate her voice at the last second.

"Shhhh!" Miriam glanced fearfully from side to side. "Come on." She grabbed Setia's wrist.

Setia didn't need any further encouragement. She hurried down the passageway with her rescuer. "How did you do that?" she whispered.

"You never attended a private school, did you?"

"I never attended any... No, I didn't."

"One of the first things the older girls would teach new students was how to break out of the dorms. And Primian security is absolute shit. All I needed was access to the panels."

"So we can get out? Do you know the way?"

"I think so. Had to pick you up first."

It wasn't true. Miriam could have left by herself if she'd wanted. She'd taken an additional risk in getting Setia out too.

"Thanks," Setia said.

Miriam winked. "Like I'd leave you behind."

Thirty-Nine

"Wait," Setia hissed, abruptly halting.

"What's wrong?"

"It's too early. We should go back and wait until later, when everyone's asleep."

"Nearly everyone's already asleep. Everything shut down a couple of hours ago. That's when I decided it was safe to find you. Come on, hurry."

Setia took a step but then halted again as a second worry hit.

"What now?!" Miriam blurted.

Setia couldn't say, only stare at her companion distrustfully.

"I know that look," Miriam said. "For goodness sake, if I wasn't really me do you think I would be breaking you out of here?"

It was a good point. It would have to be a seriously screwy, convoluted plan that involved allowing her to escape.

"All right," Setia said. "Let's—"

Footsteps approached.

Shit.

They shared an alarmed look, then both simultaneously looked back at the room they'd just left. They would never make it there in time before—

A guard rounded the corner. His eyes popped and his mouth opened as he took a breath, preparing to shout. At the same time, his hand moved to his gun.

Setia threw herself at him. Her punch knocked him into the wall, eliciting a heavy grunt. As he collapsed, she whispered fiercely to Miriam, "Get his weapon!" She ripped off his helmet, ignoring the pain from her knuckles, silently grateful his head covering wasn't made of metal, and clamped a hand over his mouth.

While Miriam grappled with him, fighting for control of the gun, Setia thrust him to the floor. Muffled shouts fought their way out of him. She couldn't maintain her grip over his mouth and get a clear blow to knock him out. He was too close to the wall.

Miriam let out a soft squeal. The guard had a hold of one of her hands and was twisting it, forcing the wrist backwards.

Dammit!

The fight had already gone on too long. It was time to put a quick end to it, despite the risks. Setia released the man's mouth. Leaping up, she kicked him sharply in the head. His exclamation was cut off and he went limp.

"Got it," murmured Miriam, holding the gun in one hand while nursing her sore wrist under her armpit.

Setia grabbed the guard's ankles and dragged him to the room. She crammed his mouth with toilet paper and tied a towel around his head. Then she tied him to the bed legs with sheets. By the time she finished he was beginning to come around. She kicked his head, sending him back to unconsciousness.

Then she took the weapon from Miriam and shut the door.

They ran.

After a minute, Setia said, "You're sure you know the way out?"

"I told you I think so. I couldn't actually *go* out, you know."

The Primian habitation was laid out in a regular fashion. Setia could remember the route from her room to Harold's lab and to the council chamber, but Miriam took her a new way. She must have been creeping around the place for a while to have figured out the layout. It probably helped that she was petite and dark and at first glance might have passed for a local. She was also dressed like a Primian, as Setia was.

Yet they couldn't risk being spotted now. The guard's absence would be noted soon, even if he didn't manage to make it out of her room and raise the alert.

Miriam pressed a hand to Setia's shoulder, signalling her to stop. She gently pushed a door open just a crack and listened. After a moment, she pushed the door again. It gave a faint squeak as it fully opened. Beyond it was a metal stairwell.

"This leads to an exit," she whispered. "Most of the exits are underground, but I'm pretty sure this one goes outside. See?" She nodded at the stair treads.

Faint traces of mud besmirched the steel grips.

"Have you been down there?" Setia asked.

"I couldn't risk it."

"So you don't know if the exit's guarded?"

Miriam shook her head.

Setia hadn't told her yet about the Fleet's military combing the area. If the Primians knew, and they almost certainly did, the exit was guarded.

They stepped onto the landing and closed the door. The stairwell was silent. Miriam approached the stairs but Setia held her back.

She inspected the gun. The grip, barrel, and trigger were familiar, but it also had to contain Primian projectiles somewhere inside. Where exactly didn't matter. What did matter was the fact there was a finite supply. Pulse weapons usually held a hefty charge when full, but this gun might only be able to fire a few times. She would have to make every shot count.

Peeking over the banister rail, she tried to see what lay below. The stairs turned five or six times before reaching the bottom. At this angle, all she could see was a featureless floor. Pointing behind her to indicate Miriam should follow, she began to descend on tiptoes, keeping to the wall side of the stairs. As she crept downwards, she strained her ears for any kind of noise.

There it was.

She froze. Miriam had heard it too and also stopped.

Murmuring echoed up from below. Male voices in quiet conversation. There was no doubt what it meant. Escaping wasn't going to be easy.

Still, if she could get clear shots at the guards, and if the door was unlocked...

She bit her lip. Firing her weapon just once would bring every Primian in the place running.

A squeak came from above.

Miriam gasped.

A set of heavy footsteps descended.

Shit, shit, shit.

Setia ran lightly down the stairs. Miriam followed at the same pace.

They turned a curve in the stairwell and then another. As they rounded the third, Setia caught sight of the top of the exit door—and two guards' helmets flanking it. She drew to a sudden halt, but Miriam didn't stop in time. She barrelled into Setia's back. Bracing herself against the wall and steps at the last minute Setia managed to stay upright, but Miriam overbalanced and tumbled down, rolling from step to step.

A shout echoed out. The heavy footsteps sped up.

There was no time to prepare. No time for anything.

Setia stuck her head into the stairwell, aimed downwards and fired. The weapon bucked in her hand. She aimed and fired again.

She'd been instantly deafened. The explosions had reduced all sound to a piercing whistle.

The guards standing each side of the door had fallen, but she had no idea if she'd killed or only wounded them. Miriam sprawled on the bottom step, groaning.

Setia flew down the remaining stairs. Miriam didn't seem to have broken anything. She only seemed dazed. One of the guards was dead, blood pouring from his neck. The other was still moving. Setia shot him, leapt over Miriam and tried the door.

Locked.

Another explosion punctured her hearing.

Who was shooting?

Miriam had turned onto all fours and was crawling over.

"Watch out!" Setia yelled, though her voice came through like a muffled whisper. She peeked upwards. A gun barrel was angled over the railing. She fired at it but missed. She fired and missed again, but the barrel withdrew.

That made five shots. How many did she have left?

Miriam had got to her feet and was staring in horror at the dead guards, her hand over her mouth.

"Open the door!" Setia jabbed a finger at the locked exit.

She fired another shot upwards.

Six.

A shout rang out from the Primian with the gun. What he'd said, she had no idea. An order? A demand? A threat? Perhaps he'd been calling up to new arrivals, warning them. For all she knew the stairs could be filled with them. She'd barely heard the shout.

Miriam tugged her arm, pointed at the door and shook her head.

Setia gave it a quick look. There didn't seem to be a security panel for Miriam to access.

"Must be a mechanical lock," she said, raising her voice to hear herself speak. "Search the guards for a key."

Miriam cupped a hand to her ear.

Setia fired off another shot upstairs.

Seven.

Then she mimed what she meant.

Dismay and revulsion filled Miriam's features.

"Just do it!" Setia could swear she could hear the thud of many booted feet approaching, but maybe it was only the pounding of her heart.

Another shot.

Eight.

There had been no sign of their attacker for what felt like a while, but was probably less than a minute. He had to be confident they were trapped and that reinforcements would arrive soon. He saw no reason to risk his life when they couldn't possibly escape.

Which meant…

Miriam's hands were bloody from searching the dead men when Setia motioned to her to stop.

"They don't have the key."

Miriam's lips formed the words, *Then what do we do*?

Setia pushed her aside. There was no handle on the door. She hoped it opened outwards.

There was the keyhole.

She fired next to it. The material burst apart, leaving a gaping hole, but when she kicked the door it didn't yield. She fired again, creating another gaping crater. She kicked again, feeling a slight give.

Thrusting the gun into Miriam's hands, she yelled at her to shoot up the stairwell.

Mustering all her abnormal strength, she drove her heel into the door at the site of the damage. The material splintered and shook, but still the door didn't open.

The explosion of a gunshot rent the air. Miriam had fired.

Screaming her frustration and effort, she kicked again and again. At the fourth or fifth try, the material parted from the lock and the door burst open.

She grabbed Miriam, but the woman resisted her pull. She looked at her in confusion.

Miriam had dropped the gun and was staring at her bloody hands. Her mouth hung open.

"Come on!"

But Miriam only touched her thigh and then stared at her hand again.

She wasn't looking at the blood from the dead guards. She was looking at her own blood.

The explosion Setia had heard hadn't been Miriam firing.

She'd been shot.

The feet of guards appeared on the stairs.

Setia thrust a shoulder into Miriam's middle, heaved her up, and ran out into the night.

Forty

The Primians hadn't followed.

Setia couldn't believe it. She'd heard them take shots, but—thank Burnap—they'd missed. Why had no one come after them?

As she ran, she risked a backwards glance and caught a glimpse of Primians clustered in the doorway, silhouetted against the light. Another glance a couple of seconds later revealed that the door was shut.

The thick, soft vegetation she pounded through grabbed at her calves. She slowed down, fearing she would trip and send Miriam flying. Her hearing was beginning to return, and soon she heard the swish of her legs running through the groundcover and her panting breath.

"Miriam, are you okay?"

The woman murmured a reply. At least she hadn't lost consciousness.

Setia checked to their rear for a third time. Even the light leaking from the closed door was lost in darkness. Maybe the Primians had killed the lights in the stairwell or covered up the damage.

The reason they hadn't come after the escapees hit: the Fleet's military was in the area. The Primians didn't want to risk running into enemy soldiers or reveal the presence of the hillside habitation.

She slowed her pace further and her breathing eased. They were out. They were safe. All they had to do was to find someone from their side. There had to be medics among the soldiers who could treat Miriam. Soon, they would be on a shuttle back to the *Bres*, where they could rest and recuperate. They would be able to provide valuable intel, and then leave it to the people in charge to deal with the Primians as they saw fit.

Figuring out a colonisation plan in the new situation would be a gnarly problem, but it wasn't hers to solve.

It was over.

She halted and gently lifted Miriam from her shoulder before laying her down. Miriam gasped as she moved her.

"How's your leg?" Setia felt for the wound. She could barely see her in the shrouded night.

"I think... Not too bad... Ow!"

"Sorry." Setia had located the hole where the projectile had hit. It was slick with warm blood. She took off her belt and slipped it under Miriam's thigh. "This is gonna hurt, but I want to try to slow the bleeding."

"All right. Do I—arghhh!"

Setia had snapped the belt tight quickly. Not too tight. She didn't want to cut off the circulation to the rest of Miriam's leg. The wounds from the Primians' weapons were odd. There was little to no burning but a helluva lot of blood loss.

She waited for Miriam's gasps to ease. "Is it okay if I carry you again? Our soldiers are in the area. I want to find one."

"They are?" Miriam's breathing laboured. "Leave me here while you look."

"I can't. I wouldn't be able to locate you, especially not if you pass out."

"Uhh... I can try to walk a little."

Setia helped her up. Miriam leaned heavily on her shoulder and hopped on her good leg. Their progress was slow but they were moving. Setia scanned around. No tell-tale glints from armour shone in the darkness, but the suits' skins were probably camouflaged.

Should she risk calling out?

"I tried shooting up the stairs like you told me," Miriam gasped, "but I couldn't get the gun to work."

"You pressed the trigger hard?"

"As hard as I could. Nothing happened."

Setia recalled firing at the door twice. That brought the total of shots she'd taken to ten. She'd given Miriam an empty gun. That's why she'd been hit. She hadn't been able to defend herself. "I'm sorry. That wasn't your fault."

"Can we stop? I feel dizzy."

They'd reached a cleft between two hills. The ground was rising and Miriam was struggling with the incline.

"I could carry you," Setia offered.

"I'd rather you didn't. It hurts more, and it makes me feel like a sack of potatoes."

It was probably just as well. Setia had a feeling blood loss was causing Miriam to feel faint. She needed to elevate her leg.

"Just a little way," Setia said. She'd spotted what looked like a hollow, somewhere to rest until daybreak. "Then we can stop for a long time."

Miriam muttered her agreement, and Setia picked her up. This time, she didn't put the woman over her shoulder but carried her in both arms.

"This is so silly," Miriam complained.

Setia carried her up to the hollow and then put her down gently, angling her wounded leg upwards. Miriam lay down with a sigh.

"As soon as it's light," said Setia, "I'll go for help." She didn't want to abandon Miriam, even if it meant the Fleet's soldiers might have left the area.

"What a pickle," Miriam murmured. "And I thought I was doing you a favour getting you out of that place. It might have been better if we'd both stayed inside."

"No way." Setia didn't divulge what Harold had threatened. The topic was too dark for their current circumstances. "You did the right thing. I didn't think..."

"I was up to it? It's okay. You can say it. You think I'm an over-privileged idiot. A stupid, spoilt rich girl."

"I don't see you like that."

"But you did, right?"

Setia was silent.

"Don't worry. I'm not offended. I'm used to people dismissing me. It's been happening all my life."

"Has it?" Setia found it hard to believe. She'd always envied the lives of the ultra-wealthy. Her upbringing had been diametrically opposite to Miriam's. She couldn't imagine anything about the woman's experiences could have been challenging or difficult. It was hard to not scoff but she kept quiet.

"I told you once my parents didn't seem to like me much. The truth was, as I found out when I was about ten, I was an accident. My mother and father had only ever wanted one child. After they had my sister, that was supposed to be it. But then I came along, and by the time my mother realised she was pregnant, it was too late for her to do anything about it. They weren't overtly cruel, but they doted on my sister while ignoring me. I was raised by a succession of nannies until I was sent away to school and forgotten."

"But it must have been nice to go to a private school," Setia countered. She would have appreciated the opportunity to go to *any* school.

"You would think so. The school was okay and most of the students seemed happy, but I didn't fit in. The other girls were into cool clothes, hair and make-up. They knew all the popular bands, the latest fashions, the best drugs. They would bribe the teachers to let them pass, but I was actually interested in the school work. The teachers liked me, which made my classmates hate me. I didn't have the social skills to change their opinion, and I wasn't sure I wanted to try. By then, I was already comfortable with being the odd one out. I suppose I still am."

Setia took her hand, not knowing what to say.

"Sorry for all the self-pity. I guess I'm not feeling too good."

"You've lost a lot of blood. I should tighten the belt."

"I don't know about that. I already can't feel my leg."

Setia patted the ground next to Miriam's thigh. It was sticky.

Lightning flashed, quickly followed by a soft rumble of thunder. A burst of heavy raindrops fell.

"Great," Setia muttered. "That's all we need." She took off her jacket and draped it over Miriam. "This should keep you dry for a while. If the rain continues I'll see if I can find us somewhere to shelter."

There was no reply.

"Miriam? Did you hear me?" Setia gave her shoulder a little shake. When she didn't respond, Setia tried again, repeating her name. Miriam's body was limp.

She'd passed out. She must have passed out.

The way to be sure was to check for a pulse or breathing, but Setia couldn't bring herself to try. She swallowed hard as the rain wet her back.

She'd been a bitch to Miriam ever since they'd met. She'd rebuffed her attempts to be friendly. She'd been disdainful and borderline rude. She'd been just as awful towards Miriam as Carys had been to her and not even realised what a hypocrite she was.

And in return, Miriam hadn't once complained. She'd been kind and gentle, and although she'd revealed all she knew about the Fleet to the Primians, it had been because she thought it would help prevent a conflict. She wasn't the traitor Setia had accused her of being. She'd been trying to make peace.

What was more, despite all Setia's coldness, Miriam had come for her and helped her escape. In spite of everything, she'd remained loyal.

Setia hung her head.

The rain soaked her hair, ran down her face and dripped from her nose and chin.

Forty-One

It wasn't until some time later the soldiers found them. Setia was crouching over Miriam to try to keep the rain off her. She'd lost track of time, and she was watching the sky, yearning for any sign of the approaching dawn.

Perhaps the soldiers had crept up quietly, or the patter of raindrops masked the sound of their movements, or Setia was simply too distracted by guilt and regret, but the first she knew that they'd been discovered was the jab of a muzzle in her back and the barked order to raise her hands.

Even then, she didn't twig the situation. All she knew was someone from the ship was here, and that Miriam might still be saved.

"Thank the stars!" She swung around. "Do you have a medic? My friend's been—"

The muzzle poked her in the chest. "Hands up!"

Confused, she tentatively lifted her hands into the air. "There's no need... We're from the *Bres*..."

The inscrutable visors of three soldiers confronted her, along with three rifles. She glanced to the side and saw two more move behind her.

"I think there's been a misunderstanding."

"Stand up."

After she complied, one of the soldiers searched her.

"Look," she said, "I don't know what's going on, but my friend needs urgent medical attention."

"Hands behind your back."

They cuffed her. *Cuffed her*!

"What the hell are you doing?! I just told you I'm from the *Bres*! My name's Setia Zees. I was sent out on a mission weeks ago with Corporal Sheldrake, Carys Ellis and Miriam Belby. That's Miriam lying behind me. We were captured by Primians and we've just escaped. Miriam's been shot."

The soldiers ignored every word.

One of them jerked his rifle towards the hills, where a patch of lighter sky heralded the rising sun. "Move."

"Okay," she said. "I get how it looks. We're dressed as Primians. I guess we can sort this out later when we get back to the ship, but can we hurry? I'm worried about Miriam."

"We're gonna hurry all right."

A couple of soldiers went in front, setting a fast pace. Directly behind her, a third carried Miriam. Two more brought up the rear. It was hard to march quickly over the rough terrain with her hands fastened behind her back. Within a minute, she stumbled.

"Get up!" someone barked. "Move it!"

From the way the men moved their heads it was clear they were talking to each other via comm. There was a sense of urgency as they walked. Although she appreciated their speed for Miriam's sake, she didn't think it was due to concern for the well-being of her friend. Something else was up.

The ground rapidly rose. Soon, she was bending forwards into the slope, struggling to maintain her balance. Even the soldiers were forced to use their free hands to grab at the strange vegetation. The sun peeked from behind clouds a little above the horizon, casting a glow over the eerie purple landscape.

"Down!"

A hand shoved Setia into the hillside. Shocked and confused, she craned her neck to see what was going on.

A brighter glow than sunlight lit the sky.

A brilliant streak of light passed overhead.

A blast exploded.

The hand remained firm on her back, but she managed to look over her shoulder. One of the hills to the rear had been blown open. A warren of tunnels and chambers was exposed like an opened ant nest, and in the distance she could see tiny figures of people lying among the ruins. A few moved feebly. Most were still.

"Burnap's balls! Was that from the *Bres*?"

"Shut up. Get to your feet."

Numbly, she complied. She didn't know what to feel about what had just happened. Though she'd become disoriented in the dark of the night, she was fairly certain the Fleet had attacked the place she'd been held captive. Not-Ahmad, Harold, the archaeologist who had shown her the cave paintings, and the rest of the Primians she'd encountered were dead or injured.

She should have been happy, but she was not.

Maybe it was only concern for Miriam that was bothering her. When she'd looked back, she'd also caught sight of her friend. Miriam's face had been chalk-white and her body was as limp as a rag doll.

No one believed her. All the way to the *Bres*, she tried to get the attention of the soldiers, but they ignored her. As the shuttle docked, they deactivated their armour and filed off the vessel, acting as though she didn't exist. She was last to leave, still restrained, along with two guards. As she was forced along the *Bres*'s corridors she didn't give up on her efforts to convince them about who she was.

"Take me to Mapper Robins. He knows me. He sent me on the mission to the planet. He'll vouch for me." She racked her brains for who else might recognise her, but she'd made precious few friends during the voyage, preferring to keep to herself. "I can tell you my cabin number and section. I'm on the manifest."

Her guards stared impassively ahead.

"Did Carys Ellis and Corporal Sheldrake make it back? You must know Sheldrake. You can ask him about me. He knows who I am."

They didn't answer, and eventually she gave up. It was pointless. The soldiers were just grunts following orders.

They took her to the brig. The place was quite extensive, as it turned out, though all the cells were empty. They put her inside one of them and removed her cuffs. As the door slid closed she ran to it and pressed herself against the transparent surface. "Can you at least tell me how Miriam's doing? Is she going to be okay?"

The soldiers left.

She trudged to the bunk and sat down, resting her elbows on her knees and cupping her jaw in her palms. What was happening? She couldn't figure it out. Did they really believe she was a Primian? Or was there another reason for locking her up?

Didn't the soldiers know about the mission she'd been on? She guessed it still wasn't common knowledge. But they had to know Ahmad had been taken prisoner, and other engineers at the settlement site must have seen her and her companions arrive from the ship and then set off.

When she'd left the *Bres* most of the passengers hadn't even known they'd arrived at Prime. They wouldn't know where she'd gone. Did they know they were in orbit now? Had the announcement been made, or were they still in the dark? Was the Fleet's military carrying out its campaign in secret? Was it cleansing the planet of the natives, removing the competition, making way for a simple, fast colonisation?

She shuddered.

Everything was screwed up.

A heavy fear hit: Was she a liability because she might reveal what was going on? Would she be silenced?

She lay down, put her hands behind her head and stared sightlessly at the ceiling. What would happen to her now?

She had to cling to the hope that her worries were needless. Sooner or later, somehow or other, the stupid mistake would be revealed and she would be set free. She could tell the Fleet commanders what she'd learned about the Primians, though the notion made her queasy as she recalled the sight of the Primian habitation, blasted apart.

Hours passed, and there was no sign of anyone. Her anxiety gave way to fatigue. She felt herself slipping into sleep. She fought, but it was no use. After the many trials she'd endured, her body needed rest. Her last thought was the realisation that her prison cell was larger than her cabin.

Muffled voices woke her.

Instantly, she sat up. Two figures were looking in.

One, she didn't immediately recognise. It was an older man in uniform.

The other person was herself. She was staring into her own eyes. Not-Setia wasn't dressed in Primian clothes, however. She wore an outfit the real Setia had packed for the voyage.

The Primian was nodding in answer to a question from the uniformed man. It was Lieutenant-Colonel Markham, commander of the *Bres*'s military.

Not-Setia's words came faintly through the barrier. "I told you they made a copy of me, didn't I? She's an alien spy."

Forty-Two

Tormented by her fears, Setia didn't sleep well after her initial exhausted slumber. As the days went by, she alternated between exhorting whatever shadowy figures she glimpsed at the end of the corridor to take her to Mapper Robins, who would explain everything, telling them she was the real Setia Zees, that the person walking around the ship was a Primian, that one of the enemy lived within their midst—and dozing on her bunk, hoping Miriam had survived and wondering what had happened to Sheldrake and Carys.

They couldn't have made it back to the settlement. If they had, they would have explained about Not-Ahmad's visit in the forest, and that she'd stayed behind with Miriam. Or maybe they had. The Fleet knew about the Primians' ability to copy, or Not-Setia couldn't have pulled her trick, setting everything up in case the real Setia arrived.

Was that the only reason she was here, or was it part of a bigger plan? Maybe Carys and Sheldrake had been captured by Primians too. Were their doppelgängers on the *Bres* right now, confirming whatever story Not-Setia had told?

What a mess.

The more she thought about it, myriad potential scenarios

fanned out in her head like the tributaries of a great river—the river of conflict between the Fleet and the Primians. Where would it lead?

She couldn't see a way out. How could she make anyone believe her? She couldn't argue against Not-Setia's story when she didn't know what it was. What else had Not-Setia told them?

Whenever her food was brought in, she would repeat her requests. When she was inevitably ignored she would ask for news of the attacks on Prime. This sometimes brought a flicker of hesitancy, as if the guard had significant news to impart if he or she were allowed, but that was it. If she could only speak to Robins...

On the fourth day, she thought of a plan. All her protestations and shouting had come to nothing, She needed another tactic and she'd hit upon it.

Two could play at Not-Setia's game.

She waited tensely for her meal to arrive.

A female guard brought it. Setia sat on the other side of the hatch, watching. The guard opened her side of the hatch and slid the meal in.

"Ughhh, not human slop again," Setia said. "How do you guys eat this stuff?"

The guard made eye contact. She pursed her lips and closed the hatch door.

The door on Setia's side clicked open, but she didn't remove the meal. "Seriously, I can't stand your food. I'd do anything for something good to eat."

The guard frowned but still didn't reply.

As she turned to leave, Setia repeated, "*Anything.* I mean it. I'm sick of pretending to be one of you. Tell your boss I'm ready to talk, but only in return for some privileges."

The guard curled her lip. "No one wants your intel. We have the situation completely under control. It won't be long until—"

"Are you sure about that? You don't know what you don't know. Do you guys even know who I really am?"

Uncertainty clouded the guard's features.

"It'll come out eventually. When it also comes out that I made an offer to talk but *you* didn't pass it on, boy, you'll be in trouble."

The guard gave her a searching look and then left without another word.

Setia sat on her bunk and waited.

She waited a long time. Her midday meal remained where it was, growing cold and congealed.

After a couple of hours, she was rewarded with the sight of three guards approaching. It could mean only one thing.

Only it didn't. Not quite.

Setia stared, open-mouthed, at the person the guards had brought her to see. "You? Why you?!"

Wulandri's eyebrow rose. "Who were you expecting? The captain? She has more important things to do than listen to the pathetic prattle of a subhuman adversary. If you actually have anything useful to impart, you can tell me."

"I don't get it," Setia said. "You're supposed to be co-ordinating the colonisation. You're not military. How come you're talking to prisoners?"

Wulandri snorted derisively. "Nice try. I see you've done your research. But I'm the one asking the questions. What is it you want to reveal that you think is so important?"

"This is bullshit. I'm not talking to you."

"I think you'll find you are."

"Take me to Bujold or Markham, or *anyone* with some kind of power on this ship."

From the way Wulandri's eyes narrowed, it was clear she didn't take the not-so-veiled insult well. "You'll talk or you'll return to your cell. Your choice."

The fact that she hadn't immediately sent Setia back indicated that Wulandri was hoping to learn something useful—not necessarily useful for the invasion but useful to her.

Things started to make sense. The entire plan had changed. A few weeks ago, the intention had been to colonise a planet devoid of other intelligent beings. Talman Prime turned out to be not quite as advertised. The colonists would have to adjust to a stark reality. But now things were even worse than anyone imagined. A human-like species inhabited the new world, taking up space, using up resources, acting like they *owned* the place.

Awkward.

Someone had decided this just wouldn't do. A new plan was needed. Whether it was only to subdue the Primians to ease the invasion, or to wipe them out completely, Setia didn't know. But she understood why she was talking to Wulandri. The woman was out of a job. All the talks she'd given, all her organising and preparations, had come to nothing. Consequently, perhaps out of pity, she'd been given a consolation prize. She had some kind of liaison role in the military. She was a nonentity, without power. She wanted to feel important again.

Maybe Setia could give her that. "Look, when I confessed to the guard I really was from Prime I was lying. I'm the real Setia Zees, and I can prove it to you."

Wulandri huffed a sigh and rolled her eyes. She gestured to the guards at the door.

"We're from the same country." Setia said hastily as the guards approached. "I know things only someone from there would know. Things not on the database. Things no one could look up." She had a hunch that when the Primians 'copied' someone, they only gained a superficial level of knowledge about them. Not-Setia would have done more research since arriving on the *Bres*, but some things about her native land weren't mentioned in the records in the ship's database, which only contained sanitised versions of Earth history.

The guard ordered her to stand, but she continued talking quickly. "Our president has had loads of affairs, one with a Hollywood actress. Uhh, I forget her name." She'd never been interested in celebrity scuttlebutt.

"That's no big secret," Wulandri scoffed.

"Get up!" a guard snapped.

"But it isn't mentioned in the database. What about...?" She hastily rummaged through her memory. "You're about the same age as me. When we were kids a pollution scandal was covered up. NexGen ChemWorks discharged poisonous waste into the water supply for Spiral City. The company kept it out of the official news channels but everyone knew about it. Everyone knew someone who got sick or died."

"Name me a poor country that didn't have a pollution scandal back then."

"Oh, come on! Who else would know that?"

"Take her away," Wulandri told the guards.

What else? Setia racked her brains as she was hauled to the door. "I know! Dumadi." It was the name of a famous TV producer. "It was a badly kept secret that he was a sleazy bastard involved in organised crime. No one dared say—"

The door slid closed. As she was frog-marched away, Setia twisted in the guard's grasp, hoping to see Wulandri emerge from her room. Surely she would come to the realisation that only the real Setia Zees could possibly know the facts she'd stated?

But Wulandri didn't appear.

The colonisation coordinator was as stubborn as she was stupid. Setia cursed and struggled. She'd had a chance to gain her freedom and she'd blown it. Would she ever get the opportunity to talk to anyone else? Why, of all the people on the ship, did Wulandri have to be her point of contact? The woman had been prejudiced against her from the first time they'd met at passenger processing. She was the last person prepared to lend her a friendly ear. Hell, she might even have guessed she'd been talking to the real Setia, but she just didn't care.

Setia was dragged through the passageways in a very undignified manner, attracting stares all the way. She contemplated attempting to break free, but both her guards were armed and she wore restraints. Once she was back in the brig, she didn't know when she would get another chance to prove who she was, if ever. When she reached the brig's entrance she'd almost given up hope, but then she spotted a familiar face.

"Carys!" she bellowed.

Carys was passing the end of a busy passageway.

"Shut your mouth," a guard warned.

"Carys! It's me, Setia!"

Everyone between them gaped. Her guard was talking on the intercom to gain admittance to the brig.

Carys had halted but she wasn't coming any closer. Setia couldn't read her expression, but that wasn't unusual. Carys kept her feelings tightly under wraps.

The door to the brig slid open.

As Setia was pushed inside, she yelled, "I saw Loki! The Primians have him."

Forty-Three

Exhausted by long nights of sleeplessness and miserable from her failure to convince Wulandri she was human, Setia had fallen into a deep slumber. She was buried in profound unconsciousness when a sense of panic jerked her awake.

She could not breathe.

Something was clamped over her mouth and nose.

Blind in the utter darkness, she tore at the thing and yelled, though the sound was muffled.

Warm breath tickled her ear as a voice hissed almost too quiet to be heard, "*Shut up. It's me.*"

She became still, and the hand left her face.

The voice continued, "We only have a few minutes."

"I can't see shit," Setia hissed back.

Fingers poked her arm and moved down to her hand before grasping it. Setia crept from her bunk. The guiding hand tugged at hers, and she followed in the direction indicated. Noiselessly tiptoeing on bare feet, she snuck out of her cell.

The lights in the brig passageway were never off but tonight they were. Setia reached out in front of her as she moved quickly along. At the end of the passageway the door slid open easily, as if it wasn't powered. A confused conversation was going on somewhere in the darkness. She sped away with her companion.

As they entered a main thoroughfare Carys said, “Act normal, but walk fast.”

“Act normal in pyjamas and no shoes?”

“Just do it.”

The two women didn’t speak again until they reached the end of their journey.

“Inside,” said Carys. “Quick.”

Setia stepped into a small cabin. Carys followed her, thumbed the lock, pressed her back against the door. She closed her eyes and exhaled, her body oozing tension. Then she went to the interface screen on the wall and checked it.

“They’ll know where I am,” said Setia.

“Hopefully not,” Carys murmured. She closed the screen. “Robins reckoned his contact could crash the security OS in this section for five minutes.”

“But people saw us.”

Even during the quiet shift there were always people about—bar flies, insomniacs, manual workers. Her attire had attracted attention.

Carys replied, “No one saw us come in here.”

“But this will be the first place they look. I didn’t know you lived so close to the brig.”

“Lucky for you I do. Don’t worry. You won’t be here long.” Carys went to a cupboard, took out some clothes and handed them over. “Get changed.”

Carys’s crew uniform was slightly too big. The cuffs hung over Setia’s knuckles and the trouser legs bunched up at her ankles. “This is never going to work.”

“It will.” Carys looked pensive. “It has to.” She put her cap on Setia’s head.

“I don’t have your ponytail.”

“I tuck my hair up sometimes. Now, listen carefully.”

After Carys had given her instructions, Setia said, “I wish we had more time to talk. I don’t know what’s going on.”

"I'll be over in a couple of hours. We can talk more then. Now, keep your head down while you're in public. The bill of my cap should hide your face from the cameras. We don't think the system is set up to detect two identical people out and about. When you get where you're going, stay there."

Her heart in her mouth, Setia tried to act nonchalant as she walked to the aviary. The corridors grew busier as she travelled along, but no one seemed to look twice at the crew member supposedly on her way to work. The aviary wasn't high-security. Carys's key card opened the entrance, and Setia made sure to leave it open, though it was much earlier than the facility's usual hours.

Once inside, she went directly to Carys's office. The birds fluttered away at her approach. *They* could tell she wasn't Carys. She passed through the office and into the stockroom at the back. Scents of bird food instantly enveloped her: musky odours of seeds, cloying smells of fat, sweet aromas of nectar substitutes. The hum of a large refrigerator and scuttling sounds filled the dim room. The source of the scuttles was a tall, clear-paned cabinet in a corner, where insects crawled and flew. Setia grimaced and turned her back on it. She found a spot to sit and settled in for the wait.

It seemed longer than two hours before she heard movement in the office. She slid into a space between two shelving units and held her breath. The door opened and the room grew brighter.

"Setia?"

She stepped out.

"Phew!" Carys moved close and lifted her arms as if going in for a hug. But then awkwardness settled on both of them. Carys's arms fell to her sides. "I have to keep to my usual routine, feeding the birds, cleaning up, etcetera. If I don't..."

"I get it."

As a member of the expedition to the surface, Carys would be under suspicion of being involved in Setia's escape. Any unusual activity might be noticed. Carys took out a sectioned box and began to quickly fill it with various types of food. "You saw Loki?"

"The Primians showed him to me. He was half-starved..."

Carys breathed in sharply and stared at her.

"I explained that he ate meat. I think the Primians were trying to take good care of him. They just didn't know how."

With a sad shake of her head, Carys said, "I have to get back down to that planet."

"So Robins knows I'm really me?"

"He can see two of you on his skein. He can't tell which is which, but he believed me when I told him we had the wrong Setia locked up. He agrees that only you could know about Loki. Our expedition was never official and the report isn't accessible to the other Setia. She doesn't know anything about my bird." Carys paused and looked Setia in the eyes. "You're sure he's okay?"

Her mind flew back to the bombing of the Primian habitation. "The last time I saw him he was alive. The Primians seemed to want to take good care of him."

Carys sighed and continued her task.

"If Robins agrees I am who I say I am, why the jailbreak?" Setia asked. "Why all the sneaking around? And why is my copy still walking free?"

"Things are weird around here. No one is listening to Robins anymore, or the mappers on the other ships. Everything is messed up. We had to get you out as fast as possible, or they could have disappeared you just to save face." She lifted the full box. "Back in a minute."

Setia waited impatiently for Carys's return. She'd thought of an urgent question. As soon as Carys reappeared, she asked, "Is Miriam alive?"

"She's still in sick bay, but she's due to be discharged today."

Setia passed a hand over her face and exhaled. "And they believe she's the real Miriam?"

"There's more than one of her too?"

"There's at least one more. They used her to trick me while I was being held captive. I don't know how many Primians can change into us, or if there's no limit. It's the strangest thing. They don't only take on our appearance, they learn our language super-fast and even seem to acquire some knowledge of the person they're copying, enough to pass as that person without deep scrutiny."

Carys was busy picking out beetles and worms from her cabinet of live food. "Ever since you pointed out that the Ahmad who visited us in the tent wasn't really Ahmad, I've been thinking about it. You know octopus?"

"I've eaten a few."

Carys gave her a disgusted look. "Octopus are highly intelligent, but aside from that, they're excellent at camouflaging themselves. They can change colour and texture to perfectly match any kind of ocean floor, sand, rocks, shells, whatever. And they can do it in seconds. It isn't impossible that an alien species could have evolved a similar capability."

"But language and knowledge too?"

Carys shrugged. "You remember I told you about the interstellar voyage my adoptive mam went on? Her partner was on an earlier voyage—the one where extraterrestrials gave humankind the information that's led to all the recent scientific breakthroughs. He told us those guys could appear from nowhere, get inside people's heads, control computer systems. And remember your buddy who came after you?"

"Arief."

"He could certainly pull a trick or two. *Now* do you think what the Primians do is so remarkable?"

"But the Primians aren't aliens, they're—"

"Back soon." Carys left with more bird food.

When she returned, she said, "What do you mean, the Primians aren't aliens?"

Setia explained Not-Ahmad's theory that his people had evolved on Earth.

"That doesn't make any sense," Carys retorted. "I know they

look like us, but how the hell did they get to Prime? They haven't even invented aeroplanes, let alone starships."

"Let me finish." Setia told her about the cave paintings. "They suspect they were brought to Prime by a benevolent space-faring species a long time ago, while they were still in a primitive state."

"But why?"

"So humans couldn't wipe them out."

Carys's eyes flicked wide. "Ohhh!" She sank onto a sack of grain.

"Does it make sense now?"

"It's starting to."

Forty-Four

Setia's next hiding place was the small observation room near Robins's office where she'd looked out upon the weird space surrounding the *Bres*. This time when she opened the viewing portal, all she saw was Prime lazily spinning and ordinary stars speckling the black, albeit in unfamiliar patterns.

She closed the shutter. "Shall we start?"

Carys occupied the same narrow bench as her. Robins sat opposite on a chair he'd brought from his office.

"We're waiting for one more person," said Carys.

As she spoke, there was a timid knock at the door.

"Here she is," said Robins, rising to open it.

Miriam hobbled in, leaning heavily on a crutch.

"Burnap's balls, it's good to see you," Setia breathed. "Here, come and sit down." She helped the woman over to the bench and took her crutch, placing it on the floor. "It wasn't until I saw Carys that I found out you'd survived. No one would tell me anything."

Miriam gave a wry smile. "I'm very much alive, or at least my leg tells me so whenever the painkillers wear off. I'm glad to see you too. I'm very glad you're out of prison."

"Wherever I go, people want to lock me up," Setia joked. "Your leg still hurts? Didn't they give you proper treatment in the sick bay?"

"They gave me excellent treatment, but the projectile from the Primian weapon had shattered my thigh bone."

"Holy shit! And there I was thinking their weapons were inferior to ours."

"Not inferior," said Robins, "only different."

"You don't understand modern warfare, Setia," Carys commented. "The best way to drain enemy resources is by severely injuring, not killing, troops. A dead soldier can be replaced by another grunt. A wounded soldier has to be brought back from the front line, treated, maybe invalided out of service and paid some kind of pension for the rest of his life. Pulse weaponry maims better than it kills. That's the whole point."

Robins continued, "Though in many ways the natives of Prime haven't reached our level of technological advancement, we mustn't underestimate them. I heard on the grapevine that our troops are beginning to suffer significant casualties."

"On the grapevine?" asked Setia. "Don't you have access to the official reports?"

"I do not and haven't for quite a while."

This was what Carys had told her—that Robins and the other mappers had been frozen out. "You guys have to get me up to speed on everything." Carys had told her a lot during snatches of conversation while trying to maintain her normal routine, but there were big gaps in her knowledge.

"It began a few days into your expedition," Robins said, "around the time we lost comm contact with you. I'm not sure if one of the other colonisation efforts had stumbled across the existence of the Primians, or if it was something to do with Ahmad's disappearance from the *Bres*'s settlement, but Captain Bujold suddenly became distant. Up until then we'd worked fairly closely, but around that time I noticed her replies to my messages were often delayed. I didn't attach too much importance to it. I assumed she was busy with settlement business and the efforts to prepare the colonists. Then—"

"Tell her about the meeting," said Carys.

"I was getting to it, but you're right, that was the next significant event. After the captain had failed to answer a question I felt to be rather important, I went in search of her in order to talk to her face-to-face. I couldn't find her anywhere, though it was normal operational hours and no notice had been sent out to say she was unavailable. I couldn't make any sense of it until someone I spoke to mentioned they'd seen her entering the shuttle bay. She'd left the ship, apparently for a classified reason—a reason even the *Bres*'s mapper wasn't cleared to know."

"We think she was meeting with the other ships' captains," said Carys.

"I never found out for sure," said Robins, "but it was shortly afterwards several announcements were made in the same bulletin. The first was that the Fleet had arrived at Prime ahead of schedule. The second was that preliminary short-range scans of the planet indicated a hitherto undiscovered intelligent, predatory native life form. Finally, it was stated that there would be a delay while the settlement sites and surrounding lands were made safe for colonisation."

"Made safe for colonisation?!" Miriam blurted. "That's their euphemism for genocide?"

"What do the passengers think about this cull?" asked Setia.

"What do you think?" Carys asked bitterly. "They're all for it. The mood on the ship's never been better, ever since the bastards learned innocent creatures were dying for their benefit. Fits right in with their life experiences."

"But they don't know it's people," Miriam said. "They might react differently if they did."

"They know it's intelligent life," Carys retorted, "and they don't give a shit."

Setia frowned. "But you met Not-Ahmad. Didn't you tell anyone?"

"Of course I did. Markham debriefed me alone. Thanked me for taking part in the mission, told me it was unauthorised and made me sign an NDA."

Setia focused on Miriam. "*You* know the Primians are people. If it's a big secret, how come you're allowed to wander around the ship? How come you aren't imprisoned?"

"I was given a very thorough talking to before they would discharge me. I had to agree I'd been mistaken about what had happened. The implication was, if I didn't, I would be put on a psych hold until I changed my mind."

"That's it?" Setia was perplexed.

"That's the gist."

"They put me in the brig!"

Miriam shrugged. "Maybe I come across as more persuadable. You, on the other hand, attacked that guy who was tormenting a bot in the refectory, remember?"

"And there are two Setias," said Carys. "That's hard to explain. You were lucky they didn't space you. Much more convenient."

Setia shivered. "Talking of Not-Setia, where is she? What's she been doing?"

"I used to spot her occasionally here and there," Carys replied. "Whenever she saw me she would walk the other way."

"But they must know she's a Primian."

"I don't think so," said Robins, "or at least there was little suspicion until you showed up. She returned not long after Carys and Sheldrake, saying that Miriam had sunk into a bog and died. I doubted her from the start, especially after Carys broke her NDA and told me about a doppelgänger of Ahmad. The Primian Setia had refused to see me, which strengthened my doubts. Then Miriam miraculously appeared, and her story didn't remotely accord with the one Setia had told."

Carys said, "I haven't seen the other Setia—"

"There isn't another Setia," Setia snapped. "There's only one. Me."

"Whatever. I haven't seen her at all since you and Miriam were brought aboard. Maybe she's gone into hiding. It isn't hard to find a place to hide on this ship."

Setia recalled the extensive search for Arief. “Hey, what about Sheldrake? What’s his take on this?”

Robins and Carys shared a look.

Robins replied, “Corporal Sheldrake has been as reluctant to talk as the Primian Setia. I have no idea what he told Markham. I am no longer privy to military debriefings.”

“I’ve tried to discuss what happened in the forest,” said Carys. “He shuts up tighter than a clam. Says the subject is classified.”

“Sounds exactly like Sheldrake,” Setia muttered. She focused on Robins. “Do you have *any* idea what’s going on? You know we’re bombing Primian habitations, right? We’re killing them. I mean, I know they captured me and Miriam and Ahmad, but to them we’re invaders. They’re scared of us and we’ve shown they have every reason to be.”

The old man’s shoulders sagged. “I feared it was so. Though I’ve been cut off from the Fleet’s commanders, I can see much of what’s happening via my skeins.”

“*Why* have they cut you off?” Setia demanded. “Surely they could benefit from your advice and guidance. They’ve relied on you and the other mappers extensively.”

He replied softly, “It must be because they know that, in this case, we would refuse our services. I am not a warmonger. The goal of all mappers is to help humankind, and military conflict—though it may benefit individuals and groups—is to the detriment of the human spirit.”

A realisation hit. “They *want* this fight,” Setia declared. “The blood-thirsty bastards. It helps solve their major problem: the colonists. They know most of the people who signed up for this venture are soft as marshmallows and spoiled rotten.”

Miriam gave her a wounded look.

“Present company excepted. What problems they would have had if things had gone as planned and there were no Primians to stand in the way of the colonisation! The complaints, the arguments, the demands to return to Earth or find another, better planet...”

“With beaches and cocktails,” Miriam murmured.

"This way, the commanders are turned into heroes, saving the settlers from danger and making everything a big adventure. It's like a freaking drama vid. Intrepid explorers forging a path in the wilderness, slaying dangerous wildlife, bringing civilisation to savagery. Only, like always, our privileged passengers are having the dirty work done for them. Once they finally get down to the surface they'll see the effects of the bombardments and, rather than noticing that Prime is a shithole where the rain never stops, they'll be relieved and grateful that they're safe."

Robins said sadly, "I think you may be right, though the official reason, as Captain Bujold put it to me, is that the Primians have shown hostile intent. They did kidnap you, Miriam and the settlement construction supervisor, after all. And I think the commanders are particularly unnerved by the Primian ability to metamorphose to look like us. The security risks posed are legion."

"But they can't possibly kill *all* the Primians," Miriam protested.

Setia wasn't sure if she meant ethically or logistically.

"Why not?" Carys said bitterly. "It wouldn't be the first time we murdered an entire nation of people."

"I know, but a whole *world* population?"

"Doesn't matter whether we manage it or not," Setia said. "As long as the locals are subdued long enough for the colonisation to get underway, the Fleet will be off to its next destination before the truth comes out."

An uncomfortable silence fell.

"The question is," she went on, "what are we going to do about it?"

No answer came.

Forty-Five

The tiny observation cabin that was Setia's temporary home hadn't been fitted up for living in. Though Carys had given her bedding and a few creature comforts, the enforced stay wasn't a much better experience than being confined in the brig. But she did have the option to sneak out. Robins's friend in security had re-jigged the access panel so it only responded to her biometrics. Now the view from the ship was ordinary no one was interested in looking outside, but it didn't hurt to be careful. It had been the last favour he was prepared to do for them.

Hypothetically, with the cap of Carys's spare uniform pulled down low, Setia could leave the cabin. Yet she hardly dared risk it. The cover-up going on within the Fleet was huge and the stakes were high. As Carys had said, it would be more convenient to space Setia-who-turned-up-out-of-the-blue than take a chance she might reveal what was really going on.

She tossed and turned on the narrow, hard bench that served as her bed, pondering the problem of how to stop what was happening. Wincing, she recalled how she'd been disgusted with Miriam for giving the Primians so much intel. Her perspective had changed. Here she was also trying to figure out how to help them.

It had been the cave painting that had made her think again.

That, and the way the Fleet had blasted apart the Primian habitation. The devastation wreaked by the attack had been horrible and appalling. Carys had said it made more sense to wound the enemy than kill them, but that only applied in wars between nations who were fairly equal. It was clear the Fleet commanders intended a massacre, and if no one stopped them they would achieve it.

To the Primians, it would be a replay of ancient history.

At the meeting with Robins, Carys and Miriam, after they'd tried and failed to come up with a plan, Carys had expanded on her theory about the Primians' origin. She'd explained that in the far past several intelligent ape-like species had existed on Earth, all close relatives of humans. The other species had gone extinct and only humans survived. The suspicion was that the survivors had killed off their competitors.

Except in the Primians' case benevolent extra-terrestrials had turned up and saved them, bringing them to Prime, a planet without an aggressive competing species. The environment wasn't as nice as Earth's. It was less stable and certainly a lot wetter, but they had adapted. They had thrived, in fact, increasing their population and developed new technologies. In many ways they weren't as advanced as humans but, on the other hand, they didn't seem as bloodthirsty.

Setia dozed.

What had it been like when the benevolent aliens arrived on Earth? Had they landed in the midst of a battle between the humans and Primians? Or a raid on a Primian settlement?

She had a vision of an ancient jungle, thick with tall ferns, vines looping between them, and lush undergrowth. Two tribes with shaggy hair and dressed in furs jabbed at each other with primitive spears and threw stones. A brilliant light appeared overhead, outshining the sun. The light was accompanied by an otherworldly hum. A dark shape descended to the level of the canopy, and the warring men and women dropped onto their bellies in fear, casting amazed and terrified looks at the strange vessel.

Pulses flew from the base of the shuttle, but the bolts were aimed only at one of the tribes. Some of those targeted tried to get up and run but they were mown down. Next, when the attacked were all dead or had fled, the pulses were replaced by beams. These fell on the protected people. One by one, they were lifted through the air into the ship's belly. When all were gathered, the hatch shut and the shuttle zoomed into the sky.

Opening her eyes on darkness, Setia smiled sadly. Of course, it couldn't have happened like that. After the aliens had assessed the situation and decided to do something to help, they would have had to locate Primian camps across a wide landscape. They probably had to sedate them before bringing them aboard their starships and keep them sedated for the journey. Otherwise, the psychological shock would be too great.

And they wouldn't have been able to transport all the Primians to a new, safe home. There must have been enough to provide a healthy gene pool, but plenty would have been left behind to eventually fall victim to human violence.

Maybe the aliens had helped the Primians in the early years. It would have been hard for them to learn how to live in the strange environment. Maybe the benefactors didn't leave until they were confident the rescued species could survive on its own.

Only now humanity had caught up to the Primians, exactly as Not-Ahmad had feared. Humans were set on finishing the job they had started tens of millennia ago.

A heavy feeling settled on her. How could she and her friends defeat the might of the Fleet? How could they stop the attack? They wouldn't only be taking on the Fleet's military, they were fighting human instinct itself.

The door to her room slid open. A figure entered, silhouetted by the light from the passageway.

Setia lifted a hand to her eyes and squinted, confused. "Carys, is that—"

The figure leapt on her. She saw the plunging knife just in time to jerk to one side. As the blade thunked into the bench next to her throat, the door slid closed automatically, throwing both her and her assailant into darkness. She blindly reached up and grabbed. The figure seemed female and not very big, but when she tried to wrench her to the floor, her attacker managed to hold her position.

Something seemed to slap her neck. White-hot pain burst out.

Setia screamed.

Agony galvanised her. She drove a knee upward, hard, and met soft flesh. There was a grunt. Together with the force from her arms, she succeeded in tossing her assailant off. A thunk signalled the woman hitting the floor.

Setia leapt on top of her, desperately trying to locate the arm that had the knife. A second stab of pain hit, from her side this time. Flailing, she managed to locate the arm as it moved away, preparing to strike again. She fastened her hand around the wrist and twisted. Meanwhile, the body beneath her squirmed and fought for freedom. Something gripped her hair and tugged, pulling her down. Then the hand changed tactics and fingers probed her face, trying to locate her eyes. She snapped with her teeth and managed to bite a finger before it was whipped away.

Meanwhile, she held onto the wrist of the knife-wielding arm with every ounce of strength she had. The arm writhed and jerked, trying to break free from her grasp.

Setia cursed. It was hard to fight an opponent you couldn't see.

I'm a moron.

"Lights! On!"

A furious face stared up at her, spattered with blood.

"You!"

Her attacker's free hand swooped toward her face, fingers curved into claws. Setia ducked the hand and head butted the woman. Her eyes became unfocused and the tension in her body slackened. Setia twisted the wrist harder and the knife fell. Snatching it up, she jumped to her feet. Her assailant was dazed but not unconscious.

Setia touched her neck and grimaced as she gingerly probed the cut. Though it was wet the blood wasn't gushing out. Her collarbone seemed to have deflected most of the force of the blow. She lifted her top. The knife had cut through the material. A long slash ran across her ribs but didn't appear to have penetrated deeper.

She sat down. Her attacker's eyes were re-focusing. A purple welt was forming on her forehead. Her lips snarling, she pushed herself upright.

"Don't even think about it," Setia said, brandishing the knife.

Not-Setia climbed to her feet and darted for the door. Setia grabbed her hair just in time and hauled her back. She thrust her onto the bench. "Take a seat!"

While I try to figure out what to do with you.

Setia sat with her back to the door. Gathering the material of her shirt at her neck, she pressed it against her wound. The pain was almost unbearable and made concentrating hard.

Should she comm Carys? Or Robins?

No. They'd agreed comms were too risky.

She also couldn't leave the cabin, not while she looked like a victim of attempted murder.

Heck, she *was* a victim of attempted murder.

What was she supposed to do with the Primian?

The mirror image sitting on the bench unnerved her.

"Could you change back to your normal self?" Setia asked. "I never had a twin and I don't want one now."

Not-Setia only glowered.

"I'm guessing that's how you managed to get in here. You had to change into me to trick the security system into opening the door. But you must be able to revert to being you. That's how you've been moving around the ship undetected, right?"

The Primian remained sullenly silent.

"What have you found out while you've been sneaking around? Figured out how to defeat us? Discover the weakness that'll turn the tide, did you?"

Not-Setia's shoulders slumped and she buried her face in her hands. "You're going to kill all my people!" she wailed. "Why? What did we do to deserve your hate?" She dissolved into sobs.

Setia hung her head. She didn't know what to say.

The Primian lifted her gaze. In a choking tone she went on, "I've heard how you talk about us. You call us vermin. An infestation that needs to be wiped out. But *you're* the infestation. Humans are the invaders. We live peacefully. We did nothing to you. Why can't you leave us alone?!" Not-Setia wiped her eyes with her sleeve before she continued, "You're so strong. My strength grows multiple times when I turn into you. You're small for a human but you're so much stronger than me. Why is that?"

"Uhh... Earth's gravity is higher than Prime's. That might be something to do with it. But me in particular? I'm just unusually strong."

Her sobs welling up again, Not-Setia said, "Your weapons are better than ours. They can kill thousands with one hit. I have tried... I have searched and listened... I couldn't find out anything to help my people. So I thought, at least I can kill one of them. I wanted to kill the one who started all this, the spy who revealed us to our enemies."

"Hold on," Setia protested. "That wasn't me. I didn't tell the Fleet about you. I was kept prisoner, remember? Under threat of death. I don't have anything to do with the attacks."

"You were snooping around that forest, trying to find us! Then when you did, two of your group ran back with the information. It was after that the bombings started. I know I'm right."

"We were on an expedition, exploring. We had no idea there were already people living on Prime. No idea at all."

They argued on. Not-Setia was reluctant to believe the truth, and, in fact, the actual course of events didn't really matter. Carys and Sheldrake had revealed the Primians' presence to the Fleet, and Setia would have too. Whether or not someone else in another part of Prime had made the same discovery, sparking the attack Not-Ahmad had mentioned, it made no difference.

As they debated, Not-Setia's appearance gradually changed. Her body became slimmer and her features more fine-boned. Over the course of twenty or thirty minutes, she reverted to her Primian self.

A wave of faintness swept over Setia and she lifted a hand to her forehead. She looked down. Blood from the cut on her neck had soaked her pyjama top. She felt sick.

Not-Setia asked softly, “Does it hurt?”

“What do you think?”

“If you let me go, you can get help.”

“I can’t get help. They’ll lock me up again.”

After a sigh, Not-Setia said, “Maybe I can…” She got up from the bench.

Suspiciously, Setia lifted the knife.

The Primian raised her hands. “I don’t want to hurt you. I was just thinking…”

So it was that, when Carys arrived, she found Setia and Not-Setia crouched together, the Primian holding together the edges of Setia’s wound.

Forty-Six

"I can't, I'm sorry." Carys's face was unusually expressive. She really did look remorseful.

"But we can't do it by ourselves," Setia protested. "Ow!"

"Stay still." Carys had returned to her aviary and brought back swabs and medical glue she used for fixing the cuts of her birds. Setia had been sceptical about its use on humans, but it was her only option. She winced as Carys cleaned the wound on her neck and then applied the glue. As she finished, she said, "I don't know if it'll hold. That cut's pretty deep. You should try to keep still."

"Huh, thanks for the tip." Keeping still was the last thing on her mind. "Would you reconsider? Please, come with us."

"No way," said Carys. "You're crazy if you think it's going to help. You'll end up back in the brig, or worse. Both of you." Her gaze travelled from Setia to Not-Setia.

Or worse meant spaced. Setia had to agree it was a strong possibility if her plan didn't succeed.

"I'm going to end up back in the brig anyway," she countered. "Or worse. How much longer do you think I have until Security catches up with me? They must be searching every cubby hole on the ship. It won't be long until someone searches this one."

"Then Robins and I will find a different place for you to hide. If we keep moving you around…" Carys lapsed into silence, perhaps realising the hollowness of her words.

"It won't work forever. It's only a matter of time before one or both of us is caught. The only way to prevent that is to put an end to this whole mess."

"Look, if I thought you had a chance of success I might consider it, but Bujold's the captain. She's never going to listen to me. I run the ship's aviary, for Christ's sake."

"You went on the mission to Prime. If she hears the truth directly from you, not whatever twisted, biased version Markham's told her, she'll—"

"What? Slap her forehead and say *Duh, I was wrong all along! Thanks so much for enlightening me, Carys Ellis?* What makes you think she doesn't know the truth? What makes you think she's been lied to? Do you think she's that dumb?"

"No, I don't, but…" Setia bit her lip.

"She's the one ordering the *Bres's* attacks. She knows exactly what she's doing and why. Your plan is a fool's errand, and I'm not going to help you get yourselves killed."

Not-Setia had stayed quiet during the argument, but at the last comment from Carys she spat, "But my people are getting killed! Don't you care?" Before Carys could answer, she went on, "Of course you don't. You're human. You're a murderer, the same as the rest of your kind."

"That isn't true! I hate what's happening, but I'm just one person. What can I do?"

"I just told you what you can do!" Setia exclaimed, rising to her feet. "You can come with us. Talk to Bujold."

"And I told *you* that's stupid, pointless and dangerous." It was like stone doors had swung closed behind Carys's features. Her face had lost all expression. She was shutting down.

Soon, there would be no way to reach her.

Setia grabbed at a last straw. "What about Robins? Could you talk to him? Ask him if he'll come with us?"

Carys also got up. "He'll tell you the same as me. He might have already tried to talk to Bujold. He didn't mention it but it would make sense. It's a waste of time." She moved to the door. "Stay here for now. If anything changes I'll let you know."

"Shit," Setia muttered as the door closed. "Looks like we're on our own."

"What now?" the Primian asked.

"I don't know."

"You won't help save my people?"

"I didn't say that." Setia was deeply reluctant to exit the small observation room by herself, let alone with one of the natives of Prime in tow. Yet she couldn't just sit here and do nothing. If only she could comm Miriam. Miriam would help simply out of the kindness of her heart, despite the danger. But comming anyone was out of the question. She might as well go up to Markham and hand herself in. And trekking all the way across the ship to D12 would exponentially increase their chances of being picked up by the security systems. They would only have a short time available before their presence in public was noticed. They had to use it in the best way possible.

The Primian stood up. "Tell me how to get to your captain's quarters. I will speak to her alone."

"No, don't. You're the enemy. If you're caught with the captain you'll be executed for sure. They'll say it was an assassination attempt."

"What choice do I have?" The Primian's eyes became watery. "I can't find out any information to help my people defend themselves, and even if I could I have no way of sending it to them. I can't prevent the attacks coming from your ship. And I can't return to my planet because I can't get onto one of your spacecraft. Should I stay here and hide while my people die?"

"Let me think." But she'd already thought everything through. The answer was always the same. She looked at the Primian. She couldn't think of her as Not-Setia anymore. "What's your name?"

The woman sniffed and replied in her own language.

"Uhh.. Did you say Waylis?" Setia ventured.

"Close enough."

It was the beginning of the active shift. With luck, Captain Bujold would be alone in her office. Of course, there was also a good chance she wouldn't be there. She might not even be on the ship. It wasn't like they could comm ahead and check. Setia pulled her cap down to obscure her face. Waylis's real appearance had never been logged by the ship's computer as far as Setia knew.

They fast-walked through the passageways and didn't seem to attract much attention. Carys's uniform lent a degree of anonymity. The passengers were used to ignoring the crew. And Waylis was just a short, slim woman in unfashionable clothes. The only thing that set her apart from humans was the strange way her eyes tilted up at the corners, but you would have to look twice to notice it.

"This place is so big," Waylis commented. "It's as big as a town. It took me so long to find where you were hiding."

"How did you manage it?"

"I saw your companion, the woman who came to see you just now, and I followed her. Then I came back later when I guessed you would be asleep."

The Primian had done better than the ship's security at finding her, but Carys would have noticed one of *their* great lunks following her around. A petite, ordinary-looking woman? Not so much. And Carys hadn't seen Waylis in her true appearance until their recent encounter.

"But how did you know Carys knew me?" Setia asked. "You never saw us together."

"I did. We watched you travel with her through our lands."

"You were watching us the whole time?"

"From the moment you left the construction site. We've been watching everything you do ever since you landed on our planet."

Of course they had. "But you had to wait until we were in the forest to try to kidnap us, right?"

"At first, we only wanted to find out more about you. There had been no attempt to make contact, so we thought perhaps you didn't know of our existence. We weren't sure if it was better to keep it that way. Many of us thought you were dangerous. Others said you only wanted a new place to live, and that we could share the planet. Some of us wanted to ask you to share the secrets of your technology, like space travel. It was..."

She said a word that sounded something like *grackler* and went on, "who suggested the idea of jamming the connections to your devices, capturing the man you had spoken to at the construction site, and pretending to be him in order to talk to you face-to-face. Grackler is one of our fastest copiers. He is famous for it."

Setia guessed Grackler was Not-Ahmad. "But you must have known we would figure out in the end that he wasn't the real deal."

"In the end, yes. We would have released your man. We were careful to make sure he never saw any of us. But that would have been a puzzle for you and not our concern."

"Where is he now?"

"I don't know. I haven't managed to contact my people since I arrived here."

"So what changed? Why did you kidnap me and Miriam?"

Waylis turned to her with a grave look. "You showed us that humans are violent and dangerous. We knew then we had to do something to protect ourselves. We needed more information. So when two of you remained alone in the forest, we decided it was a good opportunity to get it."

"What made you think we're violent and dangerous?" As far as Setia knew, no attacks on Primians had been launched at that time. "All we'd done was begin to build a settlement and do a bit of exploring."

"*You* showed us. When Grackler entered your tent, you drew a gun on him. And when he tried to leave, you attacked him."

"I..."

Shit.

"That was because I suspected he wasn't Ahmad, the man you kidnapped. I didn't know who or what he was."

"Was he aggressive to you? Did he try to hurt any of you?"

"No, but…" Setia swallowed. "We were on an alien planet. We'd been followed by those rain monsters… We were under constant threat of…" Her words petered out.

"Rain monsters?"

"The rain things," Setia replied irritably, her stomach squirming. "You must know. Creatures appeared behind us during a heavy—"

"Oh, sprites. You saw sprites? I understand better now. We fear them too."

"What are they?"

"No one knows. But Grackler doesn't resemble a sprite, even when he's copying a human."

"I know."

What else was there to say? Her reaction to Not-Ahmad's visit had felt rational at the time. Maybe her career background had fed into her behaviour—maybe her entire life experience had fed into it. Yet she didn't think she'd been wrong to challenge him. She hadn't overreacted. Or had she? She couldn't deny that her actions had led to her and Miriam's capture. Not now Waylis had told her so. What other repercussions had resulted? The image of the blasted apart Primian habitation came painfully to mind.

Forty-Seven

The passageway leading to Bujold's office was empty. Setia peered into the corners for cameras, but she was unable to spot them. No change there. She'd never been able to see the pinhead lenses viewing everything that went on in the public areas of the ship. Of all places, they had to be here. But tighter security? She didn't know. There were no guards stationed outside the room.

Taking a breath and grabbing Waylis's wrist, Setia stepped into the corridor, muttering. "Carys was right."

"What?"

"This is insane."

All she knew was they would have to talk fast. She pressed the door chime.

"Yes?"

Bujold clearly hadn't bothered to look at the screen to see who was outside.

A bolt of inspiration struck. Setia replied, "Uh, your breakfast, ma'am."

The door opened. Drawing Waylis with her, she stepped in.

The captain didn't look up nor even say anything. She clearly expected someone to put her breakfast down and leave. It took a second for her to register that wasn't happening.

A second was all it took for Setia to reach her.

She grabbed Bujold's wrists and pressed them into the desktop to prevent her from reaching an alarm button. There was also the danger she could summon guards with a voice command.

"Speak, and I'll kill you," Setia said. "I can do it faster than anyone can get here to save you."

The captain looked steadily into Setia's eyes. Her face stony, she lifted an eyebrow.

"This is Waylis," Setia went on. "She's from Prime, and she was pretending to be me. That was how she got onto the ship. You're killing her people and she wants you to stop. *I* want you to stop. The Primians are intelligent. What you're doing is genocide. It's a war crime, and if we were on Earth you would be imprisoned for life. You must stop and make the other commanders stop too, and the Fleet must leave Prime."

The eyebrow lowered. "May I speak?"

Setia's grip remained firm. "Go ahead."

"The natives of Prime have committed hostile acts, and they present a credible threat to human life. We must—"

"Bullshit. When I said you could speak, I didn't mean you could lie."

"I am not lying. Even if I were, how exactly do you imagine you're going to persuade the Fleet to do as you say? Are you going to hold me here forever? You don't even seem to be armed. Do you think the Fleet values my life above the lives of tens of thousands of colonists?"

Setia stared at Bujold's face.

Something was wrong.

She released her hold on the captain's wrists and turned to Waylis. "Run!"

As they sped through the doorway, guards appeared at one end of the corridor. They raced in the opposite direction. The area around the captain's office was devoted mostly to admin, and everyone was arriving for work. They buffeted shoulders as they dodged through the workers. Lift doors opened, and Setia and Waylis ran in, eliciting surprised glances. A deck below, they rushed out, straight into a group of people waiting.

"Hey!" someone yelled. "Watch out!"

They had to slow down. Travelling at a breakneck pace was too noticeable. Guards would already be searching for them, closing in on them.

"This way," said Setia, making a turn.

"Are we going back to the place you were hiding?"

"Can't risk it. It's quiet around there. Now they know what you look like the system will pick us up for sure. And fast. We'll go to one of the main thoroughfares. It'll be crowded right now and we'll be harder to spot."

"It's no use," said Waylis. "We have to stop sometime, and then they'll catch us."

Two guards appeared ahead, scanning the pedestrians. Setia seized Waylis's arm and dragged her into an alcove. They pressed their backs against the wall.

"They're gonna see us!" Waylis softly whimpered.

Setia was forced to agree. Even if the guards didn't know what they looked like, what they were doing made them look highly suspicious. Yet if they stepped out they would be spotted immediately. If only they'd managed to make it to a busy section, but Waylis was right. They couldn't escape detection for much longer, no matter what they did.

Setia wished she was Arief, able to dissolve into gas and float away. He'd been able to hide with the entire ship's military searching for him. He'd only come out when Robins had used her as bait. Until then, he'd been inside the...

She breathed in sharply. Could there be? She swung around.

At the base of the wall behind them was a slatted panel. She crouched and gripped it.

"What are you doing?" Waylis asked.

Setia slid the panel upward, silently thanking Burnap it wasn't fastened to the wall. Beyond it yawned a dark tunnel. "Get in!"

Waylis didn't need to be told twice. She crawled quickly into the hole. Setia followed but she went in backwards. As soon as she was inside, she picked up the panel and slid it into position. Through the gaps between the slats, she saw the legs of the guards pass by.

"What is this place?" Waylis's voice was muffled.

"An air vent. Starships have environmental control systems to keep the air moving and fresh."

"You don't need to explain. We have the same systems in our buildings. We use them to dehumidify the air too."

"Of course you do. Sorry."

"How long must we stay here?"

The space was only just large enough to accommodate them, crouching on their hands and knees. There wasn't room to turn around. They were stuck in position, backside to backside, as long as they remained in the ventilation channel. "I don't know."

"I-I'm not very comfortable like this."

"Neither am I."

"I think I'll try to lie down."

There were shuffling sounds and the metal walls flexed.

"I've moved down a bit," Waylis explained, "if you want to make use of the extra room."

"Thanks." Setia stretched out her legs and lay on her stomach. "If you're feeling claustrophobic, we can swap places. You could crawl over me."

"I'll bear it in mind. I'm okay for now."

A pause.

Waylis said, "This is quite silly, isn't it?"

"Yes, it is."

They chuckled.

"We will have to leave eventually," said Waylis. "We can't stay here forever."

"I know."

"And then the guards will quickly find us, unless you can think of a way to...?"

"Working on it."

A longer pause, then Waylis asked, "When we were in the captain's office, how did you know guards were coming for us?"

"Oh, that. Bujold had lost her twitch."

"Her what?"

"She has a facial tic. Only when I was talking to her, it stopped. I guessed she was doing something, maybe thinking something? I don't know. It wouldn't surprise me if she had a brain implant allowing her to connect directly to the ship's system."

"Electronics in her head? I can't imagine anyone choosing to do that. Humans are very strange."

Setia was forced to agree.

An entire active shift had passed. Setia and Waylis had taken turns at staring forlornly through the slats at people walking along the passageway. Lying in the vent tunnel had been several kinds of torture. Along with the fear of discovery and recapture came discomfort, thirst, hunger, and last but not least, the ache of a bladder fit to burst.

All the while, Setia had mined the depths of her memory and ingenuity for a solution to their predicament. None had come. No matter what way she looked at the problem, the answer was always the same. They would have to leave their hiding place. Neither she nor Waylis was Arief, able to last indefinitely within the EC system. They had physical needs to be met. Remaining where they were was only delaying the inevitable.

"Setia," Waylis said quietly, "I really need to—"

"Me too."

"I think I must leave. Unless you don't mind getting wet."

"I could tolerate a lot of things if it meant we stood a chance of not being caught. I don't think it will, but could you hold on just a bit longer?"

"I'll try."

If they were going to be spaced, it might be better to stay here as long as possible. At the end of the day life was life, even if you were unbearably thirsty and yet paradoxically soaked in someone else's pee. In truth, Setia simply didn't know what would happen to her and Waylis once Markham got a hold of them. She, as a ship's passenger, might survive, however inconvenient her existence.

She had a strong feeling that Waylis might not be so lucky. She was Primian and therefore the enemy. Markham might even decide to make an example of her. The presence of a spy aboard ship might bolster the charade that the natives were a threat. A public execution might impress upon the passengers that the military were 'doing something about it'.

She couldn't expose the woman to such a horrible fate. "Waylis, I have an idea."

"You've thought of a better way to hide?" the Primian asked excitedly.

"No, but can you change back into me?"

"Why? What difference will that make? They're looking for both of us."

"I know, but it's better they don't know who's who. Trust me."

"Um, all right. It'll take me a few minutes."

The passageway had grown still and the lights had dimmed to the half-brightness of the quiet shift. Whatever Waylis had to do to transform herself, the process was silent.

"I'm ready," the Primian said.

"Okay, let's do it." Setia reached for the panel, hoping they would at least make it to a toilet before they were discovered.

Before she could touch it, a shadow descended over the exit.

Setia gasped and drew back.

Waylis whispered, "What's wrong?"

Fingers poked through the slats. The vent cover was lifted up and away. An older man's face appeared, looking in.

Robins said, "I thought I would find you here."

Forty-Eight

Setia pulled down her hood and looked around. "What is this place?"

Robins had brought clothes for her and Waylis to hide their faces as they followed his directions to the rendezvous point. He wasn't here yet.

"More importantly," Waylis said, "is there a bathroom?"

"Good point. Hey, could you change back into yourself while we're at it?"

By the time they'd relieved their discomfort and Waylis was back in Primian form, Robins had arrived after travelling via a different route.

Setia repeated her question to him, frowning at the rows of half-open doors that ran around the room's perimeter, revealing reclining seats. On top of each seat was a thick, open suit with legs and arms, and on the headrests sat VR sets.

"Uhh, hold on..." She already regretted her query.

Robins replied, "I believe its official title is Ecstasy Oasis. Where—"

"Technology Ignites Passion," she finished. "I've heard of the company. Didn't know they had a venue on the *Bres.*"

"Venues. It's one of the most popular activities on the ship. There are several suites."

"Why am I not surprised?"

Waylis asked, "What is it? What do humans do here?"

"Never mind."

The Primian's impression of humanity was already bad enough.

"If it's so popular," Setia said, "how come it's empty?"

"This suite is scheduled for cleaning. The bots will arrive soon."

"You mean all those booths are *dirty*?"

Robins sighed. "It's the only public facility I could think of where there are no cameras. Perhaps you would rather we talk in the corridor?"

"I was expecting to go to your office or maybe the aviary. We won't be able to stay here long. Considering how *popular* it is."

"Everywhere I, Carys, and Miriam live or regularly visit is too dangerous. It's becoming increasingly difficult for us to move around the ship unobserved. I was taking a huge risk to go to the ventilation tunnel where you were hiding."

"So Security might know you've come here too?"

"Perhaps."

"Then we should leave."

But where could they go? The situation was hopeless.

"Wait a while," Robins said. "There's more to this than you think. I only found out some vital information myself today."

"And?" Setia demanded when he didn't go on. "Are you going to let us in on the secret?"

"Please wait."

"All right, while we're waiting..." she wanted to sit down, but after casting a glance at one of the reclined seats she changed her mind "...I want to know how you managed to find us. Did you search every vent on the whole freaking ship?"

"That would have been extremely stupid. I mapped a skein to find you."

"You can see my location?!" Setia's jaw dropped. "I didn't know you could do that."

"You didn't guess that might be the case? You said at our first meeting that you understood all things are connected. People and places are just forms of matter. Time and events are more tenuous. They are what makes mapping so difficult."

"You mean you know where I am—where everyone is—all the time?"

"I'm limited by what's in the system. While you were on Prime I had no idea where you were. We relied on your trackers and comm connections to trace you. Once they disappeared I was blind. But as soon as I heard you'd tried to speak to Bujold, I created a map and found where you were hiding. I couldn't come out to you, however, until the quiet shift. It was too risky for you to emerge from the vent while there were people about."

"So it's common knowledge that we went to the captain?"

Before Robins could answer, the door opened, and Captain Bujold entered.

"Shit!" Setia launched herself at the woman, threw her to the floor, and straddled her, pinning her by her shoulders. A hasty look at the entrance didn't reveal any guards. Maybe they were outside.

"Ms Zees," Bujold said calmly. "I am far too old for this nonsense. Please get off me."

"Yeah, like that's going to happen. You're staying right where you are. You're going to be my and Waylis's passports off this ship."

If she could hold the captain hostage, she might be able to bargain passage to the surface. It was clear her days aboard the *Bres* were over. She would take her chances with the Primians. If she brought Waylis back they might accept she was on their side.

Robins gave a quiet cough.

Bujold met his gaze with an exasperated look. "Could you please explain?"

"Setia," Robins said, "the captain is our ally, not an enemy."

"The hell she isn't," Setia protested. "She called on guards for me and Waylis this morning."

"I had no choice except to summon them," Bujold explained. "My office is observed. If I had listened to you, if I had done anything except immediately signal an alert, I would have been under suspicion. Now, please, get off!"

Setia turned to Robins. He nodded.

Reluctantly, she clambered off the prone woman. Bujold got to her feet and straightened her tunic. "Thank you," she said with dignity. "If it's worth anything, I did delay as long as I felt was reasonable before raising the alarm."

"Well, we managed to get away, I suppose," Setia conceded.

"It was very foolish of you to visit me."

"You're not the first person to say that, but I didn't see what choice we had. You realise the Primians are like us, right? You know you're killing people down there?"

"Believe me, I'm all too aware." Bujold's expression was pained. "I have been against the attacks since the very beginning, even before Ahmad disappeared, before I heard Carys and Sheldrake's debriefings, and after you and Miriam were kidnapped. The Fleet's response has been extraordinarily heavy-handed and utterly misguided." She sighed. "I have seen more than my fill of war and death. I have no desire to see any more, and I would never have signed up to captain the *Bres* if I had even imagined this might happen."

"Wait," said Setia, "go back. Did you say the attacks were planned *before* the Primians took Ahmad?"

"The *Bres* is not the only ship involved in the colonisation," Bujold replied. "Scientists from the *Balor* and *Banba* discovered evidence of intelligent life not long after the Fleet arrived at Prime."

"And the immediate reaction was to decide to bomb the shit out of them?!"

"Not the immediate reaction, no. But the Primians didn't help themselves. If they'd come to us—"

"If we'd what?!" Waylis stalked towards her, hands clenched into fists. "We don't owe you anything. You're the new arrivals. Prime is our planet. You don't belong there. You can't just turn up somewhere and act like you own the place."

"Faced with a technologically superior life form," Bujold replied evenly, "there were wiser courses of actions your people might have taken. Regardless, what's happened has happened. There's no undoing anything. We have to find a way forward. The problem is, though my sympathies lie with the local people, I am outnumbered. The other captains don't agree, and neither do their military commanders. Markham is especially bullish. I appear to be the only dissenter, and I've increasingly felt that if I didn't mind my words my own safety might be under threat. We are a long way from Earth. The Fleet is accountable only to itself. If there is an attempt to turn the tide, it must be undertaken with great care. To be frank, I am not sure it's possible."

Setia rounded on Robins. "Why didn't you tell us she was against the attacks?"

Bujold answered for him. "Mapper Robins is the first person I revealed my true sentiments to, just a few hours ago. I knew of the connection between you and thought he might be able to guess where you'd gone."

Her attention not leaving Robins, Setia pointed at the captain. "Didn't she know about the location-finder aspect of skeins either?"

"Some aspects of mapping are best kept quiet."

The door opened again. A herd of cleaning bots had arrived. The hand-sized cylinders fanned out and began to scour every surface.

"Excuse *me*," Waylis said between her teeth. "While you're all standing here chatting my people are dying. I want to know what you're going to do about it."

"So do I," said Carys, stepping in behind the bots.

"Me too." Miriam had also arrived, hobbling on her crutch.

Forty-Nine

Setia stepped down from the shuttle, helping Miriam. At the bottom of the steps, she took a look around. The *Banba's* shuttle bay was similar to the *Bres*'s. No surprise there. The three starships comprising the Interstellar Fleet had been constructed along the same lines and, as far as she knew, for the same purpose: an initial colonisation, disembarking the passengers who had paid for most of the Fleet's construction, followed by onward journeys into the galaxy. What exactly those prospective journeys entailed was shrouded in secrecy.

Captain Bujold knew, no doubt, but she wasn't about to give any hints. Certainly not until the current crisis was resolved.

The captain looked more world weary than ever as she followed Miriam down to the deck. Robins was already being greeted by his fellow mappers. Carys Ellis was last to descend. Setia only had time to notice the state of the *Banba*'s utilitarian six-legged 'bug' shuttle—marked with holes and absent two legs—before her group was escorted from the bay by armed guards.

Setia hung back until she was walking next to Bujold. "Is it usually like this when you attend these meetings?"

"Like what?"

"The goons with guns. What do they think we're gonna do?

Shoot up the ship?"

"It isn't usually like this, no. Markham and the other military commanders must perceive our party as a threat."

"Some threat. Two female passengers, one half-crippled, a bird expert, and two, er, senior people. No offence."

The captain gave her a sidelong look but didn't reply.

The mappers who had met and now accompanied Robins were also getting on in years. Was it a coincidence or was skein mapping easier the older you got? Certainly, from what she'd seen, it was highly skilled and complex. She doubted she could ever be able grasp it no matter how long she lived.

Depending on how things went, that might not be long.

Markham was already in the meeting room with his military commander peers. The three uniforms sat together at the table, flanked by two guards in full armour. Each man held a rifle across his chest and surveyed the newcomers through their visor slits.

Burnap's balls.

The commanders really did feel unsafe.

The escorts left. Bujold gave a curt nod to a man and a woman also wearing captain's attire before joining them. The rest of the party from the *Bres* and the mappers were left to find their own seats around the oval table. A large interface screen looked out blankly from one wall. Within the open middle of the table sat a holo projector.

Miriam put her crutch down and Carys helped her sit. Setia sat on her other side, resting her elbows on the tabletop, tension tightening her every fibre.

"You have ten minutes, Bujold," Markham growled. "I hope you understand the depth of the concession we're allowing. This is highly irregular, and I strongly recommend that *that* individual..." he jabbed a finger at Setia "...is taken into custody as soon as this meeting is over. She is an escaped prisoner and extremely dangerous."

Setia raised her eyebrows, looking mildly shocked. A titter ran around the room, and she couldn't help a bemused smile. Her size and build didn't exactly scream Dangerous. Her appearance belied her abilities. She was glad Lieutenant-Colonel Markham had made himself look stupid. It would help their cause.

He continued to dig. "She could even be a Primian."

"A what?" asked his neighbour.

"Unfortunately one of them slipped aboard the *Bres*," Markham replied, "camouflaged as that woman. There's no telling them apart. I thought we had the right one in custody but now I'm not so sure. The one in the brig escaped, thanks to inside help—I suspect from some of those present. They've both been sneaking around the ship. You see the risks the natives of Prime pose? This is exactly what I've been warning against all along."

Mapper Robins said, "Ten minutes may be insufficient for our purposes, but we will do our best." He briefly consulted with his counterparts before giving the command to dim the lights.

The room was enshrouded in shadow. The remaining light glimmered from the suits of the armed guards, and the attendees transformed into grey shades.

The three mappers had brought personal interfaces. They spent thirty seconds working on them before green lines fluoresced from the projector, filling the central space. Brilliant dots marked the places where the lines crossed. Some areas held only a few thick strands. In many others, thousands of filaments tangled in dense webs.

"A skein, ladies and gentlemen," Robins announced. "Perhaps you've seen one before. They are difficult to understand and, to the untrained eye, they may all look the same. Nothing could be further from the truth. Every skein cast is unique. Even applying identical elements and constraints, a difference of a few seconds between casts will result in changes, sometimes very large and entirely unanticipated changes."

"Get on with it!" Markham barked.

"Forgive me, Lieutenant-Colonel. I am merely setting the scene so everyone present has a clear understanding of what we're about to say."

"Well, what you've told us so far is that you have no idea what the future holds, so by all means, carry on. Nine minutes."

"When we arrived at Prime," Robins said, "my colleagues and I perceived many complications in forthcoming events. That was to be expected. Humanity's previous forays into planetary colonisation haven't been successful. I don't need to go over old history. We all know what happened on Mars, Ganymede and Ceres. On a rocky planet roughly the size of Earth and with a very similar atmosphere, things should have been easi*er*, but not easy."

He gave a short cough. "It may not come as a surprise that many of the complications derived from the colonists. Mapping large populations always produces unreliable results due to the copious variables, yet we saw consistencies across the board. Predicted colonisation failure rates ranged between 15 and 33 percent, despite adjustments. It was these forecasts that prompted me to send to the surface a party of individuals the skeins flagged as extremely significant."

"For god's sake," Markham muttered.

"I was attempting to either shake loose more favourable variations in the outcomes," Robins went on, "or to at least provide better clarity in the skeins. What you're looking at now is a mapping from before the team embarked on its expedition." He murmured to a colleague, and the skein disappeared. It was quickly replaced by another.

Even to Setia, this one appeared less of a mess.

Robins said, "This skein was cast a day into the expedition. I hope you can see the effects of those twenty-four hours our intrepid explorers had spent on Prime. Predicted failure rates for the colonisation dropped to 10 to 13 percent. It is to be noted that these results are not derived from any data from the planet. We have no access to local surface systems—"

"Systems?!" one of the military commanders scoffed. "Do they even have them?"

"Indications of success were looking better. Then, as we know, the existence of Primians was discovered in the area of the *Banba*'s settlement. An unfortunate conflict arose, during which a shuttle was damaged."

A ship's captain interjected, "Our people were lucky to get away with their lives."

"Without any consultation with mappers," said Robins, "an attack was launched."

Markham said, "Less of an attack, more of a retaliation."

"Since then, against our advice, the assaults on intelligent life forms have continued." Robins spoke to his colleague again. "And *this* is the result."

A third skein appeared. Setia inhaled. Compared to this mapping of the proposed colonisation, the first one had been clear and simple. The lines in this new skein had multiplied, the entanglements had grown larger and more complex so that many were large blobs of brilliant green. A multitude of lines branched away to the edges, where they cut off.

"The likelihood of the colonisation failing currently stands at roughly 80 percent. Let us be clear. That means if we were to send the colonists down to the surface today, as a group they would have only a 20 percent chance of living out their natural lifespans. Unless these attacks stop and we attempt to repair the damage the Fleet has inflicted, the men, women and children we leave behind when we depart are likely to die horrible, painful deaths."

Robins returned the lights to the normal brightness. The chaotic skein faded to near-invisibility. The mapper leaned forwards and rested his palms on the table. "I have made as clear as I possibly can the effects we are creating. Yet they are only the effects on our own people, on humans. I cannot imagine the devastation we are causing on the surface to the innocent people of Prime." He straightened up. "Thank you for this opportunity to speak. It's something we mappers have been requesting for a long time. I hope you now understand the severity of the situation and will act accordingly."

He sat down.

"Twelve minutes," Markham said. "You overran, Robins. Tut tut. Yet we have been gracious and allowed you to have your say. I hope you will now stop bothering us with your mumbo-jumbo and allow us to get on with doing what we came here to do—provide a safe, habitable environment for our passengers, who have paid a great deal of money for the chance to take part in humanity's first deep space colonisation."

"Skein mapping is by no means mumbo-jumbo," the mapper retorted evenly. "I could, for example, predict with some accuracy the date of your death. Would you like me to do that?"

Markham's face paled. "No, thank you very much." With a slight tremble in his voice he attempted a light-hearted tone as he said, "Besides, I won't be around to congratulate you on being correct."

Setia slammed the table. "While you geriatrics are sitting here trading jibes, Primians are dying! Who the hell do you think you are, Markham, you blood-thirsty maniac, killing people just so you can pretend to some other people that you're doing a fantastic job?"

He retorted with a sneer, "In any military offensive some collateral damage is to be expected. You wouldn't know that. You don't have a military background. So kindly shut up and allow those with the relevant experience to do the talking."

Captain Bujold said, "The agreement was that you would listen to the mappers *and* the members of the team who encountered the local people face-to-face."

Markham waved a dismissive hand. "Go ahead. Let them speak. It won't make any difference. You were outvoted once and you'll be outvoted again, Captain. You know we're doing the right thing in the circumstances. We cannot tolerate the threat these life forms pose. They vastly outnumber our colonists. We cannot afford to show weakness. If that results in loss of life, so be it. We have the lesson of history to tell us what successful colonisation involves, despite what the new-fangled 'science' of skein-mapping tells us. Perhaps you find it distasteful. If you don't have the stomach for it, thank the lord the rest of us do. That's all I can say."

Bujold only turned to Carys, signalling for her to speak.

It was testament to the captain's dignity and what had to be her reputation and regard among the Fleet's commanders that she'd managed to get them to agree to this meeting.

Setia chewed the inside of her cheek as she awaited her turn.

Fifty

Carys gave a detailed account of her experiences on the planet surface. For the first time, Setia heard of the gruelling march Carys and Sheldrake had undertaken to return to the settlement and send out a rescue team. Neither of them had slept or even stopped for more than a few minutes the entire walk back. They had also encountered the rain sprites again, though without incident. Carys wryly joked that the sight of the strange beings had leant them extra speed just when they'd been flagging.

Carys's demeanour was calm as she related the ordeal to her audience. It must have been harrowing, but Carys betrayed no signs of self-pity or distress. She was a real stoic. The only times Setia could recall her displaying vulnerability was when, drunk on tequila, she'd spoken a bit about her childhood, and when she'd been worried about her bird.

As she began to talk about the rescue team's attempt to locate Setia and Miriam, one of the captains interrupted, "Everyone present knows about the slashed tent and the missing members of your party. Go back to the time the native creature disguised itself as the construction site supervisor in order to get past your defences."

"It isn't really a disguise," Carys replied hesitantly. She glanced at

Setia out of the corners of her eyes. “They seem to kind of *become* us.”

“You really couldn’t tell the thing apart from the person who had been kidnapped?”

Carys seemed to deflate. “If I’m completely honest, not at first. I was confused about how he’d managed to get there and what had happened to our interfaces, but the man was identical to Ahmad. He even sounded the same.”

“Hmpf,” said the captain. “This is bad. Very bad.”

Markham said, “That’s exactly what I’ve been saying all along. The natives of that planet simply can’t be trusted. If they manage to infiltrate our settlements, who knows what might happen?”

“They wouldn’t do that!” Miriam protested. “They’re too scared of us. They just want us to leave them alone.”

“It is *not* your turn to speak,” Markham snapped. “Ellis, do you have anything to add?”

“That’s about it. Only...” she bit her lip “...if what I hear is correct, that there are millions of Primians, then they could have attacked us at any time. We were armed but we would have been outnumbered. We had no idea what we were doing or where we were going. But the Primians didn’t attack us. They just tried to find out more about us.”

Markham gave a derisive *Pfft*!. “I shouldn’t have to remind you that the site supervisor is still missing. And your party can hardly claim to have survived unscathed. The correct thing for the creatures to do would have been to declare their presence and propose negotiations over land ownership.”

“Burnap’s balls!” Setia exclaimed. “What’s to negotiate? It’s their world!”

“Negotiation is the only sensible option when faced with a superior force. Negotiation or immediate surrender.”

“We’re a colonisation fleet, not a freaking army. We aren’t here to make war. The reason Ahmad is still missing is because you bombed the shit out of the place he was being held. You probably killed him.

But wait, that's okay, right? After all, it's just collateral damage!" Her voice had risen to a shout. She found herself on her feet, and her face felt hot and sweaty.

Bujold thundered, "Sit down! Or I'll have you thrown out."

Mastering every remaining iota of self control, Setia sank into her seat.

"Thank you for instilling some discipline into your delegation, Bujold," Markham said. "I was about to suggest that Zees spoke next, but let's give her time to calm down, shall we?" He focused on Miriam. "I believe your name is Belby?"

"It is. Does anyone mind if I don't stand?"

"We're fully aware of your injury," Markham replied. "I would be delighted to hear about *your* time on the planet."

The story Miriam told sounded ridiculous even to Setia, who was sympathetic to what she was trying to do. She talked up her captors, scraping the barrel for incidents of kindness and compassion while glossing over her capture, imprisonment and threats of torture. At the end of her narrative, a strained silence fell.

Markham broke it with an icy, "I see. Just to be clear. These lovely, gentle creatures in whose company you spent such a wonderful time... Are they the same people who *shot you in the leg, fracturing your femur to such an extent the bone had to be entirely reconstructed*?"

Miriam flushed deep red. "We were trying to get away... We shot at them first."

Setia cringed with second-hand embarrassment.

"My dear," said Markham, "I say this with the utmost respect, you are a well-meaning but utterly blithering idiot. And anyone here who pays any attention to anything you said, matches you in the idiot stakes. That is all. Now it's your turn, Zees. Make it fast. I can't wait for this farce to be over so we can continue this colonisation the good, old-fashioned way."

"I'm not going to tell you what happened to me."

"Oh, that's wonderful to hear. Let us—"

"I'm going to talk to you about the Primians."

"That isn't why you're here."

"Miriam's already covered her time with them. Mine wasn't much different. I don't have anything worth adding. But you should know what you're doing and what the repercussions are going to be."

"We've already heard from Robins and his magic crew." Markham smirked.

"Oh, let her have her say," one of his fellow commanders said. "It won't hurt to find out more about the enemy."

"Right," said Setia. "The first thing you need to understand is the Primians are from Earth. They aren't aliens, even if they do live on an alien planet. We think they were brought to Prime by benevolent beings trying to save them from being wiped out, like we wiped out all the other variations of humans in the distant past. So you need to understand that's who you're killing. The people down there aren't—"

"Slow down, Setia," Robins interrupted. "You aren't making a lot of sense."

A captain asked, "What do you mean by 'benevolent beings'? Who are they? Where are they now? Did you meet them on Prime too?"

"They aren't there anymore."

Markham chuckled. "Then how on Earth—or rather, Prime—do you know about them? What evidence did you see of all this nonsense? Or are you just making it up, hoping to tug on our heartstrings?"

"To do that you would need a heart," Setia shot back. "The Primians have cave paintings showing what happened."

"Cave paintings? Ha! Rubbish. A cave painting can mean anything. I can't say I've made a big study of them, but if this great exodus happened, why isn't it represented in *our* cave paintings, hm? Got you there, haven't I?"

Setia clenched her jaw to prevent herself from saying something that, while she wouldn't regret it, definitely wouldn't help her cause. "I don't know if the events aren't represented in our cave art. Maybe they are and we haven't found the paintings yet or we've misinterpreted them. But anyway, *we* weren't the ones leaving. We didn't have a good reason for recording it."

Carys lifted a hand. "If it helps, I think the Primians might be Denisovans, a hominin—a human-like great ape—that went extinct. We don't know a lot about them. I'm guessing they're Denisovans because they don't look like Neanderthals, another hominin we know a lot more about. But tens of thousands of years must have passed since Primians arrived on Prime, so their physical characteristics might have changed. Some of us carry Neanderthal and/or Denisovan genes. It should be easy to establish the relationship."

"Exactly!" Setia exclaimed. "The people you're killing are your distant relatives."

"For what it's worth," Carys added, "I think Denisovans might appear in our ancient stories. It only occurred to me when I saw..." her eyes widened in alarm and she spluttered "...I mean..."

Markham growled, "We all know you've met the Primian spy. I'm looking forward to meeting her myself, right before her execution."

Carys sagged. "The first time I saw her I made the connection. She looks like... well, you're going to laugh, but she looks like an elf. It's the way her eyes turn up at the corners. In my cultural history, elves lived in hills. They abducted babies, exchanging them for babies who looked identical but were really what we would call changelings." She heaved a sigh. "You get the picture. I would put good money on Denisovans being included in human oral histories."

It was the first Setia had heard of Carys's guess, and she was struck dumb at its outlandishness. She wished the woman hadn't added that little tidbit. It was so odd it made the rest of what she'd said less believable.

A slow clap started up. It was Markham. "A gold star to Carys Ellis for the most ridiculous drivel we've heard today. Zees, sit down."

"I haven't finished!"

"Yes, you have. Sit."

Setia remained resolutely upright.

He ignored her. "Bujold, you've wasted more than an hour of precious time with these ridiculous presentations. We have three ships full of colonists champing at the bit, impatiently awaiting their opportunity to set foot on a new world. We have swathes of land to clear of hostile organisms. We have other, more interesting voyages to embark upon. Captain, you will return to the *Bres* with your delegation—except for Zees—and continue the search for the Primian spy. Meanwhile, those of us with real jobs to do will do them. Do I make myself clear?"

The fury in Bujold's eyes was so intense Setia wouldn't have been surprised if laser beams had shot out and turned Markham to smoking ash. "What do you mean, *except for Zees*?"

"She's under suspicion of being Primian. If she can't prove she isn't, the safest course of action would be to execute her. She will go to the *Banba*'s brig, which she is far less likely to escape."

"I'm not going back to the brig," Setia declared. "I haven't done anything wrong. What crime did I commit, huh? And how the hell am I supposed to prove I'm not a Primian? That's the biggest load of bullshit I ever heard."

Markham smirked. "You say that as if your opinion mattered. Perhaps you are the real Zees. I don't care. I knew you were trouble as soon as I met you at your final interview at the passenger processing centre on Earth. If it weren't for Robins you wouldn't be here, and we would have one less mischief-maker to deal with. So much for the effectiveness of skein mapping."

"I'm not going back to the brig!" Setia reiterated, louder.

Markham replied with a sly smile, "Oh, I think you are. Guards, seize that woman."

Setia leapt from her seat and dashed to the door.

It was locked.

"Thought you might try a trick like that," Markham remarked. "I sealed the exit the moment you entered the room. Guards?"

But the two men didn't move. Their heads were turned toward each other as if they were talking on internal comm.

"Guards! Apprehend that woman this instant!"

Setia had her back pressed to the door. Confusion emanated from the distracted guards and spread through the meeting attendees like a shockwave, an incensed Markham its epicentre.

Then one of the guards abruptly jerked his weapon around and shot the other in the leg. At the close range, the shot must have penetrated the armour.

Everyone froze. Setia gaped. Time seemed to slow down.

The wounded guard staggered. His attacker snatched his rifle from his grasp, and before the injured man had even hit the floor, tossed it across the room to Setia.

She caught it reflexively, shock turning her numb.

Who was her unexpected saviour? Had Primians infiltrated the *Banba* too?

She found herself aiming her weapon at the military commanders. A captain took a step backwards. She swept her rifle's muzzle around to target him.

Markham made a move on the rogue guard, but he was too slow. The guard poked him in the chest with his weapon. "I'm sorry, sir. But I have to do this." He gave his comrade on the floor a little kick, as if urging him to do something. The man's armour dissolved, revealing an injured soldier, features contorted with pain.

For the first time, the rogue guard spoke on external comm. "Zees, put on his suit."

"W-what?" Everything had moved so fast. What was this guy thinking? What was his plan? Did he even have one? His voice had sounded familiar...

Recognition hit. "*Sheldrake*?!"

"Move it, Zees. We don't have a lot of time. If we're fast, we can make it to the bay."

"What the hell are you doing?"

"What does it look like?"

"In case you hadn't noticed, we're locked in."

"Put on the suit. We'll figure it out."

"You're deranged."

As they'd argued, Bujold had risen to her feet. "Very heroic, but unnecessary." She activated the room's interface.

Looking out from the screen was a second Captain Bujold.

Fifty-One

"What!?" Markham gasped, eyes popping as he switched his gaze from the screen to the Captain Bujold standing opposite him. "You... What?" Then he somewhat regained his composure and snapped, "Guards, arrest that woman! She's a Primian!"

But one of his guards was rolling on the floor in agony, and the most generous description of the other was *not currently obeying orders.*

Markham frowned and his eyes became unfocused, as if he was mentally transmitting an order.

"There's no point," Bujold told him. "It's over."

One of her fellow captains asked, "Marigold, what have you done?"

Marigold?

But Bujold's attention was on her double. "At least, I think it's over. Waylis?"

"It's done," the Primian replied. "The transfer is complete." Her eyes filled with tears and her chin trembled in an expression entirely at odds with the captain's usual look. "Thank you. I can't thank you enough. We stand a chance now."

"Transfer?!" Markham had turned puce. "What transfer?!"

"From the *Bres* to Primian centres all over the planet," Bujold answered coolly. "Waylis has transmitted a copy of the contents of the ship's database, including our current understanding of the various branches of science, the ship's entire military supply specs and operation, the design of her engines and all other technology..." Emotion entered her features and she waved a hand dramatically as she concluded "...the lot! The 'enemy' now has access to the exact same information as us. They're going to level up, and then what are you going to do, Lieutenant-Colonel Markham? What are you going to do when your enemy is capable of defending itself? What are you going to tell our passengers when you're dropping them off to be slaughtered?"

"You're a madwoman! A traitor! I'll have you executed for treason!"

"You're getting very fond of executing people, aren't you? Which is strange, considering I am your superior, and *I* have final say on what happens to every soul aboard the *Bres*. I can hardly betray myself, can I?"

"You've betrayed the Fleet."

"I declare my ship independent from the Fleet. I will no longer be participating in your genocide. There will be no more debates, no more votes. From now on, the *Bres* will fly under one authority. Mine."

Markham slumped to his seat, floppy as a rag doll. "You've ruined everything."

Tension seemed to resonate at a high pitch, like the sound created by running a finger around the rim of a glass. Then it eased. People shifted in their seats. On the screen, Waylis began to look a little less like Bujold. Her hair was darkening and lines on her face were softening.

Sheldrake's armour deactivated. Within a few seconds he wore only his regular uniform, though he retained his weapon. "Zees, what's going on?"

"The captain changed the game." She added, "What the hell were you thinking? We would never have made it to the bay."

A roar erupted from the lieutenant-colonel. He leapt to his feet, snatched the rifle from a shocked Sheldrake and lifted it to fire at Bujold.

Setia shot him.

There was no time to try to only wound him and, looking back, she wasn't sure she'd wanted to. She aimed high, and the pulse round hit his neck. He couldn't even scream. His throat was a burning mess. The arteries carrying blood to his brain must have been scorched shut. He toppled, gaze fixed, mouth lolling open, and landed across the back of his chair. His upper half sprawled across the table, He was still.

A horrible barbecue stench filled the air, and the vent fans whined as they strained to extract it.

One of the mappers vomited.

Setia lowered her rifle. Addressing Robins, she asked, "Did you predict that?"

As the delegation from the *Bres* slowly made its way to the shuttle bay, Sheldrake pulled Setia to one side and said quietly, "What just happened? I don't get it."

"Don't worry, you weren't supposed to. Only the captain, Robins, Carys and me were in on it. No one else knew. But..." she swallowed "...what you did in there was really brave. I'm touched. To be frank, you're the last person I would have expected to disobey Markham's orders."

"It was obvious you wouldn't have lasted two minutes in the *Banba*'s brig. He had it in for you. And I didn't agree with what he was doing anyway. I joined the military to defeat the bad guys. It was looking more and more like *we* were the bad guys. I didn't want to be a part of that, and I wasn't going to let One Punch Girl die without a fight."

"I wish you wouldn't..."

"What?"

"Nothing." *You can call me One Punch Girl as much as you want.*

"So the attacks on Prime are over now?"

"I'm not sure. Captain Bujold has given the Primians the information they need to mount a proper defence, but it'll take time. On the other hand, there are millions of them and they're well hidden. If the commanders of the *Banba* and *Balor* want to continue the assaults, they're going to have their work cut out. And their colonists are going to have miserable, dangerous lives."

They walked a few moments in silence, then Sheldrake said, "There was no point to that meeting at all, right?"

"There absolutely was. It just wasn't the official point. We needed a distraction to give Waylis time to transfer all the data. Only the captain could directly comm Prime, but Markham was having her watched. If she'd tried to beam a ton of information down to the surface it would have been picked up immediately. We figured that if she was at a meeting on another ship, there would be no point in monitoring her. It was a gamble that no one would notice she was both here and in her office."

"And the Primian had to become Bujold to circumvent the security?"

"You got it."

"The mappers' presentations, the reports you, Carys and Miriam gave were just—"

"Playing for time."

"You arguing with Markham, trying to escape...?"

She gave him a small smile.

"I didn't need to save you?"

"I don't think so, but I appreciate it."

Fifty-Two

Setia took a sip of her drink and cast a glance around the bar. It was full, but within a few weeks it would be nearly empty. The programme for disembarking the colonists had begun. Soon, the only patrons in the drinking establishment would be off-duty military and crew, plus perhaps a few passengers who'd managed to wrangle a berth for the onward journey. The *Bres* would be a glorified, space-travelling tin can with a few beans rattling around in it.

Miriam was the next to arrive. Setia waved. Miriam quickly spotted her and came over. She hadn't used her crutch for a while, but she still walked with a slight limp.

Hopping up onto the neighbouring stool, Miriam asked, "Heard anything yet?"

"Nope. I hope we'll hear it from the horse's mouth."

Miriam tapped in her drink order.

"What are you having?" Setia enquired.

"Guess."

"Margarita?"

"You know me too well."

Setia had the same. The drink brought back good memories. It reminded her of sitting inside a tent, cold and damp, while rain hammered on the roof. It made her think of sharing stories with friends.

The second arrival caused more of a stir. It was Carys, in uniform. But that wasn't what attracted the revellers' attention. A bird sat on her shoulder, meeting every gaze with an imperious stare.

Setia jumped from her stool with joy. When Carys reached their table her face was wreathed in a rare grin.

"You got Loki back?!" Setia breathed. "When? How?"

"He arrived today. A Primian gave him to one of the engineers, who brought him back at the end of his shift."

"Is he okay?" Miriam asked.

"He doesn't seem too much the worse for wear. I don't know what he's been doing since you guys saw him, but someone must have been feeding him the right stuff and looking after him." Carys sat down. "I can only stay a little while. I should be in the aviary but I put a notice up to say it's temporarily closed. I don't get a lot of visitors these days anyway. Everyone's too busy preparing to leave."

Miriam said, "But you must be busy getting ready to transport all the birds."

Carys shook her head and picked up Setia's glass. "Can I?"

"Go ahead."

She took a drink before replying, "The birds won't be going to the surface. It's official. The higher-ups decided that nowhere on Prime has a climate that will support avian life, and it would be pointless and cruel to attempt to establish it. I heard today."

"But that means..." Miriam paused.

"That means I won't be going to the surface either. Or else who would look after the birds?"

"That's amazing!" Miriam gave her a tight hug. "You're coming too!"

"I am. I can't believe it. For better or worse, I'll be with you for at least one more voyage."

"What do you mean for better or worse?" asked Setia. "What could be bad about sharing a ship with us?"

"Oh, you know..." Carys chuckled. She really was coming out of her shell. "I still don't know how you persuaded Bujold to allow you to stay on board, Setia."

"Uhh, why *wouldn't* she allow me to stay? I don't know what you're implying, but maybe the captain's decision was something to do with my promise to quash the rumours about her, er, addiction."

Miriam burst into peals of laughter. Wiping her eyes, she said, "Who would have thought anyone was paying attention to who used the Ecstasy Oases and how often?"

"I don't know," Setia replied, "but someone's keeping count."

An unfortunate fallout from the plot to trick Markham had been the besmirching of Captain Bujold's reputation. To evade capture, Setia and Waylis had locked themselves in a booth at the Ecstasy Oasis, and in order for Waylis to learn to copy Bujold, the latter had been forced to make frequent, regular visits. Setia had observed the odd looks the captain had received while going about the ship.

The real reason Bujold had allowed Setia passage for the onward journey was twofold. Firstly, she'd simply asked and the captain had granted it as thanks for her help in stopping the attacks on Prime. Secondly, Robins had announced that, according to his mapping, outcomes were more favourable when he factored in Setia's presence on the ship.

But the reason she gave her friends was far funnier.

Miriam had successfully argued her right to remain aboard because she was disabled and therefore not suited to colony life. She also might not have wanted to stay on Prime because there were no beaches or cocktails, but Setia hadn't asked her yet. No one in their right minds would choose to live on the planet once they'd been there a while. It was a fact many thousands of people were about to discover, but by then there would be no going back.

"Here he is." Setia had spotted a certain one-hundred-and-eighty-pound beefcake entering the bar.

"He's free to roam," said Miriam. "That has to be good, right?"

"I'm not sure," Carys replied. "He doesn't look too happy."

Sheldrake joined them. Glumly, he pulled out a stool and perched on it. His head down, he gave his order. Physically, he looked okay, considering the weeks he'd spent in the brig. However, his face told another tale.

"How'd it go?" Miriam asked gently.

His shoulders sagged another few centimetres. "Dishonourable discharge."

"Oh no." She touched his arm. "I'm sorry."

"I should have expected it. You don't shoot a fellow soldier and get away with it. I guess I should be glad it isn't any worse."

"What happens now?" Setia asked.

"Don't know. They're still deciding. They can't send me back to Earth. The only other option is to join the colonisation."

"That isn't the only alternative," said Miriam. "You could stay on the *Bres*."

"Doing what?" When Miriam didn't answer he continued, "There's no two ways about it. I'm screwed."

"No, you're not," Setia said. "Don't give up hope." She didn't want to raise his expectations, but she would talk to Bujold and Robins. It would be a criminal waste to lose this brave, principled man to the wet planet.

A slot in the centre of the table opened, and a platform bearing two drinks rose up. Miriam took her Margarita and slid Sheldrake's beer in front of him. He grabbed the glass and gulped the drink down before tapping in an order for another. The women shared a look.

Standing, Carys said, "I'd better go." She patted Sheldrake's back. "Keep your chin up. I'm sure we'll figure something out."

Before she could leave, another figure approached.

"Waylis?" Carys asked. "I thought you'd gone home."

"I did," the Primian replied, "but I'm back for a visit."

"How long will you be here? Only I have to get back to work."

"Actually, in a few days I'll be here for a very long time. So if you need to leave..."

Carys frowned and sat down again. "I'm not in that much of a hurry. What do you mean, you'll be here for a long time?"

Waylis took a breath. "In spite of everything, I loved being on this ship. I loved all the amazing technology you have. It's like magic. And I loved the spirit of adventure. I never knew it was possible to travel to the stars, and the idea fills me with excitement. I spent ages thinking about it, and I spent many hours talking with Grackler. Finally, I made my decision, but I still had to ask your captain's permission. She's just said yes. When the *Bres* leaves, I will be aboard her."

Setia's mouth fell open.

"You mean," Miriam said, "after everything we did to your people, you still want to be around us?"

"Humans aren't all bad. *You're* all nice, and so is Captain Bujold. Only a few of you are wicked. The rest of you are just, well, silly and lazy."

Waylis had been heavily involved in the reconciliation process between the Fleet and the Primians. From the sound of it, she'd also encountered many ordinary colonists. In return for helping to repair the damage from the bombardments, the locals had allowed the colonisation to go ahead. Though it was true that many colonists were indeed 'silly and lazy' they also happened to carry a wealth of knowledge and experience of living with the technology Prime was about to develop. The Primians understood that humans could be an asset. Most importantly, the Fleet had ceased the attacks of its own accord. Setia doubted the locals would have allowed humans on the surface in any other circumstances.

Miriam laughed. "You seem to have a good handle on us. I'm glad you're coming on the voyage."

Waylis was staring at Carys's insignia. "Where did you get that?"

"My badge? I didn't get it anywhere. It's just part of my uniform. It means I work in the animals section."

Excitedly, Setia said, "You recognise it, don't you, Waylis? The three hares. You know that symbol."

"I do. We have it on my world."

"I saw it there myself," Setia said. "What does it represent?"

"I'm not sure. It's very old. It's carved into rocks, but no one knows exactly what it means. Some say it's so old our ancient people couldn't have made the carvings. They're too sophisticated and we didn't have the skill at that time."

"Huh." Carys's lip curled in puzzlement. "That's funny. This symbol is found in all kinds of places on Earth, places that don't seem to have been connected in any other way in the past."

The table's central slot opened and Sheldrake's second beer arrived. He drank it at the same speed as the first, and then tapped on his screen.

Carys said, "Maybe you should order more than one. It'll save time."

He nodded morosely.

Setia sensed a disturbance in the immediate area. People moved about and the chatter of the bar's patrons rose a notch. Someone was making his way through the crowd, and it was parting like a shoal of fish in the presence of a shark.

Tall and shaggy-haired, his clothes wrinkled and no doubt odorous, Dr Jacobs had arrived. He noticed her and his lips parted in a smile, revealing yellow teeth. He gave her a thumbs up.

Setia grimaced.

The voyage of the Interstellar Fleet continues in...

STEADFAST STAR

Sign up to my reader group for exclusive free books, discounts on new releases, review crew invitations and other interesting stuff:

https://jjgreenauthor.com/free-books/

Author's Notes

Welcome to the end of the first book in the Interstellar Fleet series. I hope you've enjoyed the story so far. It promises to be a long one, featuring a wide range of characters and travelling to the far reaches of the galaxy.

Many thanks to my editor, Liza Wood, Substack subscribers, Patreon supporters, and all the shipmates at Starship JJ Green Shipmates, without whose support none of these books would be possible.

Now onto the background, notes and interesting tidbits about *Talman Prime*.

If you came to the book from my Star Legend series, you will already know some of the character backgrounds and references, but for those who don't...

Star Legend is a science fiction/Arthurian legend mashup, detailing the events that follow the fall of the Britannic Isles, which triggers a return of the mythical hero, King Arthur. I won't give spoilers by going into more detail, but suffice to day Carys Ellis and Setia Zees spring from that story. Carys Ellis was closely involved with the children of one of the heroes of the story, Taylan Ellis. As hinted at in *Talman Prime*, Setia Zees was unknowingly caught up in the conflict between the aliens controlling Earth affairs and the people trying to stop them.

Another aspect worth knowing is that the founder of the colonisation project in *Talman Prime* was Lorcan Ua Talman. With an ego as large as his project, he naturally insisted that the colony planet carried his name.

In no particular order, here is some of the research that informed or inspired the book.

The Caves Under the Primian Metropolis

You will remember that Not-Ahmad shows Setia and Miriam cave paintings created by early Primians. As they travel down through the cave system, Setia notices that the tunnels are fairly regular and smooth-walled. This is because they're lava tubes, formed when volcanic activity forced lava through surrounding rock, melting it. When the lava subsides, long underground tubes remain. Lucky tourists on Hawaii can visit the tubes there.

The *Bres*, *Balor* and *Banba*

This origins of the Fleet's ships' names is mentioned in the notes to one of the Star Legend books, but for those who haven't read them I'll explain here too. Lorcan Ua Talman has an Irish background, and his ships are named after characters from Irish mythology. Bres was a king of the Tuatha Dé Danann, a supernatural race who dwelt in the Otherworld but interacted with humans. Banba was also a member of the race and is a matron goddess of Ireland. Balor was a king of the Fomorians, another, hostile, supernatural race who opposed the Tuatha Dé Danann.

Forest Trees

The odd trees in the Primian forest were inspired by an extinct group of plants called Cladoxylopsida, the first trees. They seem to have photosynthesised via stems and didn't grow leaves. Though they had a central trunk, this is believed to have been hollow, with the outer, water-transporting channels expanding and splitting apart each year as the tree grew. The base of the trunk was wide and flattened, and the trees would have somewhat resembled palms. As modern trees evolved, they out-competed Cladoxylopsida, growing taller due to their more efficient growth system and hogging more of sunlight with their wide leaves.

Prime: Water Planet?

I had a lot of fun annoying Setia with the near-constant rainfall on Talman Prime. Personally, I try to escape the dark, wet British winter and spend a couple of weeks in the sun somewhere else in the world, so you can perhaps guess the source of my inspiration for the planet's climate.

It's a bugbear of mine that alien planets are often portrayed in fiction as having a single, homogeneous climate. Knowing what we know about other worlds, that doesn't make a lot of sense. I don't go into much detail, but Prime has a range of climates, the only unifying factor being a buttload of precipitation. Earth's water cycle is influenced by a range of factors but, as far as I'm aware, nothing in our current understanding of climatology excludes the possibility of a more watery world and greater turnover of water across the planet.

Primians' Origins

Carys speculates that Primians may have originated as Denisovans on Earth, but in fact they could have been any of a number of very closely related homonins. (Homonin is the new classification for modern humans and related species, all now extinct. Homonid now refers to all Great Apes, modern and extinct.) She isn't strictly correct that Denisovans looked different from Neanderthals. According to our sparse knowledge, there were several anatomical similarities, but she's right when she says some modern humans carry Denisovan DNA. The fossil record for Denisovans is extremely sparse, but they're believed to have died out about 50,000 years ago.

If you'd like to discuss *Talman Prime*, the Interstellar Fleet series or my other books, or if you'd like to meet other Starship JJ Green shipmates, come over to our Facebook page. I'd love to see you there.

Jenny Green, Cambridge, March 2024

PATRONS

Deepest thanks to patrons:

Paul Hanrahan, John Treadwell, Joseph Lau, Peter Samuel Harness, Geeraline Marrs, Bobby Borland, John Stephenson, Chris, William Retsin, Dan Archibald, Grant Ballard-Tremeer, Dale Thompson, Jean Gill, Christopher E. Marshall, Cheryl Kuchler, Shan Shwe, Steve Glasper, Donald Swan, Wayne Lampel, Janette S. Mattey, Brian Kelly, Jim, Sarah Woods, Richard L. Adams, Frank Menendez, Patti DeLang, Elizabeth Hickey, Linda Liem, Russ Kirkpatrick, Kate Wilson, Duff Kindt, Catherine Corcoran, Shaun, John Gancz, Dave, Archie Strong, Struggle Session, Susan Cook, Annie Hsiao-Wen Wang, Julian White, Dane Elliot, Iffet a Burton, Gary Johnson, Tracey Paine, Randy Berlin, Ed Cleeves, Amaranth Dawe, Neil, Alex Green, Ann Bryant, Neil Holford, Michael Phillips, Michael Claremont, and B. Rowan

COPYRIGHT

First Edition.

www.ingramcontent.com/pod-product-compliance
Lightning Source LLC
Chambersburg PA
CBHW070431170726
48291CB00002B/457
9781913476656